Hostage to Her Heart

by

Chriss Hill

authorHOUSE®

AuthorHouse™
1663 Liberty Drive, Suite 200
Bloomington, IN 47403
www.authorhouse.com
Phone: 1-800-839-8640

This book is a work of fiction. People, places, events, and situations are the product of the author's imagination. Any resemblance to actual persons, living or dead, or historical events, is purely coincidental.

First published by AuthorHouse 4/30/2008

ISBN: 978-1-4343-6044-1 (sc)

Library of Congress Control Number: 2008901386

Printed in the United States of America
Bloomington, Indiana

This book is printed on acid-free paper.

Dedication

This book is dedicated to all of my family, especially my husband Bruce; my children Keifer, Kayla, Tracy & Lori and their spouses, Chris & Rick, and to all of my grandchildren: the girls, Mariah, Morgan & Preslee and Da Boyz: Ethan and Andreyes (Bubba & AJ). Much love to my mother, Margaret, for always being there for me. Many thanks to my best friend, Dot, for forcing me to think about sequels from the very conception! Maybe, if I'm lucky, we'll take that long awaited cruise! Also many thanks to my Urbis buddies (Mika, Aimee and Sherri- you know who you are!) for their straight up critiques on each submission. Last, thanks to the staff from AuthorHouse in making this book into a reality. To all readers: Many stories can be hypothetical tales (about dragons, vampires, and fairy tale romances) and can be deemed believable by the end of it. I simply attempted to intertwine my interests of faith, pop/rock music, multi-birth families, and how fame can affect lives. Hopefully, as you read about these characters, they will lead your heart to a memorable connection. Happy reading.

Chapter One

If God has a plan

NYCPD Detective Marras sat at his desk studying yesterday's arrest file, dated December 15th, 1977- a file summarizing the detective's notes so far. The case involved a nun known to travel through the US and even abroad. She walked right through customs and borders as if never seen. She possessed no passport or even a formal picture identification card. For many years, she had lived and worked in orphanages, homeless shelters, and even halfway houses. Most recently, she had been employed at a Catholic facility for trouble teenagers and orphaned children.

During her stay there, she dished out medications to those entrusted into her care. They were never prescribed by a doctor and how she got them, no one knew. No one ever reported suspicious activity or complained. However, she rocked the boat when she offered the headmaster at her present employment some pills to help curb his many anxieties, because of his reputation for being a mean, overbearing man. Suspicious of her overall motives, he sent the medication out to be tested. A poisonous substance was found mixed within the powder, so the police were summoned and she was brought in for questioning.

At police headquarters, Sister Elsa, an elderly woman with brown skin and a European accent, threw the detectives for a loop.

"God is a mystery. He can heal all things," she said with a crooked grin, revealing a couple of missing teeth, "He can give or take away life. God has a purpose, a plan for everyone. This can be good or bad. One must believe in him beyond everything. He has the power to change lives. I am simply a messenger that delivers forth what he brings."

"So these pills came out of thin air?" Marras asked, staring down at the petite lady before him, "Incredible! You must have broken in somewhere to get them. Everything you have said sounds so far fetched. "

"But it's the truth. Two of the boys in my care are permanently cured from their chronic medical conditions. They no longer suffer from diabetes or asthma. Just ask their doctors." Sister Elsa adjusted the wimple on her head and stared directly into Marras wide eyes almost all-knowingly. "I tell you they are cured forever."

His partner had stood silent throughout most of Marras's interrogation, but now Frank pulled him aside.

"Her story is so crazy, but do you think there is anything to this?" he asked, his eyes wide like saucers.

"I don't know. Go check this out. Call the headmaster for his story again. Then check with the nurse at the facility. They will surely have something on record about it."

Frank rushed out to comply and Marras stepped out of the room too. Perhaps leaving the nun alone awhile would make her think about consequences. It just wasn't wise to make up stories to the police. An hour went by and finally Frank returned with a full report. Visibly, his hands shook while he laid the notes on Marras's desk.

"The headmaster is very long winded. I thought he'd never stop," Frank stated and looked around nervously, "According to the nurse, the state ordered checkups for anyone who took what she gave. Luckily, there were only three this time. The two boys are completely healed."

"Really?"

"Yes and it's really made me skittish. When you think about it, this is quite surreal. No pharmacy in the world possesses what she gave out. If they did, they would be mobbed by thousands to get the same cures!"

Detective Marras nodded in understanding. Frank made a point.

"I asked if we could question the boys, but the state decided to transfer them upstate. They have a chance to be placed in permanent homes instead of foster ones since becoming healthy," Frank explained and ran a hand through his thick, brown hair.

"What about the other? Didn't you say there is a third person?"

"Oh, yes. A girl. Now, this situation is very strange from the others."

"How so?" Marras asked and Frank filled him in. The story seemed very phenomenal and so Marras wanted to get to the bottom of it quickly.

"Get Joe to bring her in for questioning. In the meanwhile, place the good sister into the holding area for awhile, will you?"

"Sure thing, boss," Frank said and did as instructed. Marras watched as the nun walked calmly down the hall seeming like she didn't have a single worry in the world.

"Remember to get that check up soon," she said to him before disappearing around the corner.

Marras muttered under his breath and felt compelled to stop by a nearby water cooler. In a non-customary way, he gulped down three cups of water, drawing stares from his co-workers in the room.

"I'm just unusually thirsty," he explained out loud. They went back to work, but it was the truth. Thirst did overpower him. Perhaps suggestive thinking on her part made him feel this way. After all, in their discussion, Sister Elsa warned Marras about having elevated glucose levels. Diabetes ran on his mother's side of the family. What if this was true? Marras shook his head. He didn't wish to be so easily gullible. He threw the paper cup away into a trashcan nearby and then noted the time on the metal clock on the wall.

"Rats! I'm late for a meeting with the chief," he snarled and rushed quickly through the headquarters building. A few hours later, he returned back into the room. Phones were ringing and several officers milled about. He noticed Frank sitting behind several stacked case files on his desk and so he went over.

"Did you get that girl in?" Marras asked.

"Yeah, she's here. Joe spooked her at the door, he said, but talked her into coming in. She's been waiting for half an hour, at least. In your office."

"Thanks, Frank" Marras said and rushed away. When he got to his door, he opened it quickly and accidentally slammed it behind him. In a dark, wooden chair, a young girl jumped like a cat at the noise. She watched as he sat down, tugging on a black sweater draped about her shoulders. Marras broke the ice by sounding apologetic.

"Ms. Reece, I'm glad you cooperated and came in on such short notice. We appreciate you telling us your side of the story. I heard that our police officer scared you a bit just showing up at your place out of the blue."

"It did startle me, but it's not my apartment. It belongs to my friend, Ross," she explained, her voice soft. She cleared her throat.

"You mean your boyfriend?" Marras asked curiously.

"Oh, no!" Tara gushed while her cheeks turned red and her eyes lowered towards her stomach. Underneath a tight white shirt, a round pooch showed, "Ross and I grew up together at the Catholic school facility. He's my best friend, not the father to my baby… er… babies."

He understood her difficulty. Receiving news about being pregnant would put any normal eighteen year old girl into a spin, but she was the anomaly that the irate headmaster unwittingly mentioned during questioning. Tara shook her head and grabbed a tissue from her purse, "The problem is that I don't exactly know how many I carry. The free clinic gave me an examination and said it could be twins or triplets."

"It's too early to confirm yet?"

"I am far enough along, but their ultrasound machine broke down," Tara explained and sniffed loudly. She looked up at him with wide eyes, blinking back tears desperately, "You have to excuse me. This is a frightening thing to learn. I wouldn't be in this mess if I hadn't taken that medication in the first place."

He wanted to put her at ease during this conversation.

"Would you like a soda?" He offered, but she declined. He went around the desk before her and propped himself on the front edge. He looked down and spoke in a soft, caring tone, "Yes, we learned of your predicament. It's very bewildering. Can I ask-where's the father?"

"Gone," the girl revealed honestly, "The headmaster forced him to move away, since Jimmy is his favorite nephew. The man never liked me, but Jimmy and I fell in love. We had a very brief involvement. Now, he's up in Canada, living somewhere with his aunt."

"Does he know about this?" he asked, studying her closely. Tara had long, brown hair that almost reached her waist. Her eyes were engaging and bright. Even if she seemed aloof in the office environment, crossing and uncrossing her legs and tugging on her sweater to hide her belly, somehow Marras felt a connection. He held a fatherly instinct to speak to Tara like his own daughter. He leaned in close to ease Tara's nervousness and she dabbed at her nose.

"No, but if he did, I'm sure that Jimmy would marry me. It's just that his uncle refused to help at all. What was I suppose to do? I had no resources or a way to find out where exactly Jimmy is in Canada. I knew that Ross had a job on the docks and a place of his own. So I ran away from Hartridge. I was finally old enough to do so and I knew that Ross would help me somehow,"

"Sounds like a good friend. You're fortunate that he's around, Ms. Reece. You do realize that Sister Elsa is here for questioning too?" he asked and she nodded.

"Yes. The officer said something about this to Ross when he answered the door. He explained that you needed my testimony."

"Yes. Just answers to a few questions. Why did you take those pills?"

Tara coughed again and then looked into his eyes.

"It's embarrassing to admit why. I have trouble with skimpy periods," she almost whispered and then spoke confidently again, "Sister Elsa came to our school during the summer. She seemed so friendly and always encouraged her students to talk to her about our problems. Henry- the boy with diabetes- wound up with her medication and in just one week, he had no symptoms. There were no more insulin shots and he could eat anything he wanted. Such a miracle! I thought she would help me too."

"So you took them," he paused to look at his notes, "one pill, every day?"

"Not exactly. She told me less actually but it didn't help my problem. So I read the back of the box and thought it would be ok to double up the dose. I took them twice a day. After that, I did become normal, but then I messed up by spending a night with Jimmy. It was just one of those things."

"I understand," Marras replied and gave a half-smile. He could recall all about the foolishness of young lovers. He was one himself, "Please continue."

"Well, then the next thing I know, I am late and so I spoke to her about this. She reveals that the pills were fertility pills. I just about died learning this!" Tara yelped and she might have cried again if a sudden thought had not occurred to her. Tara dug into her purse to pull out a full bottle, "Maybe these can be used as evidence. These are all I have left."

"Excellent. Do you mind? I can get the lab to test them," He asked and she willingly handed them over. He placed them into a plastic bag and wrote a description on it with a black marker. Tara watched for a moment before speaking again.

"If this is all you need, am I free to go now?"

"Yes, I think so. I thank you for coming in. If something else comes up, we know where to find you," Detective Marras buzzed his assistant into the office and handed over the pills, "Miller, send these out to the lab for analyzing. ASAP."

"Yes, Marras. Will do," The man took the package and then exited the way he came in. Tara stood up and commenced slowly to the door. She stared back at the detective.

"What will happen to Sister Elsa? Will she stay in jail? Will she wind up in prison?" Her tone expressed a genuine concern, "Growing up was tough at Hartridge. It's not often when a stranger seems kind."

"Yes, but don't forget that this stranger only changed the outcome of your future, "Marras replied skeptically, "For this, we will take care of her accordingly."

Tara looked to the ground absorbing his words. He couldn't help but sympathize. Such a sad predicament for one so young, he thought.

"By the way, will you be ok? Do you know someone, other than your friend, who can help provide better for your pregnancy?"

"No, there's no family, other than Ross. He's like my brother. Somehow, I will manage to get by," she said, her brown eyes narrowing in determination, "Without a diploma and no job, there's no choice but to leave our lives in God's hands."

Then she walked out, leaving Marras to shake his head. He returned to his desk and commenced typing out details onto a carbon-filled, three part report. About thirty minutes later, the power in the building shut down momentarily. He looked around the dark room, which was kept minimally illuminated by a nearby generator light on the wall. A thunderstorm approached the area. He guessed that lightening possibly hit a transformer nearby. After a few minutes, the main lights returned and Marras resumed his task. Just then, Frank rushed into the room.

"Marras! The nun's gone!"

"What?" Marras jumped up from his desk, "What do you mean gone?"

"We let her use the woman's bathroom. Someone inside said she just disappeared! We didn't see her come out or leave by the front door. There's no other way out of that area. Bars block all the windows."

Together they ran down to the holding area to check things out. What Frank said was true. The woman was long gone. Another woman, who had been in lock up with the nun, sat in a chair explaining what she saw to two officers.

"I tell you the truth. The nun stood next to me, near the sink, as I washed my hands. It seemed weird seeing someone in jail wearing a black and white dress like that, with a wimple on her head. She even prayed in a strange language," the woman relayed as she clutched at a tissue and wiped away the sweat on her brow, "We finally got a turn to go to the ladies room. While we were in there, the power surge hit. The lights went out- say about ten seconds. When they came on again, she was nowhere around. I don't recall seeing her go out the door, but I guess she could have. I'm an old woman. My mind plays tricks."

After hearing her story, Marras ordered that the security video tapes be pulled. They showed everyone entering and leaving the building, but after viewing them, they offered no clues at all. The power surge affected the cameras for about thirty seconds and everything seemed blurry on playback. A manhunt of the station and the surrounding city blocks came up empty. After that, Marras didn't know what to believe about this mysterious nun. She said his sugar levels were up, so before he went home that afternoon, he called his family doctor, an old friend, who ordered blood to be drawn in the morning.

The next morning, the usual routine played out at the police station, the same as any other day. Marras's morning went on without a hitch, but by 2:00 o'clock in the afternoon, the telephone rang on his desk. He listened carefully, slumped in his chair, chewing on a pencil. Glumly, he hung up. Up until that point, he never thought of himself as a religious man, but now he wondered if he should reconsider. The call was about his lab results. Sure enough, he could be diabetic. Sister Elsa had been right, but how did she know? Marras felt compelled to pray and he gathered his hands closely together.

His plight didn't upset him. Ironically, there would be medicine to help out appropriately. No, it's just that he never forgot Tara. After their conversation, she lingered in his mind, like the scent of good perfume on a beautiful woman passed by on the streets. Something caused him to care. Something- perhaps in the way she had looked- with lovely, dark eyes.

After bowing his head for a brief minute, Marras picked up another set of lab results about the pills that Tara gave. He stuck it in a file and then jabbed it into the back of his file cabinet. With the accused roaming at large again, Tara's current testimony lay useless and this made him angry. Yet, there were other cases to go over and perhaps he would never learn about her outcome.

"Poor thing. They were just sugar pills," he murmured in confusion. Yes, perhaps only God knew her destiny.

Later that same afternoon, in an ethnic Brooklyn neighborhood, Tara walked down a long, cracked sidewalk, returning from the market. She approached a drab brownstone and took a flight of steps up to a secured door. She punched in the security code to enter. The three-flights of stairs inside led up to a one-bedroom apartment she shared with Ross. It was a bit run-down, but it was home.

Once in the apartment, Tara went to the tiny kitchen, opened up the refrigerator, and stuck a gallon of milk inside, along with eggs and orange juice. She took out nickels and quarters from her coat pocket and stuck it into a large pickle jar nearby, collecting all loose change. "Something for a rainy day," she sighed, knowing that Ross worked too hard at two jobs just to support them. Currently, he was in-between shifts and changing clothes in the bathroom. When he heard her scurrying around in the kitchen, he came out to join her.

"So, how did things go at the station yesterday?" he asked as dark eyes narrowed and he tucked in a thermal shirt into his jeans , "You were sound asleep when I left this morning, so I didn't disturb you to talk."

"Fine," she conveyed honestly, taking off her coat and putting it on a coat rack in the corner of the living room, "It seemed a bit scary, but the detective made me comfortable. He asked a few questions. I gave him the pills. He wanted to have them tested."

"Good. Maybe they'll have enough evidence to throw that fake into prison."

"Ross, you didn't know her well enough. Sister Elsa was always nice to me." she declared, staring up at her tall friend, who buttoned himself up in a warm flannel shirt. His black hair stuck out under a pull on cap.

"So was Jimmy, but don't you realize what he did to you? You're too gullible and trusting, Tara. You have to learn to toughen up," He said as a grimace hardened his facial features.

"I'm sorry! I'm not perfect!" she snapped and pushed him aside. Ross spun around and grasped her arm.

"No, look…I'm sorry… for blowing up about them. I'm just tired. They screwed you over and I realize it's not all your fault. Please don't be mad," He asked, staring deeply into her eyes. Tara noted the puppy dog look on his face that begged for her forgiveness. It was an expression that was usually effective, but not today.

"I'm tired too, Ross -that you keep bringing it up. Go on to work and leave me in peace for awhile, shall you? We'll talk tomorrow," Tara wriggled free and rushed towards the bedroom. She didn't want to argue anymore and like a good friend, he would obey. He just had to understand that the past could not be changed. Sure, he was smart enough not to trust Sister Elsa, but he was also dumb enough to constantly quarrel with Jimmy over her friendship, both determined to be most important in her life. Well, Ross could certainly stop feeling so protective and possessive, especially since Jimmy lived so far away and Sister Elsa landed in jail. She also realized that Ross couldn't help himself. As her best friend, he remained steadfast, true and true. No matter how much he got on her nerves, of course, she would forgive him. She needed him, as he needed her.

Wearily, Tara lay down to rest; her thoughts going over what he said. She did trust in people too much and she did need to toughen up. For every time her heart laid open for someone to have, they left. Time and time again, she found herself abandoned. A pattern established since birth, ever since her mother did the same at that Catholic facility. "Perhaps a pair of steel handcuffs adequately placed could keep them from running away," she mused out loud and then noticed a wooden crucifix on the wall. Ross had bought it off someone peddling them on the streets and he thought it decorative enough to place on his wall. For the moment, she needed comfort, so Tara slid off the bed and kneeled down to pray:

"God, if you are up there, please help me. I can't do this alone. This will put a strain on my friendship with Ross. He loves me, but he'll only get mad if I don't give in to be his wife. Then what will I do? I'm all alone in this world. I'll leave it in your hands. Just send a solution for all of my problems. I do need one. Amen."

Tara scooted back onto the bed and snuggled under all the soft covers. After awhile, she fell asleep and began to dream. In her subconscious, somewhere far away, she stood upon a valley road laden deep with fresh snow, with scattered heavy trees lining up on different sides. Up ahead, there stood a large house in the distance that she felt determined to reach, but this would not be an easy task. The snow drifts were thick and uneven. Bitterly, the cold winds nipped at her ears and at her legs, even if she wore rabbit fir-lined boots that hugged her calves. The blue anorak didn't feel sufficient to keep in her body temperature and she felt unusually heavy in it. After several minutes, she stopped in her track. She gazed at the brick house that sat beautiful and wide, centered upon an expansive piece of land. Black smoke poured out of the chimney, making coal-colored swirls float up towards the stratosphere. The place, looking like something off a Christmas card, had windows decorated with full fur wreaths and red ribbon bows.

Inside, she knew it to be warm; filled with caring, loving people.

Just then, a young man stepped out of the house, dressed in full naval dress attire. His thick head of blond hair seemed illuminated by the mid-day sun. Even the brass metals on his dark jacket reflected in the sunlight like diamonds. Tara called out against the brisk breeze. The man turned, scanning the field nearby, but he couldn't make out where the sound came from and Tara was obscured by a snow drift. From the house, she saw someone rush out to join him and together they raced to a compact car. They stuffed luggage into the trunk and quickly jumped into the front seats to be on their way.

In a panic to reach him in time, Tara struggled again to get through the thick snow, but her efforts felt agonizing. Every muscle in her legs stabbed like sharp needles. Flawed from the start, her effort was not sufficient. The car pulled out of the driveway, lurched forward onto the gravel road, and then went around a sharp bend at a hurried pace. Fazed with defeat, steam rose around her face as she came to a halt and watched it disappear. Her lungs ached deep as she tried to catch her breath. She swallowed down a lump that rose sharply in her throat. What a disaster! She felt a staunch realization. That blond man was significant to her life. Someone important. And much too late, she realized the love she felt for him in her heart. Now, he was gone and she collapsed to her knees in the cold wet snow and threw her arms up to the sky to argue her case with God. "No!" she screamed, as it was all that she could do, as the sun blinded her eyes while gazing helplessly upward and beyond.

Tara's eyes flickered awake at this point, her heart pounding hard in her bosom. Jolted at the swirling emotions worming its way out from her soul, she sat up in bed and noted there were tears flowing down her face. How vivid the dream? She took a moment to realize her surroundings again and regroup her careening thoughts. No, she was not kneeling in snow. Indeed, her arms were cold, but it wasn't from the trek towards that house. She was in her bedroom in that cold brownstone apartment. The furnace that stood near a window had stopped working again. The clock on the dresser flashed seven o'clock in bold red numbers. Ross, now at work, wouldn't be home until after midnight.

Rain pounded upon the building, so Tara listened to it for a minute or two while cuddled up in a thick blanket. She got out of bed, dragging the blanket, and went to the window. For a long while, she watched the heavy rain drops fall and splatter upon the glass. Her mind kept thinking over the dream. After several minutes, she struggled to recall what the blond man looked like, but simply remembered that his face seemed fair and handsome. Perhaps his eyes were blue or green. Other details of the dream were beginning to diminish too.

Wherever that lovely house sat was not in Brooklyn, New York. Somewhere, far beyond the familiar drab brownstone buildings and distant skyscrapers, a man existed to shake up her heart in a big way. Was he the answer to her problems? She hoped this to be true, but how would she find him? By dawn, all would be forgotten. Only God knew where such a man could exist.

Tara looked up at the sky, but only could see pitch black and the occasional streaks of lightening. "I'm such a wayward romantic fool," she sighed. This seemed to be the only truth to her, other than her future: dark and obscured.

Chapter Two

Love is a fickle thing

The luck of things, circumstances worked in her favor far across the Atlantic Ocean. A blond man stepped hastily down a long metal ramp way with a gray warship docked behind him in the harbor. Dressed impeccably in a naval uniform, he saluted his top commander who waited on the pier for his report.

"Sir, the men are off for R&R. They have their orders. We'll deploy at 6:00 a.m. in two days time for our assignment to the US," Danny Cross announced crisply in an English accent, placing both hands to his sides and waiting further instructions.

"Very well, Lieutenant Commander. Let's make sure the paperwork is up to snuff," The top ranking commander saluted back. They walked towards the main headquarters office across the way, "I say, Danny, what are your plans? Can you stick around London to have dinner with us? Lilly would love to see you again and our children enjoy hearing all of your silly, bad jokes."

"Indeed Harry, I would like to see them too, but I promised my mother to visit her in Wiltshire. After all, it is Christmas Eve."

"That sounds unfortunate. How can you meet anyone stuck out in the country side? How can it compare to London's nightlife?" Harry repositioned his hat upon his fading brown hair and squinted at his younger companion, waiting for a response.

"It's not so bad, sir. I actually appreciate the fresh air."

"Fresh? I think not with your mother's horses in the nearby stables. Why not stay around? After dinner with us, you can visit your brother. Michael always throws a lovely holiday gathering on Christmas Eve. Surely he can introduce you to someone new, some lovely actress. I wouldn't throw in the towel because of last year's disaster," the commander teased, his tummy wiggling underneath the crisp shirt as he chuckled, "She didn't mean to douse you in eggnog."

"I don't think so. It's just that I feel out of place at his parties, the women gossiping about their fellow actors and all the men lighting up stogies and bragging about their new theater productions," Danny lamented and his shoulders slumped to recall that awful evening, "When I said the room stank, I referred to the rank aroma of the cigars. Not that woman's perfume or her talent. She misunderstood,"

He remembered it all like it was yesterday, the embarrassment and the way the frothy, cold substance felt upon his head when she dumped it there. It dribbled down into his ears and the back of his neck. Everyone turned to stare. He wanted to run out of the room, but somehow managed to walk to the bathroom with a dignified demeanor. Even if Michael begged him to stay on, Danny drove home to Wiltshire, where he felt secure being in the presence of his parents, especially his over-affectionate mother. She always coddled him a bit much, much to his father's lament. When Danny joined the Navy, his father thought it would make him immune to such flowery emotion. Wasn't a grown man supposed to be tough and indifferent? Still, there were times when Danny needed affection like his mummy gave out growing up. A good wife would do wonders for a remedy. If only he could find one. Harry always tried to help out.

"Well if you can't digest his sordid crowd," Harry egged on, "Lilly's younger cousin is visiting us tomorrow. That's why I want you to stick around. Let me introduce you. She's from Wales and isn't terribly gruesome, but is stalwart, faithful to attending services, and eats delicately. Doesn't that sound like a lovely dish? I won't place any eggnog in sight, I promise."

Danny smiled in spite of Harry's feeble attempt to help him meet, and possibly keep, the perfect girl. Such was his bad luck. No one ever stuck around. Along the pier, a pair of seagulls squabbled while attempting to land in the same place. Danny pointed to them.

"See that, Harry! It wouldn't matter if a girl were an angel sent down to save me. That's what happens with any woman I date. We end up bickering. The relationship dies before it even gets off the ground."

"Now, now," Harry disagreed. Danny felt determined to make a point.

"No, its true, Harry. In their eyes, I do something wrong to throw it off. I've never been lucky, like my brothers. The 70's are changing times, but no one appreciates my conservative attitude. Just ask my modern sisters. Sorry. Perhaps I should have been born in a previous century. There I might have fit in, like on our ship, with conventional methods and traditions. I never feel out of place at sea. Of course, it's all men on board. I swear on my life that I do not frolic with any," Danny joked, but Harry remained optimistic.

"So sorry about your luck, Danny, but please don't give up yet. What are you? Twenty five? One day soon, a nice girl will come along. Then it will be a match made in heaven."

"I certainly hope so," Danny sighed and tucked both hands into his pant pockets. Harry, offered a grand smile.

"Yes, it can happen. Love is a fickle thing, based on my experience. Women are all very female- quite odd in their habits and expectations. I think they view us the same way," Harry said and then realized that Danny looked out of sorts beside him. The youthful spring in Danny's usual step seemed slow and weary and his head hung low. Harry crinkled his nose in dismay of this. Indeed, out of all of his officers, Danny was most respected among the crew for his easy candor and broad efficiency when it came to his duties. Even Harry enjoyed long conversations whenever the missions were long away from home. He couldn't allow his friend to be totally despondent, "Look, we do what's best to keep them happy. Like now, for instance- I should hurry to get home on time for dinner. Lilly promised to cook up a succulent lamb dish with plenty of horseradish mash, even chocolate pudding. Forget leaving right away and have dinner first."

"Very well, sir," Danny smiled. He held the door open for Harry, "I do like Lilly's cooking. You are indeed lucky to have such a lovely wife."

"Thank you," the Commander replied, beaming about the compliment.

Danny looked at his watch while the Commander went about his business. He could drive to Wiltshire later that evening. Hopefully it would be too late for his mother to be up. Or he could wait until morning, when his mind was fresh to stand up to her complaints about his lifestyle of being single. She meant well. Lucky for him, he had two brothers and two sisters that gathered the same admonishment. Danny was the middle child of five, all very career minded.

He tried to do the right thing: to meet a girl and settle down. It's just that things never evolved as he hoped. Danny picked up a family picture on someone's desk as he waited. They all seemed happy; all smiles, sitting so proud. "Ugh! Lucky bloke!" he remarked. All he knew was that the years rolled by at a fast pace. Most friends from school were married now, with homes and families of their own. When would it be his turn?

The Commander saluted a fellow officer and rejoined Danny near the door. They exited the building and Danny looked around. The sun sank beyond the blue-gray horizon. Many pelicans rested on the edge of the wooden beams, without squawking. Danny picked up again on their private conversation.

"I think those birds have it right. Once the squabbled is over, they settle down quietly together. Why can't men and women? All I want is one girl to accept me for who I am, with all of my old fashion thinking. Drinking is one vice, but I'd give it all up for true love. I would accept her vices willingly. I wouldn't care what she'd look like or what bad habits she kept. Even her past wouldn't matter."

They had walked into the secured, fenced-in parking lot. Danny opened up the passenger door to the Commander's car. He sat inside and Harry turned on the ignition.

"You'll get your wish soon, my friend. I can feel it," Harry said sincerely and drove the car up to the security exits. Danny rested his head against the leather seat. All the weight of his one conflict sat squarely on his shoulders. For a moment, he could almost imagine someone sweet holding his hand, kissing his brow, embracing him tight. He closed his eyes to hold onto that vivid daydream and smiled. *Yes, a woman is what I desire, more than ever; someone warm to hold at night.*

That evening, he dined with Harry and his family. They drank too much wine, so he stayed over. In the morning, he watched with envy as the Commander opened up presents with his children. Later, Lilly's cousin showed up, but they were like oil and vinegar and their conversation stalled within an hour of meeting. It was awkward making small talk when there was nothing in common between them. She liked ballet and he loved rock and roll. She didn't drink where he did, and so on. Sometime later that afternoon, Danny snuck into Harry's study and called his mother to wish her Merry Christmas. He apologized for not coming home, but there would be another time to visit. Not a word was mentioned that he was in London or she would have really cried on the other end. It was best that she thought he was offshore, stuck on his ship.

Then, in two days time, Harry and Danny were off with their crew upon the Atlantic Ocean, on their way for the United States. One night, Danny stood out on deck with binoculars, studying another freighter about 10 kilometers out. He made notes on his log and walked his way towards the front bow, ensuring that the men were at task. Astronomy had always been a favorite study so he looked up above him. The night sky seemed magnificent, with hundreds of twinkling stars. He always felt so small and insignificant underneath the wide expanse of the universe. Surely, somehow he mattered. Danny huddled in his all weather coat and pulled tight at his leather gloves. A shooting star streaked across and he remembered something he did as a boy.

"Star light, star bright. First star I see tonight. I wish I may, I wish I might," he said out loud and closed his eyes, "Have the wish I wish tonight. Please, please, oh please- bring forth a wife."

Then he realized that just making a wish may not be enough. Under the presence of so many stars, perhaps the creator of such beauty would listen this time. He bowed his head to pray, "Lord, I'm so lonely. Let me find someone to love in this New Year. Anyone. No matter what her circumstances. I promise to love her for all eternity."

Yes, all he needed was that one special girl who would change his life forever.

Chapter Three

A night in the City

On Friday night, New Year's Eve, 1977, Danny walked into a crowded neighborhood bar and took a seat near the center aisle. He looked around to size up the place. The smoked filled room packed at capacity had many out celebrating the evening, dressed up in polyester suits and backless glittery dresses. The jukebox blasted an infectious beat and upon the wooden dance floor, several couples danced to the Hustle. Mingling drinkers surrounded a long glass bar. Several tables were decorated with party hats, paper horns, and string confetti for the occasion. People meandered their way through the aisles: hardy partiers, social queens, and lonely people seeking out dance partners. Perhaps one would be interested in him. A few girls did look his way from the bar.

Out of habit, he smoothed back his bangs, even though it had been trimmed earlier that week. His attire felt right for a night's outing: bell bottom jeans and a cotton shirt, along with his favorite platform boots - comfortable clothing to move on the floor if he needed to prove that he could dance disco. He didn't shave that morning, so fine whiskers stuck out on his chin, making his baby face seem mature. Surely, he stood a chance to attract someone. Suddenly, a young brunette came out from behind a door. She approached his direction. He instantly inhaled.

"Oh, my," Danny's pulse raced as he watched her struggle through the crowd, drawing closer and closer. A sultry expression graced her soft features and diamond eyes seem to cut through the dark like bright beckoning beacons. Absolutely irresistible. He had to know her name. As she came close, Danny grasped her hand. She looked wide eye at his audacity.

"I'm sorry. I didn't mean to startle you," Danny offered a warm smile as he jumped off his stool and gazed her body over. He realized that her stomach stuck out just a bit, just enough to suspect a pregnancy.

"Oh, dear. I didn't realize ..." Danny gulped, embarrassed and disappointed that he could make such a reckless mistake. At this, the girl jerked her hand away. She tugged her thick sweater tighter to hide it, her white cheeks turning red. Even her lips pouted, but she seemed so beautiful doing it.

"Come on, Tara. Let's go back to the table." A tall, young man interrupted; appearing out of nowhere. He stood behind her in an ominous stance. A boyfriend? A husband? Danny wasn't sure, but betted that they were possibly man and wife.

"Sorry. Is she married to you? No worries, right?" Danny offered an apology.

"Uh, yeah. No worries, "the young man replied, but the woman flinched away from his tight grasp. Her eyes flashed in the light.

"I am *not* his wife!"

This immediate outburst was unexpected. *Why is she upset?* Danny wondered. *Is it because I thought she is married or because her friend makes it seem presumed?*

The petite brunette stormed towards an empty table to sit down. Once there, she glared back at Danny, arms folded, like a dare.

The other man sat down beside her too, slumping into his seat. He smoothed out the thick mane of jet black hair into place again as he pouted. Now, their actions only fueled Danny's curiosity, so he went to join them. A waitress walked by and he pointed at the near empty bottle in his other hand.

"Look, can you bring more of the same for our table? In an ice bucket-and a soft drink for the lady," Danny gave the waitress a large bill.

"Sure," she said, sizing him up for a moment. Then she smiled, "By the way, I like your accent." With that, she turned and went about her way. Danny felt his cheeks warm up. He couldn't deny his British ethnicity or the way he sounded. It did charm a few women, but the look on the young girl's face at his table made him think different. Her eyes were stone cold, but the younger man seemed agreeable that Danny sat down with them.

"Say there, thanks for buying the drinks. My funds are low for the night."

"No problem."

"Are you visiting New York?" the young man looked Danny over carefully too, putting a finger upon the naval insignia pin out of curiosity. Danny didn't mind.

"Oh, yes! I'm from England, yet most people react like I'm from Mars. By the way, let me introduce myself," he offered a handshake, "My name is Daniel Cross, but please call me Danny. And yours?"

"Ross Kelly. This is my friend, Tara Reece."

"Well, then, it's a pleasure meeting you both!" Danny patted Ross on the back. If the girl was only introduced as a friend, then perhaps there was hope that the pair was not involved after all. This refreshed Danny's hope. He stared at Tara for a long moment. She seemed young, but this didn't dissuade him. "*She's so pretty,*" he thought and marveled at such an expressive face.

Tara looked him over again and then squinted. She turned to stare about the room as the men conversed getting to know each other.

"Where exactly in England do you live?" Ross asked politely at one point, toying with the noisemakers on the table. Danny shoved the ashtray aside on the table since he didn't smoke.

"It's in Wiltshire, a great place in the country, mostly land for farming and raising sheep," Danny revealed and went on a bit about the place for a few minutes. Ross seemed eager for friendly conversation. He asked a lot of questions. Perhaps it had something to do with Tara, who only sat there underneath an invisible storm cloud. Tara took off her sweater and stood up again.

"I'm going to the bathroom," she announced and went down the aisle. Danny stared at her a moment. Ross leaned forward.

"You have to excuse her. She's not in a great mood."

"I thought she sounded a bit icy. Is she always this way?"

Ross laughed and shook his head.

"Just lately. I brought her out in hopes to show her a good time. She's been so moody being pregnant and alone. Our Christmas holiday was a big disappointment as she moped about my apartment."

"Oh, so you live together. I see." Danny said. Again, he felt his luck was fizzing out too fast, like a sparkler, but Ross didn't mind spelling out details and that inflated Danny's determination again. In his mind, this rollercoaster ride made things extremely interesting.

"Yes, I offered a place to stay. I didn't want to start off the New Year all down and out," he complained, "I told her too. I said, "Tara, let's get out of this place for awhile." I forced her into a coat and hat and brought her here, to have some fun. As you've noticed, this venture is failing miserably. Once she's in a mood, it's difficult to change her mind. Actually, I'm grateful that you joined us."

"Well, I hoped to make new friends while I was visiting New York," Danny explained.

"What brings you here?"

"Ah, I'm on assignment for the Royal Navy," Danny explained, "We came to Norfolk Virginia for a two-day combined simulation. Our warship is out in Federal waters now. I am here with my top commander. We had business in Washington, DC to meet with a few Pentagon officials."

"Wow! You must be smart for that kind of job. That sounds so interesting,"

At that point, Tara returned. Danny wanted to impress her, since she looked in his direction.

"In my job in the Navy, it is fascinating working as a liaison, meeting with the top military commanders of your country, but really the meetings can get rather dull. Luckily, we didn't have to stay there very long. Now, we are visiting officials at the World Trade Center concerning NATO / ALLIED affairs. We'll be here for awhile."

Danny tapped fingers on the table, fidgeting like one with uncontainable energy. He observed the self-absorbed people in the bar that made their way around with beer bottles in their hands, cigarettes dangling off their lower lips. They were a loud crowd, only occupied with their own needs. It was a lot like the pub back home, but then again, different.

"In England, I grew up in quiet serenity. How do you manage to cope with this entire ruckus and a view full of skyscrapers? What else is there to do for fun?"

"I'm surprise you are not at Time's Square watching the ball drop. Almost all the tourists like seeing that," Ross suggested, "It's really neat how the city goes all out to prepare for such a spectacular event, with confetti, streamers, music and fireworks."

"Oh, no! Much too crowded! There are thousands of people lining up the streets, all along for several blocks. Like I said, this city is beyond me. I just came to this bar as I wanted a few beers, perhaps to meet a pretty lady. Even with them, I'm at a loss."

"Why's that? There are a few in here. They're not bad to look at."

"Yes, but most are very liberated. It's become a fad in my country too. I can't get use to it! Bah- humbug, as Scrooge would say!" Danny banged a hand upon the table, "Do I light their fags…"

"Fags? What's that?" Ross interrupted. His dark eyebrows rose.

"Cigarettes, my friend. An Irish friend of mine refers to them that way. Sorry, I forget there are different terminology for some things," Danny explained. He went to thinking about what he planned to say next, "Oh, yes, their fags… or do I let them light up? Do I pick up the whole tab or let them pay half? Damned if I am polite; damned if nothing is offered."

"I guess that is a dilemma. Never thought it out like that before."

"Right. It's very difficult these days, even to resist temptation. The women just throw it out there. Look at them! They can barely stay hidden behind their halter tops! God, there is no mystery left! No challenge in discovering what's underneath. Give me an old fashion girl for goodness sakes!"

Clearly they were different in their opinions. Ross couldn't help but stare at those who walked by scantily dressed, some in bare-back, one-piece suits that outlined their large breasts. There were several women dancing in mini-skirts, exposing long, silky legs. Danny shook his head.

"I'm for real. Things seemed bad until this lovely dish passed me by, all covered up very respectfully. Sorry, Miss Tara, I meant nothing wrong grabbing your hand that way. I was out of line," Danny's tone was sincere, but he also offered a flirtatious smile. He couldn't help it.

"Sure, that's ok," Tara mumbled. Just then, the waitress finally returned with a bucket of cold beer. It was heavy and she hefted it onto the middle of the table.

"Sorry it took so long. The place is just packed and it's hard to keep up," she complained and then tried to give Danny his change for the $50 currency, but he refused it.

"Naw, keep it. You work too hard as it is," he said and the waitress burst into a smile and walked away re-counting the bills in her hand that was now her tip. Tara gasped in surprise, along with Ross. What a generous man? Danny took a bottle out of the ice for himself. He handed one to Ross.

"I like company when I drink, so bottoms up! No one is paying any attention to us. I bet most of the cops are in Times Square, not here sniffing out under age drinkers. This street bar is just a piss-ant place, hole in the wall. We're safe."

Ross really liked Danny's easy going mannerisms. Grateful for being treated like a man, instead of just a nineteen year old boy, he took the bottle. They drew them together in a toast. *Clink*! Ross drank down the malt yeast brew. It was cold. It tasted great. A new friendship was born and Ross felt pretty good about it. Tara only shook her head and sipped at her soft drink, staring attentively at the blond man.

Chapter Four

Something about the man

Tara listened to everything as they sat in the bar and she sized up the stranger in her mind. Ah, Danny's English accent. Yes, it was neat to hear. He seemed like a droll man, with an angelic tenor voice, that made several attempts to tell a joke. It was difficult not to giggle when he screwed up the punch line. Tara stared at his profile. She noticed the five o'clock shadow on his chin. He was older, about mid-twenties, she judged, and he did possess the sexiest smile. Whenever he looked over her way, she tried to look off in another direction. It was a lucky thing that Ross kept their conversation flowing. She learned plenty without declaring an interest. With every beer, he said more about his life, dreams, and passions. The alcohol did wonders to loosen up his keen gift of gab.

Someone walked up to the jukebox to drop in several quarters. A nice selection of 1950's music changed the sound from disco to the twist. Danny tapped his fingers, counting along with the beat.

"You know, once when I was sixteen, I started a band of sorts, with my brothers."

"Who are they again?"

"I have two. Michael is the oldest. He didn't think much of my music and would spout off, 'Danny, you need an occupation where you can apply yourself seriously.' Hmff, serious! Well I guess he's happy with what I do now," Danny placed his bottle down next to the other empties, "Right now he works as a theater producer, so I guess it's all right to be so critical."

"I see."

"My youngest brother is in the navy too. When Sammy turned eighteen, he talked me into joining the academy. It's such a big world out there. Sammy always desired travel to distant places, other than going around Europe."

"How old is he?" Ross slurred, placing an empty beside the pile too. Danny was up ahead by two bottles, but Ross felt the effects early. Everything looked woozy.

"He's ten months younger as my mother wasted no time between us. Anyway, the missions that we took along the Mediterranean and Spain have been extraordinary. It suits me being at sea, but then I was recruited into this NATO/Allied Forces Liaison Project. I do meet a lot of interesting people in various countries."

"It does sound fascinating," Ross leaned over to pat Danny on the back, just as Danny did before. He practically slid out of his seat. Tara raised a curious eyebrow. Ross couldn't care less about anything at that point. He was on his fourth beer and felt good. The conversation was great. The man was terrific and it was great how he just went on and on, talking as if there were no tomorrows. Danny raised a new bottle to his lips.

"I don't really care what Michael thinks about my music. Whenever I can, I get out the guitar. While we are sailing, it soothes away my homesickness. I always liked the music this country introduces, especially from the fifties. Lots of times I attempt to write similar songs. The melodies are great, but the lyrics don't flow easy. Michael thinks they sound silly. One day, I'd love to prove to him wrong. I think there's an audience somewhere who will like them. They just have to possess an open mind."

"I know how to play too, "Ross confessed. They found a new connection. Ross wanted to impress Danny, "I improvise tunes to fit my lyrics. It's a process that works best. However, I am ridiculed with a critic too. "

Ross turned to look at Tara. He waved a finger at her.

"Tara doesn't like any of it."

Tara glared at Ross in a stern motherly fashion. His drinking annoyed her. She couldn't stand that he spoke funny and looked loopy.

"Oh, why not?" Danny was glad something came up to warrant her attention. Her nose wrinkled and delicate lips parted. He wanted to touch her nose and kiss her lips. She was so darn cute. For the most part that night, even if she remained silent, he noted from the corner of his eye those lingering expressions. This only fueled his curiosity, along with desire. Something tugged at his heart staring into her eyes. *Those magnificent eyes.* However, at this instance, she seemed agitated by what Ross said. She rose to her feet, hands upon the table, her feet apart.

"Ross can't come up with a better subject matter, so he writes about me!" Tara revealed in a huff, "I'll be right back."

She bolted towards the ladies room again.

"Please explain," Muddled by her less than enthusiastic reaction, Danny leaned in close to hear. Ross shrugged.

"I was taught to write lyrics that conveyed true emotions, about any real situations. My life was pretty much boring, except for Tara being my friend."

"How long has that been?"

"Since we were babies. We grew up in a foster home facility. Let me tell you, she has this thing about her. It draws me in, with the way she laughs, the way she thinks, which is sometimes eerily psychic. It's easy to fall for all of those strange subtle nuances," Ross revealed. The alcohol did wonders to loosen up his tongue, but he sounded almost lovesick, "I don't want to break free as she's a terrific girl, an awesome friend. I can't help but write about her."

"You must let me in on that material." It appealed to Danny that Ross spoke candidly. He definitely liked this young man, who in a lot of ways seemed very mature for his age, except for his handling of alcohol consumption. He noted Ross's slurred speech, the slightly bobbing body. Perhaps it was a mistake to offer the alcohol. Danny took the last bottle of beer out of the ice bucket. As the waitress came by to pick up the empties, Danny took Ross's full beer bottle to place on her tray. She deposit all into a trash can near the bar.

Ross didn't care one bit as he felt his body was lighter than air. When Tara returned, she watched suspiciously as they exchanged information to reach one another. Before she could speak, the hour struck midnight. The entire bar burst into wild applause, cheers, kisses and embraces. Someone threw lots of confetti into the air. It fell in their direction and landed into their hair. Danny looked at his new friends with a huge smile. He lifted his bottle into the air.

"Here's to a new year and great adventures ahead. Let destiny bring us love and good fortune," Danny deliberately stared into Tara's eyes. Perhaps it was the jovial atmosphere that finally made her smile. It captured him whole. He winked and her eyes grew wide. With this, their evening came to an end, "Look, I must get going. There's a meeting in the morning."

Danny stood up at the same time as Tara. They were so close and he could sense her warmth.

"I'm ready too. Get up, Ross," she instructed and reached for the sweater on the back of her chair.

"Here, allow me," Danny took it to wrap it about her shoulders, taking his time to do so. The aroma of her perfumed hair filled his nostrils and he wanted to touch it. Tara turned around then so that they were face to face. His eyes gazed into hers and she looked at him with a quizzical expression. He wished he could read her mind. They were so close. However, Ross jumped up out of his seat like a kangaroo. He didn't even wait on them and burst towards the front door like a damn fool.

"We best catch up to him before he does something dumb," Danny suggested and took her arm to lead her out. Tara didn't flinch or seem upset that he did this. She simply went along, allowing him to maneuver through the crowds first. Once outside, she saw Ross jump up and down on the sidewalk. As she drew closer, she saw he did it to squash bugs near a lamp post. It was a silly thing to do.

"You are making a scene, Ross. Stop it or you'll attract the police," she warned and darted to catch him by the arm. Ross laughed but obeyed. There was a cabbie coming down the street. Danny held up his hand to flag it down.

"Do you want to share?"

"No, that's all right. We can walk," Tara remarked in a brisk tone. A cab ride would have been nice. The night air was cold, but she didn't want to sit close to him. What if he tried holding hands? Danny made her feel strange and it was too soon to think of a man in this manner. Why couldn't he just disappear into the night so she wouldn't have to think about it? To her chagrin, this wasn't what Ross wanted as he suddenly told Danny where he lived.

"I wish this night wouldn't end. You're a great guy, Danny. We have to get together soon. Really, my apartment is around the corner. You must promise to come by and we can work on our music."

"Well, all right. I will. Goodnight then," Danny nodded and entered the cab. He waved and stared at Tara as the car lurched away from the curb. The two watched the cab go down the street.

"What's up with you? You weren't very nice to Danny at all," Ross complained as they made their way down the sidewalk. He was weaving and jumping over the cracks along the way, "I thought Danny was fun- extremely interesting."

"So what?" Tara replied in a catty tone. "All you talked about is his work, his life, and all about music. I have nothing to add to that. Besides, I wasn't comfortable that he sat with us. All he did was look at me all night."

Ross couldn't disagree.

"Well, Tara - I think in spite of your ungracious behavior, you only made him more curious. You didn't discourage that man one iota! No sir. You only presented a challenge."

"I don't want to be a challenge. In fact, I don't want to be anything to anyone at all. Especially that man! He's too old. He's not even my type!" Tara fumed. She marched up the sidewalk. Ross didn't think she really felt this way. He sprinted to catch up. She wasn't waiting on him. Some instinctive connection occurred between them all. Yet what could occur in the short time Danny remained? Time was clicking away quickly and fate must intervene to find any answers.

Chapter Five
A difficult situation

A few days later, Danny stopped by as promised. Tara was away at the local market, so it gave the guys time to hang out. Danny looked around as Ross offered a drink. The apartment only contained mismatched furnishings. There was a separate kitchen area, a bathroom, and one small bedroom large enough to fit a full size bed with one six-drawer bureau. Nothing more. A cold draft came through the creases of the window sill. The barren walls were in need of fresh paint. They settled into the living room and took out their guitars.

"So, Ross, what sort of work do you do?" Danny noticed an employee badge lying upon the coffee table. He picked it. There was a picture of Ross, along with the company logo. He didn't mind revealing anything personal.

"I work in the shipyard, unloading cargo. We break down the crates to transport the merchandise into the warehouse, before it gets sent out statewide. They are training me to use a forklift. It's enough to pay the utilities and rent. I also stock shelves at another place during the evenings," Ross listened closely as Danny played something arbitrary. The melody was soothing. Danny's intricate prowess with the instrument was remarkable.

"Why do you need the second job?"

"It's for Tara. I'm the only one who can help her."

"Isn't there any family?"

Ross explained a little bit about their childhood at Hartridge.

"We were orphaned. As children, we vowed to stick together. People were always coming and going, except for us. After awhile, it just didn't matter anymore. Who needs family?"

There was a determined look upon his face.

"I can't imagine. It must have been difficult." Danny conveyed sympathy as he didn't know what else to say. Their childhood was harsh when he was accustomed to an easier lifestyle growing up. It didn't seem fair. Ross and Tara were tough, but sweet. He was powerless to change their past, but perhaps he could influence their future – somehow- but he wasn't sure how. Ross leaned forward and looked about his apartment.

"I was kicked out of that school. After awhile, I found this place. Tara showed up out of the blue, in trouble. It's not a palace, but it's a roof over our heads. She deserves better and she thought that Jimmy was the answer. I never trusted the guy. He's been long gone since September."

"Jimmy?"

"Yeah, Jimmy's the one that got her that way, a guy we knew in school. He was forced to move to Canada before she could tell him about the pregnancy. If he did know, my suspicion is that he wouldn't keep his promises. I think he was a liar all along."

Ross seemed agitated by this. Perhaps the two young men faced many stormy confrontations about Tara. Danny could relate to this, and then he worried about quarreling with Ross too. Wasn't Ross crazy about Tara? It didn't make sense to interfere, as he'd be leaving again for England. A huge part wanted to stay, now that he thought about Tara's situation. Damn it. Danny felt tugged in different directions.

"Tara seems resilient. He sounds like a rotten egg. When's the baby due?"

Ross was grateful that someone took his side.

"She thinks in mid-May, but aren't any first pregnancies unpredictable? She's my best friend. All I can do is work to provide comfort."

"Well, that is honorable. So, there's no romantic involvement to some degree?" Danny quizzed, but Ross shoulders slumped. For a moment, he looked resigned to his fate.

"I would give anything for that. It's just that Tara is so stubborn, love-struck. She hopes that Jimmy will return and find her. Merciful heaven! The girl just won't accept reality. He's out of the picture! Meanwhile, I hear her cry in the night as I pretend to sleep on that lumpy sofa bed. This situation is uncomfortable for a whole slew of reasons-other than the fact that the sofa doesn't accommodate me!"

Ross studied his long legs. This made Danny laugh.

"Well, I can understand your sincere feelings. I must be honest with you. When I first saw her, there was something about her eyes that grabbed my attention."

"I sort of gathered that already, but I understand." Ross said, nodding. Danny stopped strumming his guitar, a hard grimace to his face.

"What a dilemma? It's beyond me. How can the guy just leave her with no means of support or stability? How can he expect someone else to take care of it? That's not being a man, if you asked me. I never would! Poor lass! It's a good thing she has your help."

"Thanks. I do all that I can. Besides, he's probably forgotten all about her by now."

At this point, Tara stepped inside with a brown bag of groceries. Was that a tear streaming down her face? Did she overhear everything?

"I'm tired, Ross. I'd like to take a nap before dinner. Are you two finished?" Tara placed the bag abruptly onto the kitchen counter. At this, Danny stood up.

"Say, I must rush off. So Ross, what's your schedule like the rest of the week?"

"I'll be at work every day until Saturday night. Perhaps we can get together then," Ross suggested.

"Oh, yes, of course!" Danny agreed. He raced to the door, "I will make it a point to drop by."

Danny departed with many mixed up emotions. Desperately he tried to rationalize the current situation, his own and theirs. "I think I can stick around longer," he mused, as his time was flexible per length of assignments in any vicinity. The new liaison role was one that the Minister of Defense and The United States Defense Secretary devised for specially selected military personal.

Trained like dedicated Navy Seals, his position allowed participation amidst world leaders and government officials within various nations, homing skills for vital security and peacekeeping efforts. The benefit: increased pay for every foreign assignment. Danny derived freedom to continue or decline his length of service at any point in time, without losing commission or suffering repercussions. He currently served half of the mandatory twelve year requirement.

He was lucky to be selected, thanks much in part to his father's astute, influential connections with members of the House of Commons and the Royal family. Sammy declined the offer. He loved rough necking with his shipmates instead. Although very well suited for the job, Danny never considered pulling in any favors before now. Knowing Tara's history, Danny felt every reason to request an extended stay, to work at the Trade Center awhile longer.

"How can they get by in that one-bedroom apartment?" He wondered as he shivered in the night air, "It's barely adequate to house two people. Doesn't a baby require space for diapers, toys, clothing, and a crib? Where would it all fit? And poor Ross! Even if he kept the two jobs, the hard work would soon wear him down. Such an honorable young man, but barely surviving on his pay. This is not good. Especially for Tara."

Ever since that night at the bar, Danny couldn't get her off his mind. Some obscure message in the back of his brain kept repeating, "She's the one."

Real desire fueled his actions. Somehow it felt right. Desperate situations can force anyone to do the extreme, especially when in need of rescue. It wasn't necessarily she that needed one. Danny walked towards the edge of the curb to hail a cab. Once inside, he barked out the address to the cabbie. As they made their way over the Brooklyn Bridge, a mad idea formulated in his head. Tara captured him with those incredible expressive eyes. He wanted to capture her forever.

Chapter Six

Making a dent in her heart

The next day, around noon, there was a knock on the door. Tara went to answer it and was surprised that Danny stood there, with a bouquet of wildflowers in hand.

"Ross is not home." Tara peeked up at him through a slit in the door. She attempted to shut the door all the way, but clever and quick, the brash young man lodged his body in-between the door and the sill.

"Ow! Come on, love! Please let me visit for a short spell."

"Why should I?" Tara didn't know what to do. Why was the man even there? He knew that Ross worked. He knew she was alone. Holding the door securely, she noted that only mere inches separated them.

"Well, surely you must long for a bit of company. It must be terribly lonely when Ross is away. It's quite boring where I am lodging. That is all to it. Let me come inside. I wish no harm. I promise." Danny gazed up, blinked intentionally, and Tara relented. She took the flowers and set them into a vase, while the man stepped inside and sat down upon the lumpy, leather couch. Gingerly, Tara sat down too. He appeared fashionable in cream colored corduroy pants, a thick green cashmere sweater, and brown boots. His hair fell long and was cut in a spiked appearance in the back.

"Quite mismatched furnishings in this apartment," Danny tried to sit comfortably, "It's not much space, is it?"

"It's adequate. It has to do."

"Still, neither this apartment nor this city seems suitable for any baby to dwell."

"What's that? This city is all we know and we are quite accustomed to it. This is what Ross can afford. What's your point?" Tara was surprised by this bluntness, but thought perhaps all Brits were this way.

"I don't wish to be rude, but this residence is a far cry from my surroundings in England. There I reside peacefully within a vast green valley. Ahh, it's just breathtaking," Danny's eyes lit up, "Our grand manor is modern, but large enough to accommodate several people. The rooms are brightly lit with crystal chandeliers and are decorated with comfortable furnishings. Even the stone fireplaces make everything seem quite inviting. It's just a vast contrast from this."

"Well, fireplaces sound nice for winter," Tara wondered why he described it all, "We do our best to stay warm. The furnace stalls out on occasion, but Ross complains to the landlord about the infrequency to keep this place heated."

"I see," Danny said. Tara looked away for a moment. Silence punctuated the room again. Their conversation was forced, but Tara didn't elaborate or give an opening for another topic. Other than speak about the weather, what else was there to say?

"So!" Danny bellowed, "Ross is interested in music. What do you like to do for fun?"

"There's no reason for that."

"What? Isn't there anything?"

Danny was surprised by her response. Did the girl give up on life? She lowered her eyes. All he wanted to do was make her feel optimistic.

"I imagine your days can be quite dull and tedious. Isn't there a hobby? Isn't there any time for amusement? What sort of life is that?"

"Apparently, it's one that is harsh," Tara's voice was barely audible. She frowned. Somehow the man reminded her of a time when she was happy. That was too long ago. The days were spinning away and she felt out of control. Danny hit upon delicate feelings without realizing it.

"You seem so sad and lost. I bet there were brighter days before," Danny did not think his words through. Suddenly, Tara placed her head into her hands. She wept.

"Oh, Miss… Tara!" Danny sputtered and stood up in alarm, "I didn't mean to make you cry!"

"Don't you understand?" Tara stood too. Huge tears fell down her cheeks, "Every day is absolute misery without Jimmy! I know that Ross told you plenty, but his version of the truth is warped. Ross was jealous of our relationship, but Jimmy was good to me. I just didn't allow him to sleep with me arbitrarily. We had a relationship. His love made me happy and now without him, I feel so alone! And now this!" Tara pointed at her belly, "What will I do?"

It seemed easy to divulge her feelings to a stranger. Ross knew too much. He always said cruel things to make her upset. She couldn't help sharing her fears. After all this time, she missed Jimmy. So she cried. Danny gathered Tara into his arms. His hands caressed her back until she calmed down. She noted that the cologne he wore gave off a spice fragrance. His arms were tight and his body warm. A kind stranger, destined to leave. Perhaps, for now, she could allow him to console her.

"I'm sorry. I sound like a stupid, blubbering fool," Tara said and then looked in his eyes. What soulful, deep pools of aqua blue. They were so inviting.

He caressed her hair and stared back at her, clearing his throat.

"I understand more than you think. There were many times in my life where I've been disappointed by love. So don't worry about your tears. Any time, just say the word and I am at your command," Danny's voice was husky.

"Well, really, it's improper to impose," she pulled away to gain distance again. She walked to the window to stare out, "When Jimmy and I were together, it seemed right. In my life, he shined like a bright star. Growing up, I found it hard to trust anyone."

"Ross mentioned you had a tough childhood."

"Yes, well kids can be cruel when someone doesn't easily fit in. Our teachers were always in transition so I had no one to confide in. I stayed an easy mark for cruel practical jokes. Jimmy didn't care that I was different. He paid a lot of attention. For once, I loved feeling so special. So, yes, we fell in love. It was easy to give of myself when he acted fun, adventuresome, and knowledgeable."

Tara thought about her words. She suddenly looked down at her feet.

"Perhaps, I should stop fooling myself. Ross may be right. So much time has passed and he still has not found me. Ross's address is filed in his uncle's office. It's easy to obtain when I had to sneak in," Tara let out a big sigh. New tears formed in her eyes, "I guess he didn't care about me. In one single night together-now my life is up in the air. So here I am left to figure out what comes next. As you can see, what Ross offers will not be enough."

Her lips quivered and tears flowed down her cheeks. Danny stepped forward to take her hand. He brought it up to his lips.

"Let me offer something that is nurturing and safe. Allow me to take his place."

"Why? I am in deep, deep trouble," Tara stared into his eyes and with one hand touched her stomach. It was growing rounder every day, "Ross apparently has not told you, but I may carry more than one child. I know it's true. I can feel it."

She explained about the nun and the medication that she took. Danny listened but this revelation only made him grip her hand tighter.

"Then time is of the essence. The navy beckons me to England soon. You are due in a few months time. What you need is stability and protection, with someone capable to provide it. Forgive this strong attraction. When we sat together at the bar, it was easy to sense your vulnerability, such as now."

She seemed to listen attentively. Could he dare continue? Everything spun in his heart like a whirlwind and he was sucked into the momentum. To offer the cart before the horse would be deemed irrational, but he remained a man of compulsive nature. At the rate things happened with women, he'd wind up middle aged and alone. He couldn't have that.

"Perhaps I have the words "sucker" painted upon my forehead, but I don't care. I've always assisted helpless creatures or tied off shoe laces for children. Something's been burning in my brain since I met you. Perhaps its fate that forces me to go along with such crazy compulsiveness. I want to do everything I can to help you. Right now. At this moment."

"Why? You don't know everything about me." Tara felt compelled to hear him out since she, too, believed in fate.

"That comes with time, my dear. We must make the most of our time together now. I want to learn everything. What makes your eyes light up? What touches your heart?"

Danny seemed excited. He was certainly spontaneous. Tara never dreamed that a rescue could come from across the ocean.

"Just give me a chance. There is so much to offer." He declared.

"Like what?" Tara defied that there could even be a spark of chemical reaction, but his body grew near. His lips beckoned. Something took the place of despair. Like a cat, she felt curious. In her lifetime, the cat was killed multiple of times. She couldn't help it.

"Well, in England, there is the manor that I mentioned. It's a marvelous place that sits in a wide valley, with nearby woods and trails to explore. It's a terrific place for children to grow up. You will learn to love it as I do. You can be comfortable there. Everyone in my family will help, especially me. I want to have you in my life permanently."

"Let me get this straight -are you proposing?" Tara clutched the fabric of the shirt surrounding her heart.

"I am but a simple man," Danny dropped down upon one knee. He wanted to do this properly, "Just be my wife and I will give you the world."

"Are you serious? Is this why you came over, to spring this wild idea?" Tara could not believe this. Was he for real? Yes, he seemed charming and so convincing- a gift he possessed.

"I mean every word, Tara. I swear!"

"It's incredulous. It's crazy!" Tara snapped her hand away. Astonishment gave way to panic, "We are as different as night and day. Your family will surely object! Such an absurd notion indeed! Out of the complete blue! After hearing all your stories and beliefs at the bar, there will be many challenges ahead. It's just inviting failure."

Danny stopped her in mid-pace.

"You cannot deny what I see revealed in your eyes. There is an attraction."

Briefly, he pulled Tara into his arms and when he took such command, she succumbed. There was no way to resist a man confidant enough to show assurance, "I see a decent, courageous person under terrible circumstances. No matter what my upbringing, you will always matter more. Let me help! I do so without hesitation."

"Just explain, please. Surely there is someone waiting for you back home. Why do you choose me? Are you mad?"

"There is no one waiting and no, Tara, I'm not mad. Just on fire. You are what I need to balance out my life. For a very long time, I prayed for the perfect woman. What was right for other men was not necessarily for me. Call me picky. I was about to give up," Danny sounded choked up, "From the moment I saw you, bells rang in my head, my heart pumped madly. Even my palms glistened. I'm at a fever's pitch. I must quench the flame. Dear Tara, I swear-no one will ever compare to you now."

By now, their lips were only centimeters apart. She sensed his breath upon her face. Tiny goose-pimples surfaced on her arms.

"I don't know," Tara responded, deeply amazed. Such daring! In spite of his desire, Tara managed to finagle free. She needed that space to think clearly. The touch of his body made her react. Could she give that sort of attention to a man?

Again, he dropped to one knee.

"Let me prove my worth. While I'm here, all I want to do is to convince you this can work. Oh, God, Tara - trust me! I will give you everything that your heart desires. All I ask is an answer about marriage before I leave. That's plenty of time for you to evaluate my word. Please?"

Tiny movements floated within her abdomen. What a daily toil it would be to feed, bathe, clothe, and hold several babies? Daunting at best, for just one person. There was Ross to consider as well. Undeserving of such a burden, surely a rift would pull them apart, especially if she could not yield to his bed. Not ready for any physical encounters, Tara insisted on a proper courtship.

"If this is to be, I expect respect whenever we are alone."

"Yes, of course. Always," Danny's face beamed like a child at Christmas time.

"And if I do choose to go with you, when the children are born, they must learn my faith. This won't upset you?"

"No, you are independent to teach whatever you feel important. All I ask is for some consideration. As their father, there is every intention to make them feel loved. No one will ever deduce the truth, as long as I can help it."

"And how do you intend to protect us? Surely, people will talk. Won't we be ridiculed?"

"Oh, to hell with what anyone thinks! You, darling, are a lass from New York City! A damn American! For the blokes in my village, I've always been called a fool. Just listen to the damn intonations of your Brooklyn accent! Enough said," Danny replied equivocally.

Tara finally laughed at this summation. Yes, she forgot about her own distinct accent. This whole situation was absolutely crazy, but Danny showed up out of the blue when she prayed for a solution. With what she construed, he did seem ready to take on all the challenges. She just needed to go along with his insane offer. Could they really make a relationship work?

"All right. I promise to think about this. I need time before giving a final answer."

"Then I will not give up until I hear a resound yes!" He grinned, happy that she gave consideration to his crazy idea.

Chapter Seven

Subtle connections

The more Tara saw him, Danny proved himself an interesting man, especially when he conversed on a whim. Many times speaking with Ross, one to one, he would spill out what was deep in his heart.

"In the service, I've visited many places in our world. Things are not what they seem in some countries. It's really quite lopsided, with religious beliefs and the distribution of wealth and rights. Women in some cultures are not even considered a person. If there husband dies, they can't keep their lands or vote about the welfare of their family. They have no say in the matter. That's so sad. Sometimes they find it difficult to thrive in the realm of military chaos and poverty. I've seen places with no fresh running water or good land to cultivate crops."

"I never realized that some people had it so hard," Ross leaned forward, listening closely. Sometimes Danny spouted off facts like his old history teacher, but he learned a lot. One day, Ross wanted to see these places that Danny visited.

"Yes, they do have it rough. I wish I can help them all, but I am just one man. I try to offer something of myself, something to lift up their spirits or pay their way for food or medicine. There are too many sick and starving children who need a better life through education. Those are the ones that touch my heart. I wish the world would wake up and pay attention- to give a damn for their plight. It's just so sad to witness these things as I travel abroad."

His stories always fascinated Ross, but there was something more underneath what Danny spoke about. Something Tara admired easily. He always revealed a huge heart. She remembered his generosity with the waitress. He didn't even bat an eye about giving away the money. She needed a good man like that, someone with a big heart who understood her own chaos and who allowed her to speak her mind.

It wasn't fair to ask Ross to fend for her future, when he could barely support himself. However, to say yes to Danny's proposal would mean leaving him behind. That bothered her, but she had to think about her future.

Every time that Danny stopped by, he'd gazed into her eyes at some point, seeking her response. It made her feel strange. He was older and a man, not a boy, although sometimes he could be silly like one. He was one that seemed assured about most things, except for how to behave around a woman. He seemed to need encouragement. So, out of the blue one cold afternoon, she gave him an inkling of hope.

Ross happened to run out his door to catch the landlord on the stairwell about the furnace. It was acting up again. Danny sat oblivious to her on the couch, tuning his guitar. She stood in the kitchen, stirring canned soup in a pot. It was now or never, so Tara went over to plop down beside him, catching Danny by surprise. They only had a few seconds as Tara could hear Ross's voice getting closer in the hallway.

"I just wanted to tell you…" she began

"Yes?" he responded

"….we should see each other secretly. It might upset Ross if… if… "

"What? If I should kiss you?" Danny's eyes went wide and he placed his guitar to one side. He turned to face her.

"No," Tara said and he instantly frowned. She had something else in mind. Since Ross was nearer to the door, she had to act now. With all her courage mustered up, she grasped his shoulders to pull him forward into a fiery kiss. When she released him, she finished her sentence, "No… if I kissed you."

Then she jumped up and ran to the kitchen just as Ross entered the room, unaware of their actions.

Danny looked at his feet suddenly. He didn't want Ross to notice his shock or the desire written all over his face for the girl. This was wonderful news. He was thrilled that she conceded. What was there to lose?

After that, he dropped by every chance, just to find a moment alone with her. In jest, he made the intent known to Ross, who repeatedly refuted it. Danny was headstrong.

"Consider yourself forewarned, my friend. That girl stirs up the coals in my furnace. My name is in the hat to win her over," Danny admitted openly as they watched smoke come out of the oven. Tara was a terrible cook.

"Well, Danny, only time will tell and it's sadly running out," Ross laughed and walked over to open up a window. His mind spun with glee. What outrageous statements? From what he observed whenever they were all together, Tara displayed no open interest in Danny at all. As they played cards or dominos after dinner, she kept to herself. If anything was happening, it was all one sided on Danny's part. There was nothing to worry about.

One day, Danny took Tara downtown to file for a passport.

"Along with state identification card and a copy of your birth certificate, you'll need this to travel abroad. I don't want any delays if you agree to my proposal," he insisted, looking into her eyes. Compliantly, she went inside. If she didn't, he would talk on about it for days, worrying needlessly. She couldn't bear that. The man got on her nerves being so organized. At least he behaved as a gentleman. To this she was simply grateful.

Later, they went to the corner market. She took her time shopping, much to his annoyance. When they returned to the apartment, she stuffed items into the cabinet randomly, "Here, let me do that," he said after a moment of observing. It was amusing how he liked to group certain items together, such as the spices or all of the soup cans.

Occasionally, he showed up with chocolates or small bouquets of assorted flowers, which she seemed to like best, instead of roses. It was difficult courting a girl who didn't say much about preferences, but by the keen expression on her face, he could tell whether he done well or not. It was nice just sitting in her presence sometimes, in that small kitchen area, whenever she was quiet and thinking. They would sip tea and she would stare off dreamily into space, with a face that was so beautifully expressive. How could he not fall in love with that?

One late February evening, he watched as long wayward bangs fell across her brow. It was hard not to reach up to push them out of her eyes. He stared intently, wanting to kiss her, but was glued to his spot. As she stared up with such sultry eyes, his mind went to another galaxy, so he took her hand and tried again to entice her into marriage, "Please, Tara. My family will support you. They are loyal people. You will like them. Marry me, and you will be surrounded with love too."

Tara stared into his eyes for a second and then squeezed his hand at the moment he looked at the table, thinking that he failed again.

"I never had a family to show love. All right, Danny. Let's do it. I will marry you."

With this response, it was time to reveal everything to Ross.

"After a lot of preparations, we are getting married tomorrow," Danny announced at the bar one afternoon as they played darts. Ross exposed chaffed, calloused hands and aimed steadily at the board nearby.

"Yeah, sure you are -and the mayor will give the bride away. When will this all take place?" Ross was totally clueless. All he knew was that Danny liked to brag about the absurd.

"This is for real chap!" Danny grabbed the remaining darts. He turned Ross to look directly into his eyes, "Ross, it's the right thing to do. Everything is arranged. It's just a small wedding with a few of my naval friends and acquaintances I know from the Trade Center. I want you to be my best man. It will calm Tara's nerves."

"Danny, stop! You are making this up!"

Ross froze as Danny pulled out official documents from his jacket.

"I managed to pull a few strings at the consulate. Tara has a passport in record time. Within a few days, we will depart home by a transatlantic cruise liner."

Ross took the documents to read over. Deep realization sank in and he slumped into a chair. Danny handed over a glass of water. The young man looked pretty pale.

"We have to be prepared for when she delivers. I can provide adequately. You know that's important. As her best friend, she is agonizing to leave you behind. We are friends too, so I can relate to her pain," Danny placed a hand upon his shoulder, "If only you possessed a passport."

"I do," Ross revealed, staring up into Danny's eyes. Would it make a difference? He didn't want to see them go either, "My boss made me get one, incase I ever traveled abroad for the company. That opportunity never came up."

"Ross! This is terrific news," Danny's eyes lit up, being very overjoyed, "You can join us. I will make the arrangements. Once we are in England, Michael will find you work at a reputable firm. Then we can continue with our music at some point at leisure. All you have to do is go with us."

Danny's instant plans made Ross feel dizzy. Still, he was happy to be included and not shut out.

"Alright, Danny. I will. I'll let the landlord know about the apartment. It's really all I am responsible for here," Ross responded. He didn't know what else to say. He was so stunned.

"That's great! Why live in such a dump? You deserve better and any work in London will be twice as better than what you do now," Danny offered a handshake and Ross took it, "There will be no regrets, my friend. You will learn to love England like I do. You will like my family. You will see."

Ross felt misgivings. This adventure to Danny's home territory would definitely be a new experience.

Chapter Eight

Crossing Over

"Is this right for you?" Ross was thankful for one last dinner alone with Tara on the eve of the wedding. Danny would not show up, fearing bad karma could jinx their future. It was remarkable how calm she remained as she set the table. Tara behaved as if nothing significant would take place in the morning to change her life.

"Yes. Danny is determined. He has so many hopes."

"What about your dreams, Tara? Do you share the same?"

"Honestly, Ross, I want what is best for my children, to ensure a better life. Danny wants this marriage too, so let him do this. It's not love that pushes me. I owe that to their father."

"You need to give up on Jimmy."

"Why should I? I promised my heart to Jimmy -then and forever-No matter where he is. I never promised Danny anything of the sort."

"You will stand by your duty, won't you?" Ross felt alarmed. How could Tara be so heartless?

"Yes, of course. I want this marriage consummated-legal and binding. Danny can have my body, but never my heart."

"Tara you can not dupe that man! For God's sake! Danny deserves something real in his marriage. He is opening up his whole world to you."

"Perhaps, but I didn't coerce him into it. This is my insurance that the children will not grow up illegitimate, with no family background. They will acquire all of his history and his fortune. They will not be denied anything."

"Well, perhaps therein lays a valid point. Still, I believe there are some feelings for that man. You just won't admit it. Otherwise, you would have stayed here in New York and made a life with me," Ross stared away. Tara reached out for his hand, but he pulled it away.

"Oh, Ross! I didn't mean to hurt you."

"It's all right, Tara. You choose a better future. I will come along to ensure that everyone gives their best effort in this so-called marriage!"

A new identity in England could bring about opportunities. However, misgivings swirled in her mind as the couple stood together to say their vows. The promises made were strange and bewildering on her tongue. The words were forced in front of that tiny gathering. It didn't help that Ross simply stared sternly. When they were pronounced, the groom kissed his bride with a very wet kiss. Then he rushed towards the Champaign to get the reception started.

After awhile, he sweltered wearing such a thick tuxedo. The room was exceptionally warm from a nearby fireplace. Danny felt sweat upon his brow and his tuxedo itched. All he wanted to do was cool off, "Let's go outside for a moment," he suggested and tugged Tara to follow along. The sun shone brightly into their eyes and it made them squint. The cold February air was bearable, but still Tara shivered. Danny held her close and they walked out to a pier. The Hudson River peaked over the floating wood beams. Danny pointed out to a far horizon.

"Out there, far across the ocean, is our home, Tara. The future is all ours. Trust me, trust my love, and good things will come of this. It's our beginning, darling. All of this is meant to be. You'll see."

Within a few days, the trio stood forth upon the transcontinental ship that transported them to England. As the Statue of Liberty vanished from view, they all sensed that their lives would change forever. Noisy seagulls soon diminished as the ship sailed along into open water. Tara walked along the rail to look down. She studied the deep crests that rose and fell in the wake of the huge ship moving forward. The smell of salty seaweed penetrated the air.

"Is anything wrong, sweetheart? You seem miles away," Danny placed his own coat over hers. Tara said nothing and only shook her head. He shivered, "We should go inside. It's a bit cold out here."

"I will. I just need a moment alone to take it all in, saying goodbye," Tara remarked as the wind forced her long brown hair in every direction. Her voice was so melancholy as she felt on the verge of tears again.

Danny looked into her eyes. Brown eyes that looked so misty. He realized the difficulty she endured in the past few days. While he was happy, Tara adjusted to his needs as a man and to the concept of marriage all together. He equaled the young girl to some free-spirited horse that didn't liked being corralled into the comforts of a well-hayed barn. Everything seemed new and constricting. He would allow his wife some space of her own.

"All right. I'll meet you by the buffet room in an hour."

Tara, grateful for the momentary solitude, watched him walk away. She could release her vented feelings of despair. Too late to change things, she had to deal with many insurmountable feelings about leaving everything she knew: Hartridge, the Apple city, including Jimmy-wherever he was now. He had loved her deeply. They had promised to be true to one another forever, so in thinking about this, huge tears fell down her cheeks as she studied the gold ring on her finger. Was this sudden marriage the right decision? She felt that she would never know for sure. She walked along again and looked at the blue-gray horizon. What waited across the Atlantic? What did the grand manor look like? What were the people like? And were Danny's family as amicable as explained?

In truth, across the ocean, the Cross Family shared doubts too. Who was the new bride, Mrs. Daniel Aaron Cross? Who was Ross Kelly, the young man that accompanied them? They received the news by letter and since the Commander arrived to London right after the wedding, Michael stopped by headquarters to seek out answers. His mother accompanied him as well, but there wasn't a lot that Harry offered.

"Quite simply, she is a quiet, respectful young girl. Danny seems happy, but they make an odd couple. In contrast, her attire is homely and makes her overall impression seem that way too. It's not my call to judge her financial status, but it's not the same class as ours. However, to be in her presence and to watch the expressions that light up her face are to die for, so I can easily see why he fell so hard. He does seem deeply enraptured with her."

"Then we must support his decision," Michael said to his mother, "Even if I do say he made a hasty one."

"Doesn't matter. He sounds in love and that's all that matters to me. Relationships have not been easy for him in the past, so when they arrive, I expect all of our family to make them feel welcomed and accepted. I will not succumb to less," Helen told him. When Michael announced her plea to his siblings, they nodded in fair agreement. They, too, only wanted Danny's happiness and welfare.

After several days, the ship docked in London's port. They were picked up by Sammy, whose curiosity needed to be satisfied immediately. He raced up the ramp way to greet them.

"Would you look at that? They could be twins." Tara remarked as she and Ross came down towards the two brothers below, who embraced each other openly. Sammy stood shorter with a rounder face, a mustache, and a huskier build. Remarkably, his exuberance matched the older sibling and he embraced Tara with a lot of enthusiasm.

"It's so delightful to make your acquaintance, Tara. Welcome to England!" Sammy picked her up into the air, but set her down quickly, surprised that she felt heavier than she looked. Yet, she wore layered clothing and a thick coat to cover up much of her physique. Sammy turned towards Ross and they shook hands.

"How do you do?" Ross said politely, eager to make an amicable impression.

"I do well, but you speak funny, mate," Sammy wrinkled his nose. There was a mischievous gleam in his eye, "Perhaps after a few pints of good lager, you will sound like the rest of us fine blokes."

"Perhaps," Ross felt agreeable to that logic. A stiff drink could be welcomed at any time with him. In the many bars about the ship, and especially hanging out with Danny, he had enjoyed tasting different brands of liquor that were available.

"Come on then. Let's get the luggage," Sammy suggested, taking the lead to acquire their belongings. Soon they were on their way out of the metropolitan area of London. Tara stared out the window, her nose pressed to the glass like a small child. The long ride into the English countryside seemed like stepping into an older century. Passing clouds made long rays of sunbeams trickle through the trees like a comb. The wide landscapes were like something out of a painting. Tara pointed to the various farm animals along the way as if they were alien beings.

"My dear, those are sheep. Haven't you ever come across one before?" Sammy chuckled as he stared at the married couple through the rearview mirror.

"This is all new," Danny explained, "They have never ventured outside their city of skyscrapers before."

"Never? Well see here! We have to give them a grand tour of this wonderful country very soon. Wait until you sample a bite of goat cheese, organic vegetables, or a fine trout! My favorite meal is simply Sheppard's Pie," Sammy bragged, "There are so many fine established inns, pubs, and farm shops to visit. Our county is so diversified in historical sites, castles, churches, and our place luckily lies secluded in the north valley."

"Do you have animals too?" Ross asked.

"Ah, we have a few mares and two gallant stallions."

"Really? Horses," Ross always admired them. Sammy nodded at his seat companion.

"Oh, yes. My mother, in a younger era, was a wonderful equestrian and well known. She remains a member of the British Horse Society. There are several trophies on display in our manor. My father built an entirely new stable just for her. We will teach you to ride soon enough. We are almost there, but I must stop for petrol first."

Sammy suddenly waved at some folks as the car drove up a narrow lane. People milling about speculated about the new arrivals as they stretched their legs. Tara's features brought on much twitter-tatter whispers. From a distance, she did not seem one of high class, nor wore makeup to improve the look. Her hair, quite long and uneven, seemed in tune to her layered clothing, which look bland at any rate. Ross appeared too thin in his grey suit, quite tall and quite pale. In truth, they were an odd pair to the traditional, healthy, blond, blue-eyed family in that supreme household. How would they be received?

Chapter Nine
Meeting the Cross Family

They arrived around the noon hour to the Grand Manor, a wide, brown brick estate centered on expansive acreage. Tara placed her face to the glass in the window as they came up a long driveway, amazed at how lovely it looked, with intricate landscape in front and even a fountain. Nearby were iron fences and a gated corral. Three stout horses milled about, feeding upon a stack of hay. Near that stood a type of wooden barn which seemed huge to her too.

Outside, by the front door, they were greeted by Helen and George Cross, who was dressed in semi-formal attire. They greeted everyone in eloquent tones and thick English accents. George's hair was white, along with bushy eyebrows. He stood trim carrying a pipe that was lit, but he held it aside to greet the new arrivals. Nervously, Tara formally shook hands with her new father-in-law. She bestowed a short curtsy as she stood before Helen. Charmed, the matron embraced the young girl to put her at ease.

"Welcome home, Tara. It is always yours, as you now belong to my family," Helen's tone sounded warm and sweet. Her scent bore resemblance to lilacs. Tara blushed as her own heart swelled in acceptance of Helen's immediate kindness. Helen stepped aside as Michael came out from the stable, dressed impeccably in riding wear.

"It's so nice to make your acquaintance," Michael shook hands with Ross. Then Michael faced his new sister-in-law, "And as for you my dear, I stand in complete awe."

He politely bestowed a welcoming kiss upon Tara's hand and her eyes grew wide.

"You see, my love. My family is great!" Danny stood proud by his father. Just then, someone else drew his attention. An elderly, gruff-looking man, wearing a long black coat, a crisp white linen shirt, and long slim pants, stood away, waiting for instructions, "Haskell! You old devil!"

"Master Daniel, *Sir*- it's good that you are home again," The butler nodded politely, waiting instructions.

"Yes. It is. Haskell, please take Ross's belongings to my bedroom upstairs. Sammy will point out the right ones. As for the rest, take it to our home. Be quick about it as the clouds are moving in. I don't want the luggage to get wet."

"Yes, sir. Right away." The old man followed Sammy to the back of the car. Tara clutched her heart to hear this.

"We have our own home?" she said in surprised whisper to Ross, whose eyes grew wide too. He nodded happily at her as she looked about the area. If they possessed their own, was it within the same grand countryside? This particular wide Georgian estate, situated within a very lush valley, was just like Danny described it back in New York: bordered by quaint, ancient forests, sparkling waters, and many villages of mellow stone cottages. Indeed, his home village was beautiful.

The family went inside for a light brunch. Helen Cross poured tea. She offered mini-sandwiches and macaroon cookies. Tara felt comfortable sitting near her. She was a delightful, pleasant woman, trim with fair skin, dark blue eyes, and summer blond hair.

"What did you think of the cruise?" Helen wanted to draw Ross into conversation. He sat aloof observing everything, but her warmth was appealing.

"It was really great. There was much to do onboard. They had bands, gambling, and a lot of great food. Danny and I checked out everything."

"And what did you think, dear? Was the honeymoon trip delightful?" Mrs. Cross noticed an instant frown come across the young girls face.

"The sea and I did not agree at all," Tara declared. Danny chuckled. He reached to take her hand, squeezing it tightly.

"She had motion sickness and was forced to stay in bed a lot. It wasn't quite unreasonable as the boat did rock a bit. We encountered a couple of turbulent storms along the way."

"Oh, poor dear," Helen Cross shook her head, "Perhaps you will fair better traveling by other means in the future. It's a shame it wasn't romantic."

"Well, we certainly must catch up on that," Danny revealed without thinking about it. Tara lowered her head, but not before noticing Michael. He sat there studying her over carefully, with a soothing smile. It didn't bother him at all that she caught him looking. His smile beckoned upon flirtation. Just then, a loud clatter came from the hallway. Heavy footsteps raced upon a nearby stairwell.

"Susan!" George Cross's boisterous voice boomed across the room as he stood up. He placed a cherry wood pipe upon an ashtray, but it toppled over, spilling the lit tobacco. Ross, sitting the closest to the angry man, brushed it in before it burnt the surface of the coffee table. Tara sighed in relief. The only other witness was Helen Cross, who suddenly fanned herself with a kerchief. Everyone else focused upon the person on the stairs.

"Susan! Come here immediately!"

Michael scurried out to bring back a voluptuous, platinum blond girl held firmly in his grasp.

"Oh, no!" Danny hummed, "Somebody's is in a bad spot, I believe. Now what did you do to get into a mess, my dear young sister?"

"Why do you care? Stop assuming you can be my parent as well!"

Susan struggled against Michael's grip. With a menacing glare, she looked up him. He didn't care at all. Danny argued back.

"Why should I, when you always behave so terribly spoiled?"

Helen Cross intervened.

"No, no. Please, don't even begin! Let's be civil," she reminded the family. At this point, her cheeks were beet red. George Cross walked curtly to his youngest daughter.

"Company or not, I intend to say my peace, since this young lady did not give that opportunity last night!"

"Oh, Father! Not that old tired speech again! For heavens sakes, I am an adult. I did nothing wrong!" Susan tossed her hair over in defiance. Ross stood aside, silently fascinated by her appealing shape. Susan glared at all of the men. That's when she took notice of him. Those dark eyes were mysterious. He seemed like someone from a classic, Gothic tale. Unnoticed by the rest, she offered a brief, tantalizing smile and whispered, "Heathcliff."

"Why did you run off with that Fredrick boy?" Sammy barked out as he entered the room, "You stayed out all night. We were all upset. What's next Susan?"

Susan's lip curled in a snare. Helen gasped to hear family secrets revealed so soon.

"You are kidding?" Danny looked at his sister in appall. He knew all about the Fredrick's boy wild reputation, "Susan! That dastardly beast? Balderdash! Now, I am disgusted!"

"Well, at least someone else agrees about your behavior!" George nodded his head.

"So do us, Father!" Sammy announced, sliding up to the disgruntled man.

"Yes. Quite right!" Michael declared.

"Oh, please stop! Stop!" Susan threw her hands up in the air. She hated that they all ganged up on her, "You all sound so medieval.... so chivalrousness! You do realize that this is 1978, not the 15ᵗʰ century!"

"Balderdash!" Danny declared again. Susan sneered.

"And besides, Gloria does exactly what she pleases with beaus. No one says one bloody word! Why do you deplore my ways? I am old enough to know what it is I want from a man! No matter what their background!"

At this, Susan's eyes strayed towards Ross. His heart skipped a beat, but he remained still.

"Oh, heavens!" Mrs. Cross gasped. She fanned herself again, her hand flinging frantically. Danny placed his hands on her shoulders.

"There, there, mother. Don't listen. We all know that Gloria has ten times more scruples. Oh Susan! Why show off such a vicious little minx? Somewhere in the sheath that yields such a sharp wicked tongue is civility."

"Stop speaking so Shakespearean!" Susan hissed. It was obvious the two enjoyed quibbling. It was Michael's turn to get in his digs.

"Then why behave so horribly? It never fails! When I graduated, you and your sordid friends became drunk at our party. When Gloria took off for the University, you ran off alone to Paris. For a whole bloody week! It took away her joy finding independence because she feared for your safety. Now that you are of age, you make yourself seem like some fancy free trollop! Frankly, it's enough Susan. How can one command respect from us when our celebrations are constantly ruined?"

Even if her actions were motivated to be free from George's strict rules, Susan offered an apology to the newest members.

"He's right about me, you know. It's horrid to bring out such revelations during Danny's homecoming. However, it is best to know what is gained by this marriage. I am not perfect and this family is not nominated for sainthood!"

Tara accepted Susan's extended hand and shook it softly. Susan offered it to Ross who relinquished it slowly.

"Forgive me. I did not think." Susan faced Danny now. She tweaked his cheeks hard to make them beet red, "My dear brother, I love you just the same. It's about time you finally married someone!"

He rubbed his cheeks profusely while Susan turned to her father.

"May I leave? I want to freshen up."

"That sounds like a good idea," George Cross took a seat, grasping for the lost pipe. Susan left the room, but her presence still lingered in the air, much like the sweet fragrance of perfume that caught Ross's attention.

Chapter Ten

The Announcement

During the late afternoon, Tara construed their separate personalities. Most of Danny's siblings settled into the living room area for conversation while Mr. and Mrs. Cross kept occupied elsewhere. They wanted the younger ones to bond on their own. Tara listened in with a keen ear.

In one corner, Sammy told lots of great stories, mostly about the women he dated in different ports. Tara watched him closely. She could understand why he was likeable. He was a natural flirt and his boisterous personality made him appealing. Plus when he smiled, he was very handsome, just like Danny. Sammy possessed a strong preoccupation for betting on the ponies or the World Cup football events. As they spoke, he wanted to make a bet about something. He kept his wallet handy, but Danny was more apt to bring up something about the navy. They discussed plenty, what they seen, what they did on their assignments.

Michael spoke to Ross conveying tidbits about his work as a theater producer. He described at length about the society scene in London. Perhaps he wanted to impress Ross as he too looked wide eyed and paid great attention. Michael spoke with such an eloquent tone. He displayed cool mannerisms, so different from his fast-talking younger brothers.

Susan eventually came down to join them. She wore a white shirt with a black mini-skirt, exposing long legs. From her chair, she gazed upon the newcomers. She didn't interact with them at all. Occasionally, Ross looked at Susan with a far away gleam to his eye. Tara assumed it was just natural curiosity.

"So what else did you do in New York, other than work and chasing after this young lady?" Sammy asked Danny at one point, winking at Tara.

"I came up with new songs. Do you want to hear one?" Now, Danny's eyes twinkled. He looked hopeful, but both brothers groaned.

"What? Please let's not," Michael gulped down his brandy. "I am sorry, but your past attempts were always lackluster. Why waste your time?"

"It's not a waste. Just give one moment to listen. I will prove it to you," Danny was not discouraged by their reactions. He ran upstairs while his brothers shook their heads in dismay. They had no belief that anything changed. Upon his return, Danny came down with two guitars. He handed one to Ross, who was surprised at the request to play at this particular moment.

"Now?" Ross balked and sat down his glass.

"Yes, it is a perfect opportunity," Danny pleaded silently to his friend.

"Well, if you insist," Ross took a moment to tune the guitar and then began a slow, familiar number. Back at the apartment in New York, Tara grew tired of hearing it. The men often practiced and tweaked it every chance they played. Now, as they took this opportunity to perform it well, everyone in the room suddenly paid great attention.

Obviously, the duo created some sort of musical wizardry, as their lilting voices filled the air with stirring, inspirational lyrics. The serene strumming of the guitars magically evoked deep reactions. At the end of four minutes, a moment of quiet reflection ensued. Then the family applauded. Even Susan stood to place her hand over her mouth, in mock surprise.

"That is brilliant," Michael said first. His eyes were warm, "What a remarkable improvement. Did you both create that?"

"Of course!" Danny grinned to win over Michael's approval. It was a long time coming. Before Ross came along, Danny was about to give up composing, "Ross and I work naturally together. We are a team."

"Well, congratulations. That certainly is terrific. I bet I'll never get that tune out of my head now," Sammy patted Danny on the back.

"It does have much promise," Michael said and then as a reflex, pulled out a thick address book from the pocket of his jacket, "There are many contacts in London who could boost your music endeavors. They will help copyright your material. I'm sure I can find a number to give you."

"Michael's black book is filled with many names, including pretty, eligible women," Sammy informed Ross. He poured the young man more brandy, "Once you are settled in London, you should borrow it."

Tara frowned to hear this. He was her exclusive friend for so long. How strange to think he could find someone else for close companionship like theirs. It just didn't feel right.

"I'm in no hurry," Ross felt surprised to see her turn away in response. He rubbed his chin absentmindedly. Susan studied their reactions, not missing a thing.

"It is smart to wait on that." Michael wrote down a number. He gave it to Danny, who tucked it into his wallet. Michael gazed into Ross's eyes, "Women are everywhere in London. You'll date soon enough. First thing is to square up contacts in different business fields. Father knows many in the financial district. He is an avid investor in several stock firms. The point is to find an interesting pursuit."

Soon enough, Haskell announced dinner. They gathered into the main dining hall. Tara marveled at the wide room. There was a proper place setting for everyone at a long table. It was decorated with fresh flowers and candles. A fresh fire burned brightly in a nearby stone-hearth fireplace. The atmosphere was quite amiable. Haskell filled the glasses with red wine for everyone. As they dined, Danny quickly consumed it. He asked Haskell for a refill, and then another, without even thinking about it. Tara mentally kept count.

During this first official family gathering, Tara was introduced to Anna Cross, Danny's elderly grandmother, and to his older sister, Gloria Cross. They were detained in London that morning and drove in late. Gloria, a year older than Danny, seemed lovely in a green velvet jacket, white linen shirt, an A-line black skirt, and long black boots. She possessed lots of long, golden curls and a lean figure.

"What is it that you do?" Tara asked at one point, when everyone was talking at once. Tara was eager to continue their friendly conversation. Gloria possessed an easy going personality within such a serene disposition.

"I once studied to become a nurse, but really, my dedication was lacking, so I quit. Now I dream about becoming a world class photographer. I love taking pictures," She told Tara and passed a plate of bread to her sister, who continually stared suspiciously at Tara throughout the entire meal.

The rest of the family conversed about several things, repeating details for their grandmother to catch up. She was dressed very cordial, wearing pearls and a fashionable Sunday hat. The family were quite attentive to her every need, especially Danny. There were several moments when Tara observed him whispering into her ear.

"It is wonderful to have one settle down," Grandmother Anna nodded approvingly, "It's great that Danny realizes how family is truly important."

"Yes, I agree," Helen looked at the single children remaining at her table, "You are all so consumed with careers and the prestige it brings. Our family has enough honors to burn many lifetimes. We need another generation to take hold. I want grandchildren while still young enough to enjoy it all, to hear the pitter-patter of little feet running around this manor again."

Helen woefully folded a napkin upon her lap. That gave Danny an opportunity. He raised a glass and seemed happy.

"Please, do not worry on that point mum. Tara will do us justice in that department very, very soon."

He took the goblet to drink some of the wine. He brought it back to the table too hard, as it tipped, allowing red wine to stain the white linen tablecloth. Danny blotted it with a napkin, but it made things look worse. Ross coughed, as everyone at the table stared at Tara.

"I thought you were just fat," Susan crinkled her nose. Tara tugged at the fabric of the oversized shirt underneath her sweater. With the right clothing, it was hard to discern straight away the extent of her pregnancy. Like Susan said, she simply appeared FAT!

"Yes, Tara is expecting," Danny announced. He seemed very proud, "She saw a doctor in New York who told us to be prepared. We will be very blessed. She may carry twins, or triplets, but I will bet my bottom dollar that it will be more."

"I'll take that bet!" Sammy jested, but Michael stared him down. Obviously, this was quite shocking to his parents. Helen was fanning herself again and staring at George, who when upset or nervous, naturally reached for his pipe to calm down. He puffed on the tobacco several times to get it to kick in. He grumbled under his breath, but it wasn't very audible. Tara felt embarrassed. Ross lowered his head. Alcohol clouded Danny's judgment to time such a personal announcement. Tara shook her head. Her eyes were wide. With a swift kick, she plunged a sharp shoe directly into Danny's shin underneath the table. Danny jumped up quickly and yelled like a young boy.

"Owww! That hurts! Why did you do that?!" he clutched his leg tight, staring at her in disbelief.

"Oooh! You are incorrigible, Daniel Cross!" Tara immediately turned to the senior ladies, who were surprised by her outburst, "Excuse me. I need fresh air."

Tara left the table. She ran down the hallway, out the front door to collapse upon the single step. She buried her head into her hands, feeling mortified. Helen was kind to put her at ease in the new surroundings. Now, what would she assume of her new daughter-in-law? Probably the worst. After a moment, Gloria stepped out to join her on the step. Without a word, she softly stroked Tara's long brown hair. She found a tissue tucked away in her dress pocket. Tara accepted it to blow her nose.

"Danny is an impulsive man," Gloria declared, her voice lyrical in tone, "He likes to brag. Really, this is wonderful news. Please don't be mad that he embarrassed you this way. Allow my brother the chance to make it up to you."

"Why should I?" Tara didn't understand, but was curious. Gloria's eyes were thoughtful.

"Let me explain. Danny was never one to be popular. He would tell such horrible corny jokes. I'm sure by now you have heard them."

Tara nodded. Yes, he always messed up the punch lines. Gloria stared off into the horizon.

"Well, they do have zero impact, but that's just his nature, to be sweet and different. The girls here never took him seriously. With matters of the heart, my dearest brother was quite out of sorts. Here was Michael, so handsome and mellow, and Sammy, so terrifically clever and modernly witty: two brothers quite successful in their chase for the ladies. Danny could never compete. For such a long time, he has been so lonely."

"Really?" Tara found this quite revealing.

Gloria wrapped the sweater tight to guard against the chill and stood up. The dark clouds went away. The rain never produced. The temperatures fell as the sun set, leaving eerie shades of pink and orange in the horizon.

"Danny joined the navy, not to venture the world, but to seek out someone special, to take him on. He has been everywhere: Japan, Asia and the Mediterranean. Even my brothers set him up with women in the last year. It never worked out. I feel he was about to make the navy a firm career. All of this time, since Christmas, not one bloody word. Then his letter arrived, spilling all about your marriage. We all gathered to see the picture enclosed from your wedding day. It was hard to believe, but now here you are, a wonderful new sister-in-law."

Tara felt encouraged. No wonder he felt headstrong about marriage. He was desperate to have things right in his life too.

"Well, your brother is so overzealous. It upsets me easily. I am not use to all of the dramatics," Tara admitted.

"He can't help his compulsiveness. Yet, his true intentions come from the heart. We have a tight bond. He shares with me things he won't tell the rest. When

I drove up, he was so anxious to reveal how happy he is. He couldn't wait to introduce us. I can see why. You are the only smart and a practical decision he's made to improve his situation."

"What do you mean?" Tara peered into Gloria's bright blue eyes.

"You set my brother straight about his foolishness. I knew that by the instant you kicked him at the table!" Gloria laughed, long blond curls falling into her face. Tara smiled. She felt honored that Gloria shared her secrets. At that moment, Danny came outside with his head bowed. His sister gave fair warning, "Be nice, dear brother. Bend your inebriated pride."

She left them alone to make amends. Danny took a hesitant seat next to Tara. He wasn't sure what to say. He stared out into the yard, his mind in contemplation.

"I do apologize, Tara. My behavior in there was out of line. I should have consulted with you first before speaking to the family. Will you forgive my outburst?" His tone was remorseful, so Tara took his hand. She squeezed it tightly. This tiny action was enough to make him feel better, "Should we go back in to continue? I did spoil your attempt to finish dinner."

Tara did not think this appealing anymore.

"It's been such a long day."

"Perhaps we should go home. We do have to unpack."

Home. Something of her own too. Perhaps, in her new home she would not feel out of place.

"Oh, yes!" Tara replied. Danny jumped to his feet and tugged Tara up from the step.

"Then let's go."

"Shouldn't we inform your family?"

"No." Danny replied. There was a tease to his tone, "We are newlyweds, after all. It's only natural to disappear. Let me get our coats and we'll be on our way. It's just up the road a bit. I will get Haskell to drive us there."

"If it's not that far, I can tolerate the chill in the air. In New York, we walk everywhere. At least it's not raining," Tara suggested.

"If you insist, my love. I know a shortcut," Danny revealed. Soon, they were off towards their home in the valley.

Chapter Eleven

When things go all wrong

They made their way up a well beaten path that twined through the dark and grassy fields. Danny knew the way well. After twenty minutes into it, Tara found it difficult to keep up.

"Oh, Danny, how much further? For some reason, I don't feel so good," Tara looked pale now. Even her hand felt clammy. There was a trickling creek nearby and they made their way towards it. On the bank, there was a large rock. Tara took a seat to rest. The gurgling water was soothing to her senses. She felt nauseated.

"It's not that much further now. We can be there in five minutes," Danny dampened a handkerchief to place it against her forehead and lips.

"Thank you," She whispered, exhaling a deep breath. She bent her head low between her feet.

"You'll feel better in a moment," Danny said, looking her over. He gently smoothed back her hair. There were many times on the ocean voyage when she succumbed to wooziness. Whenever Tara felt this way, he left her alone in the cabin and occupied his time with Ross elsewhere on the ship. Later, when he snuck into the room, he lay gently beside her, not disturbing her as she slept.

Thinking about this now, perhaps the travel was grueling for her in some degree. When they encountered the storms, the ship rocked to the frequent high waves. Tara stayed nauseated a lot. Now on dry land, this took on a new perspective. Perhaps it was not all due to motion sickness. This made Danny worry now. After a few minutes, Tara regained composure, but she rose unsteadily.

"No. You can't over exert yourself, Mrs. Cross," Danny gallantly lifted Tara up into his arms.

"What are you doing?"

"What do you think? I can carry you the rest of the way."

"Danny, you can't. You will hurt yourself," Tara cried out but to no avail. He was determined to do this. He made hasty steps to get back on the trail. Tara marveled at his strength.

Soon the house came into view in the dark. They approached a wood fence lined heavy with thick thistle of hearty brush. It went all the way towards a stone gate entrance. Slowly, Danny made his way up the cobble stone drive, surrounded by winter-sleeping grass. Standing watch in the wide lawn were several large trees, with dark and ominous branches, reaching out like swords towards the moon in the sky.

"This is all ours?" Tara was overwhelmed by the size of the house and landscape. Danny was out of breath. She weighed more than he anticipated. Every muscle in his back ached.

"Yes. This foursquare house is a solid place, where my mother and her two sisters played as youngsters, visiting their old spinster aunt. She had visited the states once and liked the look of South Carolina homesteads, so she had this built in the manner of a plantation house. She even had that hanging swing put in for effect. Folks around here thought it always odd, but she didn't care. This is known as the Briggs House, but it is good enough to accommodate our own children. So now it is our house, in spite of what the villagers want to call the place."

He walked upon a wide porch to open a thick oak door. Ceremoniously, the man carried Tara across the threshold. At that point, when placed upon her feet again, she took it all in. Danny stretched out his weary back. They stood in the midst of a large entry foyer with pretty intricate wall paper and solid wood floors. Adjacent to this was an ample living room. It had a huge stone fireplace, already lit and glowing. It gave everything an inviting ambiance.

She could see that one room was a massive library with rows and rows of shelves. It lined the dark panelled walls. On the floor lay a Persian rug. An upright piano sat against the wall. In the direction past the center stairway, she noticed a large, bright colored kitchen with an open pantry. There were two other rooms nearby, but the doors were closed, so she didn't know what was behind them. Yet underneath the high ceiling with the huge crystal chandelier lit up so pretty, Tara felt small in comparison.

Danny kept his word. He brought her home to a secure place to raise the children. Tara suddenly felt insignificant. What in the world did she have to give in return? She realized all he wanted was her love. Instinct directed her to embrace her husband tightly. It totally surprised the young man. Never in their short time together did Tara initiate so much affection. He was amazed at the hot feelings evoked in this one single action. They pulled apart. He felt mesmerized by the look in her eye, "Thank you, my husband," She whispered, with enough seduction and spark to set off an atomic explosion in his soul.

Tara wanted to resolve everything. At the start of their courtship, his boasting always seemed like a grand stand gesture to win her over, whereas she would prefer simple reassurances that came from his heart. He indeed accomplished the one thing she always lacked growing up: a foundation to build upon. A home meant everything to the young girl.

"Let's go upstairs. I'll show you around. There are lots of rooms, but we'll start with our own." Danny suggested with that gleam in his blue eyes. This time, Tara nodded and squeezed his hand.

They made their way around the oversized master bedroom. It contained several pieces of furniture. There was a roll top desk, a six-drawer upright dresser against one wall, along with a dark-cherry armoire. The large four-poster bed occupied the space of another section, in-between two end tables. A fireplace glowed on another wall that contained colorful high borders of clouds and angels. Danny added a log to the low fire. Colorful hues made his blond hair seem darker. He walked over to a hope chest near the bed and pulled out an extra blanket, "When the fire dies down at night, this will come in handy."

Then he strolled out to another room and came back with extra pillows to place on both sides of the bed. One for him and definitely one for her. Danny painstakingly recalled the very first time they slept together. It was on their wedding night, in a cold hotel room. Sometime in the pre-dawn hours, he shifted to cuddle closer to her warm body. He found that his neck was stiff and discovered that his head was flat upon the hard mattress. Somehow, Tara stole his pillow. She slept comfortably. Did she do it on purpose? He wasn't sure, but it happened every single time since then. On the cruise to England, he grew determined to remedy that situation once they were in their own home.

He looked around the room. The luggage was set aside where Haskell placed them earlier. Danny scooped one up to lay cockeyed on the dresser. Inside, he found the fuzzy socks that matched her bright pink robe. He laid it out on the chair. The young woman should be comfortable in her new bedroom. Tara watched closely. She tried not to give away a smile.

In the meantime, she walked idly about, checking out the dresser and the armoire. The more she moved, the more she winced. A nagging pain sharpened deeply, somewhere in the lowest region of her expanding abdomen. Perhaps she overdid it on the walk over. In a panic, Tara scurried to the bed in one smooth motion. Danny looked up with a puzzled expression. Tara seemed as pale as a ghost.

"Danny. Something's terribly wrong," Tara panted and then passed out. Danny leapt to her side. He felt her forehead and noted that it was clammy. He took a blanket and wrapped her body within it. Then he called his mother.

"I'll summon the doctor. It may take a little bit before he gets there. In the meanwhile, I'll send Gloria over," Helen Cross told him on the line, "She will know what to do."

Chapter Twelve
A bitter pill to swallow

When his sister arrived, she was not alone. Michael drove her down, along with Ross, who wanted to know all the circumstances about his best friend.

"Where is she?" Gloria demanded as she placed her coat and scarf upon the coat rack.

""Stay here!" she added after Danny pointed up the stairs.

"I don't know what happened. Tara looked white as a ghost, clutched her stomach, and then fainted on the bed," Danny told the men.

"Well, she's always been prone to fainting in the past," Ross revealed to Danny. Indeed, under considerable duress, he witnessed Tara do so. Only this time, she was pregnant, and it couldn't be a good thing, "I can explain it later. We should just wait to see what the doctor says."

Within half an hour, Helen arrived with the doctor following her close. He promptly went up carrying a black bag. Helen greeted Danny with sympathetic concern.

"Things like this one cannot predict. She is young and seems strong-willed. That in itself is a blessing," Helen Cross said, "Perhaps a cup of tea might soothe our worry."

She hastened to the kitchen, lit the stove, filled the kettle, and set it upon the stovetop. For a woman accustomed to everyone waiting on her, she felt relieved to do something caring for others. It helped to keep her mind occupied. The next twenty minutes went by agonizingly slow, but then the doctor came downstairs and summoned Danny aside.

"She is awake now and very alert. There is color back in her face."

"Ah, that's great." Danny sighed in relief, but since the doctor kept a stern expression, he braced himself for more bad news. "Is she going to be all right?"

"From this limited exam, I can tell you that this pregnancy is at great risk, since she is already showing signs of trouble. Her body is simply feeling the strain of carrying those babies. By my exam with the stethoscope, there may be triplets or quads. The placenta is at risk of tearing. It's not a good thing. I suggest that there be no marital relations until the delivery." Danny's eyes grew wide. He didn't know which news to digest first. Quads? It was unfathomable! No marital relations? Oh, God!

At that point, the doctor turned to address the others.

"Tara's activities should be restricted and she is to stay in bed as much as possible. She must carry those babies as close to 36 weeks as possible if they are to survive. Premature babies are always at great risk for complications. At the first time of trouble, take her to London, as they have good medical facilities equipped to hand medical emergencies."

No one liked thinking of the grim possibility of such an event occurring too soon.

"Thank you. It's such a chilly night." "Helen interrupted. "I've boiled the kettle for tea. Let's go to the other room before you head out."

She politely pointed the way and they departed into the kitchen. Danny looked down at his feet as the others gathered around him to comfort him.

"Perhaps we should have flown home. Tara was sick the whole time on the cruise."

"How would that have change things? There is no way to be certain." Michael declared, not understanding the reasoning behind this. Danny sat at the bottom of the staircase and placed his blond head into his hands.

"Really, it's all terribly my fault. If something happens, Tara will never forgive me." Danny felt the need to confess things like a man. "She married me to protect them. They are not of my blood, but belong to someone she loved with the full scope of her heart. Her past mattered not, as her fiery, stubborn pride has been my source of fascination. Only a fool would make grand promises such as mine. If all is lost, then I have failed her too."

Ross ran his large hands through his jet black hair; feeling relived that Danny was not as naïve as he let on

97

in New York. He was dying to go upstairs to comfort Tara, but knew this was Danny's place to do so, if he was capable. The blond man suddenly dashed outside for fresh air. Sooner or later, the arduous task to reveal the doctor's summation needed to take place.

This set heavily upon Danny's mind and it felt like the weight of the whole world pressed down as he headed up to the bedroom once he mustered courage to do so.

Indeed, the grim news stole away the look of respect that previously shone in her lovely brown eyes. Tara turned away to weep. Surely, everything gained that afternoon now crashed to the ground. Danny couldn't take it and he dashed downstairs to escape the house. Far away at the pub in the village, there would be comfort in the bottom of a glass of lager.

"Danny, wait for me." Ross called out as Danny burst forth outside, but it was too late. The man was disappearing down the twining, dark road. Everything became so complicated. Michael reacted too.

"I can't believe it! How can my brother abandon his wife in a time like this? There's no honor by this action. In his stead, I'll have a word with Tara before we leave." Michael insisted as Ross reached for his coat nearby. "Instead of walking, wait in the car. I will drive us to the pub in town. I'll only be a moment."

"All right. Thanks." Ross replied and headed out the door. Slowly, Michael ascended the stairs. Gloria touched his arm before he stepped into the room.

"Tara's so upset with everything." Gloria whispered and a deep frown graced her fair white features. She tossed her curly blond curls aside over her shoulders. "I will bring up some tea. Perhaps it will make her feel better. Honestly, Danny should be here by her side, not me."

"I so agree." Michael whispered back and watched her make way to the kitchen. Inside the bedroom, the lights were turned down low. Long shadows flowed along the wall. He stood by the side of the bed and noticed that Tara's pillow was moistened with tears. Her long brown hair covered the fabric in several different directions. With great compassion, he spoke softly.

"Tara, our family will help through this unfortunate circumstance. Don't hesitate to ask for anything."

Michael rubbed his chin thoughtfully and then reached for a chair nearby to sit closer. Delicately, he took a free hand and caressed it slowly. It was very soft and silky. She looked up at him then and her face was flooded by emotion.

"I'm so worried." Tara admitted as she now watched his finger run small circles against her skin. His demeanor was protective and endearing.

"I understand, yet everything will turn out fine; just as long as you follow the doctor's instructions." Michael encouraged, looking deeply into her eyes. His blond bangs were long in front. When he leaned forward, they swept across his brow, covering some of the characteristic frown lines that popped up there.

"But how can I just lie here? I've just arrived! I want to see everything. Sammy made it sound so exciting on the way here. And look at the luggage. I should unpack. It's my place to do it."

"Nonsense. We'll send over help. You are now the mistress of this household, not one of servitude. I suggest you get use to that new perspective. Now, you are suppose to stay in bed, but maybe if we are cautious, perhaps we can borrow my grandmother's wheel chair to get you around. I can bring it over," Michael offered on a whim.

"Won't your grandmother miss it?" she asked. His presence was something she appreciated. He made her feel special.

"Well, I surmise she's too stubborn to use it anyhow." Michael said and then as an afterthought, chuckled. A peculiar subtle smile also stole a way across her fair angular cheeks and her eyes revealed something sultry in response. It struck the man like lightening. Michael felt very warm. It couldn't be from the roaring fire in the hearth. "I will place you into the chair myself."

"Even if Danny is nearby?"

Such a profound question! Tara eyes blinked quickly. To think- he would have to place both arms around her to accomplish this!

"I can ensure the coast is clear." Michael offered in a husky voice. An eyebrow rose, producing more lines upon his forehead. What was he suggesting? Did she like it?

"I see." Tara replied, deciding to give him permission, "That will be quite fine."

Michael departed as soon as Gloria brought in the tea. There was a secret bond established somehow and Tara relaxed into the stacked pillows that allowed her to sit up in the bed. The hot jasmine liquid was soothing as she thought their brief exchange over. She felt better after Michael's impromptu visit.

Attentive, wise and blessed with subtle humor, the prestigious man was so far beyond anyone she ever known. It seemed funny how high his brow would crease upward, with tiny rows of skin curling up towards a thinning hairline. In an instant, it conveyed, *"Now, Tara? What is really on your mind?"* It was enchanting. After awhile, Tara laid her head on the pillow to fall fast asleep. She already made up her mind to seek out Michael for comfort and advice, not her half-capable husband.

Chapter Thirteen

No strings attached

The winter days slipped away before they knew it. Spring was upon them and sometimes that meant lots of rain. Whenever it stopped, Ross looked forward to any intemittent sunny day in that late March. The brisk walks along the roads allowed opportunity to become familiar with the surroundings. Ross enjoyed meeting the neighbors the most.

"Good morning, Mr. Kelly," Mr. Merten yelled from a passing field, as he checked the plowing equipment for his crop. He lived a couple of miles near a crossroad. One direction went towards the village. The other, Ross learned, went past the railway station, a connection to London, "Are you heading to the pub?"

"I think it's a bit early to be drinking, wouldn't you say?" Ross remarked, knowing that it wasn't even past ten yet.

The old Belgiun man cocked his eyebrow to stare up at the sun. He leaned into the fence line in an all-knowing stance. A large hand wiped away specks of dirt that splattered against the dark work pants. He tipped up his flat cap.

"It's never too early if you were married to my Emma. Did I ever tell you how we met?" Mr. Merten's eyes dared to share a great story with Ross, so the young man came closer, "I was so young, visiting Paris sometime before the first World War. She sat along at a sidewalk cafe, sipping roasted coffee, so pretty in a yellow dress, with large brown eyes, nice long legs. You can never forget the way a girl looks when she catches your eye. She invited me over. We both spoke French and loved the city. Soon enough we fell for each other. I thought I was blessed, but I didn't want to be tied down."

"So what happened?" Ross asked curiously.

"I asked her to run away with me to Brussels, without any strings, but she wouldn't stand for it. I was forced into marriage. We raised our family here in Wiltshire in a house left by Emma's grandfather. So now I'm stuck, on land that's too stubborn to produce crops well unless I work myself to the bone. It's all Emma's fault for making a carefree man like me take on such responsibility. Why I married her, I don't know."

Mr. Merten's attitude about his wife made Ross scoff.

"Mr. Merten, you always imply that you don't love her. I know it's all in jest. She says the same thing about you and then bakes the best cherry pie for your supper," Ross snickered, after meeting Mrs. Merten at the grocers previously. She scurried about the aisles gathering all the ingredients and complained just as much about her upcoming task to bake that pie. Ross found them to be such endearing folk.

"Hmmff. Believe what you want to there, young man. I still say that Emma can force a man to drink away a day into oblivion. No woman should have that kind of effect. Take my advice: wait a long time before getting trapped. Sow a few wild oats while you have energy to do it. That's the best part of a relationship anyway."

"Yes, sir," Ross laughed. The weathered-face man pulled out an envelope from his back pocket . He handed it over the fence shrubbery.

"You walk by here like clockwork when it's nice out. Would you mind mailing this? It's a letter to Emma's sister, the stewardess. She's married to an American aristocrat. They settled up in Scotland where the golf is better. He thinks there is a boom in investing in California technology. Claims there is a rush to produce compact computers. That jerk thinks everyone will have their own one day. What does he know? All I want is for Emma to take a trip up, so she can be away for the summer. We'd both appreciate it."

Ross nodded kindly. The envelope was wrinkled from being in the man's pocket all that morning. He stuck it in his shirt pocket and went on his way. It was nice knowing the neighbors. They all opened up about their lives, once he proved himself friendly. Ross thought about the technology tip that Mr. Merten mentioned. He could envision the possibility, so maybe he could persuade George to look into it too. George didn't mind taking risks in foreign investments. Ross recalled reading something about it in a magazine. Perhaps

George would even offer Ross an advancement to do it himself. What would it hurt to ask?

Ross continued on his way to the village. The hyacinths along the way bloomed. The brush on the fence line was turning greener. Even the birds sang and Ross couldn't help but whistle along too. He felt happy to be alive.

It was a taste of rich eloquence, staying on at the Georgian estate, always catered to by the help, and entertained by the family, especially the elder Cross men. Michael was in between productions and in no rush to return to London. The two became good friends during this idle time. It seemed a shame that Danny was away in the midst of attending some Allied/ NATO planning meeting in London. Sammy's ship was out at sea again, somewhere along the African continent. Just the same, he would send in mail about his mini-excursions inland along the coast. Also, at every opportunity, he sent pictures of any pretty lady he met along the way.

"He likes showing off," Michael scoffed while studying a picture of Sammy sitting at a bar. There was a raven hair beauty by his side. Puffing his cigar back to life, Michael tossed the picture onto the mantle, "Sammy believes he's the better Romeo of us all."

"What do you think?" Ross liked it when Michael divulged things at random. It made for an interesting way to know the man better.

"He can take the sea. I prefer staying on solid ground. London has my kind of pizzazz and a nightlife that can't be beat. There, I'm surrounded by pretty actresses that like being seen. They use the publicity for a boost up in their careers. There isn't anything wrong with being a stepping stone, as long as I get lucky too."

"Don't you want commitment?" This peaked Ross's curiosity. Michael sipped at his brandy, but choked at the mention of the word. His eyes grew wide and he placed a hand upon Ross's shoulder.

"What? Oh, no! Believe me, staying single in a paradise surrounded by such flowers is ideal. I am the only bee buzzing about with the perfect sting, the kind they demand. When you get established in London, you will understand what I mean. I'll show you the ropes."

"Thanks. I guess," Ross looked down at his shoes. At that point, Michael studied him over for a moment. He sampled more brandy and then stuck the stogie in his mouth to adjust the collar on Ross's lapel.

"First thing is first. You must bulk up a bit. There is an excellent gym where I have exclusive membership. You can be my guest. Women like men that respect their bodies. They sell excellent vitamin supplements that can spruce up your energy too, as you may need it."

"You think so?" It was weird to be evaluated by another man, but he trusted Michael's opinions. Right now, Michael peeled out of his expensive tan blazer jacket and forced Ross to put it on.

"Yes, I really do. We must do something about your wardrobe too."

"My clothes do lack sophistication, but these were all that I could afford in New York."

"Well, not for long. Father has made phone calls on your behalf. He likes you and that is a major accomplishment, believe me. Soon you will work in a nice high rise where you can use your brains. We did note that you have one."

"Thanks."

"You can stay at my flat for awhile. I have closets full of suits and blazers with shirts that I don't wear half of the time. You can borrow them. Although, you are taller than me. There we may have a problem. Ah, I got it. We'll just stop by Saville Row to make your pants. They are well known for their excellent tailors. All I suggest is that until then, you strive to add on weight so that your jackets and shirts won't hang so droopy."

"I'll try. Since I've been here, it seems I've gained about ten pounds. The food is so good."

"Yes, I think so too. Just think, once we are seen about town in Soho, all the ladies will want to sit at our table. Believe me, it will be nothing like you've ever experienced before."

Ross didn't know what to think about Michael's generosity or his advice. He couldn't wait to get to London and the concept of love-them-and-leave-them was a real eye opener. After all the pining he did over Tara, what good did it do to stay so committed to one woman alone? Tara did end up married to another man. That hurt.

Michael seemed exceptionally relaxed with no one weighing him down. Perhaps Michael and Mr. Merten made a point. Sow some wild oats. Bulk up and let the ladies swoon. Yes, this did sound appealing. Now if he could forever rid the longing kept hidden in his heart for Tara. Perhaps in time, it would eventually disappear.

Chapter Fourteen

Ross and the Vixen

In the meanwhile, there were other things to occupy his time. Helen took Ross out to the stable to see her favorite horses. The foreman showed every aspect of their care and grooming. An eager student, he worked long hours ever since: cleaning out their stalls, hefting fresh hay, dishing out feed, and learning to shoe a horse properly. It was pleasing that Ross possessed such passion, "I trust Mr. Kelly, so he can do what he wishes," Helen informed the staff, "And ride whenever he chooses."

It perched upon Susan's ears one night that Ross returned from an evening run. The foreman left early that night. All of her siblings were away. Even her parents retired early for the evening. It was a perfect opportunity. The moon barely peaked beyond the horizon as she made way to the stables.

Vivacity was a two year old which Helen acquired from a horse show. Many times Susan took the fine stallion out. He possessed his own distinct behavior and one stubborn way of thinking, but was a very easy ride. Ross felt connected with Vivacity too. He took time brushing out the mane and course underbelly. It was then while looking down that he noticed the pair of dark boots on the other side.

"Susan! I didn't even hear the stall door open. You snuck up on me," Ross sputtered and stared at the blue-eyed vixen.

"Sneaking is popular these days," She said coyly, "Don't you agree?"

"What do you mean?" Ross paused. He wasn't sure if he liked this cat and mouse game she liked to play with everyone, but tonight, the girl looked very cute, with black slacks and a tight cotton white shirt. The makeup, as always, was flawless and the platinum blond hair was long and thick. It would be nice to run his fingers through it. She ran a slow hand across the stallion's ears and stroked the mane gently.

"In the last few days, while Danny's been away, I noticed that sometimes you sneak up the road towards his house. I suspect that you see Tara."

"I didn't realize that you kept watch," Ross went on to brushing down the horse in a nonchalant manor. He didn't mind being candid, "Tara is cooped up. There isn't anything wrong with a friendly visit. Besides, Danny is aware that we are close."

"Yet, you do avoid her when he is around. Do you have something to hide?"

"Hmm. Ok, I'll bite. Like what?" Ross challenged back. This was the most conversation they shared since his arrival. Sammy once declared that Susan had more bark than bite, so he didn't feel threatened. She now offered a smug smile that was magnetizing, almost sexy. She seemed pleased he was playing along.

"I heard this little rumor," Susan said, with a sassy gleam to her eye, "You did not see her on the night she became bedridden. Isn't that a bit odd, if you are a best friend?"

"Why shouldn't I support Danny too? He was at wits ends. They said she was alert and much better, so there was no reason to rush upstairs. Look, what are you insinuating? There is nothing going on."

Susan came up to the front of the horse to stare at Ross with an all knowing expression.

"Yet there was some time ago. It shows by your actions. Let me tell you what I think. You still love that girl."

"Love? Well, I guess you can call it that, but we did grow up together. Why shouldn't I care deeply for her welfare?"

"Please don't say it's like a sisterly kind of love, because I saw everything right from the start. You are too careful not to create malcontent in her eyes. Actually, why care? To me, Tara seems to be a selfish little creature that has married someone that provides the most: my poor ignorant, love-sick brother. You couldn't do it for her in New York and it's maddening that he has her."

Ross stood there with his mouth partially agape, but he couldn't really argue with her words. They were ringing on the truth. Susan didn't mince what was on her mind.

"It would only take one look to see all those feelings written all over your face. Danny would notice and surely call you out on it. That would have complicated things further. And do you know what else I think?"

"No, but you will tell me anyway," Ross replied, but he wasn't angry. In fact, he liked her down-right honesty at the moment. There was something very real to that sassy know-it-all attitude.

"It makes thing easier by befriending my brother. You keep the enemy close at hand, and only when he is away, you can visit his premise at peace, just to satisfy your longing to see her. Yet is it enough? How long can that last before your needs smolder into oblivion?"

Ross looked deeply into her crisp blue eyes.

"All right. So I admit to masquing my feelings. Is that so wrong? I happen to owe my presence here to your brother. For that alone, I should respect him. Tara and I both have stability, which is something new. Besides, you can't say that Tara is selfish for doing what's best for her unborn. If anyone behaves selfishly, it seems to be you, always grumbling how she gets all the attention lately. Before we came along, I'm sure it was easy for you to be the center of it all. "

"It's not sought out deliberately, Ross. Right now, you and Tara are a much needed distraction," Susan admitted, "All I want is to escape. Nothing exciting ever happens here. My mother's social outings with the ladies guilds are boring. My father is always stuck in his newspaper. When he's not, he fumes the house with that awful pipe. He preaches how his children should do grand things with our lives. My brothers must earn honor and respect. His daughters are expected to settle down properly."

"They only want what's best for you." Ross reasoned. He would love to have devoted parents such as hers. She didn't agree to his thinking on this.

"It's all just fabrication of the standards of being rich. I am to finish college, marry a man of prestige, and then have a family. How can I give up my dreams, like my mother did.? She once could compete in a grand equestrian championship tournament, but she threw it away just to marry father, just because it's tradition!"

"No, I never heard that." Ross replied. He liked Helen. It was a shame. Now, he realized why her horses were so important. Love and tradition forced her to do the proper thing. Susan let out a loud sigh and looked around.

"That's why he built this huge stable, to mend his guilt and make it up to my mother. Well, that's not for me. I refuse to give up on my dreams and I do not plan on sticking around this absurd place much longer. My father's ideals are too rigid for my taste."

"Where are you going? Will you run off with a lover?" Ross teased. He couldn't help it, knowing that she swayed easily to provocative behavior, or such was her reputation. Now he wondered if that could be swayed in his favor. She sure was tempting.

"I could tell you, but you must promise not to spill out the secret."

This only built up his curiosity

"Ok, I promise." Ross playfully crossed his heart and then pretended to seal up his lips. She smiled.

"There is an opportunity in London to get into modeling. Someone has requested me personally. How can I pass on the opportunity it presents? I'd like to be famous. Don't you think I have what it takes?"

Susan suddenly posed with her hips cocked to one side and her arms up over her head. Ross looked at her up and down as she showed off her body. Yes, she definitely had something.

"You'd be perfect. Look, I'll keep your secrets if you'll keep mine. And since we've laid down such a devilish pack, why not spill out the real reason you are out here. There must be one. I never imagined a guy like me could occupy much of your attention, so tell me."

At that point, she edged close to Vivacity. With a keen nose, he shoved it at her tight bossom pocket. She looked down and then slowly dug into it to produce a couple of sugar cubes. Holding it palm up, Vivacity was very pleased with the offering.

"You like that, big boy. I bet there's plenty more sugar." Susan cooed provocatively and stroked the horse's mane. Ross was determined not to give any indication that this blatant suggestion set him on fire, so he kept a stern expression. Unfortunately, the horse butted again into her bossom so hard that it forced Susan to slip backwards. She fell flat onto her rump onto a small pile of hay within the stall. Ross grabbed the reins and took Vivacity to a different rail to give them space. In true gentleman form, he assited Susan off the ground and tried desperately not to laugh out loud.

"Are you all right?"

Her eyes were wide and her cheeks were crimson red. For once, she reacted with vulnerability.

113

"Wow! That totally caught me off guard. I wanted to stay in control while I suggested dishing out sugar," Susan revealed openly and only now did he show a reaction. His dark eyes were twinkling and a smile crept across to reveal a left dimple.

"You must be careful. You can get hurt."

Susan dusted off the black pants, turning around to get her backside. She muttered, "All I wanted was *your* attention."

"Yes. I realized that," Ross took a deep breath and waited. They stared at each other momentarily, gauging the moment.

"Well, I've never been a stranger to danger, but I've been danger to a stranger." Susan teased and then slowly reached up to brush away a wayward black lock of hair. With that hand, her long fingers slid down the nape of his neck and continued until she could unfasten the first button of the shirt. The slow movements were tantalizing, her eyes were bewitching to watch. She seemed enthralled by his hairy chest that was revealed more one by one. Ross felt electricity rush through his body that created goose pimples upon his skin by her soft light touches.

"Careful sweetie. It's my first time." He told her, but it was the truth. Ross decided to be upfront since she remained honest all the while. Susan took his hand and placed it on her waist to encourage his involvement. They walked over to a larger pile of hay in a dark corner. Yes, he never made love before, but apparently she knew what she was doing. What a teacher! At that point, Ross pressed forward and kissed her passionately. . They fell into the hay and then she unzipped his pants.

Later that evening, as the moon sat high in the eleven o'clock position, Susan walked to the barn door. She paused to flick off pieces of hay from her wardrobe and hair. Before exiting completely, she looked back. Ross was fully dressed again. He returned Vivacity to the inside stall, whistling low like nothing spectacular occurred at all. A smug expression crept over her face. Best secrets remained absolutely confidential at heart and this one was exceptional to keep. That man was exactly like that horse and even then some. She couldn't wait to saddle up again.

Chapter Fifteen

An unhappy wife

Meanwhile, at the Briggs House, another free spirited thinker struggled to settle down into a new life. Something Tara desired turned into a nightmare. "I'm a prisoner in my own home," she complained. As the days sped by, her pregnancy bloomed. Her unborn babies grew at a rapid pace. Her energy waned. Always stuck in bed, it was rare to venture downstairs.

Even the idea of the house servants fussing over her in this modern age, day by day, went against a modest upbringing. Tara felt accustomed to picking up after others. "How can I declare orders?" she wondered. Servants were something rich people possessed in the previous centuries, not in the 70's, the era of disco music, pet rocks, mood rings, and cassette tapes.

"These people live in a time warp!" she grumbled, thinking about their aged old traditions and family customs. Going from absolute impoverishment to wealth was a tailspin in adaptability. The servants adapting to the new mistress was difficult too.

"Mrs. Cross said that the potatoes were too salty," one maid complained to another.

"Just the other day she said it didn't have enough. The woman is never satisfied," the elder one sighed. "If she keeps this up, I can't work here."

"Me either. I would rather work around the elder Mr. Cross. At least when he barks, it is consistent what he wants."

They both giggled, but it was aggravating to work around the younger woman. Misunderstandings. Misinterpretations. Mistakes. The simple solution for the moment was to trade out between the Grand Manor and the Briggs House. After a month, two servants were found that tolerated the young lady best.

"Lila, can you bring up tea?" Tara requested one afternoon. Lila was busy dusting the bedroom furniture. She pushed away brown hair from her face for Tara to evaluate. Lila was minimally attractive, being thin and freckled face with green eyes.

"Do you prefer it hot or cold?" Lila asked. Since Tara was American, she preferred things usually iced down.

"Cold, please. Thank you Lila," Tara smiled and Lila complied. She went downstairs to tell Marta of the request. Marta was an older local country woman. She possessed plenty of experience and a sweet motherly temperament.

"I just made fresh scones. Take this up with you. I'm sure she'll love them," Marta placed two onto a plate and Lila took the tray back to Tara. The offered treat was splendid.

"Did you make these? They are so delicious," Tara asked while wiping away a few crumbs off her bosom. Lila shook her head.

"Marta did, Mrs. Cross. She is an excellent cook. I mostly am apt for cleaning," Lila replied. Tara looked about the room. Everything was wiped down; the window was open to let in fresh air and sunlight. It all made her confinement easier to swallow.

"You do a nice job, Lila," Tara complimented. Lila smiled, relieved, "Please tell Marta the same too. You both must stay on."

"Yes, Ma'am," Lila went on about her duty.

Tara reached over to straighten up a frame containing a picture of her husband. That dashing smile, those twinkling blue eyes. She studied it for a moment, frowned, and then placed it flat on the table. "Ugh, how can he be away? Why did he leave me alone in this strange house? Damn Navy!" It was understandable that he returned to duty; still she didn't have to like it. She thought about Ross. Her dearest friend only showed up on occasion now that the season warmed up. "Why does he ignore me? There must be something going on to preoccupy his mind. I can sense it. Stubborn man won't reveal it."

She felt jealous whenever they did talk. She saw a twinkle in his eye and a skip to his step. So thrilled by new found circumstances, it seemed unfair that he found such bliss. The only person who could chase away her gloom was Michael. Sometimes he would bring a poetry book to read out loud. His low voice was soothing and magical. With expressive blue eyes, that natural thinning blond hair, and a personality that was so suave, he never failed to surprise her.

"Oh, Michael, these are so pretty," Tara proclaimed seeing a bright bouquet of wild flowers. He picked them on the way. They filled the air with a sweet fragrance, "Put them in that vase on the nightstand. That way they are close by."

"Of course. How are you getting along?" Michael asked while pouring water from a pitcher into the wide glass vase, "Marta said that you ate your breakfast today."

"Yes, for once I was starving," Tara shifted her position on the bed. She propped the pillows from behind. The pretty flowery nightgown worn seemed a nice contrast to the crisp white pillowcases. Tara was bubbling over to talk, "Lila and Marta are both so talented and they whip up such wonderful meals, never undone or overcooked. The others always scorched my eggs or bring out burnt toast. It seems deliberate. If I wanted something like that, I would have cooked it myself."

Michael laughed and pulled up a chair.

"Now, now. I'm sure you can do just as well."

"I don't think so. My skill in that area lacks severely. Always has. Besides, why take it up as long as they can stay? Who would want to sample my offerings? Of course, I could let Ross have a bite. Perhaps it would make him ill. Why not? He's already been hit with spring fever."

"Do I detect dismay in your voice?"

"I can't help it. Ross has been roaming about the territory like an explorer on a mission!"

119

"Well, this place is new and he likes meeting people. Talks about it all of the time. Anyway, I'm here to cheer you up. Nothing can dissuade me from that."

He offered a warm smile but to his surprise Tara pouted. She tossed her long brown hair over her shoulders. She handed over a letter that lay hidden in the nightstand drawer and he opened it up. As he skimmed it over, Tara twirled a long strand of her hair in tight twists and then declared out loud the contents of it.

"It's from Danny. His schedule has changed until the next assignment is confirmed with the Royal Navy headquarters. Oh, Michael, this won't mean that you'll stop coming over, will it? It means the world when I see you walk in."

This came as a surprise, but Michael couldn't deny Tara his time. He patted her hand kindly.

"For as long as possible, you will remain my top priority." Michael promised, even though knowing that he and Ross would be in London soon. No need to bring any of it up. It would only upset the young girl and for just right now, it was nice having her full attention. Her brown eyes always seemed suggestive and sparkly. He couldn't resist that sensational smile. It was now clear why Danny fell for her, "It doesn't matter to me that he's coming home tomorrow night. Somehow we'll continue our visits."

"Thank you, Michael. You are so sweet," Tara sighed happily, "Since you are his older brother, surely there won't be any objection to whatever you say."

It was easy to declare such a statement when Tara only viewed her husband as weak. He would never go against someone he respected greatly since birth.

As specified in the letter, Danny arrived late the next night by train. Haskell went to the railway station to pick him up.

"Set the bag in the back servants' room. Since Tara is sleeping, I won't disturb her at this late hour," he told Haskell, who immediately complied to put it behind one of the closed doors that Tara observed on the first night there. It was a large section with three, small separate rooms containing single beds and a bureau.

"Thank you, Haskel. Good night," Danny said and watched the man depart. He undressed from his uniform, placed it into the closet, and then crawled under the bed covers. He stared at the open window. The bright moon shone through. There were crickets chirping outside and a barn owl was 'who-ing' in the dark. Sometime later, the calm penetrated his racing thoughts. His blue eyes closed.

Somewhat a peaceful slumber, he dreamt about their first clumsy nights together, before they boarded the luxury cruise liner that made her sea sick. There in New York, she allowed him to touch her. Their lovemaking was awkward on her part. Her moves uninvolved and robotic. It wasn't totally unexpected, when she barely knew him. His dreams he relished. For in them, she was a changed woman, one seductively receptive with sultry bedroom eyes, a sensual expression, and soft, soft skin. That vivid illusion caressed his face, stroked back blond wayward hair and allowed his head to rest between ample breasts. What a great feeling of contentment? If only that could carry over into real life? Her resistance did bother him, but they were married. He was in it too deep. One day surely she would love him back like that. As long as there was hope, anything was possible.

As the morning broke, Danny jumped out of bed feeling pretty optimistic. The dream conjured up a lot of desire. He grabbed a pair of khaki pants and a green cotton shirt from the wardrobe. After he dressed, he ran out to take the stairs two at a time, catching up to Lila who carried a breakfast tray. It contained hotcakes, syrup, bacon, juice and milk. At the top landing, the young man took the tray away.

"Let me do this…er, what is your name?" Danny asked with a friendly smile. She was surprised, but was told to expect him.

"Lila, sir. I'm new, along with Marta. She's the cook this morning."

"And this smells delicious. Why not produce another so I can sit and have breakfast with my wife?"

"Why certainly, sir," Lila replied and then scurried down stairs to comply.

Danny went to the door, knocked loudly, and then went into the room. A month had gone when he saw her last. What he found behind the door wasn't totally unexpected, but still he took in a breath. Her face was drained of color. Her belly really stuck out beneath the blankets. One thing he also forgot was that she hated to wake up abruptly from a sound sleep. The girl sprung up straight and glared with outright displeasure.

"For heavens sake! Must you be so loud?" she cried out.

"I'm sorry, my love. I didn't mean to startle you," Danny apologized and heard Tara grumble in a low voice.

It was incoherent and in a fit, she propped the large pillows against the headboard. Once done, she sat back and stared up for a moment noting the breakfast tray. Then, she rubbed her eyes to take a good look at the man. This husband. Practically still a stranger. Umph! She patted at her lap.

"Are you going to stand there all day?"

"I'm sorry," he stammered and placed the tray of food down easily, "Careful. Don't spill the syrup. It can make things quite sticky."

"I won't. I'm not that clumsy, you know," Tara replied crisply. She fluffed out the linen napkin to place under her neck, and then commenced to pouring the thick syrup over the hotcakes. He pulled up a chair to watch her.

"I missed you while I was away," he said sweetly, "There wasn't a single day that went by that I didn't think of you. I couldn't wait to come home."

Did she hear? The seconds on the wall clock ticked accurately. The time felt like an eternity waiting for a reaction.

Tara took the knife and sliced the hotcake. She stuck a forkful that was gooey and creating steam into her mouth. With surprise, she blew out a little air at the same time, as if it would cool off the offending substance faster. She waved a hand in front of her face.

"Thawank you," She muffled out a reply before swallowing. Next, she grabbed the orange juice to drink half of it down. That's when she noted the strange look on his face, "What?"

"Thank you? Thank you?" Danny could not believe that kind of response, "I just thought you would feel the same. Surely you thought about me?"

"No. I didn't," Tara didn't even bat an eye about it. His eyes seemed crestfallen. It must have brought about second thoughts as she added, "Everyone stopped by to make sure I was comfortable. My mind was preoccupied while you were away. That's all."

"Oh, I see. Well, that's awfully kind, of my sisters and mother," he muttered.

"And your brother," Tara said with sudden enthusiasm. She took a deep breath and decided to speak her mind anyway instead of waiting for Michael to act. She always was an impulsive creature, "In fact, Michael is very diligent, more so than the others. I can't tell you how much it is appreciated. After all, you were with your crew and friends, out in the world doing your thing."

"It's called work, my dear. I was stuck at sea with a thousand or more gruff, cursing, horny card-shark men all the way to Omen and back. The beauty I saw was mountain terrains, but they didn't amount to near what I have here."

"Still, you were free to move about, while I couldn't do much at all," Tara argued, over looking the snuck in compliment, "Michael has been a lifesaver! Believe me; it has kept me from going crazy! You owe him that I'm not locked up in a loony bin. So please, do not disapprove our visits together. It's all that keeps me together."

That native New York attitude was shining true, but Danny couldn't appreciate it now. His mind only focused on the fact that in her eyes, Michael was a hero.

"I didn't realize," Danny replied with a distant stare, "He's easy to admire, but don't let him fool you, Tara. Michael isn't serious about anything except his work."

"He certainly is about me, Danny. He comes by here like the sun is sure to rise."

All she wanted was to eat in peace. She didn't want to hear anything detrimental about the man she so greatly admired. Never in her wildest dreams would she think Michael would lie or disappoint her. Danny was just spouting off, like a teakettle blowing hot steam.

"Would you mind going down and letting Marta know that I would prefer the pork chops for dinner? She asked yesterday morning, but Michael was visiting and I simply couldn't think of anything else after he left."

"Sure. No problem. I'll just have my breakfast downstairs," Danny retorted stiffly and stood up. His mind was spinning. He didn't know how to feel or how to react. He didn't want a fight with Tara right now. Not in her condition and not on his first full day home, "There are things to do around the house. Later on, I should run by to visit mother for a bit."

"Fine. Fine. Don't worry about me," Tara waved him off, "I'll see you around."

He stepped out into the hall just as Lila came up with his tray. He took it from her glumly.

"It was sweet that you were so prompt, Miss Lila, but I'll just eat it downstairs. My wife prefers me elsewhere."

Lila watched him go down. She noted that his bright smile was gone, along with the spring in his step. Poor man! She suspected greatly what caused it. She couldn't wait to reveal everything to Marta later.

Chapter Sixteen

A terrific idea

After breakfast, Danny walked up to the Grand Manor. He needed his mum. She was delighted that he was home. He didn't dare hint anything was wrong. He couldn't. Instead, he plopped upon a stool near the large island counter. Helen was scurrying about the kitchen, baking home-made cookies from a secret recipe carried down by her aunt.

"Your father and Michael are in town right now," She mentioned as she took out a tray from the oven. She sorted the cookies to the cooling rack, "George wanted more of those horrid cigars. I can't stand it when he smokes. Michael mentioned that he needed his hair trimmed. They should return in a little while."

"I can see them later," Danny replied. It was good that he didn't run into Michael feeling out of sorts. This was no time for confrontations.

Helen noticed the frown on his face and the way his head hung low. She took a few fresh baked cookies and placed them before him. Then she went to the refrigerator. Her humming brought Danny a sense of peace. It also brought back lots of warm memories of their childhood, when they didn't have problems like this. Uncharacteristically affectionate, she always doted on him and Sammy, simply because George groomed Michael to be like him. She handed Danny a glass of milk.

"You are so quiet today. Eat up. Warm cookies are quite yummy," She smiled and placed the cool ones in a canister. Danny obliged and bit into the warm cookie, which tasted absolutely delicious indeed. Somehow, his mother always made him feel better.

"Sammy will be so thrilled when he gets this package. I hardly ever bake anymore and when I do, I am reminded how much fun it is," Helen filled the canister and placed the sealed container into a box. She wrapped it up for shipping, "Danny, when you leave, perhaps you can mail this off? We can't let Sammy think that we have forgotten his birthday coming up."

"Of course I will," Danny gobbled down the last of the cookies. He looked around, "I should speak to Ross first. Do you know where he is?"

"Check the stables. He loves it there," Helen smiled and Danny left the kitchen to walk outside and investigate. He found his friend shoveling manure out of a stall. Dark black bangs fell into his eyes as Ross dug into the stinky pile just to scoop the chunks into an old wheelbarrow.

"Now that's a sight I didn't expect," Danny laughed, "I thought I took you away from manual labor."

Ross wiped the sweat off his brow, took off the crinkled leather work gloves, and then reached out to shake his hand.

"This kind of labor I actually enjoy, believe it or not. Welcome home again. I heard that you were expected last night. Did you speak to Tara this morning?" Ross didn't waste time getting to the point. He looked at Danny with quiet contemplation, so obviously he was in tune with Tara's recent attitude.

"Yes, I have. She made no bones about her feelings. Makes me wonder why I even bothered to come home. It's so discouraging," Danny grumbled. Ross kept an even smirk to his face.

"Don't give up, Danny. It seems that lately-well-she is always in a bad mood. The fatter she gets, the more she balks. That's why I don't visit much anymore. Who likes being a bull's eye target?"

"You're kidding? You too?"

"Oh, yes. Don't they say that "you only hurt the ones you love"? I think we are in that category. How else do we explain getting dumped on? Especially when we don't deserve it."

"So, I'm in good company, yes?" Danny felt blessed. Ross made it easy to talk without getting into a lot of personal details. He was intuitive when it came to knowing Tara.

"Yeah, I think so," Ross placed back on the gloves to get back to task, "Tara sees it this way: You're gone to hear her complaints, but I'm not. Instead, I'm knee deep in crap because I am happy here. So, I wouldn't worry about facing such a cool reception this morning, if you did. Believe me, once she has those babies, everything will return to normal. We'll all breathe easier."

This was the exact encouragement needed. After chit-chatting awhile longer, Danny went off to mail Sammy's package. The walk gave him time to collect his thoughts. It was disappointing that Tara didn't pine away in his absence. Why should she when Michael gained her favor? It never mattered in the past whenever his clever brother dazzled the girls in their village. It didn't matter when they chose the gallant man over such a clown as he, not until now. This was so different. This was his wife.

After stopping by the postal office, Danny went into the pub for a quick pint. The atmosphere there always made him relax.

"What's your pleasure today?" Leo, the barkeep asked. Danny pointed to the tap and Leo grabbed a large glass. As he poured, Danny gave him and the place a quick once over. Leo was a big burly guy with a talent for hunting. There were several stuff heads of deer, foxes, and even a bear upon his walls. He handed over the glass. Danny went to sit at a nearby table. There were elderly men playing cards in the corner, a couple of guys playing snooker. Rosemary, the waitress, was an old classmate. She noticed him and waltzed over to say hello.

"I heard you got married awhile back. Never seen your lady in town," She asked while studying him closely. Her long black hair spilled over her shoulders. The dress she wore was short. It exposed heavy legs. Still the woman seemed ample in all of the right places.

Danny remembered that she once sat a few rows back in math class. She always snuck in candy and was reprimanded for talking too much. He assumed on a rowdy night, she could keep up with all the blokes who told wild stories.

"My wife is expecting. She has to stay in bed," he explained and took a sip.

"Why is that?" Rosemary looked very curious. Her dark eyes focused on him keenly. It made him feel warm to gain that sort of attention.

"We think she is expecting quads."

"Good Lord! Did I hear you correctly?" Rosemary cried out in a high tone. Danny felt embarrassed by this, but she instantly plopped down in the next seat and leaned in very close to his face. She asked slyly, "Is it a natural thing?"

"I guess so," Danny coughed, not sure exactly what she conveyed. If it was a question of how Tara got that way, he wasn't providing answers. No one needed to know about the medication she took or about Jimmy, "You could call it a miracle."

Rosemary laughed and touched his arm.

"I always knew you were something, even back in our A-levels. Several times I tried to get your attention, but you always chased after the wrong people. I sure would gladly give out your money's worth."

"Really?" Danny sputtered, caught off guard. Rosemary leaned over just enough to expose curvy round breasts. Just the sight of them made Danny's mouth water. To quench that urge, he took a big gulp of beer.

"Everyone always preferred your brothers, but I never cared for them. To me, they were too uppity and clever, while you were such a sweetheart. After school was out I landed this job. You came in a few times, but then you and Sammy ran off to join the damn Navy. I've waited a long time for you to return. Then I learned you went and married that damn American girl. Now with quads on the way, I guess I can quit dreaming. Quads. Wow! You've certainly proved something to everyone, eh? She's certainly a lucky girl."

The woman winked and went onto the next table. Danny felt his cheeks warm up. The whole time as he sat there, she kept looking his way, gracing over his body like he was a candy stick, but he politely ignored it. Instead, he dwelled on her words, "She's certainly a lucky girl," Right. Tara didn't feel any interest at all. She was too hung up on Michael. Danny made a low growl and took another long swig.

As lieutenant commander on his ship, there were countless times when the men told stories of what they encountered at home after being away on long missions. The pain they felt when discovering that their lovers, girlfriends, or wives were unfaithful. Danny had witnessed first hand how jealousy could be destructive. It could suck the rational reasoning out of a man faster than a ship caught in a whirlpool. Foolishly, the men wound up with broken families, in bad fights, in jail, or did dumb things just to kill their pain. He didn't want this. There was no need for this kind of friction in the family. There must be another solution. He rose from the chair to lay out a generous tip for Rosemary. Kindly, he nodded his head towards her as he departed.

"You come back again soon, Danny," Rosemary cooed at him and batted her eyelashes, "I'll always be here waiting. I promise,"

That week, true to his word, Michael stopped by every single day. Usually just opening the door and walking right in without a verbal acknowledgement. He always went up to see Tara immediately. From downstairs, Danny could hear them conversing and laughing. This didn't set well at all. Danny could recall how as a boy, he didn't think it too unreasonable if Michael happened to intrude into his bedroom. Now, they were adults and this was his home. The situation felt too personal. For Michael to intrude this way felt like an insult. Michael claimed no right and Danny had to figure a way out of this mess soon before he exploded.

One night, Danny settled down for a light supper in the kitchen. Again, Tara had denied that they dined together. This brought his mood low and Marta could tell he wasn't himself. She set a bowl of hardy stew before him, along with a glass of milk. He nodded appreciatively.

"Thanks, Marta. This is plenty. It's late now and if you want to go on home, then do so. I noticed that Lila has gone. When I'm done, I'll just leave the dishes in the sink," Danny told her and adjusted a napkin upon his lap.

She nodded and placed the fresh bread she made away. She noted how he lifted the spoon slowly to his lips and slump in his chair. His eyes gazed across the room, seeming almost haunted by his deep thoughts. This wasn't right. She wasn't stupid about the situation brewing in the house nor did she think he was either.

She survived a bad marriage once and felt she needed to give the man her best advice.

"I'm going now, but I won't sleep well if I don't have my say, sir," she began and came around the table to stand before him, "You have been so kind to us since your arrival. You could be my own son. Please allow my intrusion."

"What's that?" Danny snapped to attention, caught off guard that she suddenly placed a warm hand upon his shoulder. The simplest affection brought forth such appreciation. Someone in the house actually cared about him and she stared warmly into his eyes.

"Mrs. Cross is young and so damn impressionable. From what I have learned, you were not around long enough to make your mark with that woman. It's not good to let another man step in your house to take over your territory. Your brother may be older, but he's not necessarily wise. With his kind of reputation, anyone's suspicions should be raised, but so far, he's not crossed over any lines here. Not from what I've observed."

"Well, I don't believe that Tara would go out of bounds in her condition either," Danny replied, grateful to have someone to spill his guts to this way. It would be horrid to discuss this openly with family, "You are right. She's very impressed by his worldly ways. He's always possessed that craft. What concerns me is that I fear he's winning her heart. It'll be another notch on his belt, if I can't put a stop to it somehow."

"Your brother only loves the attention from that girl. For someone so outwardly uncomely on first impression, once you get her to talking, she possesses such an expressive face and a willful personality.

Once near enough to see these things, any fool knows there's something magical taking place. Her persona is enrapturing overall. For a man that gets that close, its pure temptation, and your brother likes the chase, not so much the catch."

"Well I prefer to keep my catch. I've bent over backwards to bring Tara here. I need her. I love her in spite of her bad behavior. What should I do about it? Tell me, Miss Marta. I do need a clear direction," Danny grasped her hand to listen closely as she sat down. There was something wise in her eyes. It was overwhelming that she realized so much.

"What you must do is force the issue out and put that man on the defense. Seek out his advice. Reveal your vulnerability. He's always been a mentor, so this will catch him off guard. He is sure to back off. Just remember you can capture more bees with honey than vinegar. You'll see. It will work."

Marta patted his hand and then stood up to wrap a scarf about her head. The wind had picked up outside and after spending a half day's pay to have it curled and hair-sprayed, it was unfathomable to have the style blow away like the leaves. Marta approached the front door and Danny rose to go with her.

"Thank you, Marta. Your advice means a lot," Danny remarked and watched as she made her way to the car outside. After her car disappeared out of the drive and down the roadway, he went back to finish off his supper. Now, he ate with a better appetite. The advice seemed splendid and he mulled it over his head as he deposited his plate into the sink afterwards. He stared into the reflection of the kitchen window.

"Of course! Why didn't this strategy strike before? Surely it will place Michael at an awkward disadvantage. He wouldn't dare put himself as an outcast in our family."

Danny smiled and then departed towards the servant's area for a good nights sleep. For once, without the benefit of whisky to put him out.

Chapter Seventeen
A Change in the Air

The following day, Danny stood by the fireplace, dressed in blue slacks, a white pull over shirt, and comfortable shoes. That particular morning he had risen early and stood awhile gazing into the bathroom mirror. Neat blond hair stuck up stubbornly on top, as it would when not brushed down properly. Fine burly whiskers graced an unshaven face. Perhaps this unkempt appearance would make him seem older. The last thing desired was for Michael to dismiss him as before, without any real regard for his presence there too. Just as he done only an hour before. As Tara's bedroom door shut securely in the upstairs hallway, Danny inhaled a deep breath. He turned to face the elder brother coming down upon the stairs.

"How do you do it? How do you make my wife so damn happy?" Danny declared loud enough to capture

137

Michael's attention, "After your visits, she remains content for just a little while before complaining loudly again."

He stood firm, with a daring expression gambling encroachment. The low fire crackled behind him and above, the iron poker pointed menacingly in Michael's direction. The standards of their upbringing suddenly nagged at Michael's conscious. Surely the daily flirtatious visits with Tara went against the grain of what the Cross Family deemed socially proper. Danny, within his right to investigate, forced Michael to back peddled fast.

"Danny, your summation disturbs me. As encouraged, I come over to make her feel better. She's an intriguing person under that quiet façade," Michael conveyed, like a thief caught so near the exit, "I realize that she is your wife."

Danny turned to throw the poker into the mantle tool holder. It clanged from the exerted force and made Michael startle in response. Then with an unreadable gleam in his eye, Danny approached.

"No, no." Danny cried out and opened his arms wide to embrace his older brother hard. Very hard. As they pulled apart, Michael coughed and stared back at Danny in disbelief. There seemed to be an air of arrogance and confidence in him never noticed before. Did the Navy teach him this? Danny had a strange smile upon his face, that was crooked and sharpened his blue eyes like daggers.

"I do not accuse you of anything. You have used every single opportunity to make Tara feel so welcomed. To this, we are both obliged."

Michael could detect sarcasm in the tone, but Danny's outward actions were damn confusing. Danny returned to the fireplace to place two logs into it.

"How can I see you as a threat," Danny added, "when ever since our youth, I can count on you like no other? I know that I can always seek your counsel."

The tone, sickening sweet, made Michael feel simultaneous guilt and responsibility: guilt for deliberately flirting away, holding hands with Tara, and then responsibility for his younger brother. Michael watched Danny rub hands before the fire. Springtime was in full bloom. The atmosphere felt very warm, even indoors.

"Of course, we can always talk. I'm most happy to listen now, if you like. However – Danny! Do you find it cold in here?" Michael asked in disbelief.

"It's not the chill in the house that bothers me, Michael," Danny knew it time to reel in the catch, "It's the chill I receive from my wife on a daily basis. I am forever cold. Do you think it's psychological? Perhaps it may be."

"Chill? From Tara?"

"Can I tell you what is most disturbing lately? We don't even share the same bed anymore."

Michael's eyes grew wide. Not once did Tara ever bring this up in their conversations, but why would she really? Was it wrong to just assume that they didn't do it because of her delicate condition? Still, it remained jarring news. Danny went on discussing the issue.

"Anyway, the fire is soothing. Every day I stand here thinking -about our strained relationship. It's been difficult to leave Tara all alone and especially so soon after our arrival from the US. After all, we were just getting to truly know each other. With my recent absence, we have turned into strangers again," Danny sighed out loud. His shoulders slumped and the confidant man now seemed in despair, "I deeply missed her being away. The Commander wanted to remedy that situation. With her condition, he agreed that I should be close to home. Harry's such an admirable fellow and friend."

"Yes, he's a thoughtful man indeed," Michael agreed in a low tone.

Danny adjusted the figurines and candles above the mantle as he conversed. They were trinkets that his mother left there, mementos of places they visited before: a porcelain bell from Norway, a replica of the Eifel Tower, a painted flower vase from Italy. Danny hoped to replace them soon with pictures of the babies. They weren't even born and yet they were a part of his thoughts.

"Still, what good does it do? She complains about everything. Nothing I say or offer makes her happy. So I leave her alone and I hate it. This should be one of the happiest times of our marriage, but it feels like hell. At night, a good pint of whisky is an effective sedative."

"I didn't realize," Michael muttered and then sat down into a chair. This was his fault, "Why again are you sleeping apart?"

"Honestly, the doctor had suggested that we have no marital relations. It is for her overall good," Danny explained, "I'm quite sure if we did remain together in the same bed, I might have tried something. After all, I am a man, her husband."

The point was well conveyed. Michael looked away, feeling slightly underhanded about his past motives whenever he spent time alone with Tara. Danny paused a moment as Marta stepped in from a side door carrying a load of wet clothes from the basement, where the washer was kept. She winked at Danny for encouragement and then proceeded to carry the laundry outdoors to hang on a line. A strong breeze swept in as she opened the back door. A newspaper scattered across the table, but Danny was quick to contain it.

"Anyway, while I was away, I did my best to ensure for her care. However, she seems very ungrateful for my attempts," Danny continued and placed the paper into a magazine rack near the couch. His moving about the room forced Michael to pay better attention, "Tara rebukes every act of kindness. Why? What terrible thing did I do? Was it my fault that she almost miscarried?"

"No, of course not," Michael scoffed, "That's ridiculous!"

"I think she believes so. Perhaps it's partly true, I don't know. Then after your visits, and only for a brief while, I find her smiling. There is color to her cheeks. It makes me wonder just how you accomplish such a feat. Obviously, something you converse about brings her great enthusiasm and joy."

"We only speak of what's happening at the manor, "Michael explained, stumbling for a decent explanation, "I tell her everything as Tara is a type of person who likes details. She loves it when I elaborate, about who said what and how they seemed. She doesn't wish to miss out on anything important. She has, after all, been left mostly alone here."

"I see," Danny paused. He sat down in a nearby wingback chair. Something came to light and his eyes grew wide, "This never dawned on me, this perspective about her. Of course, she mentioned how alone she felt, but I didn't pay attention. I thought that the maid's company would be enough. If I was confined as long like this, I would go mad too. Perhaps it is best to return Tara to the manor, just until she delivers."

"That's an excellent suggestion. She can stay downstairs," Michael agreed. It did make perfect sense, "Gloria has returned from a photography workshop offered at the university in Oxford. I'm sure our sister will be happy to share her sleeping quarters. With a new environment and more people around to sooth over worries, perhaps Tara will be more receptive of you."

"I surely hope so. Her love and respect is what I crave. I suppose while everyone is out, the extra bedrooms upstairs can be painted for the children's homecoming. Yellow is a neutral tone, don't you think?" Danny suggested suddenly, "Why not use this time to spruce up those rooms? The current furniture needs to be stored away and replaced by cribs, changing tables, and colorful children's bureaus and bookshelves."

"Yes and I think mother would love to decorate the nurseries."

"It will make a lovely surprise for Tara," Danny declared, "I bet she hasn't even thought of it as she's been too occupied with her unhappiness."

"We should embark on these plans today," Michael said, with a different gleam in his eyes, one of encouragement. Perhaps the open discussion hit the target. Feeling better about things, Danny called out to Lila.

"Please run upstairs to pack some of Tara's things. We will be staying at the manor for awhile. You and Marta can come later, after you've taken care of securing this house."

"Yes, sir. Right away, sir," The maid hastened to do the tasks. Within an hour, the trio was on their way, driving up by Michael's car. It was not that far up the road. Tara was anxious to get settled there.

"Oh, it will be so nice to be around everybody. I can't thank you enough for thinking of this great idea," Tara smiled at Michael. He looked over at Danny, but his brother shook his head, and so Michael didn't tell her it was Danny's idea.

Chapter Eighteen

Settling in at the Manor

When they arrived, Danny escorted Tara to Gloria's room, which was situated downstairs in the back of the manor. It was once a servant's quarters but when it became unoccupied, she took claim of it right away.

"Oh, this is quite lovely," Tara said as she looked around. The wall paper was taupe, with Victorian type borders near the ceiling. There was a curio cabinet of delicate glass figurines near the doorway. On another wall, a wide vanity was filled with various perfumes, hair bows, scarves, bath powder and make up baskets. There was also an exit to the flower garden outside.

"I like that there is an outside door. I can come and go as I please without anyone being concerned," Gloria explained and then whispered into Tara's ear, "A lady does have secrets sometimes."

"Of course," Tara giggled and looked out the large bay window that allowed much sunlight inside. The twin beds nearby were decorated with large, plush pillows and lovely green bedspreads

"These will be quite comfortable. I usually sleep on the one to the right. You can take that bed," Gloria pointed and Tara sat on the one offered and smiled. Now, she wouldn't feel so bored and alone.

During the next few days, the ladies came up with their own daily ritual. After Tara's morning bath, Gloria brought her a breakfast tray and they would nibble on the crisp bacon, homemade scones and drink tea with plenty of milk and sugar. Gloria read the paper out loud as if she was a school teacher. They were like two peas in a pod, giggling about silly things and studying the pictures in the stacks of magazines that Gloria collected.

Meanwhile, Danny took up sleeping in Sammy's old room upstairs. He didn't want to remove Ross from his room. It distressed him that an alert situation came up at the Allied/NATO Headquarters right after they settled into the manor. He was to go back to London every couple of days just to log in an appearance.

"It's the best that I can do right now, Danny," His commander said over the phone, "There is political unrest in Afghanistan and all ALLIED/NATO military command is on standby alert. This temporary duty is just an alternative so you can remain inland. Just report to Commander Walsh at the command center. Not much there except fielding phone calls and the usual logistics paperwork. It may be that I can get you at

Dartmouth Academy to fill in as a guest instructor, but this has to be confirmed. I will call as soon as I know."

"I appreciate that sir," Danny replied, "So all I have to do is log in for a twelve hour shift every 72 hours, correct?"

"That's right. Lilly can put you up for the night while you are in London, since our ship will be off shore. Or you can stay at the Command Center, but I figured you want to get away after duty."

"Yes, I would. Michael has a spare key to his flat. He's been here visiting for awhile. I'm sure he won't mind at all if I stay there."

"Very well. Then just drop by for dinner. Lilly and the kids always look forward to seeing you just the same. Well, I'll give you a ring soon."

"I'll look forward to it. Goodbye, sir."

They hung up and Danny was greatly dismayed. Now his job interfered with his attempt to get his marriage back on track. This was not good news at all and so began the trips back and forth. This time he drove his car up to London. It had been stored in the garage and needed to be driven. Danny left in the wee hours just to get to base by 7:00 a.m. After the shift, he stopped by to see the Commander's family, eat dinner, and then go to Michael's flat, exhausted. The next day he would make the drive home and begin the process again two days later.

It was during this time at the manor, the girls tried out makeup, jewelry and clothing. The older woman possessed fashion sense. She wanted to try out ideas from the magazines. She just needed a guinea pig to doll up for pictures. Tara seemed perfect. The overstuffed closet was full to the brim. Surely she could find something in there for Tara to wear. Her long blond curls cascaded down her back as she leaned into it.

"This should fit you," Gloria reached for a garment way in the back, which was a one size fit all, button down tunic. It was stretchable and almost gypsy-like, with dark hues of violet and browns, "It will surely fit over your belly and the browns should highlight those gorgeous eyes. Mother bought it, but I drown in it. It was a closeout sale, so we couldn't return it. You must try this on."

Tara seemed receptive and changed into it. She stood up to turn around in front of the long mirror. Gloria studied the girl. There was something else that needed to be changed as well.

"Why don't we trim your hair? You have such a slim face and all this bulk just makes you look haggard," Tara was agreeable and sat down in a wooden chair. Gloria covered her up with a large towel and proceeded to comb out the uneven hair and feathered the bangs. She took the sharp scissors and snipped away six inches all the way around. Now, it reached just below Tara's shoulders and held a nice soft bounce.

Next, it was styled with hot curlers and then Tara was given pointers on how to apply foundation and blush, eye shadow and liner. What a huge difference it made to her overall features. With a little mascara, Tara's eyelashes were immensely long. With the stylish hair clip, the pretty bright tunic, and the touch of color to her face, Tara was indeed very beautiful.

"Wow, it's hard to believe! Let's show off a bit," Gloria announced after she took a few profile shots with her expensive camera.

With the borrowed wheelchair, she took Tara to the conservatory, a large sunroom filled with comfortable furniture, large flower pots, gardening racks and tools. It was an odd room, more practical for George to sit and smoke his pipes freely than to hear Helen's balking of this practice. Near the window, Gloria parked the chair and went to fetch the others.

Tara looked outside and noticed budding red and yellow tulips up against a far border by the fence. It was lovely. Even the fruit trees were blossoming as well. What was once barren seemed promising now. She patted her ever protuberant stomach and smiled.

"Wow! You look wonderful," Michael declared as the men entered the sunroom to take a look, "It's so remarkable, the huge difference it makes in your face."

"This can't be the same girl my son brought home?" George teased, nodding. He lit up his pipe. The cherry tobacco aroma filled the room instantly. He winked at Tara and then stepped aside to let Ross move up closer. Scrutinizing his friend from top to bottom, he suddenly leaned down to take in a deep whiff. She blinked at him. He smiled.

"Gosh, you smell good too," He said as his dark eyes twinkled.

"It's Gloria's perfume," Tara conveyed, pleased with his warm attention.

"Well, no wonder it is so nice. It's perfect," Ross stood up straight. He looked directly at Gloria, who was nearest. The brief acknowledgement in their eyes lasted only a second, but everyone could deduce a subtle connection. Tara seemed thrilled with the burst of attention, but then it waned. Her husband stood in a defiant stance near the doorway. He had just walked in from a long drive and looked like he hadn't slept. The casual clothes were frumpy. Even his hair was out of place. There were circles under his eyes.

"It's too much rouge and too much lipstick. Balderdash! If you insist on wearing it, you must lighten that up considerably. It makes you look like a street girl," He clicked his tongue and then went out the room, colliding into Susan in the hall. Without even an apology, he stormed upstairs.

Susan rubbed her elbow as she stepped into the conservatory. When Ross saw her, he backed away from Gloria.

"How rude! What the hell is wrong with him? He just slammed his door!" Susan complained.

"Danny's just not himself lately. Let's not worry," Michael suggested. It was difficult to make any excuse. Yes, what was wrong with Danny, when the woman he married looked so damn fabulous? It was as if a new person was born. She seemed far natural and splendid than any actress he knew.

Later, Gloria and Tara returned to the bedroom to discuss everything that took place.

"Danny doesn't like the makeup at all. No matter how much is applied, he will still belly ache," Tara felt glum about it, "He is rather quite conservative in nature. Really, I don't care. Michael and Ross both say I look pretty. I care more of what they think. Is that wrong?"

"No, but perhaps we should tone it down just a little. It's not my wish to cause any discontent with my brother. He does seem so put out lately. Maybe it is stress from work. Let's both try to be civil," Gloria suggested and Tara nodded, as she was eager to please her favorite sister-in-law.

"Ok, but only because you ask. I really do like this attention," Tara fluffed out the pretty blouse. Long fingers ran through soft silk strands. It was the truth. Never did she hear of so many compliments at one time. Still it nagged that Danny darted off that way. She didn't want to linger on that man. There was another that made her thoughts go in several directions. Tara leaned into the pillows.

"Did you notice the way that Ross looked at you? Or was I dreaming?" Tara found a new sport: matchmaking

"Oh, yes! I did detect it. Frankly, I was greatly surprised," Gloria sounded a bit flustered by this. She sat on the bed to talk, "I wasn't sure what to make of it."

"He's a great person and smart too. You've been away in London or the workshop. There hasn't been opportunity to know one another better, but you are here now. I bet with a little encouragement, he will talk to you," Tara urged, surprising herself at putting Ross in a good light, but she liked Gloria. They were lovely people with even personalities-a perfect match. Even if Gloria was older, what difference would a few years make?

"Well, yes, I am here, but there's no time. I suppose I can swing by in London once he settles. Then I can decide."

"London? What do you mean?"

"Oh, didn't anyone tell you? Tomorrow, Michael is taking him there. Ross begins a new job in the financial district, as an apprentice. My father has given a very good reference. They'll be sharing the flat until Ross can get his own place. Michael has two guest bedrooms, so it should not be any inconvenience."

"No, I didn't know," Tara tried not to overreact. Michael and Ross were leaving? This did not settle well. Her stomach felt like knots. Danny's warning haunted her, "I feel tired. Perhaps I should take a nap before dinner."

"That's a sound idea. I'll visit Grandmother for awhile. You rest and I'll fetch you when dinner is ready," Gloria pulled the fabric of the long drapes and left the room. Tara tried to sleep, but she couldn't. Why didn't Michael say anything before? He promised to make her a top priority, but how if he was in London? It didn't seem fair that they both were taking off just as she arrived.

Later that afternoon, Tara followed Gloria into the dining room. How could she eat with such sadness in her heart? This was their last opportunity to be all together. Everyone seemed in good spirits, except Danny. He stared from across the table, tapping fingers on the linen. Perhaps it was because she didn't wipe away the makeup. In fact, before she came down, she applied a brighter shade of berry lipstick. The fine meal presented didn't begin to wet her appetite. There was pot roast with potatoes, asparagus, hot rolls, and pudding for desert. Ross was first to say his goodbye.

"It's been fun, but I can't wait to begin a new career. Your hospitality has been extraordinary," Ross looked over to George and Helen. He lifted up his wine goblet to toast them, "I can never thank you enough. "

"Here. Here. Well said," Michael applauded. He studied his family and noticed how fidgety Danny seemed, so he announced their plans, "We'll be leaving around four in the morning. Headquarters arranged a flight from London into Dartmouth. Danny should check in early. It's a quick hop. You will be at the academy by 9:00 o'clock. Don't worry, brother. You'll get there on time. I promise."

"Yes, I know. I can't help but feel anxious, although this is a good opportunity. Harry encouraged that I give it a go. A short teaching stint, then I can accumulate ample time to be off whenever Tara delivers. I couldn't turn it down," Danny explained to his mother.

"Well, it's better than risking a long assignment for months out to sea," Helen agreed, "You should be here. In the meanwhile, you'll be sorely missed, just the same. I can't stand it whenever you are all away. Here we are gathered at this lovely table and even Sammy can't be among us."

"Now, mother. It will be all right," Danny patted her hand. Helen took out a handkerchief.

"What if the unrest in Afghanistan increases and you get called away? What about South Africa too? Your brother is right off the coast of those barbaric nations. At any time, war can begin. I'm quite sure that our Prime Minister wouldn't hesitate a second to get us into the action, just for the publicity! We must keep pace with our affiliation in a NATO military partnership. No one thinks how it devastates a family. Why can't the world just remain civilized?"

"Hmmpf! Women have no idea," George muttered and stabbed at his vegetables.

"Now, Father," Danny retorted but continued to pat Helen's hand. He brought up another subject at random. Michael was quick to respond to it; anything to stop his mother from weeping.

This made Tara think. My, what a fuss their mother was making? Tara didn't think this bad news. Sure, she was surprised by this sudden circumstance, but with Danny far away, there would be freedom gained from his constant smothering and bad karma. After the entrees, they all adjourned for coffee, desert and brandy in the main living room. Tara lagged behind as she waddled down the hallway, but before she reached her destination, Danny grasped her hand to pull her into the library. He barely shut the door.

"First of all, I want to apologize for my bad behavior today," he looked straight into her eyes, "You do look lovely Tara. I over reacted. I feel better after a long nap."

"Yes, you did over react," How kind to admit a mistake? "You marred the moment. Everyone gave away compliments that I never heard in my life. It was special."

"I said I was sorry, dear. I really mean it."

Tara didn't want to hear it, but he pulled her near.

"In the future, I'll watch what I say. You are my wife. I don't believe you need all that to be special," he confessed, "In my heart, you stand out above everyone else. Please remember that."

A giddy look came into his eyes. This made Tara feel nervous.

"Where is this leading? Why did you pull me aside?"

He looked down at his shoes momentarily.

"Look, we have so much to amend, but there's no time to say it all. When I return and can stay around longer, I promise we will sort things out. Everything will be better between us."

"That isn't necessary, Danny," Tara replied, but he wasn't listening.

"Please have faith in us, Tara. Don't push me away when I do desperately need you," Danny pleaded. He pulled her closer. It wasn't so long ago when he did this. In fact, it was their first night in their house, when she desired him too. Long forgotten feelings surfaced from this physical contact. Tingles raced through her body everywhere. Yet in her mind, desire longed for someone else. His brother. How could she admit it when he looked like everything hung by a thin thread?

"Danny, please," she stammered, but he interrupted.

"Look, I won't wake you in the morning, Tara. It will be too early. You like to sleep. If it is ok…as my wife… can we kiss goodbye?"

Such a question. Now, Tara panicked. A kiss? Incomprehensible! Outrageous! Oh, Jesus! If only his eyes didn't pierce through her soul. His lips drew near. Still, he wasn't Michael! Tara felt alarmed. No, she couldn't do it. Like a dutiful wife, she pecked him on the cheek and not on his lips.

"For heaven's sake, Danny! We will see each other again soon enough!" Tara pulled away. She edged towards the door, "You are not going on some long tour like Sammy."

Tara escaped to join the others in parlor. Danny paused to pull his feelings together and he exhaled deeply. So close. So very damn close. Perhaps if he succeeded, she would surrender everything to him, but she didn't. This hurt. Somehow, he walked dignified past the servants in the hallway, up the long stairway to adjourn for the evening. At the top landing, where the lights were dim, he didn't hesitate to wipe away a few tears that fell onto his cheek. He pushed the bedroom door open and sealed himself within. Across the way, his grandmother saw everything.

Chapter Nineteen

Great Expectations

Danny arrived at Dartmouth. Within a few days, he instructed the modules for the class at the naval academy. The new cadets, a curious bunch, asked Danny about his special line of work. He answered freely. He seemed to be an easy-going, affable fellow. In spite of a comedic personality portrayed while lecturing, the men deemed him quite intelligent. At meal time, they invited their teacher to share about his life in Wiltshire. It came as a nice surprise to learn that he was an expectant father.

"Triplets or quads? Which do you think it will be?" a muscular brown-eyed cadet asked. Danny shrugged his shoulders.

"It doesn't really matter to me. The more the merrier."

"You won't be saying that when it comes to feeding and changing them all. Especially if it's at 2:00 a.m.

They'll keep you very busy." the cadet laughed, along with everyone else. Danny just smiled.

"I do suspect that, especially if they wind up being quads. Judging by my wife's size, I'd almost wager that they will be."

"I'll put down something on that wager," Another cadet took out his wallet. The men all wrote out their bets on a long notepad. They guessed on how many would be born, the time and date she would give birth, and the weight. The one closest would win the pot. "You must let us know, so we can figure out who will get this."

"Sure, no problem," Danny agreed, "The important thing is that the babies are born healthy. Just keep us in your prayers, eh?"

The men agreed. It was his hope that nothing bad would happen, although he was forewarned about the risks. Something major would only compound his problems with Tara. Right now, he simply missed her, but could guess that she didn't feel the same way. It was all rather bleak. Every night, when he went to bed, he prayed to God that somehow her heart would change in his favor.

At the manor, the days were long with everyone away. To occupy her time, Tara took up classical music. She loved playing the grand piano in the library. She studied the books that George brought over from the minister in town, who also loved playing. Helen Cross delighted that Tara's skills improved every day.

"It's so nice, as I read, to listen to Mozart or Bach." Helen remarked as she looked up from a book, "It brings about a nice atmosphere."

"This is better than being cooped up in bed," Tara agreed. The music soothed her soul, along with the bright sunshine through the open window. Everything hummed outside, the birds, the butterflies. Primroses, buttercups, wildflowers fragranced the air. Still, she was sad, as all of the men that really mattered were in London.

"Pardon me, madam. There's a letter here for you," Haskell announced. Tara retrieved it from his hand. She expected it to be from Michael or Ross, but her heart sank when noticing the return address on the envelope.

"Who sent it Tara?" Helen asked.

"It's from Danny. I'll just go to the bedroom to read it over, in private," Tara masked disappointment. She tucked the letter into her pocket. Once inside there, she closed the door firmly. Of course, Danny didn't call because Tara refused to linger long on the telephone. There wasn't anything to say. This letter was an attempt to express his feelings. It was awkward to pretend excitement to see them. Tara sat upon the bed to skim over the contents, only noting the brief descriptions of Dartmouth.

It was enough to begin conversations, because the Cross family was so familiar with everything there. They interrupted with their own stories, like the time they attended Danny and Sammy's graduations or toured through the Teign Valley just to see the highest waterfall in all of England. They visited the castle there as well.

"Another letter?" Gloria asked as she came in from the kitchen. The scent of cinnamon bread drifted in behind her, "They are stacking up since he writes almost every day. Why not put them away for safekeeping."

"In what?" Tara looked around. Gloria clicked her fingers. Out of the closet, she pulled out an empty hat box.

"This should do nicely," Gloria handed it over. Tara piled the letters inside. Then placed the box beside her bed, where the letters were kept out of the way.

Tara's pregnancy slipped into full bloom in mid-April. Miraculously, with a lot of careful diligence, she was three-quarters of the way through her eighth month. Yet it was very difficult doing any simple tasks, even walking to the lavatory. Only now did she begin to appreciate the servants' assistance to bathe, to dress, or to simply sit up for awhile in a real chair. There were days when she felt lightheaded. There was internal pressure towards the bottom of her belly. Sometimes she noticed leakage. This worried Tara, so she told Helen. They wanted advice from the local doctor. On their phone call, they learned he was away on a fishing trip.

"This is horrible timing," Helen lamented, "What if something happens?"

"Hopefully, if it does, there will be plenty of time to get Tara to the hospital. We'll just pray on it," Gloria said and handed over a suitcase for Haskell to take to the car.

They were gathered downstairs to say goodbye. Gloria was leaving for London on the train.

"I will miss you so much," Tara declared sadly. She sat into a chair near the door, "How I wish you didn't have to go."

"I must. This is a terrific opportunity. I will work as an understudy for one of the finest photographers in London," Gloria sounded excited, "I want to be a freelance photographer. This will provide a way to gain experience. I'll miss you. If something should happen, I will be by your side in an instant. I promise."

Gloria hugged Tara tightly. They embraced for several moments before letting go.

Tara and Helen dabbed their eyes as they watched her step into the car. She looked beautiful wearing a red and white polka dot dress. She rolled down the window to wave. In a matter of minutes, the car made its way far beyond the bend.

"It's just us, now," Helen sniffed, "All of my children are in pursuit of their happiness. I can't say that I'm happy with Susan. She left without a word last month. At least Michael knows her whereabouts in London."

Helen and George were upset that Susan ran off again. She was of age and they couldn't do anything about it.

"Yes, at least he called you," Tara felt so forlorn to know this. The man conversed with his parents for almost an hour. Not once, did he ask for her. Not once. She felt such disappointment.

"He's been so busy with pre-show scheduling and casting. He also mentioned that Ross loves his new job. They are getting along so well and seeing all of the night life," Helen remarked. Could she read her mind? Tara wanted to know what preoccupied them this way. She missed the attention once given. It wasn't right that they didn't care any more. What changed? Except that they were free to do anything and she was stuck at the manor.

Now, Tara only relied on the company of Helen, George and Grandmother Anna. The house grew unusually quiet. Her in-laws stayed busy with their local meetings and social outings. Helen and George participated in a new organization that helped to preserve the local wildlife and wild flowers in their county. They actively sought out other interested parties to join the effort. However, this only gave opportunity to know Danny's grandmother better.

Danny always preferred calling her 'Grams', a name that seemed odd to Tara. The older lady always spoke proper English, like someone born into royal blood. Tara was afraid to approach her. One day, while his parents were out, she sucked in a deep breath to begin friendly conversation. In her wry smile, a special glow appeared in Gram's eyes that could not be denied. She liked Tara, so a new bond took shape.

Tara soon learned about Gram's idiosyncrasies or peculiarities, subtle things that made Danny love the old woman dearly. Grams always wanted tea served promptly at four o'clock, with lots of macaroon cookies on the platter. She would dress up for the occasion and wear different hats. Sometimes brown with red ribbon, sometimes blue with black polka dots and if the whimsical mood struck her, they would have ostrich feathers or neatly pinned flags upon them. She always smelled like vanilla musk. Tara loved whiffing the fragrance as she walked about the house. Anna also liked playing cards, especially rummy.

"Do you miss him?" Anna asked as they played a game one day. Tara pouted as she studied the pairs in her hand.

"What? Who?" Tara jumped. Surely the old woman could not deduce that Michael was on her mind again.

"My grandson, Daniel, of course," Grams said, but she was no fool. She was privy to their situation, but didn't want to escalate the distance between the couple. She just wanted to bring up the subject that plagued her special grandson, "Who else bids your thoughts? Not Michael, although I have seen you look at him fondly."

"I… I… I admire him," Tara stuttered, shocked to be called out this way. She was caught off guard on how to reply. Grams looked over her glasses at her.

"Michael is an intriguing person, but I fear he will never love anyone more than he does himself. You must be careful. It's not wise for a married lady to keep her heart upon a sleeve, especially for that one."

"But…" Tara began, but Grams cut her off.

"I don't mean discontent with Michael. He's a playboy and will probably remain that way. Danny is a dedicated man, to his family, to his duty, and especially to you. I would think appreciation is in order. My husband was once a military man, did you know that?"

"No, I didn't," Tara hid behind her cards, ashamed of her feelings. Grams placed a pair of cards down, acting as if nothing was different. She adjusted her glasses and looked at Tara thoughtfully.

"He served in the First World War. We were all very proud. Like your husband, he was a Royal Navy man. I suppose that is why the younger boys wanted to join up too. They heard all my stories about my Henry. They looked up to him. He was a hero. They touched his medals fondly that I keep in my closet."

"Henry. What happened to him?" Tara wasn't afraid anymore and she was curious to learn more.

"Ah, he was mortally wounded in combat during a confrontation between the Royal Navy and the German High Seas Fleet. At the end of May in 1916, over sixty years ago, the navy lost three battle cruisers, three regular cruisers and eight destroyers, with over 6,000 casualties. It was a terrible loss. When I learned of it, I was so afraid. Somehow, he lived through the gunfire and blasting. He was flown to an outsource hospital and then transferred to London. I drove there to see him, one last time. He lingered on for a couple of days and then he passed on quietly."

"Oh, I'm so sorry," Tara replied, "I'm sure it was difficult."

"He did wake up enough once so we could talk very briefly. It was enough for me to express my love, so I'm satisfied that he knew it when he passed. George was just barely a few months old when that happened."

"What did you do?"

"We moved to Cornwall for a while. My brother stepped in to help raise George. I suppose that is why my son is so caught up in worldly politics. My brother was very in tune to it. George took forever to marry and only did it in his thirties. I was blessed that he met sweet Helen so I could relish my grandchildren. I never remarried as Henry was my only angel. It was a privilege to have been his wife," Anna placed several cards down onto the table. She paused to look at Tara with compassion, "However, as a military wife, I do recall how it feels to be left all alone. When your spouse is away for duty, the days seem endless and the nights are dreadfully lonely."

"I do feel lonely," Tara admitted. She felt ashamed of how she treated Danny before now. She could now realize Helen's lament at the dinner table. One in the military was always the first to be called directly into the middle of action.

"Your sacrifice isn't in vain," Anna placed her hand upon Tara's hand, "Whenever Danny is home, you must make the most of that time. Life is so precious. I know he loves you very much. Keep faith in yourself, your marriage, and in your husband. Never let anything pull you apart. Not even Michael. That's all I ask."

"All right, Grams. I will try," Tara promised. Her feelings were spinning. Could she do the right thing? It was even more difficult to accept the advice about Michael. That was two recent warnings about his dedication. It made things seem very confusing. All she wanted to do was lie down, "Can we stop this game? I suddenly feel worn out. We can continue tomorrow."

"Sure," Anna gathered all the cards together to put into the card box.

"Gram, thanks for sharing," Tara remarked as she rose, "I appreciate your confidence."

"Certainly," Grams said and then watched the young girl waddle back to her room. Tara did say the truth, yet the blues got the best of her thinking. It pressed upon her like a dead-weight. Once in the bedroom, she stood in front of the long mirror and studied the reflection. With a huge belly, Tara felt unattractive and gruesome. No wonder Michael and Ross bailed out. The only man that attempted to hold her was Danny. Perhaps he was the only one who cared. She could not wait for delivery to get her looks back.

Chapter Twenty

When the storm rages

The next day, she woke up with swollen hands and feet. Her energy that day was next to nil. Even at dinner time, she couldn't eat. Helen and George sat at the table. Everything was quiet, except there was a terrible storm brewing in the night.

"I'll take this tray up to Ms. Anna now," Lila took a couple of napkins out of the cupboard.

"Mother wasn't herself today. Guess it's her sinuses flaring up," George remarked to Helen, "That wind sure is kicking up a lot of pollen and dust."

"I'll follow you up, Lila," Tara offered and slid her plate away, "I want to see for myself that she is ok."

"Are you sure?" Helen looked up concerned. Tara patted her belly.

"I'll go slowly. It's just that we are close lately. I worry about her."

"That's nice, Tara. Just be careful."

Tara followed behind Lila as they made their way up the dark stairway. Lila tapped on the door and didn't hear anything.

"I bet she is sleeping," Tara said and tried the door. They tiptoed in and saw Grams cuddled within the sheets. Her breathing was even. Nearby, a pretty afghan lay upon the chair. Tara placed it over her.

"This tray isn't needed. I will just take it back to the kitchen." Lila said and departed quietly. Content that Grams was all right, Tara walked about the room for a moment. On the bureau, she noticed an old picture frame containing a black and white photo of a lovely young couple. There was lightening flashing outside, so Tara could see it clearly in the dark.

"This must be Henry." Tara whispered out loud. She studied the handsome man, with a square jaw, light colored hair and a friendly smile, just like Danny's. He stood by Anna proudly, wearing a Royal Navy uniform. How dignified he seemed. How much like a prince. It dawned on Tara that she never saw Danny in uniform. He always wore casual clothes or left before she could see him. The only time he ever dressed up was wearing a tuxedo on their wedding day. That was eons ago. She couldn't remember if he appeared dashing in it. She simply didn't care then.

Tara placed the picture back on the bureau, departed the room, and then went slowly towards the stairwell. The wind outside caused the tree branches to scrape against the windows. The storm, upon them now, made the thunder clamor outside. The ground shook. The floor felt the vibrations. It made her skittish. She

167

paused at Danny's old bedroom. Ross stayed there, so she entered inside.

It was a tidy room, with hunting memorabilia on one wall and nautical instruments and old world maps upon another. She studied the bookshelf nearest the bed. She found an assortment of reading material, from mystery books, astronomy books, and picture books of submarines and other marine war craft. There were reference books, puzzles and samples of blank sheet music at the bottom shelf. Curiously, she looked through the bureau nearby and sorted through a collection of old coins and unusual rocks. In the closet area, there were rugby trophies in a large box and further in, small feathery fishing lures were contained inside an old wooden tackle box.

She found a picture of Danny and Sammy, around ten years old, standing on rocky terrain near a rolling stream, holding up a string of large fish. They stood proud, bundled up in large hooded jackets, wearing long scarves and thick hats. The word "Scotland" was written on the back of the picture. For a moment, she circled Danny's face with her fingertip. She thought about his facial features, the way he smiled, the way his eyes lit up. No, she didn't want it to matter, so she placed the photo where it belonged.

Tara felt odd for being in that particular room. She learned more about her husband in the scope of ten minutes than he ever explained. "God, I never let him get close. I'm a wicked wife," she pondered. Disgusted, Tara went to the door and turned off the light. She felt lightheaded again. A bright flash brightened the night sky. A sudden booming bolt struck ground close by. It caused a thud inside the house as well. It scared Tara out of her wits.

Tara scurried downstairs to get to Gloria's room, never noting the dripping all-weather coat hanging up near the front door. The descent ended up too much. When she arrived to the room, she was panting. Tara reached for the bedcovers and threw it back. Somehow, a hairbrush dropped onto the floor. In disgust, Tara tried to retrieve it, but her huge belly was in the way. She managed to kick it with her foot, but it went beside the hat box. Tara stared at it. The thunder boomed again and she covered up her ears. Maybe it was a sign. Surely, Danny's long written letters would occupy her mind from the terrible storm.

So Tara took up the box, laid down under the covers, turned on the light beside her bed and began to read. This time the words struck home. He wrote tender thoughts that conveyed his confusion of her cold feelings towards him. It was hell to pay for a crime he did not commit; hell of complete loneliness even within her close company, leaving only the immense sadness that nothing brought them closer:

"Sometimes I sit up at nights and stare up at the stars. They beckon for a wish, and then I wonder, if perchance one is made, would your feelings change? Disillusionment hardens my feelings, but not my heart. I still love you, dearest Tara, in spite of everything. Just give one kind word, a chance smile, even a look -anything to prevent the ice of despair from stabbing my soul. I am miserable, lonely, and it is a cruel sentence. Perhaps when I come home, you will give back your heart. If I could just hold

you again, it would bring such wonderful contentment and peace."

Strong words of his conviction, against the backdrop of the beautiful terrain at Dartmouth. Tara noted that the last remained unopened. It came that morning and she only tossed it aside without caring. She ripped it open now. It was to the point: Why didn't she ever write back? It didn't matter now, as the teaching assignment was complete, and he was on leave.

Tara was surprised by this. If so, then where was he? The postmark was four days ago. Dartmouth wasn't far away. Lightening hit the house. Electrical energy made her hair rise in static. The lights flickered and then all the power shut down.

The dark made her afraid. She listened, but could only hear her own pants. The wind forced a window to fly open, as the latch was not secure. Rain poured into the room. She threw the letter aside and ran to shut it, but was struck cold by another realization. Her gown was soaked and she suddenly thought that the room was spinning. To compound these problems, a sharp, burning pain pushed down into the deepest part of her lower abdomen. She cringed and slumped to her knees.

"Ahhhhh-help!" She cried out, but it was incomprehensible. She gasped for air. Tara couldn't cry out or move. Nearby was a chair. She grasped it to knock it over forcibly. It collided into the lamp that shattered onto the wood floor. It made a ghastly noise. At this, she slumped into a half-stupor.

Suddenly, the door flew open and someone with strong arms whisked her up from the floor. Then in a commanding voice bellowed: "Bring the car around!"

Outside, the rain came down like buckets. Everyone huddled around with large umbrellas and raincoats as she was laid gently into the passenger seat. Someone jumped into the drivers seat, the ignition turned, and the car plunged through very muddy, narrow lanes, twining quickly towards the main metro that led to London.

Luckily, the burning pain subsided. Tara rested upon a man's shoulder. After awhile, they reached the hospital in London. Several attendants placed her onto a gurney and rushed her towards the obstetrics wing. The man ran along side as far as he could. Tara woke up briefly. Who came to her rescue? Who was her knight in shining armor? Could it be Michael? She gazed down the hall as she passed through thick steel double doors. Danny's stern face was shut out of view.

Chapter Twenty One

A sensational birth

It came as a complete surprise when the nurse stepped out from the Labor and Delivery surgical suite about five minutes after Tara went there. She found Danny in the waiting area, along with other expectant fathers. "Follow me now!" she ordered. They went into a staff lounge. She grabbed a blue scrub bottom and top from a long shelf, along with a blue tie on mask and paper shoes, "Put these on and then step out into the hallway so I can take you back. Hurry! There's not much time."

Danny did as ordered without question. Within minutes, he found himself inside the surgical suite. The nurse made him stand by the glass baby warmers. Tara, fully sedated, laid on a steel table, her feet in stirrups, her lower body draped by blue sheets. The sound of her breathing came through a large device. It frightened Danny as it echoed throughout the sterile environment.

The anesthesiologist sat upon a stool near her head. He nodded at the OB surgeon who waited for his signal, along with three teams of nurses, quite aware of their special patient. The surgeon took a sharp scalpel from a sterile steel tray. Danny watched as an incision slid across the bottom of her round, distended belly. When the scalpel was placed back, there was blood on it. This made Danny feel off kilter, but he squelched it by swallowing hard. Next, the surgeon's gloved hands groped deeply into the fresh surgical wound. There was a lot of tugging and pulling. Danny winced, but somehow, out came the first baby.

"It's a boy. Mark the time please," The doctor requested as he suctioned out the mouth repeatedly, cut off the umbilical cord, and then handed the child off to the nurses. They wiped down his fragile body, took measurements, weight, vitals and then wrapped it in a clean blanket. His foot was pressed against a page of his own medical record. An identity band went around its tiny foot. Only then, did the nurse hold up the baby for Danny's inspection.

The infant was small, with reddish-purple tinted skin and microscopic eyelashes. When he was held up, his small arms shook and flailed. Danny smiled. How tiny and helpless? He felt instantly protective. Within the boys' naked skin, tiny veins coursed along its arms. Only a feint cry escaped from his tiny mouth. The nurse tucked the infant into a special monitored warmer. The respiratory and cardiac monitors were turned on. It was an exciting event to witness. Within ten to fifteen minutes, this process took place over and over again until all were born.

As the doctor sewed Tara's incision closed, the nurses took the infants down to the special neonatal nursery to place under careful watch. Danny followed along. He was given carte blanch to stay as long as he liked, which was a privilege not usually bequeathed. Everyone smiled and gave him congratulatory pats on the back. He marveled over each child, but the last basked in attention.

"Is something wrong?" he asked. The head nurse looked up, but didn't reply. Instead she used the phone to page one of the doctors. She read over the vitals and statistics that were displayed by the monitors. Within five minutes, he appeared: a tall, lean man wearing spectacles. He took out a cold stethoscope and placed it upon the baby's bare chest, which made him jump slightly.

"We need further diagnostic tests," He said, wrote out the order, and looked at Danny, "It's a heart problem, but after we get the reports, we can determine what to do. It's not a matter of a simple heart murmur. He may need surgery."

"How soon?" Danny's eyes narrowed.

"He's very small; perhaps, if his weight comes up some, we can do the procedure. I'll keep you informed."

The doctor went on his way. The nurse brought over consent forms for Danny to sign.

"The boy will be watched over," The head nurse looked around, "The others are doing well so far. Why don't you run along to rest? We'll keep you posted if there are any changes. I'm sure your family is waiting for news."

"Yes, of course. I forgot to call with all of the commotion. Good idea," Danny stammered and his wide-eyed expression made the nurse laugh. She placed a warm hand upon his shoulder.

"It's an exciting occasion, sir. Very big news. Congratulations, Mr. Cross."

"Yes, thank you. Thank you for everything."

Danny left the nursery to stop into Tara's room. She slept soundly under sedation. One lone IV stand pumped the saline solution and sleeping medication into her veins. He stroked her hair and kissed her forehead gently.

"Congratulations, Tara. They are all here," he whispered, "You've done very well. When you wake up, you will be so surprised, as I was."

Next, he went down to the main hospital lobby. From a phone on the wall, he dialed the number to his mother. He decided to let her tell the rest as she was certainly making a ruckus on the other end. He held the receiver away from his ear. Two men stood near, one using another house phone and the other leaning on the wall. The man on the phone hung up. He stared at Danny a moment. When Danny finished his call, the man approached with a salute.

"Hello, sir. I'm Ian Walsh. I saw the commotion in the hallway, with the nurse…," he began and Danny nodded, "You seemed very familiar. Aren't you that officer rumored to be having quads?"

Danny was caught by surprised. After all, he still wore the blue scrubs.

"Yes, that's right, but how did you know it's me?"

"I've seen you around, at Dartmouth recently. My wife gave birth awhile ago too. By the way, this is my brother-in-law."

The men shook hands politely.

"So how did the delivery go?" Ian asked, "I remember the men were betting on it. I can pass on the news, if you want."

Danny didn't hesitate to share.

"With the wild storm, it was crazy driving up from Wiltshire. However, we are very fortunate. She delivered by C-section, as it was a medical emergency, all by midnight. All seven are in the neonatal unit now. They are thriving."

The brother-in-law choked on his chewing gum. He gasped, dumbstruck, and once he caught his breath, his eyes were wide in amazement. Ian showed an equal reaction.

"What? I think I heard wrong! Did you say *seven* babies?" Ian bellowed.

"That's right. So, I was wrong about the count. She gave birth to three more. They hid in her belly somehow," Danny said in a calm demeanor. Inside he turned cartwheels.

"Hell, man! This is world news! Can I quote you for my paper?" The brother-in-law demanded after finding his voice again, "I am a reporter for The Sun."

"Well, I don't know."

"If you don't give me the scoop, surely the hospital will have to report something. This isn't something that happens every day. Why not let it come from you first," The reporter argued. This indeed made sense.

"Ok, but you must respect our privacy," Danny agreed reluctantly, "Let's find a break room."

The men headed down the corridor to talk. Danny found a vending machine and drank a soft drink while he relayed a brief history to the reporter. He told nothing more personal than just the facts. The man from the Sun didn't waste another moment getting it to the pressroom, just in time to make the early morning edition.

Chapter Twenty Two
On different tracks

After that, Danny left the hospital, got into his car, and made the way back to Wiltshire. In the operating room, the doctors ensured him that Tara would remain asleep for quite awhile. The storm knocked down several branches into the narrow lane. There were deep, mud holes. Now, the tires sank into them. Dirty water splashed back upon the car. It was a miracle that he didn't wind up with a flat tire with the speed he had driven.

God must have protected them on their way. Now, as he neared the manor, the air was crisp and cool. The clouds were clearing in the horizon as the moon nestled close to the earth. He could see the pre-dawn pink haze from the sun filter into the black. It was going to be a beautiful day. He crept into the manor, slipped off just his shirt and shoes, and fell into Tara's soft bed.

The sheets and bedspread were changed, the lamp replaced, but Tara's perfume scent lingered on the pillowcase, which was untouched. He whiffed at the intoxicating fragrance. He closed his eyes tight. Sometime before mid-morning, he thought he dreamt his father say, "Damn it! He's in here!"

But it was not a dream! George pounded on the door several times to wake him up. It was like being back in basic training, when the drill sergeants wake up new troops with large sticks rattling inside metal trashcans.

"Danny, boy! Get up! Get up now!" George stomped in. He shook the daylights out of the bed covers. Danny sat up alarmed and looked around. Was he a schoolboy again? When was the last time his father roused him up that way?

"What's wrong? Why are you yelling?"

"I received a call from Mr. Gosney at the local paper," George barked and threw Danny a clean shirt from his garment bag, "People and reporters are showing up in droves in the village. You are in the news, boy!"

"What? But I didn't give out my name!"

"Doesn't matter! Reporters are masters at digging up pertinent information. There are spies everywhere!" George hissed. He glared at Danny for his stupidity, "And somehow they *know* that you live here."

"Go down and handle it, Danny," Helen encouraged as she stepped into the room to intervene. She shoved George out of the way to protect her son from his overbearing wrath, "I am going by train to visit Tara now. Gloria and Susan will meet me there. I say, this is terribly exciting!"

"Hmmf! You wouldn't let me sleep adequately after Danny called you," George complained to his wife.

"Oh, tisk! Tisk!" Helen replied patiently, "What a bear you can be! You will get over it. Besides how could I go back to sleep when I am finally a grandmother! And not just four babies, but seven! Good Heavens! This is a terrific blessing! I'm so excited!"

Helen helped Danny slip into his clean shirt, as if he was a boy again, and he just smiled at her actions. Helen stopped, looked into his eyes momentarily, and then she suddenly embraced him hard. She was crying.

"I wanted grandchildren. I just never expected so many at once! Thank you for marrying that girl!" Helen dabbed at her eyes, immediately composed herself, and then tucked a scarf around a coifed hairdo, "Its best that there are no distractions at the hospital. I bet Tara is still out and when she wakes up, she'll be glad for our company. We can't be swamped with reporters. You're the father, so go down there and act like one."

"Of course, mother, right away!

Danny slipped into his shoes, grabbed his flat cap, and followed his grumpy father out the door. Within ten minutes, he was stepping out of the car in front of the pub.

"That's him!" one of the reporters shouted. Danny was mobbed by everyone there. They whisked him inside as George watched with mouth wide open, still grounded safely behind the driver's seat.

At the hospital, Gloria paced about Tara's room about 1:00 o'clock in the afternoon, with the paper in hand, and read its contents out loud:

"<u>*Septuplets born to English couple!*</u>" *The headline reports in the Sun "All of the preemies were delivered by C-section late last night. They miraculously survived with no obvious neurological defects and the average weight were between 3 pounds and 3 ½ pounds. The fraternal septuplets will remain on respiratory assistance and heat monitors, which is routinely precautionary. These are the couple's firstborn children. At this time, the American-born mother is under sedation, but is expected to recover well. The English father hails from Wiltshire County. He is currently a Royal Navy officer on assignment as liaison with the Special Teams/ Allied/NATO Command based in London."*

"Doesn't he sound important?" Susan conveyed with an attitude. She tossed long locks of platinum blond hair over her shoulder and shrugged. She noticed that Tara woke up, "It's you that's done all the work!"

"Well, I'm just relieved that the wait is over," Helen soothed Tara's hair aside, "How are you feeling, dear? Are you exhausted? Your color is still pale. I am so terribly proud."

Tara blinked eyes wide awake to focus on Helen, who was sniffing and searching her pockets for a handkerchief. She seemed so incredibly happy. Of course! Tara reasoned to herself. Michael and Gloria swore secrecy to the babies' true paternity. Helen naturally thought the babies were Danny's. No wonder she was so emotional! Tara studied the room next, which was full of flowers, balloons, and cards of best wishes. She attempted to sit up against the pillow, but was cautious of the fresh Cesarean scar.

"Where did those come from?"

"From everyone!" Susan stated in a crisp tone while perusing over a few cards. "This whole country is ga-ga over the babies. It's been a stream of gifts all morning. Some major baby manufacturing companies have called. They want to donate several items, like diapers, clothes, and so on! All you have to do is endorse their products!"

"Really?" Tara gasped. "That's so unbelievable. Why?"

"You and my brother are celebrities! They can't wait to interview you. They already caught up with Danny at the pub."

"What do you mean? Celebrities? What's going on? I don't understand," Tara struggled to rise up.

"So many questions!" Gloria teased, "Relax. Would you like me to read this again?"

Gloria showed Tara the paper. She grabbed it to read the headline herself. Tara fell against the pillow in great surprise, but this action only made her wince. She rubbed her tummy.

"I can't believe it. Seven!" Tara sighed, "Holy Cow!"

"The press swarmed into the village this morning. Danny is there handing out cigars and several copies of the Sun paper. Of course, they caught him last night to get his official interview," Susan told her. Tara looked to Gloria for confirmation.

"It's true. Danny is in his element. We spoke by phone an hour ago and there is a village celebration brewing on your behalf. Perhaps it's best that he's kept busy this way. You have time to rest," Gloria took a vase filled with huge assortment of flowers from a nurse, "Another one? Let me place it by the window."

Tara was amazed, but she did not relish any media intrusion.

"I don't want my picture taken. I don't want any interviews, simply because I don't trust anyone outside of this family," She said. Helen understood.

"Don't worry about the fuss. We will protect you," She admired the new flowers and opened up the card, since Tara wasn't interested, "These are from Ross."

"Ross? Where is he? Doesn't he want to see me?" Tara felt betrayed. Surely this could not be!

"Unfortunately, Ross is tied up in a training seminar today. He promised to swing by later to see you," Susan revealed. Everyone looked at her, "Ross called while everyone was out getting lunch."

Did the phone ring? Tara wasn't certain, but it was a possibility. She was pretty much out of it that morning.

"Do you want to see the babies now?" Gloria asked.

"Won't they be hooked up to machines? I don't think I can bear witnessing that yet."

"But Tara, it's the only way. You must see them. Danny went in already."

"He has?" Well, this was certainly incredulous, "Did he get to hold any?"

"No," Helen replied, "They won't let you yet. They are very delicate. Danny did describe their skin as thin and their heads seem bigger than their bodies. He said he placed two hands, side by side, up in the air and it covered his view of just one baby. They are incredibly small. Right now, they are inside Isolettes."

"What's that?" Tara crinkled her nose and listened intently.

"It's like an incubator, a special bed surrounded by a glass cover and they keep the babies warm. Preemie babies have trouble keeping their body temperature," Gloria explained patiently, knowing this from her background in nursing.

"Oh, I've got to see this for myself," These details made Tara reach for the robe nearby. Helen helped the girl cover up and slowly get out of the bed. They instantly brought over a wheelchair. Tara was determined since Danny knew more. After all, she was the one who endured the anesthesia and the C-section.

"The isolettes have holes on the sides so you can reach in. You'll see what he means. They'll let you go inside as you are the mother," Gloria took her there.

The head nurse greeted Tara at the secured door and then wheeled her inside the room. Everywhere, there were blood pressure monitors, IV holders, and other parents with babies inside their own isolettes. It was frightening to see some of the glass domes covered up with blankets, but Tara didn't realize that this shielded the bright lights. The other nurses on staff nodded as she approached one of her infants. He was wrapped up in tubes and respiratory equipment. Everything Danny described was right on target. The head nurse reassured Tara.

"They are fine. All the monitors show good readings so far. That is very encouraging and a huge blessing. We just have to get their weight up."

"What will they have? I did want to breastfeed, but with that many babies, it may be easier sticking to a bottle."

"You can pump the breast milk for a short while and that way they can get natural immunization. If they adjust well to sucking to bottle nipples and their intake develops, then they won't be here very long. It's a matter of time. Now, your last son will require a longer hospital stay. I ordered a study this morning. There is a problem with blood flowing properly which could indicate surgery to correct it."

"Oh, no! Does Danny know?"

"He knew there was a problem last night, but the doctor has not discussed it fully with him, or you. Dr. Bishop will make rounds again tomorrow morning, since he works at two hospitals. However, your husband has signed the consent forms."

"Without telling me first?" Tara sputtered but the nurse placed a warm hand on her shoulder.

"It's procedure, in case of an emergent action. He was expected to do it, since you were under sedation. "

"Oh, ok." Tara sighed. "Can I see the baby?"

The nurse nodded and wheeled her over to that particular unit. The baby was so incredibly small, with a patch of soft, delicate brown hair, and very fragile skin.

"Babies recognize your voice. Go ahead and talk to him awhile. I'll leave you alone." The nurse walked away and Tara felt tears flow down her face as she gazed at his tiny face. All the monitors, respiratory help, and tubes on him made her frightened. The label above the isolette indicated he was Baby F Cross. Tara wasn't happy with that impersonal label, but she leaned closer to the unit.

"I love you, sweetheart. You have to stay strong. Mommy needs you, just as much as the others. You are part of us now, forever. Don't ever leave." Tara cried and then bowed her head to pray.

Chapter Twenty Three
The lost art of persuasion

Later that afternoon, after staying awhile with the tiny infants in the neonatal nursery, Tara returned to her hospital room. Helen and her daughters were still there, waiting to hear about Tara's experience in seeing the newborns, six boys and one girl, for the first time. Gloria seemed optimistic that the last boy's outcome would turn out fine, while Helen wept to hear that something was not right with the baby's heart. Susan stood by the window and didn't say much at all. To witness their attention all surround Tara as if she was a supreme motherly goddess only played on her nerves. She rolled her eyes.

It was around three o'clock when the nurse brought over more pain medication, which would help Tara relax. "We best run along." Gloria remarked, kissed Tara on the head, and Helen did the same. "I'll stick around for awhile," Susan remarked and turned down the blinds, "in case more gifts arrive." Tara nodded, the other ladies left, and the tired mother nestled snuggly into her pillow. Within minutes, she was sleeping soundly. Around four, there was a light tap on the door and Ross peaked in.

"Hello?" he paused to look around the dark room. Susan had been sitting there with her eyes shut, but she was not asleep.

"Shhh," She instantly placed a finger to her lips, pointed to Tara, and whispered, "She's sleeping."

"Yes, I can see that," Ross whispered back, walked inside, and gaped at all of the flowers and balloons. "Wow!"

Susan searched out her purse and found a pen and paper inside.

"Write her a note. She is worn out." Susan suggested. The last thing she wanted was for Tara to wake up and have Ross offer all of his attention. *No, sir.* She gave them over. He wrote down his personal thoughts, as the pretty blond woman hovered close intentionally. Teasingly, she ran her fingers up and down his spine and peaked at what he wrote down. His magnificent dark eyes narrowed. Ross focused upon her bright blue eyes. A subtle smile came across her face and he shook his head. The note was placed where Tara could see it later. Then he took Susan's hand.

"Grab your things. Let's get dinner," He whispered.

"Oooh, I like it when you take charge," She whispered back.

"Yeah, yeah, right," Ross remarked and they went out into the hallway, down the elevators, and out the corridor to the main hospital doors.

Around six thirty, in one of the finest hotel rooms in London, they sat nude upon a soft bed, with the bedspread halfway off and the pillows thrown about on the floor. The Chinese take out food was re-heated in a microwave oven that sat on the counter. Ross thought the microwave was one of the best new products of their decade.

"If I possessed money to invest when this first came out, I might be bloody rich today," Ross remarked about it when he toyed with the settings. Every modern home or hotel business in 1978 seemed to have one and it amazed him. Now, as they enjoyed their hot meal, Susan took a long noodle using the chopsticks, sucked it into her mouth, and then studied the young man before her. He was gaining weight and the recent work outs with the heavy equipment at the gym helped his overall muscular prominence. She stroked a finger along the length of his bicep.

"This is improving along."

"Don't expect me to turn into King Kong or something," He teased offhandedly and she giggled.

"Stop it, Ross! You are so witty with such a straight face."

"I've got my tricks, little darling. Look, why can't a street guy like me entertain and interest a new photographic sensation like you?"

"You do both very well," Her fingers ran up and down his hairy chest. She tossed her long blond mane over her white shoulders and then growled low, "I like this."

"You like secrets," Ross speculated honestly, but was amused by her expression as she played her fingers through that hair, "It's a lost art of persuasion, which you so keenly possess; of how simply well you keep me in line, just so that your family doesn't learn about us. I guess they would be knackered knowing what we do on a constant basis."

"Hmmm," Susan replied, found the pillows on the floor and threw them behind her. She leaned into them near the headboard, "No, I can't have anyone knowing about us. Danny would know for sure that I seduced you first. Sammy would find some God awful way to hound me about it, and Michael… well I don't think he'd care really, come to think about it. He has his own reputation in London."

"So I've learned," Ross nodded and his eyebrows rose up, "He doesn't think much about commitment."

"Why should he when there are women everywhere that he can have anytime of day or night. They practically throw themselves at him and open up their apartments, pocketbooks, and calendars. Just for his attention to their work or projects. He's his own hot commodity."

"At least he is cautious. He's got all kinds of protection in his flat. It's funny actually, where I've come across them," Ross chuckled, "Behind the sink stand, the bottom bookshelf, taped on the side of the refrigerator, underneath the coffee table. All camouflaged by something else, of course. They are not directly obvious."

"You never know when or where the mood may strike one. They have to be in easy reach. At least I don't force you that far. The pill is a miracle. It's a good thing. I don't want to come up pregnant and then have to explain us to the family."

"I suppose that's a good excuse to keep things under wraps," Ross opened up his fortune cookie, frowned, and then tossed it aside momentarily.

Susan took another bite of noodles from the container and stared at Ross seriously,

"You have just as good a reason to hide this. Wouldn't it disturb dear sweet Tara to know that you don't sleep with the perfect sister? I learned that she thought Gloria is so right for you."

"Let's not talk about Tara or Gloria," Ross retorted and placed the carton of Lo Mien onto the night stand. There was a bad taste in his mouth from her bringing up sore subjects, "Like I said, I was simply there, admiring Tara's transformation, and I wasn't trying to get Gloria's attention on purpose. It just happened."

"Yet, the infatuation didn't end there, my friend, because ever since she's arrived to London, she comes by the flat for dinner, over and over again. That's all I heard ever since Tara stuck that crazy idea into her old-maid head: how you are so kind, so sweet. She's definitely smitten! I can swallow it down once or twice, but not several. It gets old after awhile."

Ross felt annoyed.

"Gee, you almost sound jealous, but I know better. Look, I didn't invite her. Your brother did. What kind of guy do you think I am? I can't diddle around with you and profess an interest there too. Jesus! If I did that, so much crap will hit the fan once she learned about you. I can't have that. Not with everything Michael and your father has done to get me this far in London."

Ross stood up to place on his boxers and grabbed the blue jeans off the chair. He slipped into them and adjusted the leather belt as he walked out onto the balcony. The lights from the streets below were bright and the night air felt warm to his skin. His jet black hair flew up in every direction. It made his usually straight hair appeared tousled.

Susan picked up the fortune cookie to read it: "You have unusual equipment for success. Use it well." She giggled, wrapped the complimentary hotel robe around her slim curvy body, and went to join him. From behind, she encircled her arms around his waist.

"Come on, Ross. Take it easy." She said but he snapped.

"Take it easy? Susan, let's be real. I didn't bargain on you and your sex games or how much I actually like it. I didn't bargain that Gloria has an interest in me and gosh, I like her sweet attention too. All I wanted to do was find a decent job, make my mark, and make your family proud to have so much faith in me. Damn! Because of them, I was lucky to be in the right company at the right time! They love me there! Think I'm clever and smart!

He paused to look at the city again. The neon signs shined in the distance and he could see the bridge that crossed over the Thames River. Life was bustling and humming and he was part of it.

"And I love sitting on top of the world, to eat at the best restaurants in this city, affiliate with such elite people from all walks of life! It's incredible and scary how a guy like me, from the poorest neighborhood in Brooklyn, can fit into such a place."

"You do fit in, darling. You are an amazing guy with so many hidden talents."

"Well, let me tell you, it's been quite an experience. In the next day or two, I will be sitting in my own place with a crème de la crème company car. How many jerks do you know advances that fast?"

"That's great!" Susan encouraged. She liked it when he got all riled up. *He's so sexy*, she thought and his face became so animated. *Tara's so stupid never to realize this before she married my brother!*

"Well, I can't screw things in your father's eyes. I know he set me up with the CEO. How would George feel if he knew we were together this way?"

"It's not that he wouldn't accept it, Ross. He likes you, but he'd want you to do the right thing too."

"And?"

They stared at each other momentarily, but Ross already knew the answer. Susan threw her hands up in the air and backed away.

"You know I can't do that, Ross, because I want my career. That means more," Susan didn't beat around the bush. There wasn't a reason to do so. He preferred her honest, "Besides, you wouldn't like it if my father dictated how your life should be if we were married. He'd really interfere. Believe me. It's just like my brothers have to live by implied expectations. Right now, being away from home like this, I never felt such freedom in my whole life."

"Yeah, freedom! Well, just remember I was there to hear how peed off George became when you up and disappeared from the manor."

"See what I mean? And besides, I told you I was going."

"Right. I was forewarned. Gee! Keeping secrets is what we seem to do best. Why should I complain?"

Susan smiled and touched his face. He was looking at her with soulful dark eyes. Perhaps he did want more involvement than she allowed. Ross seemed to be the type of man who played by the rules. He couldn't have her and he couldn't be with Gloria either. What a dilemma! It must be so because he looked lost momentarily.

"What should I do about your sister? How do I lose her interest? God, she would have made a perfectly good wife too!"

"Be a scumbag." Susan remarked. Her smile smug.

"Now, be serious."

"I am. Just ignore her subtle flirtations. She's pretty dull anyways. You'd be bored with her eventually, trust me. Sooner or later, she will move on as long as you don't show any interest."

"She isn't dull, she's gracious. Are you sure this will work?"

"I know her. Yes, I'm very sure." Susan replied confidently.

Ross nodded and thought deeply. *How can I honestly do that to Gloria? I wish she showed an interest first and then I wouldn't be up here with Susan now. I feel like a cheap, male slut. What's happened to my dignity?* He sighed loudly.

"You ready for round three, Superman? I am," Susan backed up towards the door. Once inside, she removed the robe slowly. Her body was so taut, voluptuous and curvy. Just a suggestive smile from her lips turned him on. Very willingly, he went to her again. All other thoughts were put on hold upon a back burner.

Chapter Twenty Four

Let's talk about love

Around eight o'clock, back at the hospital, Tara woke up. Still, there was no sign of her husband, but a nicely printed note was placed beside the food tray. Eagerly, she opened it to read:

"Dear Tara, you sleep so soundly. Very peaceful, very lovely. Just couldn't disturb you. We can talk another time. Congratulations. Love, Ross."

Oh, this was a disappointment! Just to hear his voice, to see him in the flesh; Tara missed him greatly. As children, they shared everything and now that the most important event occurred in her life, he wasn't there to hear about everything. This was disappointing. Now she sat alone, in a standard sterile hospital room. It was like dark gloom, partially because she no longer felt pregnant either. The constant movements in her belly were gone. She hated being abandoned or left alone, ever.

On top of that, she felt anger too. How dare Danny give permission for that operation, even though the nurse explained it? *They are not even his flesh and blood,* Tara fumed thinking it over. *What right does he have? If he feels so strongly about me and the babies, then why is he away?* Surely the limelight is more important. *That's what it is; he just wants to ensure that everyone thinks he is the father.* Disgusted, Tara rolled the meal stand forward and the leg was caught somewhere underneath. She tugged, but it did not cooperate at all.

"Here! Let me get that for you," Michael insisted as he entered the room and saw what took place. A brown bag was placed on the bed. There was good aroma coming from it. Michael tugged and adjusted the stand in place.

"Michael! Thank you! You are a God send!" Tara declared. She was so thrilled to see him, so handsome within black pleated pants, a blue striped shirt and an appropriate matching tie, and a dark blue blazer. Michael smiled and then offered a congratulatory kiss upon her cheek. To feel his touch was dazzling, to smell his cologne musk scent was wonderful. Then he showed what was inside the bag. It contained lamb with red currant sauce, with a variety of spring vegetables: peas, asparagus, and potatoes, and fresh baked bread rolls; hot food from a wonderful restaurant nearby.

"I figured it must taste better that what is served here." Michael lifted the top off the tray just to see what was brought up. He winced. The entire tray was placed elsewhere, "I am quite right."

Tara laughed and the stitches hurt.

"Thank you Michael, but how did you know?" The fragrance of the food roused up her appetite and she was eager to eat.

"I had my appendix out here. Nothing has changed with the dietary department. You are a lady in constant need of rescue. I'm merely playing a part."

There was a suggestive look to those shining blue eyes, a tease that he couldn't help but express.

"You do wonderful." Tara looked deeply into his eyes, "I've always believed this so. You are a better man than my own husband."

At this, Michael's eyebrow went up, causing those familiar fine lines to crease up to his forehead. The frank conversation with Danny came poignantly to mind. He was breaking the rule, his silent word to help, not hinder. *Damn it! Why did I see Danny that morning?* It was his fault that Tara found discord with Danny. In all good faith, he should swing her mind around, at least a little. Michael pulled in a chair to talk seriously.

"That's a touchy statement, Tara. Really, Danny raced you to safety last night. He's the hero you should be thanking. The storm was terrible! You were out and didn't realize it," Michael revealed. "My father told me this morning that Sammy's battle ship sailed back into London for provisions. Danny found out and went on board to visit him. The commander allowed him to stay on. The men on board aren't allowed shore leave right now, with the alert continuing about the conflicts in Africa. Sammy will have to go back. It was a miracle that Danny decided to come home at all"

That explained Danny's delay for not coming straight home from his teaching lecture at the Dartmouth Naval Academy. In all fairness, Tara bowed her head to think about it. Yes, if not for his unimaginable strength to carry her heavy body to the car, something serious could have occurred, to her, to the babies. George didn't have that kind of brawn. Yes, she should be very thankful to Danny. Still, it was mystifying why all a sudden Michael took Danny's side of things, unless perhaps Grams spoke to him too.

"Ok, so Danny finally gets kudos for being at the right place, at the right time. He's suddenly a super hero. Am I supposed to swoon because of it?"

"Be fair" Michael urged. Tara shook her head stubbornly.

"Michael, I can't help the way I feel. No matter what he does or says, it's all irritating. We are just different people, complete opposites. The man is so full of exuberant energy, like he is permanently on happy pills. And it drives me insane. He tries too hard to ensure my happiness, but what did I do to deserve that? No matter how mean I am, he doesn't fight back. If I say it's white, he'll agree. He won't argue that it's black!"

"He's a new husband, Tara – and now a new father. I've heard that minor adjustments are tough for any couple in their first year together. It takes time to work out the kinks in sorting out your differences, your tastes," Michael rubbed his chin thoughtfully, "In your case, it can't be easy because he's always off with the navy ever since you've been here.

"Actually, I'm glad when he's away," She retorted and meant it.

"Tara… let Danny get a grip of priorities. He'll have to do something now that the babies are here. It's not just a case of just one baby, it's seven. Surely, he'll have to find a way to be home more somehow."

"Well that just brings up something else entirely. Are you aware of how much he drinks?"

"No, not really," Michael replied, "Although he did mention that he drank to help him sleep recently, only because you slept apart."

"Well, that's partly right. In one week, he drank every single night, before we left the Briggs House. I heard the maids gossiping about it; how it was odd he could hold so much liquor and seem perfectly rational. I don't like knowing such things."

"Why let these gossiping maids bother you? If he only drinks a little…"

"A little?" Tara cut him off. "Did he tell you so?"

"Well, yes," Michael stammered but based by the fiery look in her eyes, it was more.

"It's simply not true Michael. Even in New York, he drank like a fish, a whale maybe. Every time he and Ross got together, he brought over the booze in large quantities. The two boys whooped up a good old time whenever Ross was off work. I didn't like it. Why does he want to seek out answers in the bottom of a glass? It's a weakness, Michael, and one that leaves me to wonder if it will ever end. I don't want that around my children."

"If Danny puts his mind to something, he will end it, Tara."

"I don't believe it. That's another reason why I feel he is weak, with no backbone," Tara pouted and leaned closer to the man. It was time to say it like it is, "The drinking is proof and I can't watch him drown within insecurities. That type of man is not what I want for a husband or a father. I should have trusted my instincts when we married, but then again, it would not have brought me here. Now I know what it is I need. It's so very clear. It's someone strong, just like you."

Michael leaned closer too as she vented, and now she looked at him closely. Those sultry eyes. They were so adorable. He was so near, they could almost kiss. That look beckoned him and he wanted to taste those lovely lips, but this was dangerous territory. Ah, perhaps another time, a different circumstance, he could quench the desire. Quickly, he cleared his throat, pulled away, and forced himself to answer appropriately.

"Look, Danny has been preoccupied, with his duty, with the troubles in your relationship. He professed everything to me quite candidly. In all good faith, I should help you both ameliorate your relationship."

"In deed." Tara pursed her lips. Why was he pushing her away? Tara could feel it and didn't like it one bit, "Still, you are the one who came to see me tonight. Ross stopped by, but he didn't stay, and Danny is at that damn pub. You are the only one who cares about me. Just admit what I say is true!"

"Really, that media mob needed someone to settle them down," Michael stammered, but she was making it terribly difficult not to agree. Maybe Danny's priorities were screwed up. Maybe he did indulge too much in booze. No wonder relationships were difficult in the past. Women can see right through bad habits quickly. From hence on, his brother should take a road towards sobriety or risk losing his wife. He quickly changed the subject.

"You won't let that get cold? I paid a mild fortune for it dear," Michael took the fork. He brought a bite from the Styrofoam container and placed it towards her lips patiently, "Please get some nourishment. It's important to keep up your strength. You use up a lot of energy when you are angry."

Tara did as he wished and calmed down, feeling content. Yes, the man would not admit things out loud, but it meant everything that he was there. That was proof enough that he loved her.

Chapter Twenty Five
Morning has broken

It was nearing 1:00 am, when Michael arrived in Wiltshire County. He took a detour by the village pub. There were signs posted all over the main square of the glad tidings. "Hmf", he remarked as he stepped out of his blue compact car to walk inside. Someone handed over a free glass of Guinness. Michael sipped at the strong brew as he looked around. Danny stood deep in a far corner, between some local villagers and outside spectators that stuck around. Michael waved. They found a spot away from everyone else.

"Isn't this something? This place won't be the same again." Danny spoke above the chatter, music, clinking glasses, and occasional laughter. He downed his shot and signaled Rosemary for another.

"I just came from the hospital," Michael said. Danny's eyes lit up.

"Did you speak to Tara? She was out like a light when I finally left. They said it would take awhile for the medication to wear off."

"That was several, several hours ago. She was wide awake when I left her," Michael admitted uneasily but Danny only looked down at his watch.

"Oh, blimy! It really is late! With all of this commotion, I lost track of the time. It's been so crazy. I've never felt so important! What a glorious day it's been! I didn't even eat dinner!"

"You have been drinking all day?" Michael studied over his younger brother's appearance. What Tara suggested earlier about this looked on target. Indeed, the eyes were red, his clothes rumpled, but his speech wasn't terribly slurred. Perhaps to outwardly appearances, he did hold his liquor well. Danny sat down into a chair at a small table.

"Somewhat. There were lots of people asking questions, so I needed to stay slightly sober. I couldn't come across like a total fool," Danny laughed, "I'm sure that by morning, my poor head will ache."

"Well, headache or not, you must see your wife. Do it early. She wants to talk and was very aware of your absence today."

This caught Danny off guard. Even his own mother insisted he take care of the reporters. Didn't anyone inform Tara? Michael's tone was saying something different.

"Is she angry?"

"Yes, but I made up excuses," Michael watched as Danny gulped down the shot of whiskey that the waitress brought over, "Tara should be released within five days."

"Her doctor did mention that. It's supposed to be standard after a cesarean."

"Well, I offered Tara the key to my flat. This way she can see the infants until they come home. She loves the idea."

Danny thought this through. It made sense to do this.

"That's mighty kind, Michael. I don't want to inconvenience anyone. If Tara is upset with me, surely we will be at odds."

Michael understood the implication of their separate sleeping arrangements.

"There are two bedrooms and a study with a pullout couch. Sleep where you want."

"What about Ross?"

"He acquired an apartment closer to his job. By the time she's released, he'll be gone. I have business in the west end district, so will stay occupied every night. So don't worry about my presence around Tara."

"I wasn't implying a word about that," Danny felt caught off guard that Michael brought up his interferences. Michael patted him on the shoulder.

"Look, I'm trying to help, but you must do your part. Just use the flat, and for right now, stop drinking, go home, and get some sleep. In the morning, drive to London. Tara is expecting you."

Danny realized the tone. He grabbed a copy of the paper for safekeeping and took off. He went to the manor to sleep and tumbled into Tara's bed after undressing. Sleep didn't come easy. He tossed and turned. Thoughts raced in his brain. *Seven babies*, he worried, staring up at the ceiling. He imagined omnipresence. *Surely, God would not give us more than we can handle. Say it's my destiny to be their father, to ensure that they grow up safe and sound. I can do that.*

At that point, feeling better, he rolled over, crunching the pillow tightly, as he wanted to hold Tara. His body missed her. He closed eyes in fervent prayer, *God, just make my wife believe this too.*

The next morning, he drove with the darkest sunglasses as the sun was very bright. "Oh, why did I drink so much?" he sighed. Hopefully Tara would be rested and would discuss things civilly. She could be stubborn, like a goat, and lately it seemed that no amount of hay could coax such a creature to budge in his direction.

At the hospital, Danny stepped into the room, holding a lovely bouquet picked up in the gift shop downstairs. He was aghast to find a sea of flowers and gifts already there. He tiptoed in to place his modest arrangement next to the others. Tara stirred in her bed and saw him there.

"Finally!" Tara patted the chair next to the bed. "I wanted to talk to you."

"I was held up at the village. The reporters swarmed into town and I couldn't leave," Danny said as he sat down. At that point, she grabbed the day old newspaper and showed it to him.

"Please tell me that you didn't go overboard with details. The last thing I want is for anyone to know the truth. No one should know about Jimmy or how I got this way or why we are together. As far as I'm concerned, it's my business."

"It's mine too, Tara." Danny remarked softly, "No, I didn't reveal anything that could hurt us."

Her attitude was a little unsettling and she stared for a moment. There were words forming in her head. Whatever they were, she didn't say them. Instead, she picked up a pen and tablet.

"It's your mother that concerns me."

"How? What has she done? She's terribly excited."

"That's why. Don't let anything slip, Danny. She has gone out of her way to accept me and make everything comfortable at the manor. It would devastate her to know that the babies are not her blood."

"I wouldn't do that to my mother. For God's sake, I do recall a promise made to make everyone believe I was their father. I will not break it."

"Well, you are doing a terrific job, with the interviews and the wild party at the pub. It seems the perfect way for everyone to know. It kept you *away* all day long."

Did she really want him there? Did he detect this clearly? If she didn't care, why did it matter? It didn't correlate to her actions or words. Somehow, this made him change his tone.

"Look, let's not quibble about what's been done. It's hard not be excited. We have been so blessed, don't you think so?"

Tara saw his smile widening and he seemed delighted and proud. Even if it seemed odd, now she felt like talking and sharing. She needed to do it with someone. Michael didn't even want to discuss the babies at all.

"It's a bit overwhelming to have seven. That surprised me, but I went to the nursery and visited for awhile. Now, I can't stop thinking about them. They are so small and so cute."

"Yes, they are. Quite fragile, but the nurses seem encouraged. That's a good sign."

"We should do the next step. I've been thinking about names all morning. It's important that we choose them appropriately."

It was thrilling to hear that they could do this together and that she would listen to his opinions on such an important process. Now that he could be part of this, he was ready.

"All right. That's a good idea. I have a few names that I like. How about Tristan? And Elizabeth for the girl? My mother suggested Edward. She thinks it sounds regal." Danny replied happily and they spent the next hour going over several more ideas. Tara kept running combinations, as she wanted middle names. His enthusiasm was soon withered down by her stubbornness. Like a buried nail stuck to the wall, Tara came up with an idea that went against his way of thinking.

"Just bring that old blue diary to me. It's in one of those boxes brought over from New York," She requested in a raised voice and threw the tablet down on the bed.

"I still say I am against it," Danny fumed, but somehow kept his cool. For once, he was bickering back, but Tara didn't take kindly to it. Instead, she tossed her hair over her shoulder just to stare defiantly into his blue eyes.

"Why should that matter? It's important that their true paternity reflects in their names. I've struggled to have those babies, so let me do this. Danny, please!"

He knew that it was hopeless arguing further. She would not relent.

"That means I have to drive back and climb into the attic, where your stuff is stored. Can I bring it tomorrow?"

"We should inform the hospital today. I don't like visiting the nursery to see their tags above the isolettes list each as Baby A or Baby B. It's so impersonal!"

"All right, Tara. I will do this for them, for us," Danny sighed wearily, stood up, and went to the door, "I'll return in a short while, barring bad traffic."

What a stubborn woman! He muttered out loud while entering the hallway towards the elevator. Danny didn't relish climbing up a ladder with such a splitting headache just to weed through cobwebs in a dusty place. Haskell nor the servants could help as they didn't know what the bloody book looked like. He griped out loud all the way home. When he got out of the car, he stormed into the manor, went up the stairs, and found the hidden pull down staircase that led to the dark storage room. There was a light, but no one bothered to replace the bulb, so he edged around the darkness until finding the right box with the diary in it.

With the task done, he ambled into the kitchen to make a quick cucumber sandwich and then he went into the living room to pour a mixed drink. "God, I hope it helps my queasiness." He complained and clutched his tummy as the substance went down. Then he drove back and slowly went up to the hospital entrance. The brisk breeze was blowing his hair in every direction, but the warmth of it was soothing and lulling.

"Ahh, it would be heaven just to close my eyes and pass out. Perhaps the hospital will take pity and place me into a nice, quiet room," Danny thought as he approached the front steps. Reporters appeared from inside the lobby and surrounded him.

"Mr. Cross! Mr. Cross! Can we have a quick update about your babies?" a female reporter ran up with a notepad and pen in hand.

"What is their condition?" another cried out and snapped the button upon a large camera. The flash was brightening. He squinted and held his hand up to block more from being taken.

"How is the mother doing? Can we interview her?"

"The babies are fine and are well looked after by the staff. They have it all under control," Danny addressed them kindly, "As for an interview, my wife wants privacy. Please respect her wishes."

"Is there anything else you can tell us, sir?"

"As a matter of fact, I can. We are naming our children today."

"That's wonderful! May we get a list?" the first reporter asked, "We want to keep the public informed about the Cross Septuplets. Everyone in the country is excited for you."

Danny was pleased by this summation. *The Cross Septuplets.* Yes, to the whole entire world, the children were considered his. Not Tara's former lover, Jimmy. *Their true blood! Bah-humbug!* His jealous disposition finally showed up.

"Quite, indeed. I will be out shortly with that. Why not stick around awhile?"

The reporters gratefully complied. In the meantime, Danny went to the room and handed over the book to the most stubborn woman in the world. "Here you are, *my dearest*," he said with a sarcastic tone. Tara grabbed it and instantly flipped through the pages. For several minutes, she toyed with the names on the notepad and then finally smiled.

"Ok, I have it. These are perfect," She said and handed over the list for Danny to read over.

"I do agree," he said as he studied it carefully. From the first born boy to the last, the names were: Vincent Scott, Tyler Jordon, Mathew Kyle, Edward Joseph, Tristan Paul, Eric James, and last, Jamie Elizabeth, the only girl in the entire Cross brood.

The names were mixed, some that were his suggestions, some that were hers, and only a few of the middle names came from Jimmy's family. It was a fair tradeoff and it seemed that while he was out, Tara took his feelings under consideration. The next day, the announcement came in the morning papers.

"I think someone here leaked this information," Tara remarked while reading a paper that the candy striper handed to her, "We only named them yesterday."

The woman nodded politely and edged out of the room, leaving the new mother to her own thoughts. Tara felt relieved to read that there was nothing mentioned about her name, or where she came from, or when she was to be released. There was plenty of glorious information about Danny and the only reference to her seemed almost as a slight offense, as they constantly described her as "an American."

Chapter Twenty Six

The Flat and the homecoming

Tara's release came around high tea time the next evening and the couple went straight to Michael's flat. Initially, Tara felt butterflies about it as Danny placed her bag into one of the large bedrooms, but then he simply went into the kitchen to prepare their supper.

"I never realized you can cook," Tara mentioned after they had sat down to dine in complete silence. Danny didn't even wish to watch the television. The silverware echoed within the wide open dining room. Tara could hear the wall clock ticking. With no attempt at conversation, the silence unnerved her. At least he replied to this observance.

"It's nothing fancy, just bangors and mash. It was my mother's recipe that I learned as a child. She liked to cook. We didn't always have servants to care for us."

"I didn't know that," she paused and wondered if this meant she should be grateful that there were several available at the Briggs House. She studied the food on the plate and picked at the meat with her fork. It was hot and delicious and he did it for her, "You have a weird way of describing sausage and mashed potatoes, but it's delicious, and the gravy is perfect. Thank you."

"You're welcomed."

"If I tried this, it would not turn out the same." Tara teased, in hopes to keep the conversation going. Danny took a bite, swallowed it down, and then a slight grin graced his face.

"I recall your attempts in New York. The kitchen would fill up with smoke. Ross just knew the fire department would show up next," Danny chuckled as he recollected those days and Tara looked at her husband, feeling melancholy. There was that terrific smile upon his face, like the one when he sat at their table at the street bar, real and friendly. So much happened since then. Now, their strain just to make small talk made their situation seemed worse. It was shameful how things had transpired. It made her feel guilty.

Around nine o'clock, Danny cleaned up the kitchen. With the dishes stacked in the cabinets, he turned off the lights and then followed Tara into the bedroom. He walked towards the closet as she gathered a nightgown from her bag. It was nothing really extraordinary, but it was lacy and pink. She was holding it close and he stared at it momentarily and then at her. She froze and wondered what his intentions were for the night, but he shut the closet securely.

"Here's an extra blanket, if you get cold. Now that you aren't pregnant, you may not get so hot. You used to complain about the cold temperatures at night," he said and laid it onto the bed nearby.

"Where are you sleeping?" she suddenly asked.

"Don't worry. I'll be in the study, down the hall." he barked, uncharacteristically.

"Danny, I..." she began to say but he waved a hand and simply went down the hall without further confrontation. In the middle of the night, around midnight, she stepped out of her room and listened. The light was out in the study. The door was shut and she tiptoed to it. She could make out a feint snore. Satisfied that Danny was sound asleep, she went around investigating the finely furnished living quarters freely. It was wide and airy with contemporary furniture in all of the rooms. Just the perfect place for a bachelor and it was kept immaculately clean.

In the living room, Tara paused to check out a sturdy oak bookshelf that contained several awards plaques, pictures of Michael with other theater friends, and hardcover books. She picked up one and studied the fine leather binding.

"Hmm, Shakespeare," she remarked and wrinkled her nose and placed it back. There was a murder thriller on the upper shelf and she took it to the couch to read.

"Surely Michael will come home soon," she wondered as she looked at the time. Yet, her eyes grew weary from reading and she fell fast asleep. When the morning sun rose and filled the area with bright light, she found Danny rummaging in the kitchen scurrying up breakfast. Not once, in all that time that they stayed did she see Michael.

Finally, the hospital finally released the infants to go home, with the exception of Eric. They did very well and weighed close to 3 ½ pounds and didn't need any respiratory assistance. Gloria, Helen and George helped transport them to the Briggs House. They were placed in their rooms, two boys to each bedroom. Only Jamie occupied her own room.

"She's my one little girl, so she deserves special attention. By separating the boys, perhaps dressing them in different color sleepers, it will help everyone tell them apart, even if they are supposed to be fraternal, "Danny suggested to the staff, "That might be helpful to determine them until they are older with defining personalities. Right now, they all look so much alike at this point."

The staff nodded in agreement. He held up pocketbook report covers with brads and lots of lined paper inside.

"Also, I want individual folders for each baby, to note their particular care of bathing, changing, and feeding schedules. We can track everything down daily and you are free to write in any other notes that you deem important."

"That's a wise idea," Marta agreed, liking his sense of order, "The doctor will appreciate that when he visits for check ups. Thank goodness we won't have to haul them all to his office. That would be quite a feat!"

They laughed and went to assist Tara with her children. Marta and Lila were staying on along with Sabrina and Caroline, two other servants from the grand manor. They would alternate their shifts and sleep in the servants' quarters. This allowed Tara to rest up for Eric's surgery. For the cardiac operation, the hospital wanted to transport Eric to a different facility with a fine baby cardiologist available.

"I hate it that we left Eric behind in London. Poor baby is all alone." Tara lamented loudly as she studied the empty white crib in the brightly yellow room. Danny's mother did a wonderful job decorating. The borders were of little ducks and chickens. There was a rocking chair in one corner. In another, a lovely green bookshelf filled with stuffed toys and baby sundries. Lila tenderly covered up Tristan in his white crib and turned on the mobile hanging there. Tara returned to her own bedroom and looked over at Danny, who acknowledged that he heard by nodding. Tara sat abruptly upon their large bed and announced glumly, "It makes me sad."

"It can not be helped, Tara. He needs strength to endure the operation. Luckily, he has managed to gain a pound this week. He's quite a fighter." Danny said encouragingly and moved some of the flower vases to different parts of the room. He wanted her to be comfortable, now that she was home, but she seemed very restless. Her leg crossed over the other and she absent mindlessly moved it in small circles in the air. Not satisfied again, she leapt up to look out the double window. It was lovely outside, but she didn't seem to care about it.

"I suppose the nurses will watch over him."

"They are professionals and will call if they need us." Danny stood behind her now and contemplated his actions. During their stay at Michaels, she attempted several times to be civil. He was so afraid to rock the boat between them; he thought it best to stay quiet. Now they were home. It should make some difference in her mind. Should he hold her? Would she let him? Gently, he placed his hand upon her shoulder to turn her around. "You don't need to worry alone. We are in this together."

It was apparent in his blue eyes what he was thinking. Tara shook her head instead. Crushed, his eyes lowered. She knew she hurt him and felt so terribly confused. In the last few days, with a caring attitude about the babies, they shared something together, something she didn't quite expect. Tara didn't know how to deal with her conflicted emotions; especially since Michael seemed to vanish off the planet. How she wished that it was Michael standing before her, because then there would be no hesitation to embrace the man tight. Why was there no remedy in sight for such a hopeless situation?

"I just feel so blue, Danny. It's just that the weight of the world sits heavily on me. I won't feel right until I know that Eric will be ok," She lied, although she did worry about Eric constantly.

"How can I reassure you?"

"You can't. Look, right now, I'd rather be left alone." Tara felt a shiver and tears filled her eyes. When he looked up, there was desperation in her eyes.

"You do seem out of sorts. Perhaps a nap will make things feel better."

He pulled the bedspread down and she complied at his nod to slip in underneath it. Kindly, he tucked her in, drew the shades, quietly shut the door, and paused in the hallway. Tara indeed wept and it tore at his heart. Did she cry for him, for herself, for Eric, or for Michael? Hurt and anger forced him to descend down the stairs quickly. He flung the door wide to escape outdoors. The air was filled with flowery fragrances. The tall grass swayed against the west wind. Danny went directly across the wide yard and leaned heavily against the wooden fence that blocked that portion of his property from the grass overgrowth. The sun set slowly in the horizon and gave off beautiful hues of red and gold.

Frustrated, lonely, and damn weary of being denied by the woman he loved, Danny felt that his heart would explode. In desperation, he pulled out a silver flask that laid hidden deep in his pants pocket. It was the only source of comfort to be found. He cursed the air and drank the alcohol down. When the flask emptied, he threw it into the grassy field. In anger, he walked over to his car, fired it up, and then drove down the road at a rapid speed. The servants didn't spy him again until the next morning.

Chapter Twenty Seven
When Something Snaps

On the day of Eric's operation, Helen stayed with Marta and Lila to help out with the infants at home. George never did like hospitals, so he stayed home. Susan agreed to a modeling job at an Italian winery. Ross was detained by business meetings. So, Tara and Danny rode the 6:00 a.m. train to London. They met Michael and Gloria at the station.

"I can only stay for a couple of hours." She said to the couple from the front seat as Michael drove them. "There is a big publicity shoot happening and my boss insists that I show up on time."

"That's fine. We understand," Danny remarked. He stared at Tara, as for the first time in days, she applied lipstick. Michael watched closely in the rearview mirror. Gloria saw something wicked flash within Danny's usual calm eyes.

"Are you ok?" she asked and that caused Tara to stop and look at Danny too. He stared accusingly into her eyes. Tara sighed, "Gee, its only lipstick. No big deal."

She stuck the lid on the product and threw it into her handbag. Michael shifted his eyes back to the road. Gloria studied them all only to offer Danny a way out of what brewed to be an awkward situation, "Are you worried about the operation?"

"I suppose we all think differently. Some worry more than others," he replied in a confrontational tone. Tara looked out the window in disgust. Not a single word more was spoken until their arrival to the hospital. They went into the holding room to see the baby. Tara cradled Eric to her breast, even with all of the IV lines and monitor tubes attached for the heart surgery. She caressed his face so delicately.

"My precious little angel. God will watch over you." She whispered, kissing his forehead several times. She placed the infant into the bed that would wheel him into surgery. Danny stepped forward to kiss the child as well.

"You keep up your fight, little man," he whispered.

This fatherly attention was so gentle that Tara was greatly surprised.

"He's a strong willed little guy." Danny mentioned out loud. The nurse smiled and tapped him on the back.

"You've kept him strong, by your visits recently."

"Thanks," Danny replied.

Tara's mouth opened wide.

"You came by to see Eric? I thought that you went …"

"Where else, Tara?" Danny cut her to the quick. "Of course I stopped by to see him. One of us needed to do it and you were incapacitated."

He went to the waiting room. Always guardian of his tender feelings, Gloria sat close to her younger brother. Gingerly, she wrapped an arm around his shoulders. He leaned forward in prayer. Michael whispered into Tara's ear.

"You thought he was at the pub, right?" he asked.

"Yes, I did, whenever he left the house for long periods of time. I guess I was so wrong."

They sat down in the reception room to wait. There were several questions that Tara wanted to ask Michael, but it wasn't possible with Gloria and Danny in the same vicinity. She would have to wait to do so. The time crept slowly by. Waiting felt like an eternity and the silence amongst them was stifling. Gloria tried to make small talk, but every discussion bombed. There were too many silent agendas, too many words hidden, too many feelings immensely raw or riddled with guilt or confusion. Gloria was never so glad when it came time to leave. She embraced Danny tightly and kissed him on the cheek.

"You'll be in my thoughts today, dearest. Please call and leave word of Eric's outcome so I won't worry long."

"Yes, of course, my best sister. Love you," he replied and kissed her back on the cheek. She offered Michael a grim smile and blew out her breath. He understood.

Gloria embraced Tara, "Everything will be fine," she remarked in Tara's ear. In a minute, Gloria raced down the hall, her boots clicking loudly upon the wooden floor that led her out. Another hour passed and Danny yawned.

"Anyone want something to drink?" He stood to stretch out his back and straighten out his cramped neck. Michael nodded and yawned too.

"Coffee sounds good. It's hard not to fall asleep waiting."

"Nothing for me," Tara replied, tapping her fingers upon her knees.

Danny nodded and went down to the nearest break room. There was a couple coming down the hallway with a little toddler, all smiles and warm hugs. *All's well in his world*, Danny groaned as he stood in front of the coffee machine. *Lucky bloke! This is how we should be*, he lamented.

A Styrofoam container popped down with hot coffee and Danny placed coins in the dispenser for another one. Five minutes later, he returned to the waiting room. Stunned, he stopped at the door. Tara now sat next to Michael, with her head upon his shoulder. This tiny physical contact made him squeeze the cups tightly within his hands. Michael suddenly looked up, but not to acknowledge him, but the cardiologist who just walked up behind Danny.

"The operation is over," The surgeon announced. At the sound of his voice, Tara leapt up to greet him.

"How is Eric? Will he be alright?" she asked breathlessly.

"Yes, indeed. Everything's great." The doctor declared.

"Oh, thank God!" she whooped, spinning around in glee. The surgeon smiled and turned to address Danny,

"The defected valves are corrected. We are sorry for the long wait, but there was a conflict with the OR room and another case, but everything worked out in my favor. Eric will be in the post-op recovery room for a short bit. Then he will be placed back in the special nursery."

"When can he come home?" Tara wanted to know. She wiped away a few joyful tears.

"There will be a short post-operative recovery. If everything goes to plan, he can go home very soon. All right, if there are no more questions, I have charts to sign. The head nurse will call you back in about an hour or so to see Eric."

He waited a moment and then departed down the hallway.

"He's going to live!" Tara exhaled loudly. Without thinking, she embraced arms tightly around Michael's neck. His eyes grew wide at her reaction. Gasping, he yanked her away and looked around, but it was too late. The nearby exit door swung wildly. Styrofoam cups were thrown to the floor with coffee spilt everywhere. Danny hastily departed down the hall in long angry strides and disappeared out the main door.

"Oh, God! Now you've done it!" Michael exclaimed and peered angrily into Tara's confused eyes, "Things will never be the same!"

The news of Eric's successful surgery brought smiles to the nurses who cared for him during his post-op recovery. Tara went inside the area alone. She studied the infant over. There were several bandages across his tiny chest where the incision was made to repair the heart valves. An IV bag hung from a pole. A thin tube ran normal saline solution to nurture his body.

"His color is good," she remarked. Nearby, the nurse agreed.

"Is your husband with you? He seemed anxious this morning. I thought he would come to see for himself."

Tara was hesitant to reply.

"Danny wanted to stay. Something urgent came up and he left."

"Oh, that's too bad. He seemed so caring. You're a lucky girl to have such a terrific husband," the nurse remarked while she wrote information into Eric's chart and then walked away to answer a ringing telephone. Tara needed a moment to compose her feelings. How could it be that everyone noticed Danny's good qualities but her? The nurse was so right and yes, Danny did much for Eric lately. He pulled a surprise, much like his older brother, and both affected her heart. It was shocking to watch Danny storm out. Never did she expect him to react quite angry. Neither did she expect Michael's attitude shifting 180 degrees in the waiting room.

"You go on alone to see your baby, Tara. I will wait here," he said stiffly at her request to accompany her to see Eric. He placed the dirty napkins and empty cups into the trash receptacle, "I am uncomfortable around children."

He really meant this and he felt disgruntled that his mother always pushed him to marry just to have a family. Marriage only tied one down and babies cried a lot. Toddlers had snotty noses and screamed all of the time. There was no patience for that in his system. None at all. It was best he hung around adults. Tara tried to encourage him, but it was to no avail.

"I understand. They are only little babies. Things will get easier the more you are around."

"What does that mean?" he looked startled. "Surely, you don't want me to take Danny's place. That's his expectations, not mine."

"But I thought..."

"What? That now we can have an open relationship? Oh, no my dear. Simple flirting is one thing, but that's all it was. I managed to stop before it got out of hand."

"Michael, what are you saying? You always came by to see me. I felt special being with you. At the hospital, you made me believe that you loved me. There was that look in your eyes," Tara's mouth parted. She desperately clutched the handbag making her knuckles turn white. Was this a practical joke? Was there a hidden camera somewhere? Why was he being cruel?

"You made up your own conclusions," he replied in a cold demeanor, but this was the hardest thing he ever did. However, now he realized that consequences could occur, that never dawned on him before, "My parents will cut me off if I dare interfere further. Danny has always been my mother's favorite child. My Gram thinks he is a gift from God. They will persuade my father to do something about me. I won't play havoc with my inheritance or my career."

"Is money all that matters? Your inheritance? Your work?"

"Why would I give that up? My life is in London, not stuck in Wiltshire pretending to be a daddy. That's my brother's choice. I never asked for that and suspected that you would stir up complications. Certainly, it was irresistible here. For five seconds, I closed my eyes. You snuck up to place your head upon my shoulder. That's what provoked my brother, to see us so close. Well I won't go down burning for such a weak moment."

Tara felt like one struck by a brick. His words were brutal. This couldn't be happening. Sick to her stomach, she took a deep breath while tears flowed down, making her mascara run. She felt so stupid.

"You led me on Michael. Now I've made some terrible mistakes. What should I do now? I've ruined everything with my husband. He probably hates me now."

Michael stared out the window for a moment to think. He couldn't just abandon her there. Everyone else was not available to take care of the love-sick girl.

"I suppose I should take some responsibility that this went of control. Look, we are family and can remain friends, maybe; but nothing more. Do you understand? There's a bond made with my brother that can't be broken, ever."

She nodded and wiped away the tears. There would be time to cry later and she must put on a brave face. There could be nothing more. "Concentrate on Eric," she thought. "I need to see him." All her trust in Michael just went out the window. Michael sat down, grabbed a magazine, and flipped through the pages.

"I'll wait here while you check on your son. When you come out, you can stay at the flat until he can come home. In the meantime, I'll look for Danny to explain. If I'm not successful, then perhaps Gloria or Susan will drive you and Eric to the Briggs House when he's released," At this point, he stared up towards her brown eyes, the ones he loved to drown his reflection into, and fought to stay true to course, "I pray that Danny forgives you, dear. He's the only reason you are with us."

Tara felt embarrassed, disillusioned even. And now she cursed how she ever loved Michael this way, especially when Danny tried so hard to make their relationship work. He wanted a family, the one thing denied as she grew up at Hartridge. Stupid! So Stupid! She looked at Eric and caressed his head. Tenderly, she covered him up with a receiving blanket. When she entered the hallway to return to the waiting room, she felt afraid of her future. Would Danny come back? Would he demand a divorce? Would the children be taken away if she couldn't provide? This was not good.

Chapter Twenty Eight
The Mother Queen

Within the next two weeks, her spirits spiraled downward. Every night, she cried, for the hurt she received from Michael and the hurt she gave her husband. The warnings proclaimed about Michael ran through her head. Danny and Grams advice were right. A day late and a dollar short. Now she realized, quite sadly, how Michael was a playboy, a lover of luxury and of himself. He could never be someone's husband or a father. He was much too selfish and much too accustomed to his lifestyle. It was a hard lesson learned.

Helen was so surprised when Tara returned home with Eric without Danny. He simply disappeared and called no one, not even Gloria. She learned about Eric's outcome from Michael, and he didn't offer any explanation, but Gloria could tell by his tone that he was involved. George thought about calling Scotland Yard, but he didn't want any publicity about his son's disappearance. At this point, Danny was too well known. Surely someone saw him recently, so he made private inquiries.

The entire household moved on to accept a rigid routine taking care of Danny's household. The seven infants simply required a lot of feeding, burping, bathing, changing and cuddling. Lila and Marta loved the challenges, but they were aware that Tara was not herself. She cuddled each child as if her life depended on it and there were always tears in her eyes. Helen came over to see the babies practically everyday, but she couldn't pry. She wasn't the only one asking questions.

"Where is that devil? Did mother have any clue?" Susan snapped as she followed Gloria through the market in the village gathering up a few baby supplies and groceries. "God, I can't believe we are both stuck doing this."

"Stop complaining. We are only helping out," Gloria sighed as she paid for the items on the counter with a credit card. She was glad that Danny nixed the ideas of endorsing anyone's products. He wanted to provide on his own and he desired privacy. It was a good thing for their family too.

Her pretty blond hair was up in a nice coifed style and many ringlet curls fell against the nape of her white neck. She was dressed casually in blue jeans and a plaid button down shirt, wearing sneakers, while Susan stood beside her in tight hip-hugger jeans, wearing red heels, and a tight black and red v-neck halter top. The register clerk couldn't keep his eyes off her cleavage. Gloria clicked her tongue to put his mind into bagging their groceries, "Your brother will be appreciative. Besides, we both have nothing else to do."

She loaded up the bag into Susan's arms and opened up the front door. They headed quickly to the car, parked at the curb, and got inside. Gloria found keys inside her purse and ignited the engine. They pulled out to the main road through the village, stopped at an intersection, and Gloria went down a different route, an alternative way to the Briggs House. Susan pouted as she watched the familiar drab scenery go by. The country was not as exciting to her as London.

"What awful timing. It correlates with my life lately. That job in Italy was the worst photo shoot I've ever done. It was hot and sticky and the director made a nasty pass in my hotel room. He really was quite ugly and I said no," Susan revealed honestly. Deep down, after being intimate with Ross several times, she couldn't be with anyone else. She never thought that monogamy would suit her, "Thank goodness Sammy taught me how to defend myself. That final kick to the groin was enough to infuriate and the director smashed a lamp going out the door. I paid for it the next morning. There was a smutty message at the hotel desk. That cold bastard had the nerve to fire me!"

"You roll with the punches, dear sister. Not every man is a saint. I learned my lesson from being fired, too. My boss thought he was a god, but he's an asinine, know-it-all jerk. I did learn enough to start up my own business. Who needs him?"

"Well, at least you have talent. All I know is how to bat my eyes and show off my body."

"You'll get another gig and find a better agency. I can shoot your portfolio while we are home now. In the meantime, let's drop these off. Marta will be grateful that we did the shopping for her."

"I'd be grateful if someone will fill me in on where my brother is. It's not like Danny to just up and disappear."

They parked the car in the driveway and stepped into the house. Inside the main living room, Marta took the needed items. The women were left alone to converse. Tara tapped liquid from the baby's bottle onto her palm. Susan wondered if she was purposely ignoring the obvious question.

"What happened, Tara? You are his wife. Haven't you heard anything?"

"No. No news since Eric's operation." Tara replied and lowered her eyes as she placed the bottle nipple upon Matthew's waiting mouth. He liked to eat. Matthew moved his mouth to seek out the nipple adequately. Then sucking securely, a small dribble of formula fell to his neck. Tara patiently wiped it away, "Really, I've been much too busy to notice. We are doing fine."

Gloria watched the young woman sit down upon a rocker. There were dark circles under her eyes.

"You have let the staff help, haven't you? I realized that Sabrina returned to the manor. You are not trying to do everything by yourself?" Gloria asked and noted that Lila folded towels nearby and shook her head woefully. Tara remained silent. "Tara, you simply can't. There's too many. No wonder you seem tired"

If only Danny was home, he would set Tara straight, whether she wanted it or not. She couldn't carry on the responsibilities of all the babies. Why was she trying?

"Something's not right," Gloria sat down beside her. "Danny should be here to help you. Surely he isn't back to duty."

"Sammy is still on his ship because of a conflict," Susan picked up a burp rag from the sofa to sit down. She threw it to another corner to get it away altogether, "and he is detained indefinitely. Perhaps Danny didn't have a chance to tell us."

"That makes sense. I bet Sammy can find out. I know a way to reach him," Gloria suggested. "It will certainly appease my mother."

"Whatever you feel best." Tara remarked. If she cared, it didn't show at all. She studied her baby and gave it several kisses on the forehead, holding on tightly as if someone would take him away.

"Let me call Sammy right now." Gloria reached for the phone. She managed to get through a maze of connections in twenty minutes and wound up with a choppy radio connection to his ship. After explaining the problem, since everyone thought it best to keep things hidden from him, Sammy wanted to work quickly.

"Sure. I'll have to call London headquarters and it may take awhile to get valid feedback. However, why would he do this? He just became a father," Sammy was puzzled.

"When we talked last, he seemed very excited to come home for awhile. What's going on? Am I needed?"

"No, not right now. Just see what you can learn. It's important."

"Ok, sister. Right away." Sammy replied and their connection was cut off. An hour flew by until the call came through. Gloria listened. When he was finished speaking, she placed the receiver down.

"Well? Where is he?" Tara didn't know why, but she felt goose bumps go up her back. She felt afraid knowing. Every night since Danny left, she had waited for the man to come back to the house to confront her. She expected him to be angry and demand that they all leave, but it never happened. She noted the stern look upon Gloria's face.

"Technically, he is on standby for a new mission."

"Where is he hiding? Under a rock?" Tara's tone was crisp and now Susan became angry.

"No. He's not, but obviously, he feels that he can't come home. Why is that, Tara? What did you do? Or rather, what didn't you do? Everyone notices how Danny adores you, but there isn't any appreciation. If you were a better wife, he would not feel unimportant. I bet he's drowning his sorrows at a pub somewhere." She snapped and stood up. Suddenly Gloria clicked her fingers, but Tara sniffed. Her tears flowed down her face.

"It's not my fault!" Tara, shocked by Susan's accusation, realized that it would be devastating to admit the truth about Michael. Instead, she revealed the other worry about Danny. "You don't understand, Susan. He drinks. He's an alcoholic, and because of that, we simply can't get along."

"That's a lie. I've never seen Danny out of control. The man has always made us proud," Susan hissed as she couldn't believe he changed that much, "Danny always puts you first, and do you care? No, because you are stupid. An absolute idiot!"

"How can you say that?"

"Well how can you sit there and remain so calm? Don't you care that he's missing? You sit like one on a throne, a mother queen, without any feelings or regards for our family or worries. You are very selfish."

"Selfish? You've never cared for anyone but yourself. That's selfish, and now you can only spout off wicked thoughts to match your deeds. Not once, while I was stuck in this house, did you ever come by to check on me. Your brother does drink! Any maid here can vouch for that. So how can you possibly know what goes on?"

"I don't, but there's enough gossip to know how you treat my brother. He's away and it's his house. He should be here. You don't care whether he's dead or alive!"

"Susan!" Gloria cried out, "Please don't say such a thing."

"Well, it's true! Maybe he has come to his senses about his wife, but he would have called you, or our mother, or Grams. Something's terribly wrong or something's happened to make him stay away. I feel it in my bones. Don't you?"

"Do you, Gloria?" Tara turned to know what her favorite sister-in-law thought about the situation. Tara felt sincerely worried this time, but they both noticed the tall, serene blond spring quickly out the door and towards her car. Within seconds she was out of the driveway and flying towards the village.

Yes, Gloria didn't want to be in the middle of their sudden quibble. Her mission was to find her brother and talk face to face. Susan's suggestion about the pub brought about a great idea where to find him. There was no time to waste.

Chapter Twenty Nine
The Village Fool's Fall From Grace

The pub was classic: white wooden building with thatch covered roof, large six-glass, thick pane windows, and a chalkboard propped by the door listing the daily specials. It wasn't extravagant nor a dump. Inside, Gloria saw workmen repairing a bar sink, a couple of women watching a small television set, a recent assassination of Henri Curiel, a political activist in Paris capturing their interest; as well as several other patrons sitting around, talking and playing cards, minding their own business. The barkeep stacked glasses below, while two guys laughed by the snooker table. The low lights and cigarette smoke lingering about the room was rank and made her cough.

"Can I help you miss?" the waitress asked, determining that the pretty blond seemed out of place. The waitress cleaned off a table, dumping a full ashtray into a paper bucket on the tray she carried. She picked up empty beer bottles and glasses to place on the bar. Gloria followed her.

"Yes, maybe. I'm looking for my brother, Danny. He frequents this place. He's fair, handsome with blue eyes like me, about 5'11 and is blond…"

"Stop. I know him," the waitress announced out of the blue, chomping on a piece of gum. She took it out of her mouth and threw it into the trashcan. Placing the tray on the bar, she pointed out the back door. "We figured someone in the family would show up sooner or later. Follow me. I'll take you over."

Gloria felt surprised but tagged along behind the slim woman with reddish-brown hair, dressed in a plain drab shirt with dark pants. They went out a back door, into an alley way, and then towards a small house on the other side. Pretty flowerboxes hung on the window ledges. A round earthen pot sat near the front steps that led inside, filled with sand and cigarette butts. They stepped through the door into a well-furnished living room with curtains drawn. An aquarium filled with tropical fish let out enough light to show the stacks of letters and magazines upon the coffee table. Gloria squinted to adjust her eyes.

"Wait here," the waitress said as she closed the front door securely. She went past another door into a creaky hallway. Gloria could hear a female voice speak to the waitress, and then Danny's voice. Her heart pounded in her chest to hear it. He ambled out in a white shirt and buckling up his belt.

"Hello, dearest Gloria. Ahh, I'm found. It's good that someone gives a damn."

Gloria embraced him hard, feeling his warmth, feeling his breath upon the back of her hair. Tears surfaced to her eyes. He wasn't hurt or dead. Still, she pulled away to take a closer look.

"Thank God! You're all right!" Gloria noticed his eyes, which were very red. Didn't he sleep? "Why haven't you called? We've been so worried."

He didn't reply right away as a woman with long black hair came to stand by the door to listen. Idly, she brushed away at teased locks with a wooden brush and looked at Gloria up and down too. Gloria recalled seeing her around once or twice in the village. Not a real beauty, but the reputation preceded her. It was known that her flirtatious personality could entertain anyone for nights on end. Danny introduced them.

"This is Rosemary Clifford. We went to school together"

Further recognition triggered Gloria's memory. Yes, she recalled that Rosemary was once shorter and not as big bosomed or curvy as now. With such a large bust swallowing up a slim waist, she flaunted it further by wearing a bright red blouse, a short black skirt and black fish net stockings with dark flat shoes. Gloria's eyed narrowed in suspicion. The woman reacted.

"I best leave you alone to talk," she said, then hoisted up her well-endowed breasts for show, flipped on a lamp light switch which brightened the room, and then she glanced at Danny as an afterthought, "unless you want me to stay. I don't need to go back for another hour."

"I haven't anything to hide from her," Danny replied and Rosemary came to caress his face. Danny smiled, but Gloria saw only red.

"What's been going on?" Gloria stared into his eyes in disbelief, "Is this why we didn't hear from you? Because of this woman!"

"It wasn't appropriate," Rosemary answered in a smug voice, "I don't think your family would be happy. He's been here all along -with me."

"What?" Gloria felt hot suddenly as her composure snapped. This was unfathomable! "Danny, you are married!"

"I approached him first," Rosemary went to the kitchen to pour a glass of brandy from a blue decanter, "He was drunker than a skunk when we took him in. My roommate and I put him up for a few nights."

"What roommate?"

"Me," the other waitress said calmly and then pulled out a cigarette from the pack stuck firmly in her apron pocket. She placed the thin mint-flavored filter tip into her mouth, barely allowing it to dangle off her lower lip, "I'm Eileen. I say, we both knew how to cheer him up."

"They did," Danny found a lighter on the table. He brought it over towards her cigarette and clicked on the flame, "I haven't felt this kind of attention since I left New York-womanly companionship. It's been quite educational."

Educational? About what? Gloria fumed. This was unexpected and deplorable!

"I can't believe this! Then stay with them! Have your fun!" Gloria cried out, "Honestly, I can't take this truth. I thought you loved your wife."

Gloria went to the door in a rush, but the handle was stuck. She pulled and tugged until it opened contrarily. She turned to let out one more outcry of disapproval.

"You can't be my brother. He's a man of integrity."

Gloria threw up her hands and ran down the steps to get to the car. Unfortunately, it was parked on the other side of the building. Two large trash bins blocked her way going around instead of through the pub. That gave Danny just enough time to come after her.

"Gloria!" Danny yelled, quickly placing on shoes upon his bare feet. He raced to catch up and grabbed her arms to make her stop, "Look, I'm sorry."

"Let me go!" Gloria struggled but he was very strong.

"I won't! You have to listen to me!" Danny looked into her eyes desperately, "Please, understand. I didn't plan this."

"Are you saying those women coerced you to unzip and drop your pants? I'm not that stupid!"

"I know you're not. Let me explain, please!"

"Then tell me, Danny. What happened?" Gloria stared at her brother, defying him to reveal all that transpired, but she bet she wasn't going to like hearing it. Danny kicked the dirt on the ground and stood with his head bowed. He thought a moment before speaking.

"Look, I've always felt comfortable at the pub, so I went there to calm myself down. Everyone remembered who I was- the man with the septuplets! They bought several rounds of drinks. I was proud being accepted as their father, but weary that my own wife doesn't. As the evening got late, I became a sloppy drunk. Rosemary sat down and for once, someone listened to me. She made me feel better about myself."

Danny ran his hands through his hair as he outlined all that happened.

"I was so plastered, more so than I've ever been in my whole life-falling out of my chair, stumbling to the bathroom, tripping in the process of coming back to my table. Rosemary made me follow her home and I passed out on the bed. Sometime in the night, I turned over and felt a warm body beside me. I was still hazy and maybe I thought it was Tara. I don't know, but the next thing I did was place my arm around her. She drew closer, with her hands everywhere. Even lips upon my neck, my ear. God! It felt so good to be touched like that again. In the dark, one thing just led to another."

"All right, I get the picture!" Gloria rebuked loudly and shook her head. Curls sauntered loosely around her shoulders, "She's the type to take advantage of anyone. Although, I can't believe you acted upon it."

"I couldn't help it. It felt too good. Besides, I was still drunk and upset."

"About what? What is it that set you off?"

So he drew out all the events that occurred ever since bringing Tara home to the Briggs House: about her close friendship with Michael, how she chose his attention over her own husband, how it was most upsetting to watch Tara embrace Michael that day. It was a hard pill to swallow. This new jealous rage instantly felt like a bomb going off. Just thinking things over made his pulse quicken Now, Danny looked at the sky to calm down again. The clouds overhead came swirling in from the east with rain close behind. The grass needed watering as some areas were dry and withering. Withering like his heart.

"I wanted to ensure that Eric got through surgery all right. I hoped to bring him home eventually to be with his brothers and sister. I wanted to hold Tara and be proud of our new family. In the course of one day, she threw our marriage out the window because of her lust for my brother. In the course of one night, my fidelity is wiped away too. The difference is that I realize my mistake. I do give a damn about things," Danny sighed, reaching up to rub his neck, "Yes I realize how difficult it is to swallow how I hide now like a coward. Still, I'm left with only realization that underneath this flesh is a simple bloke. I'm sorry for the fire set ablaze in the night, but the smoldering embers only leave me to realize that my physical needs are just as important."

"Don't talk to me about needs,"Gloria scoffed but tried to remain reasonable, "I've been spinning wheels to find you. That was mine- to make sure you were all right."

Surely Rosemary used her womanly ways to convince Danny to stay. It was reasonable to assume that he would enjoy her attention after Tara denied even the simplest acts of affection. She crossed her arms and stared.

He placed his hands upon her shoulders, placed his head against her brow, and stared into her blue eyes.

"Well, I'm grateful that you care about me, dear sister. Really, I am."

Gloria nodded and sighed. She could never stay angry with him as he was her favorite brother. She did agree about his generalization of Tara's recent actions, but things were not all her fault.

"Tara does deserve a good scolding, but she's very naïve and impressionable. What about Michael? Will you ever speak to him again?"

"Michael has always been too easy to admire, so I know why Tara found him fascinating in the first place. It just went on too long, that's all. His bond he will keep. There are no doubts in my mind about that. As for Tara, our marriage vows never meant anything. That was obvious when she blatantly ran to him. I can't change that," Danny looked very disillusioned, "In her eyes, I falter as a man. Those constant rejections made me miserable and drunk enough to react to a woman's touch elsewhere. In your eyes, it is a huge mistake, but so what? She doesn't care what I do."

"I bet she will when she learns about this," Gloria remarked, disappointed. How could he just give up? Danny disagreed with her opinion.

"No, this fall from grace will not make any dent in her feelings. I've asked headquarters to release my leave status. It would be nice to stick around, but Tara is happier by herself. Besides, I think it's best to put distance in-between me and Rosemary."

"That's a good idea," Gloria nodded. It should stop before complications came out of it.

"Orders are being cut, as we speak, to go to sea. I believe starting off in the Mediterranean, near Barcelona. Perhaps tomorrow."

"So soon? Why?" Gloria gasped. This didn't suit her well.

"The sea gives me so much solitude. Out in open waters, breathing in the salt air, I can think alone. Think seriously about my marriage. Tara can remain at the Briggs House for now as I promised her security. Later on, when the children are older and more manageable, if she wants it, then we can discuss divorce."

"Oh, Danny. Let's hope it doesn't come to that. You must give Tara another chance," Gloria pleaded but he waved it off without considering it.

"I've made my decision. Before I leave, I will bid everyone goodbye."

"Look, it's been crazy since you disappeared. I believe Tara has a change of heart. She was crying this afternoon and I could tell she hasn't slept much. I think part of it is her worry about you," Gloria revealed and now wondered if Tara cried too out of some kind of guilt. Perhaps this is why she insisted on caring for the children all by herself- in case Danny ended their marriage abruptly. This seemed a reasonable fear, but Gloria could also hoped that Tara felt remorse over her actions, that she regretted the behavior with Michael. Perhaps she was ready to set things right, but Danny didn't seem ready to think that Tara had changed her mind.

"Unimaginable, but if true, what about the damage I did? To my promise of fidelity and faithfulness? How can I go back and pretend nothing took place? How can I touch her knowing I broke a huge part of our vows? No, I can't fake it and I won't lie about it. Besides, before I deal with her, I must heal myself first."

"Heal yourself? From what?"

"Lately, I'm easily stressed out. When I left the hospital, I stormed out into the parking lot. There was a metal support beam, about an inch thick, which held up a part of a covered walkway. I hit it hard with my fist and now there's a huge dent in it. Perhaps I should reimburse the hospital with a check for it. Just look at my knuckles. They are bruised and scarred from the nicks," he said and held out his hands for her inspection, "I am out of control, with the temper, with the drinking. With being a top officer, I can't risk behaving that way around the men. Something has to give or I'll do something really stupid down the line."

"You mean other than sleeping with Rosemary?" Gloria's left eyebrow shifted up, almost teasingly, but he couldn't accept that.

"Gloria, please! This isn't a laughing matter. Tell no one. Let's keep it secret for awhile," Danny took her hand and she agreed, but not before he did something for her.

"Ok, I won't reveal your sins, but clean up your act. Get your life under control again. Just promise to see our parents for breakfast and then go by your house to bid your wife goodbye. You should explain it to her personally about your plans. You owe her that," Gloria insisted and then offered Danny a goodbye embrace. He nodded limply and didn't balk about it.

Gloria walked briskly to get around the large bins. She went down to her car and got in. She drove away feeling better that she saw him after all. Rosemary came outside just then to meet Danny in the street. Just down the way, Mrs. Henry, the nosy grocery owner threw out boxes into her trash bin. She noticed Rosemary kiss the man upon his cheek, right as she led him back into her house.

Chapter Thirty

Out of time

Early the next morning, Danny arrived to the manor. In his pocket were orders with the specific information for the next assignment, delivered that morning by a courier. He thought about things this way: Tara didn't want him around and that hurt. Sure, he wanted to spend time with the new infants. They were cute and preemies. He wanted time to bond further, even if in his heart, he felt deeply attached. His name appeared on their birth certificate, so in every right they were a part of the Cross family. He must provide for them even if Tara didn't show regards for his love. Yes, he felt it best to return to the ocean, where on board his ship, among his crew members and colleagues, there stood respect.

Danny stopped at the doorway, took a deep breath, and then went inside the brick Georgian manor to bid farewells. He saw his father at his customary place at the head of the table, while his mother sat at the opposite end. His snobbish sister, Susan, sat in the middle and took a bored yawn while pouring milk into a bowl of cereal. They looked up when he entered the dining room and the women rushed over to greet him.

"Where have you been? Gloria didn't breathe a word of your whereabouts after she saw you," Susan fussed while Helen gave him a motherly once-over. He was glad that he took time to shave that morning. He wore his best blue jeans, a blue polo shirt, and dark boots. It made him feel comfortable traveling in them.

"That doesn't really matter," he said and clenched his jaw squarely to drop his news, "I just stopped by to say I'm shipping off again-today."

He watched them react.

"I can't believe this," Helen sat down again. She took out a handkerchief. Danny already suspected she would behave this way. His mother always cried at the mention of anything disagreeable or painful, "You just returned to us from the brink."

"I was not dead mother. I needed some time alone," Danny struggled to admit this out loud, "It's just that I'm having problems. Tara and I – we don't get along."

"I knew it," Susan walked over to the silver serving tray on the credenza to refill her cup with coffee. With a nose turned up in the air, she remarked, "That girl is just a thorn in your side. You'd do better off without her. Why do you choose to stay married? We don't live in the 18th century anymore, brother. You can divorce."

"Our family does not believe in divorce," His mother glared at Susan to stay quiet, "Besides, Tara just delivered seven infants. That is a remarkable thing to adjust to and she must focus on those little babies. A man isn't a woman's first priority under these circumstances. That girl has suffered nothing but transition since she's arrived."

Suffered? Tara? Oh, no! Danny shook his head. He provided everything for her comfort. To each their own perspective. He bit his tongue though. Feelings were too close to the surface of how he dealt with such suffering lately. He still couldn't get over the fact that Tara turned to Michael for emotional support at the hospital. He could try to overlook this minor infraction on her part, just to appease his guilt for doing worse.

Just then, his grandmother entered the room and sat down near him, wearing a red dress and a white bonnet with a red scarf wrapped around it. She overheard the hubbub. It distressed her. Danny stood near and she patted his hand.

"How long?" Grams looked at his face.

"Several months, I'm afraid. The assignment takes us down to Australia and Argentina. After that, our fleet will go to the Falklands. I'll miss you, Grams. I'll miss everyone."

"Hmff," George remarked and then came around the table to offer his son a handshake. Out of a grey jacket, he took out his favorite pipe, lit it and the air filled with the aroma of cherry tobacco. Helen waved her hand at the smoke and so he stalked off to the solarium to smoke in peace. He never said much when he felt sad. It pleased Danny that this time his father kept his opinions quiet.

Later on, after eating breakfast with all, he mustered up the courage to go home.

Trekking down the familiar trail, he recalled the first time he and Tara went hand in hand in this direction towards the Briggs House. Such high hopes then, for their marriage. What happened to those dreams? Why did her love slip away time and time again? He thought that just being married would solve all of his difficulties, but Tara never made things easy, even while being pregnant. Now, she was a mother, of seven tiny tykes. They were so cute and he had promised to be their father. Just recalling how helpless they were in the nursery made him react, so he took faster steps. He wanted to see the children. *God, I miss them,* he realized now.

At the Briggs House, the front wooden door opened wide and he stepped into the house. From the kitchen, Marta heard his familiar steps across the floor. Instantly she ran out to greet him.

"Mr. Cross! You are home!" the servant wiped her hands upon the apron, which bore sprinkles of flour upon it, "Thank the good Lord. You look well!"

"Yes, Marta. I'm perfectly fine. Thank you."

"Can I get you anything? How about tea? I just put the kettle on," she pointed towards the kitchen.

"No, thanks. Right now, I only want to go upstairs to see the babies. It's been over two weeks. Besides, I'm being deployed out today. I won't be staying long," He turned to shut the door securely. Marta watched him ascend the wooden staircase and patted her heart.

By this time, Tara overcame her initial shock to hear his voice downstairs. When he had entered inside, she ran to the bedroom mirror to stare at red eyes and fly-away hair that was greatly out of place, "I look horrible," she panicked and ran to the bathroom. With a wet washcloth, she scrubbed her face vigorously and then applied powder and blush. She dabbed on a bit of light lipstick and powdered her eyes.

She returned to the bedroom and paused to look at her attire. Her top smelled like formula spit up. "Gross!" she thought and within five seconds, she threw it off to gather a fresh shirt from the closet. There was a decanter of light perfume on the dresser and she sprayed it upon her body in various places. Then she grabbed a brush and ran it through her thick stubborn hair to lengthen out the curls. Her hands were trembling. What could she expect? Would he let her stay? Would he kick her out? She might as well look good to face the firing squad.

His footsteps progressed into each of the children's room. He spoke to Caroline first about their progress and then she could hear him speak softly to the babies. It was easy to imagine how Danny held each one tenderly before returning them to their cribs. In Jamie's room, he said in a playful high voice, "My little sweetheart, you are so pretty. I love you," There were sounds of voiced kisses, probably upon her soft tummy, which only stirred up Tara's beating heart, "I must calm down," she thought and went to sit on the bed to wait. Still, her foot patted upon the floor like a drum.

Finally, Danny stepped into the bedroom, but he merely nodded and said nothing. He went directly to the closet to grab a suitcase. While he packed, Tara unraveled waiting for a more emotional reaction.

The clock on the wall ticked loudly. The birds out the window cackled and tweeted. The smell of Marta's baked cinnamon bread drifted throughout the house. She could hear Lila sweeping a floor below with a straw broom.

Danny eyes stayed focused to the task, so she took notice of his features. He acquired a recent haircut and his chin seemed shaved and smooth. There was a nice scent of expensive cologne that she could determine. He looked extremely handsome in blue as it highlighted his blue eyes. For once, it felt right to be in that room together, but the silence and the packing made her apprehensive. This killed her patience. She must break the ice.

"Are you going somewhere?" she asked in a timid voice, "Is it because of me?"

"No, not because of you," he lied, but then decided to reveal the rest in truth, "I have a new assignment, so I have to pack. This won't take long. I'll be on my way and then you can carry on as before."

He did not speak in his usual droll candor, so Tara went over to him. Brave under the circumstances, she realized that she must make the first move towards rapprochement.

"Danny, I'm so sorry... about that day, with Michael. I... I didn't mean to upset you."

"Forget it, "he remarked and secured the suitcase. Then he went to the closet to take out a brown garment bag that contained several cleaned and pressed uniforms, along with shiny black shoes. Carefully, he placed it beside the suitcase and gave her an in-depth explanation.

251

"There is a flight out of London to the Mediterranean this afternoon. The ship is off the coastline. From there, we will cruise to the islands off the Argentine in the South Atlantic, head to Australian waters to participate in exercises with their Royal Navy fleet, and then for several months, I will be near the Falklands."

Tara didn't know what to say, but placed a hand over her mouth. This isn't what she expected. He dug out a wallet from his backside and placed a wad of bills upon the bedspread.

"There are documents at the bank for you to sign. It's to give you access to my account. An automatic allotment goes to it every month. Use it for the household, unless you want my father to handle things."

Tara was totally surprised by this request. She never handled expenses or bills before. However, she didn't think she wanted her father-in-law always poking about the house. She liked George, but sometimes he behaved like an overbearing bear, especially to her mother-in-law. Helen was a patient soul, but Tara couldn't depend on herself to do the same. He made her uncomfortable and the maids too.

"I can handle it," Tara said softly, "I think."

"Sure you can," he encouraged, staring into her eyes. Then he snapped his fingers with an afterthought," Oh, yes-I usually get a separate check from the finance office for handling ALLIED/NATO foreign affairs, things not usually a part of ship duties. I'll send that by mail," Danny informed her and returned the wallet to his back pocket, "Somehow, you must deposit those in the bank. Just ask the manager if there are any questions about the transactions."

"Ok," Tara replied and stared at the money. She never saw so much all at once, yet it was all English currency, "How much is this?"

"In American money, it's about five thousand, give or take with the daily exchange rate," He replied, but he gave a slight smile because of her naivety. With that, he picked up the garment bag and suitcase and went to the door.

Five thousand dollars! Tara was flabbergasted by the sum and stared at it. All the while, she assumed that George and Helen provided for everything. Just how dependent was she and the children on Danny?

They should have spoken about personal affairs way sooner than this, just like other ordinary couples did. Now Tara realized that everyone worked in the family. George took care of Helen and Grams. Danny took care of them. This put Tara into a quandary. She didn't like being this dependent, especially when there were seven children to look after. One day, she must find an occupation, one where provisions were made without sole dependency on any man. Even with no particular skill to offer now, Tara wanted an equal role or a superior status, but until that came about, it wasn't wise to let the man of the house leave altogether without knowing the status of their marriage.

"Danny! Wait!" Tara ran out of the room with the money in her hands. He stopped in the hallway to listen, "What….what exactly should I do with this?"

Tara's eyes reflected that for once she needed his clear instruction.

"Pay the staff. They get paid regularly from my parents, but taking care of our children is extra. Ask mother what amount they agreed upon. There should be plenty left afterwards to do what you wish," He said and took a few steps down the stairs. How can she let him go without a kiss or something? Tara panicked. She must act.

"Danny! Please wait!" she cried out again and clutched the money to her stomach.

Now he paid better attention. Her hypnotizing eyes engaged. Lovely pink lips parted. Perhaps Gloria's words rang true. Perhaps Tara did cry for him. He placed everything down on the step and went to her. They met at the top of the landing. With courage, he took her free hand and they stared. Regret on his mind. Hope on hers. Danny seemed to struggle for words, but she felt grateful that he acknowledged her at all.

He looked around and then cleared his throat.

"Look, things haven't been easy for us. I know that I mess up a lot. Still, I wanted to make sure that you'd be fine while I'm away. The utility expenses are paid from my account and if anything needs repair, my father or Haskell can hire someone," he stared into her eyes, "You should use most of this for yourself. Go out and buy new dresses, pamper yourself really well. Perhaps take a trip to London, by yourself. You've been cooped up for so long, a break is deserved. It will do a world of good."

She couldn't agree more. It was difficult to be confined during her pregnancy. How amazing that he offered such kind gestures. Especially after the way she treated him. Did he just say she deserved it? The man must be out of his mind, but she adored his consideration.

"Are you sure? You hate it when I draw attention, although I wouldn't mind compliments," she teased and he suddenly laughed at this.

How could he demand constraints about little things when he couldn't do it himself about major ones? However, by cheating, he walked away with a better perspective.

On the very last night over at Rosemary's house, they talked until dawn, naked on the bed. The women smoked long cigarettes and drank lots of cheap red wine. They offered a free style Ménage à trois, an exhilarating taste of sex without any rules or expectations. Danny never experienced anything like it before. The girls wanted to hash out his problems, like marriage counselors.

"It must be incredibly difficult for any woman to carry a load like that," Eileen mused as she read again the faded newspaper article about the septuplets birth. She drank wine from a chipped glass, "I would worry about everything, especially if I would miscarry."

"With a body that large, no man would find me desirable," Rosemary agreed and puffed at a cigarette. She offered it to Danny, but he didn't want it, "Still you tried, didn't you?"

"Her size wasn't the consideration," Danny watched the tip of a vanilla incense stick turn to ash and fall on the bureau. The lights of the bedroom were low and so the burning end of it gave off a fiery glow, "I only wished to be near her, to offer comfort. Frankly, she couldn't have sex as it wouldn't be safe. The doctor objected and now that the children are here, she must wait six weeks for any intimacy. "

"Uh, poor thing, with such a handsome husband and no way to enjoy each other, I'd die if I couldn't do it. And besides that, she's stuck in maternity clothes. These are all reasons to feel crass and blue."

"Still, she flirted with my brother, the cad. He knew better. She fell blind into his lair. In spite of that, I find that I still want her. Maybe I'm just insane."

"If you return, Danny, then do something nice," Rosemary suggested. She liked him, but realized that they lived different lifestyles. She just couldn't break it when he was down in the dumps.

"Like what?"

"Send her on a shopping spree. Any woman likes that! If it's safe to do so. Are the reporters still after you?"

"Yes, but I'll force them to speak to my father from now on."

"God! I've seen him at the bank! He's frightening as a bull when he gets mad. How did you survive growing up?" Eileen gasped and clutched a pillow.

"It wasn't easy," Danny laughed and leaned forward to look her in the eye, "The reporters will surely grow weary dealing with him. After all, we need respect for our privacy. I don't want Tara to worry about their intrusions while I'm away."

"It's a long tour. Most likely, you will miss the babies, Danny, and your wife too," Eileen patted his hand, "You'll miss watching them grow and working things out. That's a shame."

Danny didn't reply but watched Rosemary take a long drag and exhale rings into the air.

"She's just not mature, that's all. That's why he's in a mess. That woman needs help growing up," Rosemary said and then added, "Why not give her independence while you are gone. Let her be the real little lady of the house and be responsible for things. It will help build up her self-confidence and self-esteem."

Danny thought this was a great idea and so went to the bank and drew out that large sum of money. Yet, somehow, upon his return, Tara already revealed choices. She looked so pretty in the smock gingham blue shirt and the white stretch pants. The fragrance she wore seemed sweet and not overbearing. Even her makeup wasn't over done. The light eye shadow made her eyes so defining! And now, on the stair landing, he never expected her to stand there and squeeze his hand so hard. That suggestive look made him want to stay, but it was too late to change things. He was out of time.

"Well, I must be going on my way. Susan is driving me to Heathrow and will keep the car for awhile. Goodbye, dearest Tara. Take care," Danny said in a lame voice and tried to turn away. Instead, her warm hands kept him at bay and he had to turn to face her again. Her pupils riveted back and forth and he wondered what she wanted. Then she clutched his waist. With an urgent thrust to move his body forward, she plastered a hard but ardent kiss upon his surprised mouth.

Their bodies melded together. Electricity flew throughout every nerve in his body. What pure ecstasy to feel a kiss like that from her. His eyes widened, but then he closed them to drift freely along within immense pleasure. When their lips finally pulled apart, he looked at her face, happy that she seemed it wasn't the worst thing to occur between them. Long lashes blinked slowly and her hands caressed his back up and down.

"Will you write, Danny? Please?" her voice, soft and sexy, charmed his mind. He couldn't move at all as it felt so good to be close, to feel the soft curves in her hips and watch the rise and fall of her bosom. Tara dumped fuel onto desire by speaking low and whispery, "The letters you sent from Dartmouth were beautiful. I never realized how much you wrote with your heart. It was nice. If you write again, this time I will too. Let's fall madly in love through them."

"Yes, of course," Danny replied giddily, feeling out of whack as she released him then. He stumbled down to the next step, "I'll write every day, every chance I get. I promise."

Was he in a surreal dream? Did he just find heaven? He fumbled for the suitcase and swung the garment bag around his shoulder. Somehow he ambled down to the foot of the staircase and only looked back once before exiting the front door. She stood there, her eyes sultry, biting a lower lip. It was a look that sent him to the moon. She blew a random kiss with her hand and mouthed, "Stay safe."

Within minutes, he was in his car, driving down that dirt road with the radio loud as he listened to a corny love song on a radio network. It seemed nowhere near contemporary. "I can write a better melody", he mused out loud, realizing it had been ages since thinking about music, a long time passion. Tara filled his heart with song.

What just happened? The woman actually kissed me! Oh, God, thank you!

Dust blew in the air and the scent of the tall grass along the road filled his nostrils. He felt so light, like an albatross was lifted from his soul. All thoughts bounced in every direction. Surely upon his return, things would be different. He just needed to write and call on occasion. That kiss inspired the low ember in his heart to re-ignite like an Olympic torch and he couldn't fathom what changed, but perhaps they were equal now, for the wrong done. Except that Tara didn't know about his sexual escapade with Rosemary and Eileen. There should never be a reason to discover it.

At the Briggs House, Tara watched the car drive away from the nearest window. She looked at the heavens and cried out fervently, "Yes!" This time they were in it for better or worse. There was lots of time to find a resolution about Danny's drinking. She looked at the money. He was a responsible man, who ensured everyone's well being. She was blessed. The babies, far too young to realize it now, should be taught his importance while they grew. As a good military wife, she knew to accept that duty came first. Tara didn't like that he was going away again, but decided she could deal with sacrifice, just like Grams.

Tara looked at the money and found a safe place in a drawer. She made grand plans, "I can save it and when I go to London, I can visit Ross. That scoundrel hasn't called often enough."

There was much to tell, much to be shared. Tara turned and studied herself in the long mirror. She lifted up her shirt, jiggled the loose skin and flab, and then grumbled. "No more bangors and mash with gravy! I'm going to whip myself into shape!"

Surely by diet and long afternoon walks to the manor and back, she could slim down quickly. By the time Danny came home again, she could surprise him with a nice curvy shape. They could work out their awkwardness of making love. Feeling frisky about this, she giggled uncontrollably. She ran to the calander on the wall and reasoned out the months he would be away. If he came home by Christmas, she could tie a bow around her waist and present herself as a present to unwrap. How funny to imagine a wide-eye expression upon that angel face. At long last, a sincere smile crept across her face just dreaming about it. Feeling better now than she had for several weeks, Tara kissed her ring and thanked her lucky stars.

"Whooeeee!" she screamed out loud suddenly, "Marta! I must speak with you!"

She ran quickly downstairs to disappoint Marta about her new diet.

Chapter Thirty One
Babies and money

The days were quite warm that late August in Wiltshire. Everything was hearty and green, and in this transition, Tara watched her infants grow healthier too. At four months old, the babies, even while they ranged between 5lbs to 6lbs, progressed well. The local doctor checked on them often and from the beginning suggested that they stay close to home. No one could come around with bad colds or the hint of a respiratory infection. On this particular check up, he looked at Tara with a wide smile, "You're doing a good job, mom. You can relax and treat them normal, just like other babies."

This was terrific news. She had the staff and family to thank for helping as they did. Just their devotion made her feel appreciative. The babies required a lot of round-the-clock work. It surprised Tara that on some occasions, even Susan came by to lend a hand. Even though she was working for a new modeling agency, Susan found it disappointing that the photo shoots were far in between, so when she was bored and came home to visit, she stopped by to bother Tara. Of all of the in-laws, Tara bit her tongue the most around Susan because she was negative about everything: the way that Tara juggled the children, the household affairs, the servants, or even how often she corresponded with Danny. They shared different ideas all the way around.

"She just wants to write to Danny and tell him how I can't handle things. We are doing fine, aren't we? "Tara fumed to Marta one day after Susan left and the older woman nodded.

"Yes, indeed. You keep everything running smoothly. With seven babies, that's saying a lot dear. Mr. Cross would be very pleased," Marta replied kindly. Tara wiped her hands on a towel and threw it onto the kitchen table.

"Thanks Marta. I hoped so because I do try hard. It's just that Susan has such a wicked tongue. It makes me feel bad about how rude I spoke to my husband in the past. Was I really that mean? God, I'm so lucky that he's given me a second chance. With her, I just want to stick a pound of butter into that big mouth- just to shut her up!"

The servant watched Tara stomp upstairs with three baby bottles in her hands. Marta shook her head and went back to chopping vegetables.

"My, oh my! Such headstrong women!" she declared, glad that she stayed out of range when they feuded.

Tara thanked the stars above that she didn't encounter problems with the rest of Danny's family. Rarely did Michael or George come over, as they stayed away unless something forced them over to the Briggs House. Gloria and Helen came by often. They couldn't stay away from the infants. Tara truly treasured their visits. The women guided and encouraged Tara all of the time. She could feel their devotion and love. Yet sadly, other than the family and the servants, there was no one available to confide with closely, since she remained stuck at home. This loneliness only made her want to see Ross more than ever. It was time to make that break to London and visit her best friend from childhood. She wanted to hear all about his new financial career and his lifestyle. She asked the family to make those arrangements.

During this time, Sammy finally came home. He had been stuck on his ship throughout the alerts and then wound up on a duty tour to the Ireland coastline. All he wanted to do was catch up with his family. On his first day home, he played cards with Grams, chatted with his parents, called up Michael, and picked on his sisters, and then rested up for a day. When the warm sun rose the next morning, he walked over to see Danny's children.

"Oh, my, they are lively and squirmy," Sammy gazed at Tyler and then into Vince's crib as if staring at aliens. Vincent moved his head to listen to the voices in the room and Sammy toyed with the mobile above the crib. Tara found his presence a bit unnerving. The man looked too much like her husband, as Sammy decided on a lark to cut off his mustache. What a difference it made to his face! Luckily, he wasn't satisfied with the look and planned to grow it back. Sammy placed his hands onto his hips and crooked his eyebrow up, "Are you sure it's all right to hold one?"

"Yes, but please wash your hands first," she instructed out of habit and he did so promptly. She picked up Vince from his crib and placed him into Sammy's muscular arms. She saw how his eyes grew wide. He walked backwards to scoot down into the rocker. After a minute or two, she giggled to hear him coo at the baby in a high voice. Vince stared up at Sammy.

"Oh, look! I think he knows who I am!" Sammy exclaimed and with confidence, held the baby upright, letting his legs dangle just above his thighs, "Hi there, little man! I'm your Uncle Sammy. Just remember-I will always be your favorite uncle. When you grow up, speak to me first if any cute little girl catches your interest. I'll give you lots of tips!"

"Uh, I don't think so," Tara gasped. She shook a finger at him, "My son will grow up to be a responsible and respectful gentleman, like his father."

Sammy laughed but then his eyebrow raised up a bit. A curious expression came over his face.

"I say, what was all the commotion about when Danny went missing? No one has breathed a word. It's like its top secret. I'm dying to know," He looked at her closely. Tara wanted to be as honest as possible. She liked Sammy as he was always kind. He deserved an answer.

"There were problems. Stress got to us. I don't blame Danny running off to think alone. Before he left, we made up. Really everything is fine again. I do miss him," Tara revealed. Sammy nodded and then held his nephew close. He bestowed a soft kiss on his forehead. It was a tender moment between them that Tara found endearing.

"Well that's a good thing for you, dear sweet boy," he said softly to Vince, "Mummy and Daddy should get along. You need both parents to raise you. That's very important for little wee ones."

There was a message there that Tara understood. She placed a warm hand upon his shoulder.

"Don't worry, Sammy. I'm crazy about Danny now and our marriage will remain intact. Honestly, we write almost everyday since he's been away. My hat box is almost filled to the brim."

"What's that? What hat box?" He crinkled his nose and tried to comprehend.

"It's a box that Gloria gave me out of her closet. Red is the color and it's perfect. I stash all of my red hot love letters from your brother there, but I won't share what he writes," Tara revealed in a nonchalant manner. He chuckled, enjoying her dry wit. It was great that things worked out for his favorite brother. Sammy suddenly patted the baby's diaper.

"Oh, oh, I think there's an accident."

"Then change it," Tara retorted but he stood up holding the baby out towards her.

"Please take him. I don't know how!" He cried out.

Ugh, he's inept too, she thought and really did think that the Cross women were far efficient. About then, Tara heard the front door open and footsteps come up the stairs.

"We are ready to go to London now, if you want to see my new studio," Gloria announced loudly as she sprang onto the top landing. She had established the studio with Michael's help. She came into the room and noticed how he was holding the baby, "Here, let me have him!"

"Thank you! I thought I was a done man. Tara insisted I learn to change his diaper!"

"You should, brother," Michael teased, but he smiled hesitantly at Tara. It was difficult to pretend nothing ever happened. At least they spoke politely. He came over to give news, "Oh, by the way, all the arrangements are set for your trip."

"Ross is attending a leadership seminar this weekend, but is free on the next," Gloria explained too while she cleaned up the infant for Sammy. He stood close, observing everything. After a moment, Gloria cuddled the fresh-bottomed baby in her arms, "Michael has spoken to Ross about the details."

"You'll travel by train next Saturday morning. I would take you, but I'm due to see a production in Wales and will be gone for a week. Gloria is booked that day with customers. So, Haskell will drive you to the station and Ross will meet you in London," Michael conveyed as he stared at her intently by the doorway, "He wants to show you everything. You'll have a great time."

"That's wonderful Michael. I can't wait," Tara replied stiffly, maybe a bit put on as Sammy studied her over and then looked at Michael suspiciously.

Gloria noticed the expression on Sammy's face. She deliberately picked up a container with the stinky soiled cloth diapers and handed it to Michael, practically shoving it in his face.

"Here take this downstairs to the laundry area," she commanded.

"Whew! Why don't we buy those plastic disposable ones? Wouldn't that make life easier?" Michael complained and held it away at arm's length.

"Cloth diapers are inexpensive and save the environment. Why whine! Either way, cloth or plastic, you will still take out the dirty ones, to the laundry or to the trash," Gloria scolded very severely, "Now, scoot!"

Michael reluctantly walked out with the can and Sammy followed behind him, snickering.

"She's so mean to me lately. I thought by helping her with the shop, she'd stop." Michael told him and Sammy shrugged his shoulders. With the men out of the way, the girls could talk.

"You are a terrific aunt." Tara complimented then.

"Thanks. I love doing this. If Danny was here he would definitely be the first in this room, unlike my other brothers who shirk the messy duties."

"Do you really believe so?"

"Of course I do," Gloria said with positive enthusiasm. "He's been writing to me too. Those letters say how much he wants to be home. He misses you and the children,"

Gloria leaned into the crib to place Vincent down. She tucked him in securely and then checked on Tyler.

This conversation reminded Tara about the military checks. During the month of June and July, they steadily came in the mail. In his letters, she learned that after the combined exercises in Australia, he had been assigned to work at the British consulate in Argentina. They suddenly stopped when he finally sailed off to the Falklands. Since there was never any time to get to the bank in town, Tara simply placed them in a drawer for safekeeping. Sometime in August, she accidentally found out that George had taken liberty to pay her household staff for all their services.

"I am very happy to hear that Marta, Caroline, and Lila are doing a great job helping you out," he had told her when she stopped to say hello one afternoon. She had been out for her walk and saw him pruning at bright flowers along the fence line. He wanted to bring Helen a pretty bouquet to place in vase. He stopped to admire the bright sunshine and then took out his pipe. They conversed a moment or two about trivial things and then he had brought this matter up, "I decided to raise their salaries. That way you needn't worry about paying them while Danny is away."

"But George, Danny told me..." she began but he growled.

"Now, now! Don't worry! It's all handled. Just take good care of yourself. I want my son to have someone at home waiting for his return," George remarked stiffly and then went inside the house without another word. Tara returned to the trail to descend back to the Briggs House. She somehow had suspected that George knew their problems. Perhaps one less burden would ease worry on how she perceived Danny overall.

"Well, don't worry, George!," she had muttered as she picked up her pace, "We are just fine."

So, along with the checks, she still had that $5000. This was too much money to just leave lying about in a drawer. She needed to do something sensibly. Besides, the checks had expiration dates upon them. She led Gloria to the bedroom to show her everything.

"Wow! That's quite a sum," Gloria surmised while she also studied the crisp paper co-signed by Britain's Minister of Defense, "Danny must have done a lot of government finessing with the bigwigs in Argentina. Britain's always fought with that country."

"Why?" Tara asked and sat down on the bed to listen.

"Danny explained it to me once. There's just a lot of bickering over who has rights over the Falkland Islands. Argentina claims its part of their regime, although we do too. You never know where that can lead if conflicts aren't squelched before it escalates over sovereign territories. That's part of Danny's job being a member of the Special Teams. Every one of those checks includes hazard pay. You should deposit them into the savings account."

"You mean his military account, don't you?" Tara asked thinking that surely Gloria was confused.

"Didn't he tell you? Danny has two, one military which receives an automatic allotment of pay from the Navy. The other is just his savings at the bank in the village. I recalled he transferred into savings quite often. To have access, you need a signature card on file."

"He said I must go there to sign one. I have never been to town," Tara explained and looked at Gloria closely. "We never even discussed signature cards or money before he left. I guess I was much too consume with my own needs. This came as a bit of a surprise when he told me about it."

For the first time, Tara seemed vulnerable. Gloria thought it was a good time to talk.

"Look Tara, Danny told me about your problems, that you shut him out a lot," Tara felt embarrassed that Gloria knew, but the woman sat down beside her and patted her hand, "I suppose the pregnancy was a big factor, but now, everything is doing better. He could have sent these directly to the bank, but he didn't. He wants you to handle it, as his partner. Money and personal finance is an important issue in marriage. You have free reigns to do anything you wish, but win his confidence. Do the smart thing. Deposit all of this and grow your nest egg together, for your children."

"Yes, our biggest problems were due to misunderstandings. I don't want to screw this up. It sure would be easier if he was just home to do this. I miss him."

"Well, Danny thinks they may return after the first of the year. Everything's up in the air with our military. Besides, it's the life of a navy man to have long missions."

"What if there is an emergency?" Tara worried. "God forbid if something ever happens to one of the children, but what if I need him here?"

"Sammy knows contacts. We can get Danny home if any comes up. Now, as for these, let's get to the bank. Sammy and Michael can wait an hour on me. Lila and Marta can handle things for awhile. I'll drive you there."

And so they went into the village that afternoon. Tara marveled to see it for the first time. There were several stone cottage buildings with thatched roofs. Nestled everywhere were many brick and wood buildings: a flower shop, a church with a tall bell steeple, a grocery store, a modern post office, and an old livery stable. Even a fancy inn with a neon light by the street displayed their rates and the time. The village seemed a mish-posh of antiquity and 20th century life. She noticed that there were several families getting an early start to their weekend shopping, as it was Friday.

"There are so many people here," Tara said as they drove against the curb to park. The narrow cobble streets were lined up with several cars and farmer trucks. They were lucky to find an empty place.

"They come from the outlying districts. We have some open markets down by the schoolhouse, but mostly people shop at Mr. Aberdeen's store," Gloria said and then crinkled her nose, "Actually, it's that nasty Mrs. Henry's store now. She's his widow. Everyone loved Mr. Aberdeen as he was so friendly, but she's a gossiping witch. You have to be careful around her."

"Why is her last name different? Did she remarry?"

"She was lucky to marry one of the city councilman's brothers, who keep her abreast of the local activities. Do you know that Judith managed to stall a giant conglomerate from building a modern grocery store in the vicinity? It was amazing, but she'd do anything to keep up her country store. Well, I must run over there to pick up a few things myself. I see her standing outside, so I'll go in quickly before she shoots darts into my back. Meet me there afterwards."

She walked up the sidewalk and ran across the busy street, passing Mrs. Henry to get inside. There were two ladies beside her near the doorway and they observed how Mrs. Henry turned up her nose. They leaned over and whispered more. Mrs. Henry stared at Tara from afar. Tara was too preoccupied to care and she went into the bank. Mrs. Henry shook her head and walked into her store.

Tara was greeted by a kind brunette man, dressed in a brown tweed suit and a long tan tie. He took her checks and cash to enter the transaction into a computer. She signed the signature cards while he went over to another office. Upon his return, he sat down to explain everything about the plastic card he handed over.

"It allows you to draw out funds from any automatic teller machine," Mr. Warner said in a serious but patient tone, "It is very expeditious."

She studied the embedded numbers along with her printed name on the front and the magnetism strip on the back. There was also a bright colored emblem upon the card.

"What does this mean?"

"Oh, yes," Mr. Warner patted his pencil on the desk, "That allows the capability to buy on credit. You can buy practically anything at any store where that same emblem is displayed."

"It doesn't come out of my account immediately?"

"No." the man replied and tried to explain everything in simple terms on how it worked. It was mind-boggling, but Tara followed his logic and timidly stuck the card into her wallet. The man let out a huge smile.

"There's no need to fret as you have more than enough to pay a full balance. All you have to do is call our offices and let us know how to handle it for you. Your account is in very high standing."

The man then printed off a deposit slip showing the amounts just added to the savings account. He pointed to both the military account and Danny's savings. Tara almost fell out of her chair.

"Wow! I can do a lot of major, major, major shopping when I get to London!" Tara cried out when it summed up her husband's net worth in both. The bank clerk chuckled.

"Yes, madam. Quite major. Your husband has been our customer for a very long time. Although, I do believe he inherited money from a trust-his grandfather's estate-when he turned twenty one."

Tara nodded and left the bank in a daze. Danny never breathed a word. The man was well off, although he made it seem his income only came from the Navy. Flamboyant in personality. Modest in style. Tara liked it that he saved what he earned. She wondered if she could handle money just as well. Until Danny came along, she always scrimped and saved for a rainy day. With the credit card, was there really a need to remain so cautious?

"Oh, imagine the fun I can have next weekend," she thought happily. There were plenty of fantastic department stores in London. Susan and Gloria shopped there all the time. With new clothes and perhaps a new hairdo, she wanted to shine like a bright new shilling. She wanted to look great in her new figure, as she lost around twenty five pounds. That by itself deserved rewarding. The diligence with exercise and eating right showed.

"I must send Danny a fancy card with a glowing love letter tucked inside. Perhaps I can scent it with perfume," Tara giggled and went to the store to find a card.

Chapter Thirty Two
What's in a little gossip?

When Tara caught up to Gloria, she was busy making a transaction, so Tara decided to look around for the romantic stationary. Suddenly, in a far corner, the two women she saw outside looked in her direction. They made it pretty obvious to point in her direction and then they scampered off to the opposite aisle. Tara felt weird about it but continued shopping on her side. Still, their voices floated over the stocked shelves.

"I tell you. That's Danny Cross's wife. Poor dear. That's who Judith was talking about outside."

"Well, she never comes to town. What happened again? Judith whispered so quietly that it was difficult to hear. She stopped when that tall blond woman came over."

"Oh, Carol! Didn't you pay attention? Turn up that hearing aid!"

"I can't," Carol whined, "this thing is shot, Tina, and I must replace it."

"Oh, very well! She said that she spotted her husband with Rosemary. They were out behind the pub. Rosemary kissed him and then held his hand to lead him to her house," Tina snickered. "And it wasn't two days later when she showed up at the store with her roommate, Eileen, and they were discussing everything that went on with him. Judith heard everything, very innocently, of course. They were reminiscing about how much fun they shared before he went off to sea again. He's in the navy, you know."

"Well, I'll be. With those flirty bar maids, what man stands a chance? Besides, all navy men have women in every port. It's just their reputation for being off to sea for so long. They must have their fun with the ladies. Why would he be an exception?"

"Well, I heard his wife was laid up when she was pregnant. If they couldn't do anything, it's understandable why Rosemary brought him home. My brother says she makes it very easy for any man. Her husband doesn't seem the type, but you have to watch out for the quiet ones. I bet there was a rowdy time in bed. And his poor wife doesn't have a clue!"

The women giggled viciously. Tara was so stunned that she couldn't even breathe. Did someone stab her heart with an ice pick? She leaned against the display of greeting cards and pretty stationary. Just then, Gloria called out.

"Tara, I'm ready to leave."

Tara stuck the stationary back into place. Forget the romance! Forget everything! How dare he do this!

Her eyes narrowed and she gritted her teeth. She was determined not to react. What she overheard put her mind into a tailspin, but she walked out of the store proudly. She passed by those gossiping ladies and even Mrs. Henry without giving them a single clue about her feelings. On the way home, she said nothing, but Gloria was too busy talking about her new shop.

For the next few days, Tara kept occupied with her children and the chores as usual. She passed the time thinking everything through. It hit her hard to realize he spent time away with both women. When she received his letter that Tuesday, she threw it into the hatbox unopened. It was disappointing because lately his letters burned with his steamy thoughts. All his words left her yearning deep for his touch. Well, he could forget about that now.

He called on Thursday, but she refused to take it. Per her instructions, Caroline was forced to make up a very lame excuse. She hung up the phone suddenly. Surely it infuriated Danny on the other end, but Tara was pleased that Caroline did it. He deserved it. That conniving, deceitful man! Every night, she tossed and turned in their bed. She closed her eyes and tried not to think about their torrid love sessions. All it did was remind her of their wedding night.

His hands were rough when he fondled her breasts in heated caresses. He didn't mean it that way; it was just that touching a woman was new. Tara tried to relax but she was not pleased that he groped in the dark. Danny fumbled to climb over her, to reach that pivotal point to become one. The hard thrusts lasted only minutes and then languished in that unwilling passage of her body.

Frankly, Tara felt relieved that it was over, but stared angry at the ceiling. The act was meaningless and she felt unfulfilled. She stifled tears while he sounded happy.

"Oh, Tara! What an experience! I've waited much too long!" Danny fluffed up his pillow and tried to snuggle close to her body. *So he's no longer a virgin. Big deal!* She cursed and turned away in the opposite direction so that he faced her back. How opposite she felt and ignored his caresses. There was nothing about him that she liked then. She was horrified when he wanted to do it again sometime later that night. Thank goodness that the cruise over made her much too sea sick to do it anymore.

"The rest is history," she thought now, about all the troubles they shared while in England. Tara punched her pillow to reposition her body on the bed. She felt angry and disillusioned.

Her thoughts didn't let her sleep in peace. Yes, she was reluctant for the sex then, but she desired him now. All her senses heightened in anticipation of his recent letters. They turned into word foreplay and everything written she could not resist.

"There are so many melodies that play inside my head when I think about you," He wrote, "Whenever I'm alone, I gather my guitar and imagine the strings as your body. I play them lightly, transcend my fingers down one by one, softly, and stroke each gentle chord to fill the air into an enchanting crescendo. The music stirs my heart, my soul, my imagination. Then I can see you, so close. You are my velvet dream that must never float away."

If the letters weren't enough, his sexy voice on the calls home placed her into giddy, super hot volcano of lust. They talked about their desire just enough for each to smolder with excitement. When she hung up the phone, she was breathless and imagined he was the same.

Now, after all of this, how can it be fair to share what she alone knew most intimately about her man, the things she learned from their very few encounters? She never forgot the way he breathed upon her face when he lay close, the way that his muscular body felt naked by her side, with the course strip of dark blond hair running just below his belly button to there. How can she forget the look in his eyes when he expressed ecstasy during his climax? These were private and carnal knowledge between lovers. They were sacred between husband and wife. How dare Rosemary and Eileen-whoever they are- know the same exact damn thing!

The wound festered to decay her reasoning like gangrene. She knew herself to be selfish, but now she realized that she was terribly possessive too. That inborn compulsive and combustible instinct set her ablaze into a jealous rage. She wanted to slap him and strangle those women, but she was not one disposed to violence. No, instead, she would somehow seek out revenge and never once, in all her thinking, did she consider any consequences.

Chapter Thirty Three
Tara strikes back

When it was time to go to London, Tara ensured that everything was right before she left her children. How she would miss them, even if her absence was for one night. Marta and Lila waved goodbye and stood at the door until the car went around the bend. Haskell drove her to the station. She checked herself in. Then found her seat on board. The train lurched forward to be on its way. She watched the lovely scenery zip by of exposed chalk on the hillsides; plush green valleys with grazing sheep; and the occasional horse riders lingering upon wooded trails. She closed her eyes to relax. She did not wish to think about Danny and those women. No, this time in London would be a grand adventure, spending one-on-one time with Ross again. She couldn't wait to get there.

The train pulled in five minutes early. Crowds disembarked and herded toward the exits, anxious to reach destinations unknown. She pushed through the crowd, catching various hellos and farewells from the mingling strangers. Due to the number of people centralizing in one area, she never thought she'd find him. Crushing her overnight bag against her chest, Tara saw a familiar face; near the ticket counter, close to a revolving turnstile, a tall and rugged man stood alone.

She gasped to recognize those dark flashing eyes, the jet black hair, and the exposed left dimple, showing as he smiled, like now. Tara placed her hand to her mouth in sweet heavenly shock. What transformation befell upon Ross? The expensive tailor-made suit, black and dapper, made his overall look magnificent. His chest, bulk and wide. His arms filled out the sleeves. Tara couldn't get over it. He bowed gallantly and then showed her a rose. She rushed forward to greet him.

"Hello there, pretty stranger," He teased but there was no way Tara would accept a simple hello.

"Oh, Ross!" she exclaimed and plowed into him with a firm, but happy embrace. She squeezed tightly and said in his ear, "You big buffoon! You look super!"

He laughed, encircled her waist, and gave her the rose. Politely, he took her bag to swing over his shoulder.

"Come on, Tara. I have big plans for you today. We are going to have some fun," He announced. His expensive car was out in the parking area. He opened up the door, placed her bag in the backseat, and then let her slide in. She sat in it only to look up at him in awe.

"Is this yours? Wow! You must be living large."

A huge grin came across his face as he closed the door. He ran to get to the opposite side, so excited to be with Tara again. Of course, as he drove away from the station, her curious nature struck immediately. Tara checked out everything in the car, pushing the lever that turned on the windshield wiper, changing the radio dial to find the music that she liked best, and thumbing through all the paperwork in the glove box. She even commented about the steering wheel.

"It's strange to see those on the right side. Plus, you drive very well in the wrong lane. I don't know how you do it, Ross. I'd end up in a wreck for sure."

Ross didn't mind that she rattled along this way in conversation. For once, it was like the old days, when she cut loose about everything. The woman could go on and on. He missed that a lot.

"Takes talent, sweetheart. I'm a man blessed with such," he teased back as he steered towards Marble Arch and Oxford Circus to go shopping within the flagship department stores. The morning time hummed along. They stopped at Selfridges to look for high fashion shoes at good prices. Tara ogled at the size of the five levels of outlet stores. By noon, they went towards Tottenham Court Road for a bite to eat in Soho. She heard Michael speak of this section of London often enough and now she was here too, with Ross, who opened up the door and pulled out her seat like a true gentleman.

"This is a great little spot as it is quiet during the day," Ross said and Tara looked around as the waitress handed them a menu. There were long mirrors on the walls and many different size cushy chairs to sit upon. The atmosphere was trendy, but Tara felt comfortable.

Ross took charge of their order, "We'll start off with halloumi cheese and chorizo skewers, two of your grand specialty salads, and make up two drinks with white rum and banana liqueur. Make the glasses the larger variety. We are thirsty."

"Ross, I really don't drink," Tara chastised but he shook his head firmly.

"You are on a holiday, young lady, so just relax for a change. Trust me. You will fall in love with this quickly," he blinked his eyes, causing her to laugh. It was so easy to be in his company again. He looked too good to be true. To play things off as they did as children was next to impossible. Too many things happened to change their perspective. They were adults now and many feelings were on fire. In this domain, Ross was in charge. Tara definitely liked the smooth and confidant bravado.

"So tell me everything," Tara asked, "Seriously, how do you like your job? Your life? Are you happy?"

Ross leaned back in the chair and studied her face. Her long lashes blinked and those warm eyes seemed very attentive. He wanted to impress her, so he told her everything about his rapid success. Mostly Tara heard a lot of unusual terms that he threw out to sound important, such as portfolio, capital gains, or profitability strategies. Surely, he was just bragging about what he learned.

"Our organization happens to sit in the midst of the most vibrant part of the city. We are so culturally diverse and it's so exciting meeting these executives that hail from Japan, Russia, or from the Middle East. Those Arabs are bloody rich!" he laughed after going on for about thirty minutes. They downed their skewers and finished their salads. He looked at Tara closely, "Ah, enough about that. Do you want anything else? You use to eat everything in sight, but you've only eaten half your salad. You look good though."

"What a nice way to say that I once ate like a pig," she laughed and he laughed too. She pushed away her plate, "No, I can't eat anymore. I've been dieting, so the salad was just right. Besides, this astronomical drink has filled up my tummy. I'm content just to sit here and listen to you shoot the breeze."

"Anything to accommodate a lady, but I did go overboard. Let's talk about you. How are things at the Briggs House? Are you more comfortable there, in your marriage?" Ross was sensitive that there were problems, as he heard different things from Susan and Michael. They never fully elaborated, but he could gather that Tara and Danny shared difficulties. It seemed reasonable in light of her pregnancy, but she wasn't that way anymore. Surely changes occurred.

"Danny and I go up and down," Tara said carefully, "We are like a pair of odd shoes. We head in the same direction, but its uncomfortable and awkward finding our footing."

"Wow, that's an unusual description of a marriage. So does that mean you aren't happy with its progression?"

"You can say that. He is away now, you know. So that makes things tough again," Tara took a napkin to wipe her mouth.

"Yes, I knew. In fact, he sent me a box full of sheet music about a month ago. They are great melodies, very creative. I've matched them with soulful lyrics and sent them back. I hope he likes them. At least he's not given up that passion, which we share. He mentioned in the note that you are his inspiration. So it's difficult to imagine you continue to have problems."

He was staring into her eyes and Tara didn't want to discuss why she was upset with Danny. There were feelings that surfaced while he was away, before she discovered his tryst with Rosemary and Eileen. She could be honest about that.

"He's gone too often. I get lonely, Ross. Real lonely. With him in the Navy, it makes it difficult to know him well. I've discovered things recently that show he lives another life."

"What things?"

"Let's just say that he has his own friends, his private activities. I don't fit in the scheme of that at all. So I decided to take some time to reevaluate our marriage."

"Oh, I'm surprised," Ross gulped and leaned towards her. She met him halfway. She wanted his deep attention.

"Honestly, I realize just sitting here, after all of our time apart," she said, reeling him in," I feel so damn comfortable in your company, like we never left Hartridge. We use to do everything together, remember? We shared our hearts. I miss that. I have never shared such intimacy with Danny, not once. It makes me sad."

She placed her hand over his. Ross was quite sensitive to her touch. There were no suggestions he could offer to make her feel better about Danny. He dwelled on the sentiments she exposed about him.

"I miss your company too, Tara. Not a day goes by that I don't think about you. Honestly. I felt that if I called more, I'd make things worse. I knew there were some problems with Danny, but not the extent of everything. I am always here for you. That will never change."

This special day together must be the best ever in her life. They were alone in London and free to do whatever they wished. She was so pretty in the bright lavender dress worn with one inch high heel shoes. Her makeup was spotless, her curves pudgy, but very appealing. There was much to reveal, other than the sites in London. Just one look, one more touch to his hand like that, would be enough to make him act. His thoughts about Susan and Gloria were stuck far away in his mind. Those women were not in the same league as Tara. They never were.

"I suppose we should go. We can hit the market square and look around. When we get to your hotel to check in, we can stay there for dinner, order up room service," he suggested.

"What about the bags? I'd hate to keep stuffing your car with more all afternoon. Sorry that I got carried away,"

"Let's go to the hotel down the street. I know the concierge there. He can make arrangements to get them to your room."

"Can he do that? Can you request it? It's not even the same hotel."

"I can make anything happen dear. I'm invincible," he raised his arms to show off his biceps, before he slipped into the jacket he took off earlier. Tara giggled, stood up a little off balance, and grabbed his arm for support.

As the afternoon dwindled away, Ross found Tara's mannerism playful and sexy. They soaked up the city like two young kids. They went to an outdoor market.

While there, he bought candles and four bottles of good wine. In the afternoon, they took in a play and right before sundown, they returned to her room. Ross called up room service for a plate of strawberries, grapes, cheese, crackers, and sausage. It would make a perfect light supper to go with the wine. He took out long taper candles from a bag to set upon the table. She went to the bathroom while he did this. She came out to see it all arranged.

"Isn't that a bit much?" Tara asked, gaping at the wine and the candles as he lit them.

"We will continue celebrating," Ross popped open the first bottle. He poured its contents into slim glasses, "It's been such a wonderful day. Let's just enjoy our conversation and our special time together."

A knock came from the door. Ross let the Room Service clerk deposit the tray. He paid a nice tip and then shut the door securely. It was a modest furnished room in a reasonable hotel in the city. Ross opened up the maroon drapes. They sat side by side to watch the sun go down. The long rays silhouetted the outline of the tall buildings in the distance. The sun melted into the horizon.

"This reminds me of New York," Tara sighed at one point, "I sure do miss it."

Her mood was melancholy as she drank. They talked about their childhood and how different that life was from the manor with servants. Truly all of the Cross siblings grew up with silver spoons. There were also considerable differences living in London versus living in the Wiltshire countryside.

"Where would we be today if they never interfered with our lives," Ross asked at one point later that evening. By that time, he felt the effects of the wine, "We'd still be back in the US. I'm sure God might have helped us overcome being poor. I'm too smart for that and a lovely girl like you deserves all the riches in the world. If you married me, I'd make things better. You'd never be miserable. God Tara, I realized something today too. I never stopped loving you."

It was dark now and the tall candles were the only light in the room. Tara let her head fall into her hands. She shook it, feeling intoxicated and sleepy. The whole room was spinning. She was accustomed to an occasional glass of wine, but not several.

"Tara, would you like more?" Ross really didn't wait for a reply but simply poured the red wine into her glass. Tara drank it down quickly and then banged the glass on the table for more. She was out of control. So was he. He fumbled to remove the cork on the last bottle. Tara watched for several seconds. He looked good and smelled good. He had muscles and a nice smile.

She needed to get to the bathroom. Her bladder was too full. Coming out, she stumbled towards the bed and fell in, throwing off the tan comforter and gliding her body across the cool sheets, slinking like a cat. She remembered that she never answered his question. How bloody rude!

"Sure, I'll take more wine. There isn't anything else better to do here." Tara blinked her eyes. She knew full well that he watched her, sensing any keen movements. He liked the way her hair fell over her shoulders. Over stimulated by the atmosphere, he sprang next to her and massaged her back in long strides. Tingling sensations burst everywhere. She delighted in his manly touch. His hands were wonderful.

"I know of something better." Ross whispered into her ear. She turned onto her back to look up. His eyes were amorous. His body, so damn close. Deep curiosity took over. An old fantasy possessed her mind. All of Danny's words rambled in her head:

'Slow stirring melodies upon a guitar, fingers playing lightly, transcending down one by one, softly, stroking, and filling the air into an enchanting crescendo… Stirring a heart, a soul, an imagination… a velvet dream.'

The words only made her body yearn for what a man could give. For the first time in her life, she wanted sex. She wondered, 'what would Ross be like? He's sweet, sexy. He's right here!'

"Then show me." She replied and Ross kissed her firmly- wet, warm, and confidante. The candle cast off long, dark shadows on the wall. She wanted this man now. Tara began to unbutton her dress, but Ross objected.

"Let me do that," He knelt on his knees to undress the quivering lady upon it, pulling off her dress, slip and bra. Tantalizing, long fingers ran along her naked sides as her ample breasts were exposed. He slipped off her shoes, kissed her ankles, brought down the lacy panties, and then he undressed. Layer by layer, his clothing came off, revealing a body Tara never seen before. She was hypnotized by the erotica as their eyes studied each other naked.

He was very muscular and hairy. His chest tickled against her breasts as he went on top, taking possession of her. He kissed her neck slowly, tickled her ears with a soft breath, and ran his lips down her sternum. His tongue went beneath her belly button to find and expose flaming nerves further below. Tara gasped and closed her eyes to delight in everything he did; an amazing lover, who took his sweet time to get her to an intense destination, not just once, but again and again. She surrendered everything that night, for his lovemaking only made her burn. Who was this man? This expert lover? Where did he obtain such carnal knowledge and expertise?

Introduced to a dazzling education of physical pleasure and endurance in different positions, she learned much about herself. She felt different, more experienced. Eventually the wine did its magic and they slept wrapped up in each others arms. Tara fell into a deep, peaceful slumber and sometime later, she stirred and peaked from underneath a sheet.

Dawn filtered into the room. Tara sat up, but nausea made her scowl and her head ached with a dull thump. She looked around confused. 'Where the heck am I?' Then she saw Ross. 'Oh, God!' For several seconds, she studied the sleeping naked man who rested partially uncovered. She horded most of the blankets that night. She now noticed that her stomach turned. Her tongue tasted bad.

Quietly, Tara snuck out of bed. She went to the bathroom before she barfed everywhere. Afterwards, she slumped onto the tile floor, with her head near the porcelain toilet. She stared at the hotel robes hanging by the door and tried to think. That night was simply lust. Now there were bigger quandaries that ravaged her mind.

For one, on her post partum check up, the doctor gave her a prescription for the pill. She never filled it. It seemed senseless since Danny immediately departed for the Atlantic. She didn't even want to think about what could happen with the lack of this protection. Second, before they slept, Ross speculated that perhaps Tara should leave Danny altogether and remain with him instead.

Was it possible? Was he crazy? Was she? Tara returned to the room and noticed the shopping bags in the corner. They contained lovely dresses, hats, and shoes. They contained jewelry, perfume, and purses- all bought by her rich husband. She dropped by the bags and stared at some of the contents inside one. She took out jewelry to look them over. Did he give Tara this money out of responsible husbandry duty, or to appease his own guilt?

'Of course! That jackal! That deceiving, no good, low-life scoundrel!' This was entirely his fault. His affair disgusted her and she felt sick, sick, sick. She threw the jewelry back into the bag and took a good look around. It was too ironic. Now she dealt with her own slip up. It wasn't wise to sleep with Ross just to get even. Another onset of nausea swept over and she ran back to the toilet to kneel before it. This was the throne she so rightly deserved. With all that she did that night, she should be flushed away with the puke filled water.

After that, she took a hot steamy shower just to wash away any scent of their lovemaking. It was very noticeable; this special fragrance of their unified body juices, derived by their frank naughtiness in the night. Such carnal knowledge should have been exposed by being with her husband like this, not her best friend. Surely Danny frequently showered after sleeping with those awful prostituting women.

"Oh, God! What have I done," Tara cried out, for she suddenly realized why Danny turned to them. She rebuffed his attentions, every single one, from the beginning. She leaned her head into the tile perimeter and banged her head lightly on the wall. The water rushed down over her head. She stared at the long strands of brown hair that dangled towards the floor. Focused on the obvious, it only mustered up a sad realization. If anyone was a victim, it was Danny, not she. Tara gulped. It felt much too difficult to accept.

With this enlightenment, Tara stepped out of the shower and hastily dried off with the towel. She must get out of that room. She must get far away from the crime scene. Not so quietly, she rushed to dress. Ross woke up. He sat there discerning his whereabouts. He watched and after vying for acknowledgement with a customary good morning, Ross tried to reason her strange actions and replies.

"What's with you, Tara? You don't have to rush back there. You can stay in London for a day or two. We can send for your belongings. I can find a bigger loft and even hire someone to help out with the children," Ross calculated, "I must earn a living, but things will adjust. It will not be like New York City as my salary is much more generous. We can be together and live happily."

"No, Ross. We can't. We can't do this," she grabbed the bags to place them near the door.

"What? Which part? Do you not want a nanny? What other alternative is there?" Ross sensed that something was not right. He quickly changed into his clothes and then went to embrace Tara, but she pushed him away.

"None of it. I simply can't stay."

"But after last night ....I thought ...,"Ross stammered in disbelief. Tara cut to the quick.

"You did everything and more, but what was I thinking? Oh, Jesus! Ross, let's blame it all on the wine. I must go home to my children at the Briggs House. That is my place. Not with you."

Ross suddenly felt desperate. The night was magic, true and true. What force in the universe was pulling them apart? Again?

"Look, if you are worried about Danny's reaction, he can't stop you. He's too far away to do anything. This is perfect timing to do this. If staying in London's not right, I can request a transfer."

"Ross, George helped you get that job. You can lose it," Tara reminded him.

"Yes, you are right. I didn't think of that. Well, I can go to a different company, maybe in India or Japan. I have experience now," Ross suggested. Were any of his ideas registering in her head? She kept moving around the room as if ants were in her pants, "It would be a new way of life, but we can adjust, Tara. We can make this work. I promise you'll always be my top priority, along with the children. I love you."

He took her into his arms, but she snapped.

"Ross! Don't you understand? I don't feel the same for you!"" Tara shouted and freed herself. Tears surfaced in her eyes. He stood still, astounded of her reaction.

"What the hell is wrong with you?"

She must make it sink in.

"I have never felt that kind of love for you. Never."

"How can that be true? We felt fire last night Tara. It's been an underlying current between us for years. Last night, for once, you acknowledge it and needed me. It was magic."

"Oh, Ross, it wasn't that. I was selfish," Tara wept, hating to admit the truth. "When I came to London, I already had this planned. I wanted to lure you to sleep with me, so I could replicate the wrong Danny has done to me."

"Wrong? What did he do?"

"He strayed and slept with two women. I just found out about this. I wanted to get even, so badly. So I must love him if I'm this angry about it. How does this help me? It only adds burden. The Cross family cannot be embarrassed by my stupidity, not when they have given much already. Please understand. This was all a big mistake."

Ross sat down absolutely stunned. Why was God punishing him? After all, Tara admitted that Danny didn't make her happy. He knew that he could do it. Still, she was rejecting him. She thought she still loved her husband. It hurt.

"Are you sure?" he asked again.

"I'm sure, Ross. Just let me go home and you go back to your world. Leave me out of it."

He toyed with an empty bottle of wine and then abruptly tossed it into trash. He grasped her arm and looked firmly into her eyes.

"All right Tara. I'll abide by your wishes. Just know that I have always wanted you. It meant everything to have you for my wife, but something always stood in the way. First it was Jimmy, then Danny, and now your warped pride for the Cross family. In spite of that, you remain the air that sustains my being. If last night was a mistake, it is in your eyes, not mine. I will always remember."

"Ross, I'm so sorry. This has to remain our secret." Tara begged. She didn't let his words sink in, fearing that it would change her mind. She snapped away to rush to the door. She stood waiting with the overnight bag and packages at her feet. "I must leave. The train departs in an hour. Can you at least see me off? I have to go home."

With his posture slumped and eyes staring in the distance, Ross grabbed his coat. He went out in the hall to bring back a luggage cart. He could use it to wheel her bags to the car. Tara ensured that everything in the room was gathered up. She left the key on the bureau, secretly happy that the deed was done in a strange hotel room and not in his apartment.

At the station platform, Tara hopped onboard. She rushed to find the assigned seat, never saying goodbye. She saw Ross through her window. He paid a porter for helping him with her purchases. What a difference a day could make? He turned and walked away with his hands deep in his pockets. He seemed too ashamed of her rejection. Tara realized at that moment that she was a very wicked woman, for it was she who struck a dagger deep into his heart of gold.

Chapter Thirty Four

When friends deceive

"She's crying again," Caroline announced loudly over Edward. He screamed in her arms. She placed him down into the playpen, right next to Tristan and Tyler. They looked at her to pout too. Edward didn't stop crying at all. He was mad, "Shoosh, now. The bottles are coming. My, you cry so, just like your mother."

"Here, I've made them up," Marta ran into the room from the kitchen. She offered Caroline a tepid bottle filled with eight ounces of baby formula. Tara gave up pumping breast milk back in June. Formula seemed faster, especially with hungry, growing babies. Marta looked down at the three infants and frowned. "Wait a minute. Jamie's not among them."

"I realize that," Caroline picked up Tristan to feed him.

Marta placed both hands upon her hips studying the boys. They were strong little six month olds, not quite ready to sit up on their own. They kicked their feet and flailed their arms. Edward turned over onto his belly and leaned up with his arms, using it for leverage to support his body. His face turned bloody red crying for attention.

"I'm confused," Marta picked him up, "You just said that *she* was crying."

"Not Jaime!" Caroline shook her head. She propped herself on the couch to feed two children. Marta placed Edward next to her, supported by a pillow. Caroline stuck a bottle into his mouth. Instant silence. The boy sucked in the formula fast. Then Marta picked up Tyler to feed.

"Then who?"

"Mrs. Cross! She's at it again," Caroline looked up the stairs. "I don't know what's wrong. She sounded like she was weeping. Then she flew out of Vincent's room with her hand over her mouth. I think I heard her gag."

The women stared at each other with a suspicious look.

"It's not our place to say anything," Marta said. She didn't like this one bit, but she loved the little babies and she liked Tara too. Besides, the babies only fussed terribly that morning because the women lagged behind in their chores. It was past their feeding time. Marta thought it very kind for Tara to consistently slip extra money into their purses for their devotion. Marta saved enough money in her bible for a grand Christmas with her family.

Still, Marta realized several things about the married couple in the house. Danny left for sea back in May. Tara just gave birth in April and so they could not be intimate during that time, not with Mr. Cross's disappearance figured into it too. Marta kept up with things with her ears and keen observance. She lived in the house and knew about everything that unfolded. Next, in August, Tara went off to London to shop for new clothes. It was a reward for successful weight loss. Even if on her return there were lots of packages, Tara simply placed everything away. Not once did she wear anything new. Marta thought this quite odd.

Now, in October, the woman puked into the toilet daily, sometimes three times a day. She felt worse last month and so missed celebrating her 19th birthday. Tara feigned a cold so Helen wouldn't bake a cake or create a fuss.

"She's pregnant, I tell you. She must have been with someone in London," Caroline speculated and shook her head woefully, "It's the only time she was out of our sight. It's only a matter of time before the family finds out. I can see it now- all the fireworks flying from Mr. George Cross's mouth. He isn't stupid, by no means."

"Shh, she's coming downstairs," Marta sat down with Tyler in her arms. Tara walked down a few steps, but looked quite green. She stopped midway and then went flying up to the bathroom again. Twenty minutes later, she managed to make her way into the living room. She sat across the ladies and Caroline stared at her. Tara noticed this, but said nothing.

"You have no color in your face, dear," Marta said after a couple of minutes, "How about a cup of tea?"

"No, thanks. I can't even think about tea or food. I feel awful," Tara admitted. There wasn't a clear way to hide this anymore. Even with the last pregnancy with the septuplets, it went well compared to this one. "I must be cursed for what I did with Ross," Tara thought gloomily. If shame developed into liquid form, it would ooze throughout every pore. She felt far worst now than for how she treated her husband before.

Danny would take this as a personal insult and she wounded her best friend's pride. How much further damage could she do? She watched the ladies tend to her three sons. Vincent was fed and napping upstairs. Soon the others would wake for their own feedings. It seemed like a never ending chore. How would another baby make things easier? This was a disaster in the making. Yet, Tara didn't want to feel this way about the new baby.

The phone rang then and Tara rose to get it, since the ladies were occupied. She picked up the receiver hesitantly and prayed that it would not be Danny on the other end. Ever since August, he tried consistently to get through to her. The first three times, Tara managed to avoid a conversation by Caroline's help. By the fourth, Caroline shoved the phone towards her. Tara heard Danny blasting obscenities loud and clear through the outstretched receiver. He never swore before, but now he was mad. Caroline shook her head and refused to lie anymore. There was no choice but to speak to the man directly.

"I've been trying like hell for weeks, Tara. It's difficult to get to a phone sometimes. Everyone here must put up with long lines just for four minutes of time. That's all I have with you. Damn that woman for wasting precious minutes! You should have fired Caroline a long time ago, that… that… oh, never mind! Are you all right?"

"Sort of," Tara said. It was intimidating to hear his anger on the other end.

"What the hell does that mean? You don't write as much and when you do, your words are so vague. Something's wrong and I want to know what it is."

Tara clutched the phone. How dare he raise his voice to her! In some ways, Tara still wanted to strangle that man, but it wasn't best to bring up the blatant affair. How can they fight reasonably if he was half a world away? It seemed best, for now, to simply discuss the children and not themselves.

"Let me tell you what's different," Tara began, irritated by his demeanor, "I am terribly busy. The children are a lot to handle now, Danny. You don't understand. You are not here to deal with it on a day to day basis. There's very little time to rest. I'm tired."

"I'm sorry. I'd rather be there to help. So what's been going on?"

"Well, the other day, Edward woke up with a bad fever. He's the second to ever be sick and I was so scared. I think he caught something from Lila's cousin, Mr. Brewer. He came over with plumbing supplies to fix the leak in the upper bathroom sink. The whole time he sniffed and coughed. I'm sure he left his nasty germs everywhere for Edward to catch."

"Poor boy, did you get him a doctor? How is my little guy now? Is he well again?" Danny asked with genuine feeling. Tara didn't like hearing it. If she wasn't mad otherwise, she could appreciate his fatherly concern.

Damn it! He forced her to share, this one common thread keeping them connected by the heart.

"He's better. Just a minor ear infection. We stayed up all night because of his crying. Now, it seems that Erik and Matthew came down with nasty colds. Their noses are running all over the place and they fuss when I clean their faces," she revealed and felt nausea come on again, "I'm not feeling well either, Danny. I simply can't talk because I feel sick. Very sick. I swear you caught me at a bad moment. I just need to go lie down. I'm so sorry to cut this short."

It was true. Morning sickness didn't just stay in the mornings. He bought the explanation with a heavy sigh and allowed Tara to hang up -two months ago. Now, his recent letters asked several complicated questions, like what changed since their moment on the stairs? Did she still want him? Did she love him? There was no way to explain it. Things must be broken in person. First, she must tell his family. Which would be worse? So now, picking up the receiver, she worried who might be on the other end.

"Hello, this is Tara."

"I have to speak to you," Gloria said, her words crisp on the line, "Susan and I fought."

"And that's different from how?" Tara knew the girls argued all the time now. Since Gloria opened up her photography studio, she found reasons to drop by Ross's apartment. Susan apparently sat on the opposite end of the fence. Perhaps she thought that Ross was beneath Gloria. Tara wouldn't put that past Susan, knowing her in-law didn't approve of her either. In light of the recent indiscretion, perhaps it was wise not to push Ross and Gloria together.

"It's different, Tara. It involves you," She revealed. Tara panicked to hear this. There were sounds of people, buses, and children in the background, so surely Gloria called from a payphone, "I'm on my way there. Meet me outside so we can go for a walk. We can't discuss any of this within earshot of the servants."

Tara agreed and hung up. She felt afraid. It became inevitable. If an angry outburst must come now, Tara preferred it first from Gloria. The tall blond showed up sometime later, dressed in a dark cashmere sweater, sensible shoes, and gray wool pants. She wore a thick black jacket and dark glasses upon her face. She parked the car closest to the road, waiting for Tara to come out.

"How are you, Gloria," Tara tried to sound civil, but Gloria grabbed the glasses off her nose to reveal red eyes. She glared at Tara.

"I just came from the worst screaming match. Susan is livid. Ross packed up out of the blue to move to Paris."

"Why?" Tara gasped as it surprised her too, "What about his apartment and his great job? I thought he was happy."

"No, lately he's been miserable. Susan and he were into it this morning. Don't ask me why she was there. I thought I'd be clever to bring over croissants and steamed coffee for breakfast. He's never stopped me from visiting before. I knew something bothered him, so I wanted to cheer him up."

"And why again is Ross leaving?"

"Because of you, Tara," Gloria glared and placed both hands upon her hips, "Ross apologized to Susan for something incredibly stupid he did to Danny. He said it would only be right to leave the company. Ross wants to make his way in the world without my father's help. Paris seemed like an exciting opportunity. Frankly, I worry about how he will swing it. He's such a mess."

"What's wrong?" Tara felt afraid to hear the answer. Surely, this was her fault too.

"He's been drinking, quite heavily," Gloria revealed and walked quickly upon the dirt road. Tara struggled to keep up, as there was still an element of nausea in her tummy. Gloria placed on the dark glasses again, "You once complained that Danny could hold his liquor well, to hide the drunkenness. Let me tell you, Ross does not. Things slipped away at work, at home. Susan stood there digging out his secret. The door was partially open and I could not help but listen. Their words escalated. You know Susan. Sometimes you just want to slap her, but as I stepped in, he admitted that you slept together when you visited."

Tara threw both hands to her mouth in humiliation. Gloria rubbed her neck profusely and stopped in the road. She whipped around to confront Tara eye to eye.

"Why Tara? I placed all my hope to be with Ross. He never gave any indication that he didn't sincerely like me too. You pushed that idea on me and now I'm just as mortified. He's going away and that hurts. By now, I'm sure he's crossed the tunnel and is in France. What happened to make you sleep with him?"

"It's hard to explain. Danny and I …" she began to say but Gloria cut her off.

"Please don't use my brother for an excuse! He wrote an incredible letter recently. He said on the day he left, things were terrific, that you kissed him and seemed committed again. Hell, we all thought so too. For awhile, he's all you talked about with mother and me."

"Yes, I know," Tara felt glum. Gloria paced in a small circle.

"He wrote that he never felt so blooming excited about his future. Recently things felt terribly off. Something he couldn't begin to understand. You hardly write and hardly talk on the phone. He wanted me to investigate your circumstances. I never expected this in a million years! It breaks my heart. When Danny learns what happened, it will kill him. He loves you and he respected Ross."

"I'm so sorry," Tara felt her heart break, "Ross and I - we were drunk. I was careless. It just happened."

"Oh, Jesus! I've heard that lame excuse before!" Gloria cried out and then she cringed. Tara stared and each deduced something true. Gloria kicked the ground because she unwittingly broke her word. Tara clutched her stomach.

"You knew? About Danny and those women?"

"Tara, I swore not to tell."

"Just hold on. I can accept it being an accident the first time because I did that with Ross, but Danny stayed at that house all week long. I'm sure they just didn't play cards every night."

"Tara, he felt upset."

"Well, good! Because finding out hurts, Gloria. I kissed my husband before he went away and had great expectations that things would be wonderful again. I kept hope about our marriage, especially with all of the love letters flying back and forth between us. For once I needed him as a wife should! And he screwed them! He went away knowing that he did. God, I feel so ill!"

Tara turned green and ran to the side of the road. She bent low as bile surfaced to her throat and fell upon the ground before her. Gloria watched, her eyes fixed on what was happening. After the onset, Tara stood up, wiped her mouth, and returned to stand before Gloria, looking a bit ashen.

"That's why I was with Ross. It was stupid but I wanted revenge."

"What happened that night?"

"We had too much wine. It made things too easy, although it was Ross's fault I wound up so stupidly drunk. Earlier in the day, we had gone out to lunch and talked about the old days, his new lifestyle. I sat there and patted his hand, gave off such dreamy looks! He's an easy pushover. I don't feel proud of myself. Sleeping with other people isn't right either, but I didn't offer my spouse money or shopping sprees just to appease one's guilt. That's why he hurried back to duty because he couldn't look at me and lie about it."

"The truth is that he went away to heal his doubts, Tara. Mostly he wants to come back to be a dedicated man to your marriage. That was my impression of what he said," Gloria revealed, "I guess it's way too late. Are you with child? You look very pale."

Tara nodded, now losing the punch to argue further. Gloria paced back and forth and tried to think out a sensible solution.

"This is not the best of situations. I'll go to the manor and inform my parents. If I say the truth about Danny first, they should not go too hard on you. At least Ross is far away where my father can't kill him. Once we jump over this hurdle, perhaps its best to go on as normal as possible-pretend nothings wrong until Danny comes home. We'll let you tell him the truth about this baby."

"What about Susan? Won't she say something since she knows that I slept with Ross? Isn't she angry too?"

As often as Susan bothered Tara about her household and commitment to Danny before, surely the platinum blond was going ballistic. Gloria's blue eyes focused on Tara.

"I've persuaded her to secrecy. Besides she is heading down to Morocco for a photo layout and will be traveling between there, Greece, and Rome. She'll be quite busy until Christmas comes around. It's a lucrative contract. I told her that if fame comes along, she wouldn't want family secrets to get out. She bought it, so she'll keep quiet about your affair."

Tara nodded and then reached out for Gloria's hand.

"Can't we still be friends?" Tara asked, needing to know how Gloria felt about this. Luckily, Gloria squeezed her hand in return.

"I sided with my brother on his secret, but now it's out in the open. I can only stay silent with yours. I still consider us friends and you'll need me to buffer out awkwardness with our family. I love you Tara, but this really hurt me too, although I can forgive you. Besides, I agree. I didn't like those women at the pub either. I can't really blame you for retaliating this time."

"This time?"

"I know what transpired with Michael and that was truly bad form. Once Danny learns about Ross and the baby, you are on your own then. We can't protect you further. Agreed?"

"All right, but I don't want to let Ross know about this right away. If he's that unstable, he'll need time to readjust to his new life," Tara requested and the women embraced in agreement. Tara watched Gloria get to her car. She pulled out onto the road at a quick speed, throwing leaves up in the air. Tara stood on the side of the roadway and thought about things. She could imagine Helen crying and George grumbling and grabbing for his pipe. This would hurt Grams, too, once she learned of everything, but luckily, she was away in Cornwall, visiting her brother until after the New Year's holiday. She loved Grams.

Tara took a slow walk up the cobblestone driveway. In some ways, in spite of all the stupidity, she wanted to remain at the Briggs House. With the children, it became her home. Tara watched leaves fall gracefully to the ground. She turned to study the look of her house. Black billowy smoke poured from top of the chimney, pilfering the clean air with the aroma of burning wood. "How pretty it seems," she mused and then tears surfaced.

How could she be pregnant again, especially with Christmas around the corner? It just wasn't right. Somehow, they needed to get past the holidays before chaos settled in about the new baby. The holiday alone seemed an emotional time of the year for most people. In January, Danny could come home and find out the truth. Hopefully by then, she would have a solution figured out, to live on her own. It seemed impossible right now, with seven children, but she could predict that Danny would let her go for sure. Just the fact that this was Ross's baby would make him burn inside. This was too personal of a slap in the face. Again, heavy tears filled Tara's eyes. Such a sad fate and after all of those beautiful letters, between husband and wife, her heart remained across the ocean with that man.

Time seemed to be her friend and then her enemy. The crisp fall days passed by quickly like sand within an hourglass. Before long, the winter atmosphere chilled everything around and there seemed to be lots of snow that particular year, as 1978 came nearer to an end. From as far away as Scotland to the southwest outskirts of London, it fell heavy. Inside the grand manor, Tara stood by the decorated mantle of ivy and long red candles to look over the recent Christmas card greetings.

She noted that there wasn't one from Ross written to the Cross Family, but she felt this to be expected. It saddened her that she didn't hear anything either. Tara pouted. Why should she, when her deception ran deeper? Briefly, Tara recalled their last Christmas together as they huddled in blankets in Ross's run down NYC apartment, with a broken furnace. They drank hot cocoa with cinnamon sticks, a treat they learned from a nun who came from Mexico. Ross gave a gift of pink fuzzy slippers while she in turn gave him a good pair of work gloves to use on the cold docks. It was all they could afford-all they had. It was enough back then.

Why couldn't they now be easily satisfied? What had changed them?

Tara gazed at the flames and softly twirled a strand of hair as she stood there, thumbing through all the holiday cards, within the happy atmosphere of Helen's birthday celebration. Across the room, all decorated for Christmas a week away, George poured Champaign for everyone there, except for Tara, who just reached four months. She went to sit down in a chair to watch Helen open her gifts.

"Sammy should be here any minute," Gloria said as she came away from the front window. She went up to her mother to bestow a loving kiss upon her cheek, "Happy birthday, Mother."

Gloria handed over a small box wrapped in a green cellophane wrapping and with a pretty bow on top. The flowing ribbons were quickly discarded as Helen tore into it. She made such a fuss about the fancy necklace within it.

"Isn't this design lovely?" Helen commented and showed it off to everyone. She studied it closer, "It's seems very familiar, like a bracelet George gave once when I expected Danny."

Helen suddenly glanced at Tara. She placed the box down abruptly, bringing up another subject, "Try the appetizers, Gloria. They are wonderful."

Gloria went to the tray as instructed. She selected one and then looked over at Tara. No words needed to be communicated between them. Tara realized that it was she that made things uncomfortable lately. No one really spoke out loud about the pregnancy or predicted what Danny may say about it. In fact, all discussions seemed to happen behind closed doors. Tara never heard a single comment or admonishment. Helen opened up another present to keep the mood in the room uplifting as possible.

"Oh, look at this lovely picture! Thank you, Tara, The babies are beautiful," Helen admired the 8 x 11 wooden picture frame. It contained the septuplets professional portrait. Gloria took it against the backdrop of a blue drape held up on either side by Marta and Lila. It looked like she took it in a studio.

They were quite cute now, at nine months old, with giggling mouths, cherub cheeks and sparkling eyes. In the picture, they sat up holding assorted toys, dressed in their Sunday best. Helen studied their bright brown eyes and long brown hair. She long suspected that these children did not belong to her son. There was no family resemblance, no blue eyes, no blond hair, nothing. Still, in every sense, she was their grandmother and loved them dearly.

Right now, they slept in an adjacent room, watched over by the hired staff. She often talked Tara into letting them stay over once in awhile, just to give them spoiled attention. This made it easy for Grams to see them too. The time by herself was a nice break for Tara and she could never argue against Helen's requests. Out of everyone, Tara respected her the most. Mysteriously, a kinship took place between them since the new pregnancy was announced. It was something that Tara didn't expect. Helen went about quietly to ensure that Tara was protected and provided for, with her medical check ups and care. Helen behaved as if nothing was wrong at all, except for the occasional slip ups.

After a lovely dinner gathering, Sammy finally made it home. He had been delayed by the thick snow and when he dashed into the foyer, Gloria sliced the cake in the next room. With such a loud entrance, Helen quickly went to greet him in the hallway. He paused to look at everyone and then suddenly noted the changes in Tara's appearance. She seemed thinner in the face and stature, but when she stood straight up, a half-volley ball shape showed underneath the blouse that she wore. Sammy gasped and then his jaw dropped. Instantly, before he could utter a word, Helen pushed him towards the kitchen- far removed from anyone hearing them.

"Is she? Is her tummy...?" he sputtered, as he knew not else how to react. "Man! I've been away at sea too long. In four months time, how can I be unaware of news of such importance? Is she...? Pregnant?"

He glared at his mother momentarily. Helen nodded. He couldn't believe it.

"No, way! How? Who?"

"Yes, she is expecting. Look, Sammy, its best not to talk about it right now."

"Why not? Why didn't anyone write me about this? Did anyone inform Danny? I bet not."

"You know that we can't tell him. It's a terrible situation. It's Ross's baby," Helen said softly.

Sammy paced about the room while he realized the impact of the situation.

"Oh, mother! This is awful. Look, I just came from the Falklands. Our ship hooked up with my brother's about 10 kilometers out. Let me tell you that there's been changes in my brother. First of all, he dives into work like a man possessed. It took me forever to convince

Danny to go with me to the mainland- so we could talk."

"That was a good idea. What happened?"

"Oh, we went for drinks as I happened to know this crazy little spot," Sammy revealed and looked at his mother squarely in the eye, "It has the best seafood and I drank fruity concoctions, while he guzzled down beer. Danny seemed so out of touch-bummed out, like the ocean plunged in on his world. He told me about his worries, about their problems in their marriage, how it began. Did you know that Michael interfered? He made a play for her while she was laid up at the Briggs House."

"No, I didn't," Helen fumed, "Perhaps I should have a word with Michael later."

"No, Danny already confronted my big brother and Michael's promised to back off, but Tara didn't have any idea of their talk. When Erik's surgery was over, she turned to Michael instead of Danny to show her happiness. That's what set Danny off to run away and then after his disappearance, Tara's thinking changed. She must have realized something about Michael, because then she suddenly wanted Danny back. Which he was thrilled that somehow, things worked out." Sammy warbled on and then grabbed a drink from the refrigerator and gulped it down quickly.

"They ended up writing, back and forth, like mad he said. Danny noted a change in her. Tara even revealed something to me about this when I visited this summer. Anyway, something happened as they weren't communicating as much and Danny thought that perhaps Michael interfered again. It was never Danny's suspicion that this change in her had to do with Ross. This news will age Danny by ten years! His heart will wind up screwed up, all because of that woman!"

Sammy gritted his teeth and slammed his drink upon the counter. Anxiously, he peaked out the door and noted how everyone chatted politely and ate the white cake that Gloria divvied out.

"How can everyone just stay so calm?" Sammy hissed and then smacked the counter again-this time with his fist. It made his mother jump, "Sorry, mum. I didn't mean to frighten you, but everything is damn confusing. When they married, I was thrilled. I thought Tara was so special- or so we all assumed. Now, poor Danny will go through hell. She's too much maintenance. Why in the world does she remain here with us? Why is she in our house?"

"Why do you think?" Helen murmured and picked up a stuffed toy on the table. She patted a spot next to her as she sat down, so Sammy slid in as directed. "Those children are every part of our family now, irregardless; as is Tara. I love them all so much. Somehow, she's made a grand mistake, but it was done out of hurt."

"Hurt? What hurt? Danny is the one who hurts," Sammy couldn't believe what she said.

"Are we so sure?" Helen looked up into his eyes. A scowl was evident upon her face, "There's been something brought to my attention that makes me question his sincerity, his character. I never thought I would do so."

"For God's sake, what? I've never known a more honorable man," Sammy defended his brother. Helen's eyes narrowed.

"Before he went away, there was an affair with two women in the village. Did he reveal that to you?"

"No!" Sammy gasped, but then he sighed, with many spinning thoughts uttered out loud. "It's hard to believe. This is terrible. There are real children involved here, quite innocent victims over all. I do say this, Danny can't learn of this slip up. His ship should be in the Mediterranean waters now. There are crews going up to replace some of the men for shore leave. There are few that know him well. Some are from around these parts. What if someone has seen her or heard something? He must fly home to find out first. That should happen now!"

"Yes, I think you are right. They should confront each other in privacy. I'll request that the children be here when he comes in. Can you find a way to make it so?" Helen touched his hand and Sammy stood up, eager to act on this plan.

"Consider it done, mother. I'll arrange it right away."

Sammy went to the next room to make several special phone calls. He knew what to do and how to get his brother home as soon as possible.

Chapter Thirty Five

Fury Like lightening and Thunder

A week later, Sammy went to the airport and waited outside in the car. When Danny came out the airport lobby doors, Sammy stepped out to assist. The two brothers quickly embraced. Sammy opened up the trunk to stow away Danny's belongings.

"What's wrong with you, dear brother? You don't seem like yourself. Did you see a ghost on the way here?" Danny kidded as he noted Sammy's stern face. Sammy shrugged as he closed the trunk. Danny looked around at the familiar airport. "At any rate, it's good to be back in England. At least in time for Christmas morning. Even if the snow seems a constant thing, I miss the landscape. I miss our home."

They sat inside the warm car. Sammy started the ignition. He wasn't in the mood to talk. Danny thought it odd. There were times when Sammy squawked away like a parrot on speed.

"Is everyone fine?" Danny placed on his seatbelt. "How are our parents? How's Tara? Did you go up to see the children?"

"They are fine. She's well as to be expected." Sammy replied and then cringed.

"Did you say something weird? You look like you swallowed a frog whole. Even your skin tone seems green." Danny surmised. Sammy kept firm eyes upon the traffic light near the airport entrance. This really made Danny worry. He thought about his circumstances that brought him home, "It did seem strange how Harry let me go like this. He called me to the office. We shared a bit of stow away brandy. He said the whole crew would get a break, but not until after Christmas. It couldn't be helped. There is far too much surveillance due with our Allied affiliates. We won't get much of a break at all. How about you, Sammy?"

"The same here, I'm afraid. I must re-board in four days," Sammy replied, steering the car out into traffic.

"Still, Harry said I didn't need to wait. My tickets were arranged. He patted me on the back, said it was an early present."

"It was a ruse," Sammy drove out to the main metro to get out London, "I spoke to him recently. I begged for his help."

"Why? Is everyone all right? No one's sick?"

"Really, everyone's healthy. Our parents are the same. Oh, the babies sit up now. They are really quite lively."

"Ah, I can't wait to see them or Tara either. Damn, I do miss her, even if she's so mean lately," Danny joked, but Sammy didn't even smile.

"Yes, you must right away," is how he replied, with an ominous tone, "I will drop you off and take your bags up to the manor."

"I see. For some reason, I'm not welcomed in my own house. My wife-she's still icy, eh?" This Danny somewhat expected, due to her lack of letters and hesitancy on the phone, "There's a saying- about absence making the heart grow fonder. In Tara's case, can she at least be receptive?"

"Just wait. You'll find out everything you need to know the moment you walk in. Now why not close your eyes to rest. Let me drive in peace. The snow is awful thick on the roadway. I must concentrate," Sammy instructed. Danny stared out the window and bit his tongue. Something didn't feel right. He shouldn't pick his brother apart for answers. He sensed he would find out soon enough.

It wasn't long before they reached the Briggs House. Snow surrounded the grounds and the fence lines. The trees, bare and low, bent with the weight. The icicles hung from the roof over the porch. Danny stepped out of the car and took a deep breath. 'Home.' He noticed the wreaths upon the outer windows. There were no other decorations, not even a tree twinkling through it. Perhaps it was too early to do this with the infants. Anticipation drove him crazy, but so did the fear of the unknown. As Sammy drove away, Danny made his way into the house.

He paused in the entrance hall, since it was so eerily quiet. Only a light shone from upstairs and in the kitchen. He yelled out, "Hello? Anyone here?" No one responded, so he hung up the thick all-weather coat upon the rack near the door. He ran upstairs to investigate further. All of the children's room seemed tidy. Several of familiar stuffed animals decorated the bookshelves, which made him smile. He walked into the master bedroom. Tara's pink fuzzy slippers sat on the floor by the bed. Danny went over to pick them up. They looked dingy and well worn.

"I must get her a new pair," he thought. He wondered why she did not replace them, but figured it was an old habit from childhood living at the foster home facility. She probably wore lots of hand-me-downs. He turned off the light to walk downstairs. He paused by the fireplace. There was a chill in the air, so he placed another log into the low embers. His hands warmed up and he gazed around the room.

The mantle was decorated with ceramic Father Christmas knick knacks and fake green ivy. The draperies were a deep forest green color, but made the ambiance feel comfortable. The furniture was re-arranged during his absence. A porcelain vase of silk flowers sat upon a small table by one of the windows. Perhaps this was a touch of Tara's effort to decorate, which warmed his heart that she tried. A clink of a glass came from the kitchen. Danny raised his brow.

"Hello, I say. Who's there?" he went towards it. There by the kitchen sink, with her back towards him, stood his wife. She looked good from behind, with a trimmer appearance of shapely hips that tempted him. Now to see her again, all he wanted to do was hold her within his arms, to nibble her ears, and to whisper things to bring out a smile. He felt confidant that he could achieve this reaction with her, considering that they were miles beyond his initial homecoming back in the spring. Yet, something happened to change her tone in her letters. With no clues, he wasn't clear where they stood in their marriage anymore. Clueless and fumbling, he begged for a reaction.

"So, you are home. Why are you so quiet? I called out," Danny walked closer, but she shook her head. He stopped. She placed a wash towel down and grasped the edge of the sink tightly. The whites of her knuckles were quite visible. Something was terribly wrong. He could sense it now.

"Are you dismayed with my arrival? Surely you can offer a cup of tea so that I can thaw out. It is very cold outside," He stood anxious, waiting for some kind of response to his presence, "Won't you at least say hello? Turn around so we can talk."

He hoped she would offer sexy eyes and a torrid kiss like she gave back in April. It was too much to hope for as she obeyed.

"All right, if you insist," she sighed, her eyes low. She bit her bottom lip in a tight grimace. The sight of her body punctured all thoughts and knocked holes into the sails of his hopes.

"What the hell is that?" Danny blurted out, staring at her tummy. He took two steps backwards as if it would attack. He could accept this if they just met and were in New York again. But this wasn't New York. This baby was not his. His fists clenched. Tara felt quite unprepared. No one gave any warning of his return. Luckily, the children were at Helen's. The staff was with their families. In fact, it was Helen that suggested their outing and now Tara realized why. Danny grabbed a chair for support, "Oh, Tara! This is such a humiliation! All this time-not one bloody word!"

"For God's sake, man! How would I do that? Did you want me to send it by special telegram?" Tara snapped. She was very rude, but she could not help it. Tara struggled to decipher her own feelings seeing him in the flesh. He looked damn good. He bore a fantastic tan from being in the warm waters off Australia and Argentina. She couldn't make up her mind what to do. A part of her wanted to run to his arms, but the look on his face stopped that. Another part ached to recall everything he did in town. Pain rose up like bile, "It's not something so easily relayed."

There was a look in his eyes that she just couldn't take. So she paced out into the living room and snapped on a light. She picked up toys; straighten out pillows on the couch, grabbed newspapers and magazines to put them into place. Anything to keep busy. He found his voice and it was sharp.

"Jesus Christ, Tara! Who is the father? Do you prefer him over me? Do you want him like that? Did you like it? Who is it?" Danny followed her into the room. She could sense the warmth of his body hovering over hers, but this only agitated her feelings, along with his damn questions.

"No, I don't want him! I did prefer you, remember? Why is it that you managed to screw that up first? Well, it was my turn to do the screwing back, dear husband!

319

This child belongs to Ross," Tara stared into his eyes, almost daring. Was she crazy? Perhaps not. What would he do with this information? Would he rant a bit? Then leave? That's always the way things happened before. He never fought back. Why did she think he would now?

Yet, her words registered into his mind like a mad poison. His blue eyes narrowed like tiny slits. There was a hard, mad grimace upon his face that looked like evil. The man stepped forward with all of his might, clasped her arms tight like a vice grip, and forced her body backwards to slam up against the nearest bare wall. Sharp pain infringed on every aspect of her upper arms. She gasped when her back hit solid against the cold wood. She stared up in shock. Danny was pissed. His eyes flashed like lightening. His voice sounded like thunder. Totally mad, he lost his senses.

"You made it with Ross? Damn it, woman! Did you not think about us or how I would feel about it! No! Why should you- when you never gave a damn! Why did I even think I could trust you again?" His grip squeezed harder. She thought her skin would slough off. It hurt like an Indian burn. Frantic, she struggled against his grip, but to no avail. He was magnificently strong. She appreciated this, oddly enough. He seemed so masculine, but when he spoke about trust, this made her declare quite a few things.

"I did care, Danny. I cared so much that I was determined to be a good Navy wife-to show that you could depend on me. Everything I ever wrote in our letters was the truth. But you ruined it for us! You slept around on me first! Not just one woman, but two!" Tara hissed in retaliation. Her words were hitting a target, "The damage was done, long before this came into being. I couldn't stand it that they knew every single detail about you as I did. That wasn't fair to me at all, when you are supposed to be my man!"

He stared into her eyes and loosened his grip, but did not let go or back away. Their bodies pressed against each other now, his face so very close. She could sense his breath, feel his warmth. This drove many other feelings into play. It was unexpected. Even if she was furious, she tingled with arousal to feel his body again. These feelings didn't register- they weren't logical. He too, stared down at her breasts, seeming bewildered, sensing his own confusion of being right on her. For just a brief moment, they looked into each other's eyes to register that connection.

'Damn it,' Tara thought in a rage, 'We won't hit the sheets anytime soon! No, not at all!' So, she pushed him off and vented her grief.

"When I went to town, I became this poor, sympathetic creature. 'Oh, poor Tara. She can't keep her man in check!' How would it make me feel? I was furious. I fought fire with fire. In my case, Ross happened to be convenient. I coerced him into it. It was stupid that I never filled my birth control prescription. We can't change any of it now! This baby is coming whether you like it or not!"

He stepped back and looked at her again, noting her stomach. In order not to hit her, he swung at the vase nearby. It crashed to the floor. Broken jagged pieces scattered everywhere.

"My new vase!" Tara cried out and pushed aside to get to the pieces. Her body trembled as she fell to both knees. "Stop it, Danny! You throw a worse tantrum than the children! Why attempt to discuss matters like a grownup? Never a man, not even when we did it the first time! So hurried! So rough! How was I supposed to enjoy that? Why shouldn't I turn to someone else if you are always running away?"

Tara clutched at the large glass pieces. With one, she cut a slice into her finger. It was accidental. There were too many pieces to pick up. With a tissue hidden inside her dress pocket, she wrapped the wound to contain the bleeding. At that point, Tara looked up. Danny glared at her. He pointed a finger into her face.

"Let me say one true thing: you forced me to preserve my own soul." His tone was full of venom. "What does it take to please you Tara? How does one learn when you only lie there without emotion, waiting for it to finish? I tell you the problem we had then was about Jimmy."

"Jimmy?" Tara gasped. He wasn't even on her mind anymore, so why was it on his, "What are you saying?"

"Whenever I tried to love you, your head would turn away. Perhaps you wished he was in my place in bed. I tried to understand, but a new husband has every right to consummate his marriage. Hell, I am the one that assumed all of his responsibility very willingly!" Danny ran a hand through his thick hair and shook his head, "I accepted you and the children, but your love is cold. No matter what I do to earn your respect."

"How can sleeping with two women be a way to earn my respect?"

"Truly, my foolishness there is a mistake, but guess what happened, dear wife? I learned from it." Danny bent down to look at Tara in the eyes. His voice was low and quivery, "Surely what I got can make you shake and moan so loud it would cause the whole house to cave in. You'll never know now-because of your damn feelings for the wrong men!"

He stood up and went to the coat rack. He grabbed his coat.

"Especially Ross! He was just a conniving worm who wanted back what I took away. He was just itching to get into your bloomer, that's all, and you fell for it."

"Yes, I fell for Ross that night. What you may offer now is too little, too late! I never felt quenched and at least Ross knew how to put out my fire! Over and over again! All through the night!" Tara cried out. It was a malicious thing to say. She knew the words were like daggers to his pride, but she wanted Danny to burn, to hurt- like she did. Surely it worked, because he was glaring in mad contempt.

"How dare you strike away with such wicked words? Don't you realize anything? What brings a man like him to slide into hissing serpents like you but foul unrequited lust? It's a disgrace and a dishonor what you two did, and I thrive by nobler qualities. I walked away from my mistake and intended never to go back there. I tried not to hurt you with it. All you can do is gloat. I won't stand for it. If that's the sort of man you desire, then go straight to hell to be with him. You can have your fire and burn into ashes that will blow away in the wind! Live with your own damn consequences! I'm out of here!"

With that, Danny slammed the door hard. All the pictures on the wall shook.

Tara looked at the jagged pieces of glass. She slumped to the floor. She never felt so wicked and weary in all of her life. Triumphant satisfaction is what she expected to feel, but instead of winning a battle, she lost a major war - her life in decay and ruin. She was bleeding. She was dying inside. This is what became of their marriage. The guilt consumed her soul. She heaved a sigh that was anchored down by shame. She drew her body up into a fetal position.

Two men hurt over stupid, foolish actions. Actions that she alone provoked. *God, why am I so stupid? Why?* She hit herself on the thigh with a fist. Ross never called, never wrote; Danny just threw away her love to the winds. After awhile, Tara rose to dispose the shards of glass into the trash can. Huge tears flowed down her pretty face.

'Danny is right. I do love all the wrong men.' she cried, but she didn't care as much right now about Jimmy, Michael, or even Ross. The man who stole her heart forever walked out the door. There were no clues how to fix her mistakes or win him back. None. This was a disaster.

Chapter Thirty Six
The intensity of snow

Danny marched down the lane next to the road. It was covered thick with snow, but even if he couldn't see the familiar dirt trail, he knew the way. He felt so angry. Surely steam rose in the air about him. Why did Tara sleep with Ross? It seemed like such a vial act that anyone ever bestowed. It made him hate and he never hated anyone before. Ross could be spit out into the wind. He'd never give a damn again. Yet, the welfare of Tara and those seven precious infants concerned him most.

Danny deeply loved them. To lose any would cut him like a knife. He felt overwhelmed by the possible consequences. He felt out of control. He wanted to hit someone and knock them senseless. As luck held out, as he proceeded around the corner, he noticed his two brothers out in the driveway. Michael pulled a box of presents out of the trunk. He slammed it down and angled the box precariously, just to show something to Sammy. *Damn, this is far too convenient!*

Danny burst forth into a full run and just before he creamed Michael into a wide bank of snow, Sammy realized what he was doing and jumped in the way to block him. They went crashing into the snow bank, rolling down the lower slope into a heap. Danny landed on top. Breathing hard, he stared into Sammy's surprised face.

"Jesus! Danny! Get off of me!" Sammy spitted out dirt and snow from his mouth.

"Sure!" Danny puffed and gave Sammy a hand up. Then he swung back with his hand and landed a perfect fist upon his younger brother's cheek. A wide eye look came across Sammy's face as he landed onto his backside. Danny pointed at him. "You should learn when not to interfere."

"What in blazes are you doing?" Michael cried out and came over to see. Danny turned and cuffed him one too. Michael fell flat onto his back, just when his sisters came running out. They came to help bring in gifts to the house.

"Stop it! Stop it!" Gloria screamed as she got to them. She yanked Danny away. "Are you crazy? Why are you hitting them? What did they do?"

"Sammy just got in my way. And you!" he pointed at Michael, "You deserved that a long time ago!"

"For what? Danny! Have you lost it?" Susan shouted and helped Michael up.

"He interfered with my marriage and when I get my hands on Ross, I'll kill him!"

"Why? What did he do?" Michael stared up. He was momentarily confused about everything. His eyes were as big as saucers. Danny spat onto the ground.

"Just know that he's toast! That bastard!" Danny's face grimaced and he took a few breaths to calm himself down again.

"Well, he's in France now, Danny! You can't touch him!" Susan scoffed and stood in an angry stance. This stunned Danny. This totally deflated his plan to find Ross and annihilate the man into a million pieces. Danny paced and then stepped out towards the road. He stared out across the fields. The sun went down some time ago. Everything was dark. He could make out the shape of the trees and the dead grass. Susan frowned. She hit Sammy on the arm.

"Do you know what's up with him? I'm always the frickin' last person to know anything! Someone tell me what's set Danny off!"

Gloria and Sammy looked at each other just as their father came out the door, hearing all the commotion. Gloria shook her head, but told Susan the truth.

"Tara's pregnant. It's Ross's baby."

Susan gasped. She clasped both hands to her head; then collapsed to her knees, which shocked everyone. Gloria assumed that she was upset for Danny. When her father reached them, Susan jumped up. She screamed into the air.

"No! No! No! Damn! Our family is cursed by that evil woman! She's ruining everything!"

"Susan, get a hold of yourself!" Sammy shouted and tried to stop her, but Susan pulled loose. She looked like a crazed woman! Susan went running into the house, saying nothing more. Sammy spat out more dirt, "Jesus! What's got into her crank?"

"Forget it! It's the first she's heard," George said. He seemed put out. "It's upsetting all the way around. Go inside now. Your mother waits for your company."

He stared out at Danny who didn't budge from where he stood. Everyone complied and went inside without any more commotion. George was undecided, but then walked out to the road to stand by his middle son. He took out his pipe, lit it, and together they watched the snow come down. They were there several moments before George spoke.

"It feels good against our skin. Sometimes we enjoy it. Other times, its freezing," he said softly as they observed the flurries build up in intensity, "A man can get lost in its white fury. Seems to lash out from nowhere, but when it's still and quiet again, we can appreciate the immense beauty and simplicity. We love it most then, naturally. Just remember for everything there's a reason. So we should respect this- especially when she falls."

Danny stared up at George then, quite out of sorts.

"I can't believe this. My life is falling apart and all you can say is something about the intensity of snow?" Danny griped, wishing his father could offer some clear instruction. He felt so depleted of direction. George's eyebrow cocked up and he placed the pipe from his mouth at arm's length.

"I was speaking of love, the love we feel for our wives. In their attempt to hurt us, they tell a truth. You just have to figure out your truth-what Tara is trying to tell you," He said and turned to go into the house.

He was at the door when he looked back to see a most puzzled expression on Danny's face. George was really upset now.

"Damn Danny, must I explain everything? You know- our wives? They can be frigid when provoked. We get lost in their fury, but when they stop long enough for us to figure them out, they are beautiful! We then realize why we love them. Trust me on this. I can't explain it adequately, but your mother can. Come on in. Its cold out here and she has eggnog waiting. We can't disappoint her on Christmas."

So Danny went inside. Helen greeted him with an embrace. They filled their cups with eggnog and went into the living room where a huge fire blazed in the fireplace. Decorations made the room pretty. Michael sat by the tree, with a nice bruise showing up on his face. He placed several gifts down around it, but kept a wary eye on Danny. Sammy stood by the fire and rubbed Susan's back. She was lost in some kind of shock and refused to speak about it. Gloria sat on the couch. She studied the look on Danny's weary face. She reached out to take his hand.

"Don't haste into divorce, Danny." Gloria pleaded. "Don't make any hasty decisions until things smooth over. Tara is just confused right now. Like you."

"No, Tara is perfectly straight. Her words were like mini daggers tonight. Practically atomic missiles! They made a cruel puncture to my heart. I am the one who has lost."

"Tara needs time to readjust. Your fooling around has left her for a loop."

"How in the hell did she find out?"

"I don't know. Honestly, she surprised me with it," Gloria admitted. This was the truth, "I'm quite sure that in spite of what you did, you remain in her deepest thoughts."

Danny didn't take kindly to this.

"Balderdash! After all of this time, after all I have given! I deserve to be in her bed. Not that man!" he didn't care if he admitted this in front of everyone, "I have been badly replaced. Tara will just deal with her abolition alone."

"You don't mean that! The child is innocent!"

"It will always be a reminder of her infidelity. I left no such thing."

Danny suffered a deep impact. There was a clear picture in his head of what happened between Tara and Ross. It left a very bitter taste in his mouth. His friends Rosemary and Eileen would never give out such details. His mother tried to reason with him next.

"You can accept this child, Danny. Accept them like the others who aren't your own."

"You know the truth? How?" Danny seemed shocked. Even Sammy and Susan turned around to listen, only learning of this now. Helen patted Danny's hand.

"It's so evident the more they grow. They never resembled any of us. Still right from the beginning, you claimed them. I believe no matter what's happened you won't let Tara go. You still love her."

"But it is not enough, Mother! Tara never has made a firm commitment to our marriage. That lack of conviction and love is what made me stray first. And that is where I really blundered in judgment! Perhaps if

I didn't go that far, she would not have either," Danny's voice was hoarse. He choked on his words.

"There, there." Helen Cross said, her eyes warm, "At least you admit your faults. Trust time to make things right again. It will happen. Now, let's not say another word about it."

At that point, Susan placed her cup down on the mantel. She ran to her room upstairs. Within the hour, everyone went upstairs to bed. The evening ended too soon. That night, Danny couldn't sleep. He tossed and turned and finally slept around one in the morning. At six thirty, he woke again. He decided to get up.

When he was a child, he couldn't wait to be the first one to the presents. This Christmas brought no joy to his heart. He was without a wife. He could lose his children. These thoughts left him miserable. He ventured out into the hallway. Down below the stairs, he saw his mother creep out of the kitchen and go into the servant's section with baby bottles. This startled him. He went down the stairs to follow.

He came into a wide open area that the staff used as a mini-break room. It contained a couch, a soft blue recliner and a table with four chairs. A console television set was in far corner. The table was pushed back. Two large playpens were in the room. Helen peaked down at one containing Tristan, Jamie, and Erik, who were awake. Erik sat up, chewing on a soft toy. He was teething again. She took one bottle to hand to him. Eric laid down, holding it in a slant.

"That's a sweetheart," Helen whispered. He looked so cute at eight months old, with cherub cheeks, a button nose, and soft wisps of brown hair that fell over his brow. Danny recognized him only because of his green sleeper, the color assigned to him. Tristan was in purple. He held out his arms to Helen. She complied to cradle him into her arms. The boy placed his head down against her shoulder. It was touching to watch and tugged on Danny's heart.

He turned to notice the playpen with the other four boys, Vince, Tyler, Matt and Edward. They were sound asleep. When Jamie saw Danny enter the room, she looked at him with wide eyes. Helen looked around to see him there, looking about curiously. She propped a pillow in the playpen and sat Tristan up next to it with his bottle.

"This room seems too small. I've spoke to George about building onto the house. I think the children need an area when they visit," Helen said. She handed Danny the bottle, "If you allow Tara and the children to remain, then it would make sense to do this."

Danny didn't know what to say. He felt delighted that the children were even there that particular morning. A nice Christmas surprise. No wonder the Briggs House was silent upon his arrival. He went to the playpen to coax Jamie into his arms. She stared at him, but didn't cry. She scooted closer where he could lift her out.

Danny sat into the recliner to be comfortable. His mother covered them up with a blanket. The tiny tot stared intently at Danny's face and then touched his nose with a free hand. He made a silly face. She giggled outrageously, dribbling formula on the side of her mouth. He wiped this off, but the fact that she felt comfortable moved him to tears. He kissed her brow.

"Oh, Mother. I can't lose them. They have been on my mind the whole time while I was away. Often, I wondered what I was missing. Would they recognize me? It's hard to be an absentee father. Last night, I stood by the road. I tried to imagine what my life would become without them. It's incomprehensible. What's worse is that I don't have a clue how to handle this situation with Tara," Danny repositioned Jamie so she was facing out from his chest, "She's expecting Ross's child. I need answers. My father is no help. He just made a nonsense comment about the snow and love; that we have to respect it, even when it falls. What the hell does that mean? He said you could say it better."

Helen sat down. There was an intense look on her face.

"Oh, your father's head remains stuck in business. He makes sense there. Once he thrived on it so much, that he neglected me and your older siblings. I married him because I loved him. Yet, he was older, with his own set of friends. I didn't think they'd have that much impact, but they did. He was with them a lot," she revealed. Her eyes seemed far away, thinking back about her life then, "I felt awkward all the time. I was this young girl, with two babies. They were all high society, with big expense accounts and foreign getaway places. I was terribly lonely."

Helen stood up to pace about. This made Danny nervous. She cried easily when something upset her. She usually paced when something unusual or upsetting was revealed to everyone else.

"We lived in a different home then, in London. I missed my old friends, from my racing days. With your father away in Scotland all the time, it was easy to escape to the racing clubhouse. I kept up with close male companions. Your Grams wasn't pleased with me at all, believe me."

"Mother! Did you have an affair?" Danny gasped and then his eyes got really big, "I am a true Cross?"

Helen patted his hand.

"You are what saved us, Danny. I told your father that he either kept his business with us or just live up in Scotland with his big wig friends. There were plenty of lady escorts around. I couldn't stand for being second. He had to make a choice. I found out about you during the course of our estrangement and yes, there were doubts about your paternity," Helen tilted her head to one side and a smile came across her face, as she studied Danny closely. He was so handsome, tucked under the blanket, with Jamie staring at her talking.

"The man I befriended at the clubhouse was an Italian, with dark eyes and olive tone skin. A beautiful man. The proof is all in your fairness. Thank goodness you came out with lots of blond hair. That was enough to convince your Father he needed to stay around Wiltshire, just to keep me at bay from others. We moved into the Briggs home and built the manor when Susan came along. It was rough going for awhile. We had our share of fights and suspicions, but that's only natural I suppose. We are happy now."

"I never knew," Danny looked at his mother carefully, thankful that she was candid. She stood up then to look over the sleeping boys.

"They'll be up in an hour or so. Like clockwork. Poor Tara's hands were full for awhile even with the servants there to help. Right after you left, she seemed so happy. Her eyes glowed whenever she spoke of you. For once, she felt like a true daughter-in-law. We were laughing and sharing things. I grew to love her as my own. I knew something was wrong before she went off to London. I could sense it. The glow was lost and she didn't eat much. It was like an ominous cloud stood above her head."

"I'm supposed to feel sympathetic, right?" Danny snubbed this train of thought but Helen shook her finger at him.

"You made that mistake first. You must consider her heart. She's just as angry with you, as you are with her now. Yet now there is more for her to contemplate than just your feelings. There's a baby involved. There is Ross too. He was her best friend. I'm sure she hurt him somehow, by what took place."

"How on earth would you know?"

"The man took off, Danny. Dropped everything, his friends, his lavish apartment, his high-in-the-sky job, which your father ensured he got. When I rejected my Italian friend, he went away and never was heard from again. Even if I bump into the same friends, they are very hush-hush about him, which makes me sad. He was just a friend. Tara will anguish over this decision forever. She grew up with Ross. Just remember that when you cut her down with your tongue."

Danny nodded with a solemn face. He tried to put himself in Ross's shoes. Obviously, Ross didn't win the girl. She came home to the Briggs House. That should count for something. Helen went to the door to turn down the lights.

"I'll be back in an hour to help with the children. Lila and Marta have offered to be with us this morning, to help. They spent Christmas Eve with their families," She told him and then looked at the room again, "I still want to enlarge the house."

"You make your plans, Mother. I'll figure something out," Danny agreed. This made Helen smile. She left them alone as they napped. About two hours later, she went to the dining hall table. Her other children sat there drinking coffee. Sammy toyed with a stuff animal. Susan looked angry. Michael had quite a shiner. Gloria's eyes seemed far away.

"We will have our breakfast and open presents around 10:00. I want to let you know that I've called Tara to come down," she announced.

"What? Mother, why?" Susan cried out but Helen glared.

"It's Christmas morning. My grandchildren need both parents here. We will all be on our very best behavior. Let them work out their own discord. Stay the hell out of it. Am I clear on this?"

They grumbled but nodded. Haskell was outside, waiting by the car. Helen opened up the back door and waved at him. In minutes, he was driving down towards the Briggs House to pick up Tara.

Later everyone came down to the living room area after eating breakfast. They all helped feed the children, who were awake and playful. Surprisingly they enjoyed time with them. The only one not so cooperative was Susan, but they expected that. The children were placed into a playpen near the tree, which was moved from the servants' quarters. They were all dressed up in fine

Christmas attire. Gloria wanted to take their pictures. With definite personality traits and looks, it was easier telling them apart. Finally, the time came to open up presents, but even Danny didn't think it was right to participate without their mother.

"It's their first Christmas with us. Perhaps Sammy could go fetch her. I could leave or go upstairs," he offered but felt torn about doing either. He wanted to watch too. Before he could say anything further, Tara stepped inside the room with Haskel. Susan gasped but bit her tongue. Everyone stared at Tara. Clearly, she was uncomfortable to be there, but she was proud. She kept her feelings contained. The children reacted to see their mother.

"Ma-ma!" Some said. Most held out their arms for her attention.

"I'll try to stay out of the way," Tara said in a meek voice. She made way to them.

"Oh, you look so cute! What darling outfits!" she exclaimed, picking up two of her children, "Thank you, Helen. They look perfect."

Helen smiled. Tara tried to avoid Danny's eyes, but he stood next to his mother. He didn't seem too upset that she was there. He even smiled when she kissed Edward's brow and allowed him to go down her leg like a slide. He whined to do it again. Gloria reacted to occupy the boy.

"Oh, you silly little monkey. Stop your belly aching. You were doing just fine a moment ago," She chastised, getting Edwards attention by snapping the flash bulb on her camera. He liked the bright lights. She scooped him up to place him center of the area. George handed him a present. Gloria poised him, then stepped back with the camera to her eye, "King Edward, you be the first. Smile! Let me take your picture."

A natural ham, Edward clapped his hands and then made the silliest face at everyone. Then he blew bubbles with his lips locked in a tight oval shape. Everyone laughed. Gloria looked at Tara to offer an encouraging wink. Between all of the adults, they poised the children around the presents, the tree, and watched them tear into the gifts.

Somehow, they all managed to be civil. Marta took Gloria's camera.

"You need a family picture. Everyone - gather together," she instructed. Tara sat on the floor with her babies, while Lila clapped hands to get the children's attention towards the camera.

"Why don't you scoot down next to Tara, so it looks like you are together," Marta suggested to Danny. It was on purpose. He wasn't so sure, but his mother nodded. "Go on," she mouthed. Danny positioned himself near, kneeling close, with a hand placed upon her shoulder. Everyone crowded close. It made for a nice photo shot, but obviously to touch each other made a great impact on the pair. They rose and stared at each other, but said nothing further. Words were in the way. There were things to say in private. At the same time, they couldn't bear being with or without one another.

At that point, Lila and Marta helped clear up the room of all of the torn Christmas wrapping. Sammy, Michael and Danny took the babies into another play area. Tara went to the hall to get her coat. She passed by Susan who glared. This wasn't a time to bicker. All Tara wanted to do was escape. Helen was surprised that she was leaving. She confronted her at the door.

"We will have lunch soon, a huge ham. You will stay?"

"No, Helen. I can't. I'm grateful that I saw the children open up their presents. That was a blessing, but you must share the rest of your day with the family, without me."

"You are still a part of mine, Tara. You don't have to rush off," Helen said and touched Tara's hand. Now, heavy tears streamed down Tara's face. Helen offered her a tissue.

"This is too hard, Helen. I can't breath. I have a lump in my throat. My heart aches -being around him."

Helen embraced her and then tenderly smoothed away Tara's bangs that fell forward. Long pretty curls angled her face. Obviously, she made an effort that morning to look good.

"Is it hurt that keeps you from staying?" Helen asked and Tara shook her head.

"Oh, no. I deserve the hurt. I just can't stand it that I can't touch him. Before my mistake-with Ross- I had looked forward to his homecoming. Everything is ruined between us. There is only disappointment in his eyes. I'm a failure," Tara cried unashamedly and sniffed loudly. She grasped Helen's hands for composure, "I can't take it. I still love him so much in spite of what he did, but he will never get over this. Please-just bring the children home whenever Danny leaves. Let them have this time together. That's my present to him. I must leave!"

Tara rushed out the front door and ran down the driveway to get to the road. Her legs stumbled along as tears blinded her eyes. Miraculously, she let out a new burst of speed, her goal to reach the dividing fence line that separated the manor from the field next door. Her beating heart thundered within her head and she thought that she heard Danny call out her name. How could she look back to be sure- because if wrong and deeply disappointed- her anguish would consume her overall? Just then, the snow fell again, hard with strong flurries, and it didn't stop for three days.

Chapter Thirty Seven
In the darkest hours

It soon came time for Danny to leave again. He awoke very early that morning to eat breakfast with the children. They sat in high chairs in the servants' quarters. They offered bits of cereal; shared their toast and juice bottles. Each child giggled as he pretended to gobble the gifts from their tiny, soft fingers. *This man was funny*! Their over-bubbling, joyful laughs came deep from their bellies and stirred his heart.

In just a few short days spending one-on-one time, he learned plenty: their preferences and the way they interacted. Tyler liked blankets, lots of them when he slept, where Edward seemed hot natured, in temperament and temperature. Jamie slept on her back, loved cookies, and listened attentively whenever he hummed. She tried it too which astounded him. Tristan although shy, liked being held. Eric babbled all of the time. Vincent didn't like juice; Matthew always smiled. He made silly faces a lot. These things became implanted into his memory forever.

"They are beautiful. I'll truly miss each one this time," he said to Marta and Lila as he stood to leave, "Please watch over my little crew. I must run upstairs to dress now. Goodbye ladies."

The servants nodded. He kissed each child on their brows. Danny went to the door, looking back once. His eyes seemed misty, but he darted out quickly before losing composure. Outside the door, he paused to close his eyes. Such pain in his heart. How many times could he endure going away, leaving them all behind? At this point, he ran upstairs.

"Blimy! I could almost cry. He's a damn good father," Lila remarked and gathered up a purse as Caroline walked through the side door to get her. The car was outside running. Marta took out her handkerchief to sniff into it.

"I am crying. Who knows when he'll return? I heard him say to his mother that he'll take on more work. Mr. Cross doesn't want to be anywhere around while Tara has Ross's baby," she told them. How did things come to such a mess? Danny and Tara were sweet people. Marta loved them both; like her own, in spite of their status. There were awful circumstances to provoke each. Marta shook her head, "I don't know how Tara will fix things now, but I'm going to pray. She needs him, and so do those babies. He needs them. You could tell that the whole time he was home."

"No truer statement was ever said," Lila nodded and the ladies sadly went about their duties.

In the meanwhile, Michael drove down to the Briggs House, his mind whirling over recent events. He felt too chicken to have a brotherly one-to-one discussion with Danny while he visited, especially after being attacked in the driveway. The sucker punch made a dark bruise to his face. It still hurt. Ever since then, he only heard brief snippets with the words divorce. He did realize both his mother and Gloria worked diligently to convince Danny otherwise. He just didn't know if it worked.

Michael focused on his own motivations. What if divorce sent Tara far away, even back to the states? How deplorable this would make things? Michael still felt very fond of that petite woman. Danny forced him to speak cruelly at the hospital just to uphold a promise. It killed him to do so. If things never progresses smoothly for the couple, then why should he uphold his word any longer? Nevertheless, he still couldn't offer an easy resolution, not when she carried another man's child. Michael deemed himself a coward. He could never accept any responsibility of the children. Still, he must say something. So meagerly, there he stood knocking upon her door, wringing his hands.

"Hello Michael," Tara wrapped a tight string belt around the long fleece robe to keep warm. She allowed the man to come into the house. She wondered why he came over, but only focused on the day, "Are you taking Danny to the airport? I know that Sammy is leaving tomorrow."

How uncanny her perception sometimes.

"Yes, unfortunately, I am. He gave me this shiner the other night," He told her, leaning forward to show off the dark bruise.

"Oh, I wondered how you got that. Why did he hit you?"

"Let's just say this: It was a way to release immediate anger. An easy mark. This isn't a good situation, Tara. Talk to Danny before he goes off to sea on a new mission. Give the man a reason to hold on to you -your marriage!" Michael pleaded.

"Michael, I can't!" Tara said, surprised that he begged her to do this. She felt too proud, too ashamed. Surely, she would wind up in hell for her sins. Tara showed off the shape of her round belly underneath the robe. "How can he ever forgive this? No, perhaps Danny is best without me. All I do is cause the man foul distress. There are other women who can soothe away his worries, better than I. They have already proven that."

Fat tears trickled down her face. Michael hovered closer. He wanted to take her into his arms, to smooth away her hurt. He stuck to business instead.

"You are merely upset, Tara. It's understandable, but things can be salvaged. Apologize for your mistakes. Let him do the same. Help drive away the demons that plague you both. You must think about stability upon our estate. Think about your new child. Think about all of your children!"

"It's them that bring the most heartache. I hate to uproot them, but if he forces me to go, then I must."

Michael wanted to ease her worry.

"I haven't heard a word about it. Maybe he's decided against divorce right now. After all, it was Christmas and there's been too much damn snow. I know that he's been playing with the children daily. That might have helped. So if you say something, maybe by now there will be an impact." Michael explained. He looked into her eyes, "There is some ceremonial tribute for a commander stepping down at headquarters. Danny got a call about it. He must participate before departing for the airport. So there's still time to act."

"Let's not hold our breath, Michael. It's too late at this point. Really, the whole discussion upsets me. Thanks for stopping by to share your feelings," She scooted the man towards the door. Michael stared down at her. Her eyes were deep pools he wanted to drown into forever, but she didn't look upon him the same way. What happened between them in the spring seemed buried in her mind. At least he spoke his peace, like a true brother-in-law should do upon their behalf. This was honorable, perhaps enough to allow her to respect him again. For now, this should do.

Michael returned to the car and drove away. Tara watched the white swirls fly in the air from the snowy road. The snow had fallen heavy that morning, so much so that there were lots on the roadway and along the slopes of the ditches. How he made it down was a miracle.

Tara went to sit down in a brown chair close to the fire, with a brown leather journal by her side. A gift from Gloria. A Christmas present. Haskel brought her gifts over the following morning since she did not stay for Christmas lunch. It was tradition for the adults to exchange gifts after their meal. The morning was for the children. Danny and Tara were the only ones with children. In Helen's eyes, this made Christmas last longer.

The journal was one of eight received. Another gift came from George and Helen -piano books, contemporary music. Tara didn't know when she would play the piano again. There was an upright piano in her own library room, pushed against the wall since no one played it. It wasn't as expensive as Helen's, still the desire to play was nil. Music reminded her of Danny and Ross. It reminded her of their days in New York City. Their friendship was in ruin because of her. With this discord, she couldn't bear thinking about music again.

When she received them, Tara absentmindedly flipped through the pages. There were plenty of music scores from motion pictures, love songs of the 70's. The decade was slipping away. It was a decade of change for everyone, including herself, 'My baby will arrive in 1979,' she thought. It seemed amazing. That morning, she tucked the book into the piano bench, and then opened up Gloria's present next.

The gesture of the journal made her cry. She plopped onto the bench. Hard tears engulfed her. Danny knew about her blue diary, the one stored up in the attic, which he brought down when the children were named. Perhaps at some point before he came home, way before he learned the truth about Ross, he mentioned to Gloria how she liked to write down her deepest thoughts. Leave it to that man to suggest a gift that would touch her heart. With sadness enveloping her feelings, she couldn't open up the rest. She didn't even look to see if there was one from him. Most likely not. Tara merely placed everything into the closet to open far later when she felt better.

Now, an hour after Michael left, Tara sat thumbing through the bare pages. She grabbed a pen and looked around. Lila and Caroline came that morning to prepare the house for the children's return. They were upstairs, stripping down bedding and wiping toys down with disinfectant. The sun's warm rays melted some of the icicles outside. One lone bird appeared from out of a barn. It chirped merrily out the window. It sat precariously on a thin limb. Tara sat Indian style on the easy chair. Her mind whirled in circles. She wrote:

Why is everything such a struggle for us? Every step forward I take, there are many steps back. Why did I agree to marry Danny and come to England? A gun was not pointed at my head. I could have said no, but I didn't. I allowed myself to be his wife. I kept none of my vows. He kept every promise, except for one, to remain faithful. He failed at only this. Why? He's obviously very human, very fallible. I perceived him as such, in bed. He never learned what it took to make me burn with desire, except when he sent those letters. Within them, he bared his soul, his dreams- such torrid aspirations. Through them, our hearts became one. We were suddenly on fire. Now, it's lost. I want his soul back again.

Sure, our physical intimacy was dull; carved in stone ever since our awkward wedding night. What else to expect when I kept turning him away? It's natural for a warm man to seek out a soft touch, a gentle look, a kind voice. I only gave this once. On the stairs. How pathetic! I must forgive him, for he is a man- a creature that's discovered the taste for sex, and must tame away desire. It's something one can't do without, like air, water, love. He must quench the endless thirst; feed the bottomless ache; fulfill the need to connect with another warm being. I understand. I did that too.

I could have demonstrated what it took to be satisfied, except I didn't know it, until I turned to Ross. With my friend, I felt electricity, an endless volcano heat, and insatiable need- a release like shooting fireworks, burning madly in the night. I think I felt it because I was too comfortable with Ross-never afraid. We are always connected by some cosmic force that can't be adequately explained. Yet I do not love him like that. I want love with my husband. I want to be comfortable in his arms. I want never to be afraid of his love. But perhaps, it's too late for us. This is all so sad. So terribly, terribly sad. No wonder the village women find me pathetic.

I could never take care of any child properly on my own. The situation remains the same, with this child I carry. His father is long gone. He probably hates me. Really, really bad. My best friend, who I've hurt. Who I still need in my life. Must I choose one man over the other? Doesn't matter. My husband is leaving. My respectable, supportive gentleman. One who accepted me as I am – once- with all of my flaws. Until I crushed him down for what I did that night. His soul died. He'll never trust me again. So I'm alone. It's a worse sentence than death.

Tara buried her head into her hands. Pride broke down. She sobbed. '*I must stop being so pathetic- such selfishness. I should stand before my husband to beg on my knees for his forgiveness. I should plead for absolution. These children need a family to help them. They need their father!*' She needed to salvage this marriage before Danny tossed it away to the wind. Michael was right.

Precious time wasted away. Tara sprang from the chair. She ran upstairs to tell the staff of her departure.

It was awkward making steady progress up the snowy road. It was thick, slushy, and her boots stuck in the white piles, making her tired. Pregnant, bundled up from head to toe in a thick coat, scarf and gloves, she tried to speed up. Everywhere, there were fresh snow drifts along the ditches. They hid her approach to the manor. Finally, she arrived to the far edge of the property. She stopped to catch her breath. Panting and puffing-there was a sharp pain in her side.

At the manor, someone stepped outside, dressed in a dark uniform. He paused momentarily to adjust a pair of gloves. The sun shone brightly upon him. He squinted at the sky. A brisk breeze blew wisps of blond hair in all directions. Was this Sammy? Was it Danny? Tara stared to make out a face. It was then when recognition took place. Her heart pounded like mad. It was Danny. She never saw him before in uniform. He looked absolutely spectacular. So tall. Drop dead handsome.

He placed on a regal hat. Something very magical took hold, some sense of great pride about the overall transformation. Even the medals on his jacket shone out like lasers underneath the sun. A true military gentleman, so proud of his profession, and he looked every bit the part. It took her breath away.

"That's my husband." She whispered. "My husband!"

At that moment, Michael came out from the house. The two men rushed to the car. Tara struggled to move forward. She must reach the drive in time. The car backed up too quickly, and then accelerated up the road. Oh why must Michael drive like a bat out of hell?

"Danny! Wait! Wait!" Tara called out, but to no avail. The car turned around a bend. It disappeared from view. Tara stood there. She pouted. She huffed. Steam rose into the air, escaping from her nose and mouth. What awful timing? What dismay? She looked straight to the sky and then dropped to her knees. The snow penetrated her pants. It was cold and wet. A few flakes fell from the overloaded trees. Tara squeezed eyes tight to pray- to vent, to argue-with the man upstairs:

"Please, God! Help me! This is so insane. I can't get things right. There must be a purpose for the children and for us not getting along. For me stabbing my best friend in the back and to carry his child. I need answers. I need to know your plans. Surely there is one for all this. I promise to stop screwing things up. One day, you'll reveal what you want from me. I'll trust you. I'll do whatever it is. For now, please know that I love Danny. Just bring him back in my life. Let him stay this time. He's the man of my dreams!"

She believed in God, so surely he must hear her prayers. In her heart, a desperate fire rose to set things straight. The sun slipped out from a passing cloud. The rays shone in her eyes. In between the trees, it skewed. It looked like a cross. Were her eyes playing tricks? Surely, this must be a sign. She believed in signs, premonitions, and intuitions. She dreamt about the man in blue. That morning, her shiny knight stepped out of hiding. Why did it take so long? Now she must hope. Hope and pray for a reunion- a chance to set things right again.

After that day, life trickled back to normal. Through Helen, Tara learned that Danny committed to stay on his mission for at least six months. She couldn't believe it. That seemed too long, but perhaps it was best. She could concentrate on her children. She could concentrate on having Ross's baby. The months crept along slowly as her pregnancy bloomed. Helen still dropped by often. She didn't treat Tara badly at all. She was very supportive, but Tara never could figure out why. The doctor stopped by to offer medication for the nausea. Now, Tara felt better.

By the end of March, Helen was sad, but found comfort visiting the grandchildren. For the exception of Michael, most of her children were out of the country. Sammy's fleet sailed up to Scotland for four months. Gloria's studio became prosperous. She hired a manager to run the place. It gave her time to freelance for various magazine companies. She traveled frequently and was now in Germany.

Thanks to an amazing portfolio created for her sister, Susan's face became a frequent cover on popular fashion magazines. She stayed knee deep in publicity shoots. In April, Susan snagged a high profile invitation to a fashion designer's birthday celebration in Paris. The ten stories building seemed trendy, with bars and dance floors on three different levels. The party was held upstairs with the elite and well known. After awhile, Susan became bored mingling with that high-society crowd. She grew weary listening to minimalist music- a new fad-which to her was dull.

So, she stumbled down the basement to check out the lower dance section. It hummed with average patrons. The floor, with bright lights over head, rocked with punk music. She strutted to the dance floor to intermingle with the dancers. No one cared. Everyone was out for a good time. Just as she turned around in a spin, she spied Ross over by the bar.

She stopped, startled by his appearance. The bartender yelled loudly. Ross fumbled into his wallet. Did he need money to pay for his purchase? Susan stared closer. His clothes, wrinkled and disarrayed, made him appear unkempt. Even his face was covered in heavy whiskers. It was over six months since they last saw one another. Never known to resist an opportunity, she went over to the bartender. Rudely, she threw the man plenty of cash.

"Leave him alone, will you? He's covered!" Susan snapped. The bartender backed away, satisfied with the money in his hand. He went on about his business. Susan sat on the barstool next to Ross, "Man, you are a mess!"

There was an odor about him, one that made her cringe.

"Did you ever hear about soap and water? It's a new fashion statement. Most folks use it," she teased. He looked at her with narrow slit eyes. Did he even recognize her? His body swayed. He took down the drink.

"Thank you," he slurred and then his head bobbed to his chest. Susan wrestled to get Ross to stand up. His weight was heavy, but he could still walk.

"Eeww, Jesus! You reek! I'm taking you with me. You don't need to stick around this dump anymore."

She whisked him out of the club. Three hours later, in a dark bedroom, she stretched out her back. With a thin sheet, she covered the nude man. With soapy washcloths and perfumed soap, she cleaned him up.

The pan of water was disposed in the bathtub. Wiping her hands clean, she stared back into the bedroom, "That should get you by until the morning, my friend."

She turned off the bathroom light and then curled up into a chair nearby, thinking everything through. Lighting up a cigarette, it glowed in the dark. Long trails of smoke drifted in the still room. Susan felt satisfied with herself. She even smiled. Nothing would hurt that man again, not if she could help it. Even if what he did was stupid, she could forgive him. There were feelings he left behind that she couldn't comprehend. Feelings that stirred up too many emotions. She liked his personality. She loved his easy-going manner. When he was on top of the world, he shined. He was so brilliant. Sexy. She loved him now, even in his darkest hours.

She took a long drag and then deposited the cigarette into the ashtray, squishing it firmly to ensure it went out. Then she drew a blanket from the bed. She closed her eyes to snuggled into it, and not against the man she so desired. There would be another time, a better place. She must be patient. And hope like hell that Tara would not interfere with her plans again.

Chapter Thirty Eight

Lost in Paris

The very next morning, about 11:00 o'clock, Ross woke up alone in that strange room.

"Where am I?" he groaned and held his head against his hand. A sharp pain pounded his brain. On the night stand, there was a bottle of aspirin and a soft drink. He gulped down four aspirin. At that point, he looked around with eyes squinting.

He noted it was someone's fancy apartment, for it was clean and furnished nicely. How he got there, he had no clue. With a wrapped sheet around his waist, Ross ambled towards the balcony door, if for nothing else but to get his bearings. From a distance, the Eiffel tower stood near, perhaps six to seven blocks away.

"Hmm, this is about ten miles from the bar," he mused out loud, "How in the hell did I get here, unless by a car. I sure wouldn't walk."

Next, he went to the kitchen. A coffee pot was already set up with aromatic ground coffee beans and water. Tape to the side of the handle, a note read: "Turn me on, darling. When you're ready." The handwriting was vaguely familiar. Then he went to check out the refrigerator. A wrapped up egg and ham croissant sat on a plate, along with bagels, cream cheese, and fresh fruit. Another note read, "Eat me"

"Hmm, someone's going out of their way for me," he thought while popping the croissant into the microwave and the bagel into the toaster. He ate some fruit while he waited for both to heat up. Afterwards, a thorough investigation of the place turned up no identifying clues about his savior. His clothes were gone too, so he searched the bedroom closet, but only found female clothing.

"Nice," Ross whistled as he touched the delicate lace upon skimpy red lingerie. He noted high heel shoes on the floor that would look spectacular to wear with it. There was nothing for a man, so now he wondered what he would do. He was naked. Either someone threw out his old smelly clothes or he was the butt of a bad prank.

Ambling back to the bathroom, he finally saw something hanging on the other side of the shower door. It was an Armani suit, along with matching socks, a dark shirt, ribbed t-shirt and fresh boxers to finish out the ensemble. Another note was taped next to a $1250 sale price tag on the outer plastic bag. It read: "Take a shower. You need one. Use the shaving cream and shaver in there. Get dressed. Meet me at 2:00 in the plaza below. I'll buy your lunch."

Ross scratched his head. "Wow, what a suit!" he thought and placed the hanger behind the bathroom door. Then he stepped into the shower. By the time 2:00 rolled around, he was fully dressed. He checked himself out by the mirror before he went out the door. "I look hot, if I say so myself," he winked before dashing out the apartment.

There were a few patrons sitting around at the outside café. Ross only ordered water since he had no money. Around 2:10, he noted a pretty blond coming his way, wearing a short black skirt, high black boots, and a tight white shirt and black blazer. That sassy look along with a pouting smile, hidden behind the fancy dark glasses, he recognized right away.

"Hi there, dark and handsome stranger," Susan cocked her hips to one side with arms folded, "Remember me? We had a long fling in London."

He smiled to see her again. Susan sat down, placing a napkin on her lap. The waiter came over.

"We'll have the special. No alcohol today. I'll have water too," she remarked, looking at Ross directly. He smirked but didn't argue. The waiter nodded and walked away.

"You are the one paying," He said, but took her hand, "This suit makes me look grand. Your generosity is surprising and I appreciate it. I just figured after the way I treated you in London, you would be kicking my ass."

"I should, but I always liked dressing you up," She took off her glasses, squeezing his hand in return. There was something more important to discuss than her feelings.

She wanted to know more of his current status, "You were a mess last night, Ross. Are you broke?"

"How can you tell?" he replied sarcastically, but she deserved a better reply after their long off and on relationship, "Of course, I'm broke."

"What happened?"

He was embarrassed to admit it, but plunged ahead anyway. They never kept secrets from each other. What did he have to lose admitting the truth?

"I lost my job, Susan. I wanted to succeed without George's backing. It was an illusion. Your father's smart. In a matter of days, everyone knew about my disregard for his kindness. I'm afraid that everything is lost. No one important wants to hire me, and so recently, I've turned into a bum. This suit looks great, but it's not me anymore. I'm simply not the man you knew."

He looked sad. This only made her disagree.

"The hell you aren't. I still believe in you, even if your world has bottomed out. It's hard to keep a good man down. It's just this place. It's lovely, but it's hard to survive without friends. You need to go home, to London. I'm here for another six weeks on a shoot, and then I'll be back. "

"That's good in theory, but…"

"No, buts. Take this money," she shoved him a wad of bills, "Don't get drunk on it. Just go back to London to look up Michael. He'll help you out. There are connections that don't have anything to do with my father. Upon my return, I'll rent out a private apartment. We can see each other whenever we want."

"Ah, Susan, not if we can't be more than just friends," he began and then shook his head, "God, what am I saying? I've really screwed things up. There's no way your family will ever accept me if I wanted to marry you. Not with what I've done to Danny."

He didn't know half of it yet. Not one clue about Tara's pregnancy. Even if it killed her, Susan must do the right thing by Ross.

"Ross, marriage is overrated. Friends last longer these days. Trust me on that. Go home. Look up Michael. Do it for me, please? It's important you make a new life there."

"All right, Susan. I promise. Maybe in a day or two. Whenever you're through with your boy-toy," he kidded and drank his water. He seemed lost in thought, "Although the words out. I'm just a rotten scumbag who screws over true friends. I'd be careful."

The waiter brought over her drink, along with appetizers. Susan squeezed lemon into her water. Her nose crinkled to hear him say that.

"You are a man with class, Ross. So, you messed up, big time. There were reasons behind it. Tara provoked you into what happened. I overheard enough conversation at home to know this. She was pissed at Danny for what he did. You always cared about her, so she trumped your ace. You can bounce back from this. Give it time."

"Yeah, I did get lost in the moment. Our behavior was very wrong. Mine more than hers. How could I be so disloyal to your brother?"

"Danny is a reasonable man. Once he's over his anger, he'll realize this mistake was not all one sided. His heart is big. Too big sometimes. He'll forgive you one day."

"You think so? Danny opened up my life to many opportunities. Yet I sucked in Michael's lifestyle like a bottom feeding fish. I thought I could be a big shot too. Just because Danny is out of the country did not delegate permission to sleep with his wife. You're right. I must go back to face the music. Music! *Oh, God*! I must face Danny again!"

He seemed somewhat overwhelmed by what he said. He clutched his head. The name of the Almighty came out loud enough for others to look over. Susan noticed. She noted too how he seemed crazed. Calmly, she dipped a shrimp into the cocktail sauce, ate it and then leaned back in the chair.

"You and my brother were very close once. Not so much now because there's been too much conflict with Tara and the Navy a lot. Can you talk about that, what took place in New York? We never discussed it before," she was determined to get to the truth of it, "Something must have happened. He paid for your way over. It couldn't all be just for Tara's sake. It always left me puzzled why. Not that I don't appreciate it now. Otherwise, we'd never met."

Ross studied her lovely blue eyes. She looked curious, sincerely interested, so he leaned over too. Thank goodness it was easy talking things over, because there was something he wanted to tell her- a rare closeness. It was unprecedented.

"It's what I said-'facing the music'- it strikes me hard. Music was a passion shared like nothing else, except for my friendship with Tara," He said mysteriously. A light shone in his eyes that surprised Susan. The words that came out next were almost hinting on erotic.

"We shared a great time *grinding* out ideas. We drank, talked, and stayed up until 2:00 or 3:00 in the morning, (much to Tara's annoyance then), with our stacks of blank sheet music, sharpened pencils, cold beer, thick pizza and tuned guitars. There were a lot of thought processes going on between us. Sometimes we argued, other times we laughed. We pushed ourselves to the *extreme. All this surging, purging, mad creative energy.* We build up the perfect Frankenstein, only it was our music. What could be better than that?"

The waiter interrupted with their entrees. Ross took a few bites and then a smirk came across his face.

"For those special moments, when a masterful, well crafted song came to life, all that was missing were cigarettes. Too bad neither of us smoked or it would have made a great ambiance. Let me be frank, Susan. I never felt so close to any *man* before in my life. Believe me, its very weird to say out loud."

He looked around, wondering if anyone overhead. Ross wanted to explain it right.

"It's just all that energy in one place seemed out of this world- all the soulful words, the terrific melodies he produced out of thin air! There's a side of your brother that really shines- one that is smart, brilliant, and outstanding. The man has a keen sense for producing catchy tunes, producing great ideas for songs. He just couldn't get his words quite right. That's why he depended on me."

Susan never heard Ross speak so candid; so much unearthed excitement. It was like he was in another world.

"When we came to England, this passion regressed. He stayed busy with the Navy, the problems involving Tara. I was hung up on Michael's feedback to reinvent me, moving to London to begin a new career. Something happened, before I spiraled out of control. Danny wrote some arrangements when he first arrived to the Falklands. When I opened up the box, I stood there in shock. I couldn't breathe. My heart pumped madly and my skin was all goose-pimples. My senses were heightened like I just had great sex!"

Indeed, Susan thought he looked aroused now. There was a look, *some crazy look*, which made him seem outrageous. His eyes were wide-eyed dark saucers. Ross took a long drink of water. Perhaps to calm down his racing thoughts.

"I couldn't wait to tackle it. I spent a whole week writing lyrics down, re-arranging his compositions to fit the rhymes. Restructuring the bridges, working up the choruses. Then I rushed like mad to mail it out. I don't know if Danny's even looked at it. What does that matter now? He's pissed at me. I stepped over the line at something else he loves, so how can he forgive enough to regain the other? Does that make any sense to you?"

Susan nodded. So lost she was in his story that she wasn't even aware that she finished her entrée. Ross slumped into his chair, thinking seriously about everything.

"It will mean the world if he does give me another chance. We could start over and dive into what we worked on so hard back then. So, yeah, I must return to find out this fate. Even if he must beat me into a pulp first, for my affair with his wife. It will be worth it. I will take it like a man if only to continue with our music. It's odd, but that's how I feel. That's the truth of our friendship."

"I never realized. It's crazy, but I understand," Susan blinked her eyes and then took his hand, "Danny always loved music. My mother threatened him several times to turn the radio down when he was younger. He was always tapping his fingers, bobbing his head to something floating in his mind. He was in another dimension. I guess that's another reason why girls thought he was weird. When Tara came along, he actually stayed out of that dreamland long enough to concentrate on his love life."

Susan coughed. Ironically, she reached for a cigarette and lit it up. The cloud of smoke was interjected into the air by thin, ruby lips.

"Pffft! We all know how much concentration that took!" Susan laughed, "My poor brother has never been in any relationship that brought him good luck. They were all disasters. I don't know why he thought by marrying the girl, it would turn out any better."

Ross looked down at his food. With a fork, he toyed with the salad. In a weird way, he loved Susan. He loved Tara and Gloria. There was love in his heart for even Danny. He just wanted things the way they were before stupidity blasted away their friendship.

"Well, maybe his luck will change. All I know is that before I was with Tara, for a very short time, he was happy. When he was happy, he produced that box full of impressive licks. The tunes were phenomenal. Magic. They could prove to be timeless. I hope he gets peace of mind in his relationship with Tara. I want them to be happy. Then we can be friends again. That would be extraordinary."

"I can appreciate that you want to work together again. For your sake, I hope it turns around. Just wait patiently."

She never knew such things about her brother, but she could recall when the pair sang their song on the first day home to the Grand Manor. It seemed eons ago, but that tune knocked them all away. Yet to speak about Danny this way was completely new. Maybe one day, Danny could forgive Ross, but with the baby coming, Susan was not so sure. She couldn't tell him about it. That was for someone else to do. Perhaps Michael or even Tara. All she wanted to do was send him home.

They finished their lunch and then went sight seeing together afterwards. Paris, a city known for romance, cast a friendly spell over their afternoon walk-a-about. Later, they came back to the apartment for supper. That night, they made love. Then in the morning, Ross went to the bus station in a pair of new jeans, a dressy blue shirt, and dark shoes, items she bought on their shopping spree. All his other belongings were stuffed neatly in a duffel bag, even the $1250 suit. She trusted that he would take it to a dry cleaner at some point. He climbed the bus and waved goodbye to her through the window.

Chapter Thirty-Nine

A world away from Wiltshire

Meanwhile, in London, Michael's days endured the busy theatrical season. In his mail, he checked out all the invitations to different plays and cast parties. His life was a world away from his family in Wiltshire and frankly, he preferred it that way. Demanding directors, bossy producers, giggling actresses, and temperamental actors. Whose life could be more remarkable than this?

He paused at his breakfast table to look over a postcard that Sammy sent from Scotland. "If I wasn't stuck on board, I'd go fishing," Sammy lamented in one line. Sammy loved to fish and he loved water, which was one reason he joined the navy, to be out on the sea. The card showed one of the best coves known for fishing. He thought it was good that Susan and Sammy were away because of their careers. Lately, when he went home, he was surrounded by gossip, given freely by the three remaining women around, Tara, Gloria, and his mother. Yet, it was hard to ignore the hot topic among them. '*Danny.*'

He discussed this with Gloria once when he stopped for a visit, after he realized she knew plenty about his affection for Tara. They could talk about the couple honestly, "I'm sorry, sister, but I feel sad for Danny. He doesn't get it. The Navy interferes with his marriage."

"He loves the navy," Gloria pouted. They were in the stables then, feeding the horses, far away from anyone overhearing them, "He can't help it that his nose remains grounded in Allied/Nato activities. It's what he does for a living. There's nothing wrong with that."

"I'm not saying there is," Michael placed the empty bucket onto a shelf nearby. He stood to look Gloria straight in the eyes, "Yes, it's an honorable profession, but it doesn't work for him. Tara needs a man's constant attention."

"Constant?" she scoffed, her nose wrinkled. "I don't understand."

"Yes, constant. Everyday. Every minute. Their marriage will never straighten out unless Danny realizes this. Perhaps that is why she turned to me in the first place, and then to Ross. We talk to her. We look into her eyes. We try to figure out what makes her tick. It's a wonderful diversion. She is a woman who relishes being the center of one's world. Whenever I saw her before, I couldn't help the temptation. She transformed, into this invigorating persona who captured me whole. Whenever she gazed at me with those eyes, I was hypnotized. It's the kind of look that pierces one soul. I know you can't understand it, but it's the truth. I simply never got over that feeling."

"Well, it's best you find a way to get over it, Michael. She is Danny's wife not yours," Gloria scolded, "You and Ross both stepped out line. He more so than you. I sure hope that Danny manages to forgive him as he has you. I think you were lucky."

He watched her storm out of the stable. At least the air was clear between them. He was glad to tell her the truth. As for Ross, he couldn't be mad for what happened with Tara. In fact, in many ways, he was envious. What would it be like too sleep with such a lovely woman? For awhile, she possessed a nice shape, curvaceous hips and a full bosom. Michael couldn't help but feel tempted, but he knew now to let sleeping dogs lie. At least until a new opportunity presented itself. If Danny kept screwing up, surely it would.

Michael considered Ross like a protégé. To see him fail was ghastly. So when Ross showed up on his doorstep later that evening, out of the clear blue, Michael knew he must offer Ross a clean slate. Heavily inebriated, Ross stepped into the apartment only to pass out cold on the living room floor. Michael covered him up with a blanket for the night. The next morning, he gave the man reason to clean up his act.

"You think it's a boy?" Ross felt dazed when Michael told him everything. Was he dizzy from the hangover or was it from excitement? The room was spinning. The bright lights from the open window shone into his eyes. Michael looked like an angel. Was it a message from God? Now there existed a child. A child by the only woman he ever truly loved in his lifetime. Their bond would remain sealed forever in spite of their mistakes.

"There is no doubt at all." Michael conveyed, "Mother told me that the doctor sent her over for an ultrasound. She was extremely nauseated for awhile, so they wanted to ensure everything was well. He's a little small, but is perfect otherwise. So yes, it's definitely a boy."

"Oh, dear, sweet Jesus! A son! *Michael*, I will have a son!" Ross felt delighted. He rose to dance exuberantly around the room, even with a splitting headache. Who cared! This was joyful news, "Where do I start? Gosh, there's so much I must do: get a new job, a new place!"

Michael smiled, happy to see Ross act this way.

"Stay here until you get your foothold again," Michael offered and went towards the kitchen to pour himself a cup of coffee. "But do it soon! From what I hear from Mother, Tara is due any day now."

Ross nodded and joined him there.

"Thank you, Michael. Thank you. I won't touch another drop of alcohol. You'll see a new man. I'll go out first thing to look for work," Then Ross frowned with new worry. "You do believe that Tara will allow me to see her?"

"Yes. I think she will. Gloria said she's been thinking about names, so seems very receptive of the baby. She's been managing quite well in spite of the circumstances. You were her best friend. I'm sure she doesn't hold any disrespect for you."

"And, what about Danny? I don't wish to cause further problems. Did they fight about this?"

"Yes, they fought and I guess they sort of broke up. It's crazy because he's off at sea and hasn't done anything about their marriage. He doesn't write or call her. Nothing. There's no filing for divorce or a word about what he wants to do. Everything is in limbo. She's stays at the Briggs House, living her life normally as possible. Mother wants him to stop dinking around to just resolve their discord. She encourages it frequently. I don't know if he heeds her words."

"What about Tara? What does she want?"

"Gloria told me that Tara wants reconciliation too, once the baby is here."

Michael sat down at the table. Ross sat down too. Michael poured him a cup of coffee and offered scones.

"Frankly, everything is screwed up. My Father has even tried. He told Danny to accept an assignment in a closer location, perhaps in Dartmouth or London. Father thinks this may help them reconcile faster if he's closer. I don't know. It's a good suggestion in theory for other reasons. We all live and work close to the manor. We can come and go as we please to visit home. It's not so easy for my two naval brothers. Their duty forever comes first. "

"There's a lot of interference from the Navy," Ross agreed, "Hopefully Danny will consider this. I do want them to make up. What happened was a mistake in our judgment, but I want Tara to be happy. I'll support her in every way. In the meantime, at least you haven't given up on me. I won't let you down again."

Michael appreciated his promise and shook his hand, consummating this agreement by a positive reaction.

Chapter 40

Baby Boy Blue

In the course of the week, Michael recommended Ross to an old friend, who offered a position in his international brokerage company. Ross was hired to be an assistant with a modest salary. When he got the job, a colleague on the 2nd floor told him about the opening for his apartment, as he had taken a position in Japan. He sublet it to Ross at a reasonable rent. It was a modest beginning. A good do-over, one that Ross felt comfortable with overall.

After the move, which was very simple for he didn't have anything, Ross waited for news. Tara's due date came and went. Another week went by. Ross grew extremely anxious as he sat at his desk, trying to work on portfolios that Friday afternoon. He punched out at 5:00, grabbed take out from a Chinese place, and then went to his barely furnish apartment. He checked out his mail, watched the BBC news for awhile, and waited for a comedy to come on television. Around nine, rain pelted his balcony and windows. He flipped the channels to watch a movie. It was very boring. Sometime around 10:00, he dozed off. Then the phone rang and it startled him awake. He placed the receiver to his ear.

"Hello?".

"Ross, it's Michael."

"Yes?"

"Gloria took Tara to the hospital about 8:00 last night. She was having minor labor pains all afternoon, so they thought it best to get to London. Same hospital as before."

"What? What time is it?" Ross wiped his eyes and looked about. The morning sun filtered through his blinds. He looked at the clock, but Michael already checked his watch.

"It's about 7:30 now."

"Jesus! Why didn't anyone call me?"

"I'm calling you now. Frankly, I just found out. Gloria's all excited. The baby was born around 6:00 this morning. Get dressed and go over there, will you?"

Ross didn't need further prompting. He hung up and was out the door in a matter of twenty minutes. At least it stopped raining, but the air was heavy with moisture. He caught the local bus. When he arrived to the parking lot at the hospital, he snapped his fingers.

"Damn! Maybe I should have brought flowers." There was no time now to stop by a florist. He rushed to the front door and flew to the information desk. He found out her room number. The elevator was down the hall. While he waited for it to stop at his floor, he looked around. The local gift shop wasn't even open yet, but the newsstand just did. Ross ran over to check out their selection.

Tara was awake when Ross tapped on her door. She was huddled under a blanket as he came in, dressed in sneakers, jeans and a striped cotton shirt with a light all-weather jacket. Not overdressed or flamboyant. He walked in with a few movie star magazines in hand.

"I know you once liked reading this kind of smut, daydreaming about the stars. I'm not in it though," he teased looking closely at the pale patient, "No one wants to keep up with Mr. Joe Average."

"Ross!" Tara exclaimed, surprised to see him. She was glad that they were alone. Helen and Gloria left the premise to get coffee and breakfast.

"Michael told me everything," Ross fidgeted. Tara struggled to sit up. She patted the chair next to the bed.

"This room is too familiar," she said, noticing his shifting eyes looking about, "Actually, I'm very happy that you are here."

"Really?" Ross's expression was similar to a lost little puppy, the kind of look that she adored, when he really wanted her approval.

Yet it wasn't her desire to bring up any details about their tryst in the hotel. Instead, she wanted to share everything, as friends; since he was the father to the child delivered shortly two hours prior. To reveal every uncomfortable detail that she endured. Tara took his hand and squeezed it hard- to prevent him from running off.

"Let me tell you, Ross…this pregnancy knocked me for a loop since day one! I puked all the time; I couldn't eat anything, or could rest properly. It about killed my marriage, but that wasn't enough to do me in. In the last week, my blood pressure shot up and gave me severe headaches. My ankles swelled the size of softballs. The local doctor thought I should check in early to be induced, but I persuaded him to let me ride for two more days. I truly thought I was cursed. Thank God my water broke last night. Gloria was visiting her mother, so that made things convenient. The labor pains were horrible after midnight. I endured ten hours worth at least. The worst thing to feel in my life! It took forever to push him out this morning. I yelled, huffed and puffed. The nurse possessed a deaf ear by the time I was done in that delivery room. It was like cramming a bowling ball through a thin coffee straw!"

His eyes grew wide with that description. Even his dark eyebrows cocked up to his forehead. She laughed to see his reaction. It was time to let him off the hook.

"Oh, Ross, it was difficult, but I would not trade this experience of natural childbirth for any other in the world. It was the weirdest feeling as they took him out from my body- just strange. And when they laid him on my chest, still bloody and screaming, let me tell you that our son, Thomas Ross Kelly, is absolutely perfect. God, you should see the full head of black hair! I bet that's why I suffered indigestion."

"That is his name? You named him after me?" Ross sputtered. He felt shock. It was more remarkable to hear it for the first time. *Thomas Ross Kelly.*

"You don't mind do you?" she asked, "I really liked the sound of Thomas Kelly. I thought it was proper to put your name in it too."

Suddenly there was plenty to consider all at once. He didn't know where to start.

"Of course not. I'm so honored. Won't this make Danny more upset? With the last name being Kelly? The way they register babies these days, it's a woman's choice to choose. You could give your married name," Ross wanted to be rational. He could imagine how Danny would feel explaining the difference in the last name, "Michael told me you separated. It's my entire fault he's mad at you."

"Ross! Don't! Please, don't apologize," Tara interrupted as she stared intently into his eyes, "What's done is done and I'm equally at fault. Yes, he was pissed, but I'll deal with Danny later, in my own way-when the moment is right. The important thing is simple. I want you to be a part of Tom's life, as morally possible. His name will remain Kelly. After all, you are his father. That is what I want. Don't you?"

"Oh, yes! That is really great. I appreciate your consideration," Ross replied running his hands deeply through his thick black hair. His heart was thumping in his chest. He couldn't believe her logic. What luck? He felt grateful.

"Do you want to see him?" Tara gushed. She pushed the button to summon the nurse. Ross felt giddy. He felt like one that won a million dollars with no deduction for taxes-ever!

"Oh, sure! Of course! Gosh, I'm so excited! My stomach has butterflies in it."

After a few minutes, the nurse came to the room with a glass lined cart. In it was a healthy 6 lb, 19 inch infant male, wrapped in a blue blanket, wearing a soft white pull-on cap. There was a mass of jet black hair peeking out. The nurse placed the baby into Ross's arms and then left the couple to themselves. There was a rocking chair nearby, so Ross pulled it over. For a long time, he sat there looking over the boy, from his facial features to counting all the fingers and toes.

"Oh, Tara ...he is just beautiful," Ross's voice sounded quivery. She saw tears in his eyes. At that moment, Tara felt absolution. Somehow, their friendship would survive. She knew that they could work things out. This must have crossed his mind too.

"This is difficult for me to say, now that I've seen Tom, but with our upbringing you know why I feel this way. The baby should stay with you always," Ross told her honestly, "You are his mother. A good one too. I still need time to get my life in order. I want to provide well for our son. If you manage to win Danny back, then we'll work out visitation, around his wishes and yours. All I want is to see my baby from time to time. That's all I ask."

He kissed Tom on the head softly. Tara nodded, feeling so grateful that he was being sensible. Just like when they were kids, he always placed her feelings first. He was a good man, a good friend. A friend that no one else could replace or duplicate. Somehow she must make Danny understand this concept, that he could never fulfill a part of her needs like Ross did. Yet, neither could Ross be what Danny meant to her now. How to accomplish all this remained a mystery.

Ross stayed for as long as possible, but he knew that Gloria and Helen would be returning soon. He didn't want to face them just yet.

"Look, if you need a ride home when you get out, I'll be happy to take you," He offered before stepping out the door, "Of course that means I have to borrow Michael's car."

"Oh? Don't you own a car anymore? I thought you had that snazzy one?"

"Lost it in Paris, I'm afraid, but I do own two legs and a bicycle. I could put the baby in a carrier and let you stand on the pegs of the back wheels."

"Uh, I don't think so, Ross!" Tara laughed and he went out the door chuckling.

Later that night, the baby slept soundly in her arms. Tara caressed his tiny face. He was indeed a beautiful child, with a perfect angled nose, dark eyes, and all that jet black hair. The baby's face grimaced as gas passed through his belly. His chin suddenly revealed a familiar left dimple. She kissed his brow and whispered:

"I worked too hard for you. Such a gift, a true treasure. Don't worry, Tom Kelly. You have a firm place in my life, in my heart, no matter which man loves me. Your father is a superman and will lift you up to the stars, but my husband will be your rock, your foundation. You'll need both. You'll see."

Tara snuggled the boy close. She felt a true bond. No matter how this baby came to be, she felt determined to get her life back on track, to secure his future. She felt happy that she and Ross made amends. Forgiveness made one feel free. She wanted this with Danny, for their love to spread wings. These last few months, Tara waited patiently-so damn patiently. Now with the baby born, there stood a new focus: Barcelona. It was time to connect with that stubborn Navy man, face-to face. Every night she missed him. Her heart and body burned for his touch. This just made determination grow like wildfire. She would go there. She would make him feel her fire too. He would take back the ashes he wanted to throw away to the winds. She would not take no for an answer.

Chapter Forty One

A woman on fire

Ross kept his promise and brought Tara and Tom back to Wiltshire about four days after Tom's birth. The septuplets were at Helen's house until later that afternoon, so Ross knew the coast was clear. He didn't relish a scolding from either Helen or George for what he did to Danny. He took Tom out of the car seat and escorted Tara by the arm to bring her inside.

It was odd having him in the Briggs House, even if it was just long enough for him to tuck Tom into his crib upstairs. Tara was happy that they made up. Still, to have the other man there without Danny wasn't appropriate. Even if he was her best friend. Her gut feeling was confirmed by the way that even dear Marta glared from the kitchen, with a sharp menacing butcher knife poised in her hand. Ross took one look at her and soon announced his goodbyes.

"I must be running off. I only borrowed Michael's car just long enough to bring you home. He has a premier to dash off to later tonight. So, goodbye for now. I'll call you soon," He said and quickly went down the steps. Perhaps he felt spooked too.

Tara joined Marta in the kitchen to see what was for supper. She did realize, too, that Marta would not make any bones about her feelings. They had grown too close to mince words.

"I know Mr. Kelly is the baby's father, but this doesn't seem right. I don't think Mr. Cross will like hearing it. He may be away and you may be separated, but you are still his wife," Marta said while dicing boiled chicken into small pieces. Her hands were moving quickly with the knife. Perhaps she thought it was Ross on that chopping board. She stopped for a moment to dump the pieces into a hot pot on the stove. The dumplings were already boiled, so Marta just added a few seasonings. The home-cooked aroma made Tara feel hungry.

"I understand, Marta, but how can I do this any other way? He must be allowed to see his child. I'm stuck out here in the country with seven other children. It would be difficult for me to take Tom to him, especially when I don't drive."

"What about Gloria or Michael? Aren't they friends with Mr. Kelly as well?"

"That's an idea, Marta. We'll see about it later on. For now, I don't want to release Tom to go to London. He's still so little. If Mr. Kelly comes by, you must be civil. That's all I ask."

"Certainly, I'll try, but it will be very difficult. I always admired your husband. He's a good soul, so I can't help but feel protective of his interests. Please, forgive me," She said, her warm eyes studying her over.

"Of course. It's just that I do wonder -does my husband still consider me his interest? I feel so badly that our anniversary came and went in February as it did, without any communication. Although, I did suck up my wounded pride and attempted to smooth things over by sending a card. I'm sure he threw it away. Why should he be happy to see it? He was very hurt when he discovered everything about Tom."

Tara sat at the table then and placed her head into her hands. She shook it wearily. Marta thought about the last time she saw Danny, at the manor.

"He was a mess at Christmas time like you are now. That man is just as proud, but he can't fool me either. I can remember everything, like when the children were ready to open up their presents. As you walked into the room, there was something shining in his eyes."

"Probably daggers," Tara mused, trying to kid about it, "He probably wished I was a dart board that he could impale. That would have made his Christmas."

Marta scoffed. She stared into Tara's eyes, determined to make a point.

"I don't believe that. You can tell the difference in a man when he feels hurt or laments. The whole time spent with the children, he always brought up tender loving tidbits about their mother, even if they didn't understand. So you see, in spite of what you did to hurt him, you weighed heavily upon his mind and in his heart. I know he loves you and is lost without your presence. With love, there can be forgiveness. Now, all you have to do is convince him how you feel, that there is a chance for your marriage. So what will you do to make this happen?"

Tara smiled at Marta. She was a great cheerleader, one definitely needed.

"What else can I do? For now, I must get stronger. When I get my six week clean bill of health, I will begin walking on that trail. The next time Danny sees me again, I want that man to melt on the spot! Every womanly weapon that I can sum up will vaporize any ideas of divorce! I don't want him to think he can turn me away."

There was a fire in Tara's eyes, one that Marta appreciated. Yes, Tara did this before with dieting and exercise. Her constant walks blasted away her pudgy stomach derived from pregnancy. All she needed now was toning.

"You can do it, Tara. I believe it. Just think positive."

As the days passed by, Tara watched what she consumed. When Tom became five weeks old, she stepped on the bathroom scales and noted that she dropped fifteen pounds. Certainly breast feeding helped too. There was something in a magazine that claimed it helped with weight loss. This only made her determined to lose more. Pregnancy played havoc with her body. She wanted control, so Tara defined her muscles in a new way. The septuplets, now active toddlers, just celebrated their first birthday in April. They were into everything and so she invented a game using her body.

"Come here, Matt," she said to the boy as she sat into a chair. He instantly obeyed. Tara encouraged him to crawl upon her feet. He sat his hind end against her ankles while she held onto his small hands. "Let mommy take you for a ride. Wheee!"

Balancing his weight, she lifted her feet straight into the air. It was enough resistance to feel her thigh muscles tighten up. Next, she tried something with her arms. She scooped Edward high in the air towards the ceiling and then brought him straight down so she could kiss his forehead. "Did you like that, sweetheart? Let's do it again!" Edward giggled. What a fun game with Mommy? After five repetitions, Tara placed him down again. Next, it was Jamie's turn. Over and over again. There were seven toddlers. Each shared a turn with mommy.

Their weight was perfect to tone up her biceps and thighs. Every night she went to bed with sore muscles, but the exercise was well worth it. Whenever she could, up that dirt trail she went, between the Briggs House and the Manor. Back and forth, two times a day. She wasn't walking it anymore. She ran. When Tom turned eight weeks old, the doctor happened to see her jogging.

"Hello, Tara. How are you?" he called out. Tara stopped on a dime. She didn't pant anymore.

"Fine. Just great."

"You look really good, now that I look you over closely. You have color in your cheeks and you look thin in that sweat suit. Maybe you look too good. By the way, did you fill your prescription?" Frown lines went towards his head and he looked over the tops of his glasses directly at her. Tara nodded eagerly. She realized the implication. He was worried. She rejected the idea to get her tubes tied.

"Good. You surprised me with Tom. Give your body a rest. At least a year, if all goes well with your husband, all right? Have a nice run. I'll see you around."

He stepped on the gas to be on his way. Tara never kept secrets from the doctor. His sentiments she took to heart. She would miss his devoted care and frequent visits. Her family would only see him whenever the children needed immunizations or because of illness, but lately, the babies were as healthy as a herd of stallions.

The weather was warming up and Tara could take the children outside to play in the sunshine. They would run and play on the lawn, not far from her sight. It was a great way to let them blow off steam. Helen always came over to take pictures of them and of Tara too, sometimes catching the young woman standing or sitting by herself.

"Helen, don't you have enough of me?" Tara laughed after Helen took several. "Do you really think I'm more interesting than the children?"

Helen smiled like a kid in a candy shop.

"Yes, I do think you are very interesting. Every day, you seem so lovely and fit. These pictures won't be for me," she revealed, "When I develop them, I will send them all off to my son, so he can appreciate what he's missing. Such a stubborn man! It's his prerogative to do what he wants with these. I'm simply a messenger,"

Tara nodded. Her mother-in-law always seemed to surprise her. It was nice she helped in her own way, but sometimes things didn't always go to her plans.

In late July, she stopped over as she had news to share. She sat down in the living room, sipping her tea for a moment as they chitchatted about the regular routine of things. Then Helen stood up to pace the room a bit, seeming a bit fidgety.

"Helen, is something wrong? You don't seem yourself," Tara asked. Helen sighed and stared out the window for a moment, composing her thoughts. Then she just blurted it out.

"I wanted to let you know that I spoke to Danny. He finally returned my calls. I tried to reach him just to say happy birthday. We talked about his missions. The reason I couldn't reach him before now is because he just returned. He was sent up to the Northern hemisphere, near Antarctica. They took a team of scientists there to gather some type of data regarding the ozone. Now the crew has returned to Barcelona and will dock for a week or so. This makes him relieved. Can you believe he says his legs are sea weary?" Helen laughed, but she sounded nervous. She also clutched her hands together. Now Tara worried.

"He went out to the mainland since he doesn't have to stay on the ship or the base. Danny has found an apartment in Barcelona."

"An apartment?" Tara cried out, her eyes wide, "Why? What is he thinking? Does he plan to stay away forever? This is ridiculous!"

"I know, dear. I had hoped the pictures I sent would foster a desire to come home. He's never been away from us this long. I understand your dismay. However, he is pleased to hear that the children walk on their own now," Helen conveyed. There was a far away look in Tara's eyes. She seemed to suffer a set-back. Perhaps this was a good time to talk about her son, "I think he should see how fast they get into mischief now."

"Yes, I sure could use his help," Tara placed Tom into a soft quilted baby carrier. Her mind was turning cartwheels. She didn't know what she should do. Why was Danny doing this? Helen sat down too.

"It was my hope to tackle him head on about his life in person. Things can't stay in limbo this way. It's not good for either of you, although there's been plenty of time to file for a divorce. Obviously, something delays this action. It's either his conviction to you or to our family."

"What do you mean?" Tara listened carefully. Helen picked up Edward as he was getting hit by Tyler unintentionally with a soft stuffed animal. She soothed down his hair to stop his crying, bounced him on her knee, and then placed him into the playpen to continue playing.

"I never told you this, but there's a tradition in our family, through the Cross side. Divorce isn't easily accepted. One should stick things through. It's believed that one should first accept death before dishonoring our family."

"It's not my intent to sound cruel, Helen, but Danny is in the navy. I'm sure he faces an element of risk with all his special teams' activities. Gloria mentioned that he gets hazard pay. Do you believe he volunteers all this time to choose death over divorce?"

Tara shook her head. This made her angry. There was no reason for the man to take on extra risks. Helen didn't believe it either.

"No. What I believe is that Danny is carried away with his work. Sammy said he is like a man possessed. It's good for the navy, but not for himself. He's always been this way, someone with an exceptional amount of energy. He pours himself into every challenge."

"But not the challenge to save our relationship," Tara fumed.

"Tara, he may not show it now, but I believe he still possesses a conviction towards his marriage. Sure, he feels everything is lost and maybe that's why he stays away. Perhaps he's afraid of another disaster or your rejection. Still, he can never deny his own feelings. My son fell in love with you at first sight. He admitted it when he brought you home. It's my strong gut feeling that nothing's changed in regards to how he loves you. I hope this gives you encouragement."

Tara sighed, so grateful that her mother-in-law stood on her side.

"Oh Helen, yes it does. I thank God that your tradition and duty are what they are in this family. It does offer much hope. Nothing is simple these days. I miss having a man's jovial face in this house, especially in the morning. Frankly, Lila and Marta aren't enough with my coffee," Tara blew out a long sigh. She gazed into Helen's eyes wistfully, "What I'd give for a real marriage, to see Danny every day, just to converse about our children or about our home. I want to hear one of his bad jokes. It's been so long since he's even shown that part of his zany side. I always thought it a hindrance, but it's not. It revealed such bright twinkling blue eyes and a crooked smile. And I learned to laugh.

Helen, you wouldn't believe how much of that man I miss. How can I wait to set things right?"

"Then why delay? Let's do something now. I can arrange a flight. Gloria can come down if she can get away from work. I can ask. We can help Lila and Marta with the children. You must fly to Spain soon," Helen insisted. Tara nodded and they grabbed each other's hands in shared jubilation of this plan. This made Helen deeply happy that Tara wanted to remain a part of Danny's life. That was just one half of the battle. Hopefully Danny would see her spirit shine through. She was a Cross woman and would remain so, come hell or high water.

There were a few days until her flight, so Tara kept occupied, just to sooth jittery feelings. She went over to the manor into Danny's bedroom and brought over all the maritime maps, his books, and artifacts. She placed these into their bedroom. At night, she reviewed the maps, read mystery books, and studied astronomy, just to feel a connection. Whenever he looked up at the stars, did she cross his mind? She wished it so.

Sometimes she took out the letters from the hatbox to read each over and over again. Tara realized something. For the longest time, she always perceived him as one with no backbone. He was simply a respectful man trying to know his wife. On the night he backed her up to the wall, he showed his true feelings. He suffered enough and would not stand for her nonsense. He knew her well enough by then. There was fire in his demeanor. She loved this, "Oh, Danny! Never lose your grit!" It really did make him seem sexy.

She took out a suitcase and decided what to pack. As she found the lovely items bought in London, Tara thought of those women in the village. She stared at a red dress with spaghetti straps that she tried on. She bought it two sizes smaller on purpose, as motivation to slim down enough to wear it.

"You will never get him back," She mused, twirling in front of the mirror. The crest of her bosom showed. It fit snug in the waist. Her legs looked slinky underneath the short hemline. What man could ever resist such visionary appeal? Especially with the sultry smile she easily showed off in the mirror. For the first time, Tara thought herself beautiful. She would use her wiles to win Danny back.

When Gloria finally cleared her schedule and closed the shop for a month, she drove to the Briggs House directly. As the car pulled into the driveway, Tara's heart soared with wings. Her flight was tomorrow. It was time to make her mark. It was the second week of August when she flew out to the Barcelona coastline.

Chapter Forty Two
Fight for your man

A fifteen minute drive from the airport left Tara in the center of a crowded city. She arrived by taxi. Before she stepped out of it, she read the address on the postcard again. Helen gave it to her before departure. Danny's apartment was located in the Barr Gothic quarters of Barcelona. Tara paid the man; then walked up along the cobbled streets to find the exact place. His note to his mother indicated it was a suitable one-bedroom apartment near an old church, containing an oval blue-stained window within its main wall. Surely, she could find such a landmark.

Tara made her way through the crowds with a brown suitcase, heaving a heavy handbag upon her shoulder. There were tourists everywhere, resting at the outdoor cafes, shopping near the Placa de Pi, eating at their many tapas bars along the way. There were many narrow passages in between tall buildings with railed iron balconies. Her senses filled with the smell of ethnic foods she could not recognize and she saw many artists drawing or pedaling their wares along the streets. It was a beautiful city, but there was no time to get lost in it now. Her mission was to find that church and his apartment. Soon enough, Tara found the right street and approached a three story cream building made of bricks. The number on the outside showed it was the right address. A middle-aged, dark skin woman stood outside sweeping a walkway. She was dressed in a mid-calf length cotton dress. Tara approached her.

"Es la casa de mi esposa?" Tara tried to enunciate the Castillian Spanish language, looking at an English/Spanish booklet. The lady stared, so Tara showed a recent picture of her spouse, the one taken together at Christmas time. As luck would have it, the woman spoke English. She recognized the man instantly.

"Yes, I know him. Are you really his wife?" she asked in a thick accent. She knew what Tara attempted to ask. Tara nodded and noted that the woman stared at her closely.

Yes, the young lady seemed harmless enough, dressed neatly in a tan two piece skirt set and toeless flat shoes. Her eyes quizzical, the smile polite, and she looked hopeful. It was hard for the landlady to resist being curious now, "Well, in the two months that the LC has been here, I never realized he was married. You'd never know it with the friends he brings over."

Friends? Male or female? This made Tara very suspicious and so she frowned. The woman sympathized to this instant reaction. She married a cheater once.

She knew that look. The woman immediately stepped forward to help Tara with the suitcase.

"Here, let me take that. My name is Sylvia. By that look, I believe what you say is very true. Everyone has a story, but you are not one that he told, that's all. The LC lives on the far end."

"Are you sure we are talking about the right man? Who is LC?"

"Why- the Lieutenant commander. That is your husband, Seniore Danny Cross?"

"Yes, that's right," Tara was pleased they discussed the same. Although there were many doubts about what he did in his free time. Sylvia offered some clues.

"Well, usually the man is out all during the week. He has friends on base and some in the city, but then he returns here on weekends. Sometimes he doesn't appear until late in the evening. It's a hot day, senora. Please, come inside to rest. Have a cool drink," Sylvia offered, "There is an extra key to the apartment, but out of courtesy to my renter, I should have his permission to give you access to the place. However, in lieu of this, I'll let you wait in my home as long as you like. We can get to know each other, yes?"

Tara accepted, although she suspected that the landlady wanted particular details about their estranged relationship.

It wasn't all bad waiting there. Sylvia was kind, friendly even. The home was lively with fiesta-type music. Her grandchildren were visiting, with books and toys scattered about the living room. Being around kid-friendly obstructions as she stepped over the blocks and toy trucks made Tara feel instantly at home. Sylvia dragged her into the kitchen to sit at the table. While she went about preparing the family supper, Sylvia told great stories to occupy the time: about her family and about the city itself.

"My family have inhabited this great city for three generations. It's such a terrific attraction as we are so vast in our culture. The architecture makes you sigh in wonderment. And our history- well, for instance: My grandfather knew the great Picasso and said it was so remarkable he learned to paint so young! He worked and lived in this section too. He was a remarkable man, but my grandmother remembers that he had children by different women. It's interesting what we tend to recall about a man, isn't it?"

Sylvia laughed and placed a hot pot into a water bucket in her tiny sink. The steam rose like a cloud above it. She fussed about placing down dishes, fine wine glasses, and even lit up a few candles. Her two sons and their wives came around five and they all sat down to eat. Tara was surrounded by lively conversation, some in English, and some in their Spanish. The food was terrific, but all she could do was look at the rooster clock on the wall. Around 7:00, when the evening moon shone on the horizon, Tara went to the patio to wait outside, sitting in a chair next to the landlady. They observed the few passersby that made their way to the nightclubs downtown.

"There are a lot of tourists that get turned around in the streets. Sometimes I give them better directions. The LC usually passes by my doorway, so we shouldn't miss him." Sylvia said and propped her feet against a footstool to wait with her.

"Sylvia, I didn't think it proper to do this before, but since you have been so kind, can I ask a question?"

Sylvia took a sip of her drink and shook her head at Tara. She liked the young woman and would divulge everything she knew.

"I already know what your question will be, and all I can say is that on most occasions, your husband comes home with two, three or four friends, usually a mixture of men and women. I think they just mainly hang out to drink awhile, to talk. They are sometimes in uniform, so it's hard to note whether they are shipmates or more. Only a couple of times did I ever note the women go home later in the middle of the night. I can hear them talking or stumbling about as my window is in the front. Whether any one has stayed all night, I do not know this, but he's only been here two months. That's not a lot of time to digest his habits when he's mostly around on the weekends."

Tara nodded. It was enough to prepare for the worst scenario.

The air was sticky and warm, but a light breeze cooled them off to bear it. In the distance, Tara could hear music, a quaint celebration of guitars, horns, and lively chatter. She sipped on a cool drink, trying to remain calm. Sylvia chatted idly about different things as an hour passed, Then two, three. Finally four. Tara tapped her feet like a drum and grew inpatient. Where was he? Finally, her worst fears transpired. Around 11:30, she heard his voice drifting up the cobbled streets. He laughed. Someone giggled in a high female voice. *Damn. He's not alone.* As he came closer to view, a lovely Spanish woman leaned all over him.

"She sounds like a hyena," Sylvia said and stood up abruptly. Politely, she went inside the house to allow Tara privacy. Still, she spied from the window. As the pair approached the building, Tara stood to make her appearance known.

"Danny!" Tara cried out, just as he took the woman into his arms. Right there, in the middle of the street. Was there no shame? Tara fumed. The drunken woman frowned suspiciously as Tara descended the steps towards them. Danny's jaw dropped in surprise.

"Tara! Jesus! When did you get to Barcelona?"

"Let go of that woman!" Tara demanded, biting her tongue to keep her cool at that point. Every nerve in her body was on heightened suspense. She reminded herself of several things in a hurry. They were estranged. What he did in this type of situation should be his business, but she couldn't buy into that bull. So she fumed.

"I will not let go! She is my company!" Danny announced, his crisp blue eyes narrowed. His jaw stuck out and he brought the woman closer to him.

"We must talk, Danny! And right now!" Something snapped to see him react like a stubborn child. Maybe all that time alone with seven willful children made her pounce with such ferocity, but she took hasty steps to grab his arm forcibly. With gusto, she separated the pair, flinging the other woman away to completely piss her off.

"Ay!" the woman shrieked. She looked at Danny for an explanation. The language she injected into the air with rapid fire was deeply accented. Tara mimicked the same without any comprehension to what she said. It was quite rude, in Danny's opinion.

"Stop it Tara! What's with you? For God's sake, she is with me. You have no right," He tried to pull away from her grip, but Tara kept it firm. He looked at her hand in surprise and then at her face. Tara stared at the other woman, giving away this total back-off look.

"I do have every right! You are still my husband!" Tara retorted. The other woman yelped. That word was understood plainly.

"Husband! You are married? You never told me this!" she cried out and hastened to walk away.

"Yes, but we are separated. Please, don't go! I need you!" Danny implored as she stomped halfway up the block. Only then, did she turn around. .

"Ay, no! I do not get into the middle of your business!"

"That's right!" Tara mimicked the accent again. *"Don't get into the middle of our business.* He's my man! Now, go away!"

The lady stormed off in a mad huff.

"Why did you do that?" Danny stumbled forward on the street. He smelled like whiskey, but he spoke soberly. She couldn't determine how drunk he was as he hid it so well. Danny pointed a finger at her, "We are no longer together, in case you have forgotten dear!"

"No, I haven't! But nevertheless, we are not divorced. I hate the way you show off your conquests! It hurts!"

"*What? What?* You want to talk about hurt?" Danny sputtered with both hands upon his hips and his legs wide apart. Even in the dark, she could tell his face was turning red, "I can tell all about that implication! Let me spell it out in four letters, my dear wife!

R-O-S-S! Talk about showing off conquests! Well, that baby is proof enough of yours! Mother told me that you finally had it."

"You are not being fair! Tom is not an 'it'. He's a live human being, not a trophy, for God's sake!" Tara retorted, but Danny waved her off to storm towards his apartment.

"Go with him!" Sylvia hissed through the blinds, "Make him listen to you, senora!"

Tara nodded and ran after him. At the door, Danny fumbled with the key, but eventually the lock unopened. He fell inside and then he clicked on the lights. She followed close enough where he couldn't close the door on her. Once inside, Tara looked around. The living room was poorly kept. It sorely needed sweeping and dusting. Clothes littered a nearby couch along with newspapers, magazines, and a lot of empty beer bottles.

"Why did you follow me in? More importantly, Tara-why are you here, damn it?" Danny folded his arms and stared closely. Maybe too closely, now that he could see her in the light. Sure he was angry, but she was a lovely sight. Her hair was long again, all curls and bouncy, in varying layered lengths. It looked soft to touch. He wanted too- No, he couldn't! He was pissed! *Stay on focus! But her figure- God!* Her figure was great!

"I wanted to see how you were getting along." Tara's voice sounded lame.

"Why on earth for?" Danny demanded.

He stood there with a muscular body, hands on hips. Did he exercise away part of his time? His arms showed hard biceps in the short sleeve black t-shirt he wore.

Even his waist seemed slim. The pants he wore were black too, very tight, and made his backside look so divine. She noted this as she followed him in.

"There are tons of reasons why!" Tara snapped, "Perhaps it's because I care about your well being, as your friend; perhaps it is to be with you in the flesh, as your wife; most importantly, perhaps it is to salvage our marriage, for our future."

Danny whistled long and slow. Was she for real? He was shocked, but still, throughout this time away, his heart died away in bits and pieces by jealous feelings and loss. Yet how did she know that there was much more to it that he missed: the lilt of her voice; those expressive brown eyes; the way that she laughed in amusement at someone else's jokes? Glumly, Danny realized a sad truth. Personally, he never discovered a way to bring out her fire in his favor. Tara never shared any deep secrets, any special looks; he always felt left out of her grace. So why was she wanting a second chance? Was this a joke?

"There's not much to save at all. Everything dissolves to dust, the moment I take you into my arms," Danny scoffed. Tara felt the thrust of these words. The truth hurt deeply.

"I have treated you horribly Danny. I'm big enough to admit it. It's miserable that our mistakes escalated to a breaking point with other people. Yet, we can stop it now. We can put it behind us. Please, let's not have our past destroy us. Let's start over. It's all I want to do."

"So you can turn on a shilling whenever not touched in the right away? Oh, no! I can't do that, Tara. What do you think lies underneath this flesh? A pin cushion?

How many times can one man take rejection? Well, your betrayal with Ross was the last straw. There is no way to come back from that final jab!"

Danny felt the alcohol cipher anger from the depths of his belly. She looked really upset too, but not in the same manner.

"Oh, Danny! I know that Ross was a mistake. I'm sorry. I never should have hurt you that way. I never should have gloated about it afterwards. It was so wrong. After Christmas, I realized everything! How much I need you in my life. You are the man for me. *The only one*. I do love you."

"Love? What do you know about love? Except to stomp all over it, with no regards for my feelings- ever!" Danny retaliated.

Hot tears fell fast down her fair cheeks. She was not getting through to him. Tara bit a bottom lip for self control and turned away from his direct view.

Perhaps it was too late to salvage their relationship. She would return to the Briggs House alone, to live out her days with her children, lonely and miserable. She blew it. This was her fate. He would remain at sea forever, never divorcing just to appease his family tradition. Yet, perhaps something did happen, for he backed down.

"Look, Tara. I can't …I can't discuss this now. I am drunk and too stunned to think clearly. I am going to bed."

Feelings remained raw. He was shocked by her words. Danny only wanted to make sense of everything. To see Tara cry was intolerable. All those hot tears streaming down such a lovely face. So in desperation, he struggled into the bedroom, slamming the door, and locking it from his side.

This gave him time to think everything out. What amazing timing that woman possessed! It was incredible that she showed up out of the blue! All he wanted that night was to have a little fun, especially with Nina, who he met at a friend's house.

She was the neighbor's sister who possessed the right qualities to stimulate his thinking. Nina was cute, with dark eyes, black hair, and so many tempting curves. They sat outside to drink and she flirted the whole time she talked. Sure he brought other women over to his place before, but they were mostly friends from the base. He didn't really want to risk insubordination with those women, but Nina was so different. She was fresh! With no hidden agenda about what she had on her mind that night, she pressed Danny up against a wall and laid one long wet kiss on his lips. Then with a frisky hand, she slid it down to get his immediate attention.

Eight long months out at sea was enough torture for any man. Add to that all the longing he felt while firing hot letters to his wife back and forth before Christmas, when he thought everything was still right in their marriage. What did he get in the end? Nothing! No, Mother Nature was calling. What was desired from Nina was pure animalistic. The wild beast in him called out a safari beat. It was exhausting remaining a martyr, being a saint. So he brought Nina over, determined to go all the way this time. He wanted sex. The wild-who-cares-what happens-next- kind of sex, a wild abandonment. Why not? Tara and Ross did that once. So why not his turn?

Now that was screwed up because his wife showed up. Jesus!

Danny took off his shirt, slipped off shoes, and pants. Then with just his skivvies, he fell into bed to stare up the ceiling, the absolute worst place for such a lonely man. He thought he wanted to cool off after the quarrel with Tara. The light turned off in the other room, but he didn't hear the front door, so he knew she stayed.

She stayed. God, help me now! The minutes ticked by. Crickets chirped in the distance. He could hear music floating in the air faintly. Danny tossed and turned in the sheets, anxious and praying. Even with the air conditioner on, his body went into a sweat. His heart pumped like mad. The more he thought about her, the more he felt desire. Strong, upsweeping desire- for his woman on the couch. He couldn't stand it. His body reacted, even in his mind fought it. Two difference impulses went on at once, where he wasn't the driver of one. And that one was winning! It was a man's doom to lose such control.

Jesus! I'm not a kid anymore! Danny jumped up to his feet and ran over to the dresser. He threw clothes out of the top drawer and came up with a silver flask. Thank God he had stored it there recently. Off came the cap and he gulped the contents down. Tiny droplets escaped and dribbled down his chin. His mind, cruel to the extreme, made him see her so clearly. Such pure torture! She looked too damn beautiful. Those bouncy curls, sexy curves. Tempting, haunting eyes! That alone did him in, along with the pouting lips, her curvy shape, and those salty, flowing tears. He was a done man the moment he laid eyes on her. Déjà vu.

Danny drained the flask empty and felt himself shaking- to think of her words: '*You are the man for me! The only one! I do love you!*' He stared at himself in the mirror, both hands running through his blond hair, fingers clasping in the back, and elbows turned towards the side. Was she for real? Did she truly want him that bad?

Yes, tomorrow would be another day to react with true reasonable thinking, not hasty, nasty-even lusty-ones. Damn his pride! He sighed- a deep, miserable breath because he wasn't by her side- and went to lie down again. Thanks to all of the alcohol consumed earlier that evening, and the flask, he gratefully fell asleep.

Chapter Forty Three
A new set of Priorities

In the morning, Danny woke up and he threw the covers back, springing out of bed in alarm. He slapped his head. *Jesus Christ! There's a special formation at seven!* How could he have forgotten? Still, the required uniform and shoes remained at his friend's quarters near the base. His original plan was to have dinner there and stay the night.

That was before Nina sauntered onto their patio.

She was the only reason he waltzed home. Yet that plan was screwed up too. All because Tara decided to visit. Now, he had to go back.

Danny dressed in a mad rush and looked at the time on the clock nearby. 5:30 a.m. He could get there in time to change –if he ran. Danny stumbled into the living room. He saw Tara laying on the couch, and she raised her head to look at him. Her eyes seemed puffy, sleepy. There was no time to explain anything, so he grabbed his wallet, his keys, and rushed out the door, with shoes halfway on. What could he expect upon his return? Would she stay or go? Fate did not cooperate at all. *Damn!*

Sylvia stopped by later that morning to check up on Tara. She had a few pieces of Danny's mail, so it was a valid excuse to stop by.

"Where is the LC?" Sylvia stepped inside, pausing to look around.

"Gone. He left in a hurry this morning," Tara murmured, her eyes downward.

"You do not deserve this as you love that man," Sylvia said "Those women meant nothing, I'm sure. I sense that he's needed someone real for a very long time."

"Really?" Tara sniffed and Sylvia nodded. She took out an extra key from her pocket and handed it to Tara.

"Keep this. He didn't throw you out last night, so you can remain. I'm sure in his eyes, you are worth more."

"Yes, you are right. I should believe it too," Tara said proudly and then took the key, "Can you show me to the market later. He needs food in the house. I looked in the refrigerator last night to get a drink. It's completely empty."

"Sure. Take a shower. Get dressed. I'll come back in an hour," Sylvia agreed. She turned around and went down the stairs. Tara closed the door. She looked around the messy apartment. If he denied their love and forced her to go, there must be reminders of her presence there, no matter what the decision. So later, Tara and Sylvia went to the outdoor market. Tara picked out a lot of fruit, cheeses, and canned items, which made Sylvia raise her eyebrows.

"Cooking is not my thing. I simply don't know how," Tara told her, "Besides, it never mattered much before. He's always been away to sea too long. I'd love to show how a real home can feel with a woman's attention. Other than sprucing up the apartment, a home cooked meal would be ideal."

Sylvia nodded.

"Well, there I can help. I cook too much for my own family. It will be no problem," Sylvia offered and Tara thanked her.

They stocked the empty refrigerator, along with the cabinets. Then for the next two days, Tara scrubbed and cleaned; caught up the laundry; placed fresh linen on the bed, and flowers upon the table. She didn't know where he was or when he'd return, but at least working kept her mind occupied. Once it was all done, there was time to snoop around. He wasn't a man that kept personal items out. In the closet, she found a large picture album.

She sat on the bed to browse through it. There were several pictures of him on board ship with his crew, along with the different places they had been. It also contained all of the pictures that Helen sent of her and the children. On one page, upon the cardboard mat, against one picture of the children, he penciled on the side plenty of x's and o's. Next to another where she sat with the children on the lawn, like little ducks in a row, he drew an outline of a heart, but then crossed it out. This disappointed her. She turned the page to find a picture of her alone, standing by the staircase in her home. It was taken at the end of July. She looked good in it, wearing a simple white dress and her long brown hair was spiraling past her shoulders. He drew a rose beside it, with petals falling, then scribbled the words "Do you love me, do you love me not?"

"I do," she whispered. Tears sprung to her eyes. "Oh, Danny I do. Just let me prove it to you, please!"

She placed the book away where she found it and bowed her head in prayer. Where was he? Why didn't he call? There was a phone out by the couch. She went to it then and placed a long distance call to Helen. After a long conversation, both she and Gloria told her to stick it out. "The children are fine. We are handling things. Make amends with your husband." That's all Tara wanted to do. It seemed forever, but on her fourth night there, he returned.

Tara heard the key jingle in the lock as she sat at the desk in the bedroom. His footsteps entered inside, the light came on, and he progressed towards the kitchen. She could hear the refrigerator door and the cabinets open and shut. Perhaps he took it all in, the visible changes that were made. She hoped it pleased him. Tara had waited forever for this moment and all her senses heightened in anticipation. Every night while he was away, she had kept up a routine:

A candle was lit for atmosphere. Soft cologne fragranced her body. It went perfect with a dark blue negligee, something elegant and sexy bought at a very posh department store in London. Suggestive -most definitely- and luckily, it was even Danny's favorite color. She washed it out every morning so it would be fresh for the evening.

At that point, he sighed out loud and then his footsteps drew near. She looked up at the door as Danny walked in, dressed in that uniform that made him so damn handsome. Her heart pounded as he took off his hat and approached. His shoulders slumped and his hands clutched his hat tightly, but he didn't seem upset to find her there. He seemed, in fact, relieved.

"Christ, Tara! You don't know how much I hoped that you would stay. We were sent out to sea and just returned this afternoon to a full military review."

He drew closer with a serious look upon his face. His eyes weren't red, so he wasn't drunk. He wet his lips and spoke in a soft voice.

"While I was away, there was only one strong conclusion on my mind." Danny paused, taking in her beauty against the backdrop of the flickering candlelight. He cleared his throat, but he couldn't contain the sudden tears, "Most assuredly, you are not someone that a man can easily forget, nor stop loving. I am simply a hostage, forever bonded to your heart, with no means to escape. No ransom but pride to give up. If what you say is true, then somehow I can try again. Just be for real this time, dearest Tara. My heart…it's suffering a fragile mend."

Did she hear this straight? Excitement flooded her soul!

"Oh, yes! I'm for real!" She gasped. Before he changed his mind, Tara jumped up to throw herself upon him to embrace him tight- so very damn tight-consumed by such incredible raw feelings, "Yes! Yes! Yes! Oh, Danny! Yes! I love you so much!"

She breathed in his scent like nectar given from the Gods. His body felt so warm, so right. He clung to her waist tight, afraid to let go it seemed. But in the instance that they did, he saw her tears stream down her face too. They laughed and each took a moment to wipe away the tears. Tara felt a lump in her throat and she choked it down to speak.

"I thought everything was lost," She stroked his face everywhere, like a blind person memorizes ones look. Her eyes stayed keenly focused on him. He was all that mattered.

Danny's eyes conveyed astonishment and a slight blush came to his cheeks. He also began to sweat.

"No. I couldn't let us go. I love you too much, Tara," he sighed and then glanced at his jacket. He let out a breath, "But gosh, I'm so damn warm all of a sudden. It's not just because of you, but because it's an incredibly long walk from base wearing this thing."

He let go of her to unbutton it, really showing his discomfort.

"I had to wear it all day. It's uncomfortable in the sun and feels like an oven wearing it at times."

He slid his hand down, but she could not resist helping him out of his clothes. It was an irresistible opportunity. Her memory was too vague. The last time she ever saw him strip down was too long ago. Like two actors in a slow motion picture, they worked together. She opened up the bottom buttons as he released the top. Tiny goose bumps surfaced over her satiny skin. She could even feel her nipples point out erect against the thin fabric of her lingerie. Did he take notice? His eyes were certainly scanning her body, not seeming like it missed any details He slid out of his coat. She grabbed a hanger and placed the jacket away into the closet. He took off his shirt and she placed it on the back of the chair. Then he kicked off his shoes, slid off his socks, along with those dark pants. He placed them into the chair too. They both stopped at this point as he stood in his skivvies and stared in hesitation.

Somehow in this magical moment, there was fear. Danny felt his heart pound in his chest. There was a look of puzzlement in her eyes. Should he take her to bed now? This one thought suddenly got him. After all, when they fought last at the Briggs House, didn't she declare their lovemaking hurried and unsatisfying? Even for what he boasted that night, he had to get this right with Tara.

"Are you hungry?" Tara asked out of the blue.

Danny's eyes grew wide. Hungry for what? For her body? '*Well, yeah.*'

"There are leftovers in the kitchen. If you have not eaten, I think I can heat it up." she suggested.

This totally blew Danny out of the water. Food? Was she really talking about food?

"Did you cook?"

"Ah, no, silly. Sylvia is a wonderful cook and has been kind to bring up plenty. She complains that I seem to thin. Do you think so?"

"Oh, no! You look great!" Danny declared with his eyes big. His voice sounded like a growl.

Tara giggled.

"Well, this is your fault. I never learned to cook as we have all of those servants. You do recall how I tend to burn everything whenever I tried. Luckily, because of Sylvia, you don't have to worry. Isn't it my wifely duty to ensure that you are fed?" Tara really meant it.

What to say, but this was totally endearing and what a wonderful feeling it gave him. He couldn't help but laugh, quite deliriously. For once, his wife was trying to please and serve him. Now, in her eyes, he was her master. How in the world did that happen?

"Well, since you never learned, I won't force you out of your element," Danny teased, "Come on. Let's see what's there."

He took her hand to lead her into the kitchen. They set out what were available and warmed things up in the microwave. She fed him and he fed her. They consumed some wine and talked a bit, but nothing about Ross, or the children.

For once Tara listened earnestly, as he explained everything about his recent trip at sea, on board with a special narcotics patrol. It was nice how she finally took an interest in what he did in the Navy. It never seemed important to her before.

"There were reports, drugs being shipped off to some of our English ports. It was a pretty exciting adventure. We confiscated several dangerous men and several pounds of cocaine and marijuana on this one frigate. They had about 75 men onboard. It gets scary when we pull along side, because you never know the extent of their weapons, but they surrendered without conflict. We turned over the items and those men to the Spaniard police. It was something I'll never forget."

Danny leaned heavily on the chair. He sat silent for a moment, thinking about everything in the past few months and he sighed.

Tara took note of his demeanor now. His hair was tousled from wearing his hat. He seemed tired. *Very tired*. Like everything he went through caught up all at once.

"You love the navy, Danny. I always knew that. You always seem excited about what took place, but you seem different now," Tara said, looking for a clue to what he was thinking, but all he did was gaze directly into her eyes and caress long strands of her brown hair. There was an odd expression upon his face which made her uneasy, "What? You look like the wind has gone out of your sails."

"It has, Tara. I'm so tired," he said mysteriously. His voice seemed raspy, indifferent. She leaned close to pay attention, "These last missions have been stressful, just because of everything we've gone through, I suppose. When I left home after Christmas, it just about killed me. It was difficult leaving our children and difficult for not knowing what would become of our marriage. I've been an absolute wreck inside ever since. And now, you showed up out of the blue. I made a decision while I was away this week."

"What? What is it?" Tara clutched the edge of the chair. His tone was so ominous that she felt frightened.

"I prayed the whole time about everything, about us; if you'd stay or go. God and I had a private conversation- in my head, of course. I asked that you'd be here waiting. I wanted my wife so badly and it came true. I explained to him that it seemed I had other mistresses- the Navy, the sea. I couldn't have that and you. Perhaps, my grandfather could do it, but my Grams lost him in the war. How could I do that to you and our children? The world is too crazy. There's been so much escalation in the Middle East and in Africa, Afghanistan. So come late September, I'm giving it up. I want to come home. Permanently."

"Are you sure, Danny?" Tara gasped. She couldn't believe it, but he took her hand.

"I've missed out on too much already. I need to be with you. You deserve a true husband. Harry and I spoke about everything. We never had secrets. He believes I should do it too, even if he's going to miss me. He's like another father, so the decision was difficult. I am so grateful that we work so wonderfully together and that he is compassionate."

Danny sipped his wine. He drew her close, to caress her face.

"I told him you were here. I told him what you said. I've been given two weeks to reconcile our hearts. It can be our delayed honeymoon. This coastal region is lovely to see, provided if it's with the right person."

"Perhaps I am that person?" Tara placed a grape within his mouth, very suggestively. Her eyes were flirtatious as she peered into his. She truly believed in him. He was the most remarkable man in the world to sacrifice so much for her, "I am so overdue for true romance."

"Yes. So am I. So am I," Danny replied in a husky voice. A strong desire swept over him. The same kind that kept him awake before. The calling was irresistible. That look in her eye lit the torch. Her breath was upon his face and she seemed adorable. Hypnotized by the seduction, Danny tugged Tara to sit upon his lap. They kissed for several minutes, torrid kisses of fire. Then they went into the bedroom. This time, he was no longer afraid to lie beside her.

Every nook and cranny of her body was explored with his fingers, with his kisses. Sometimes, within the teasing and the careful nips around the nape of her neck and her raised nipples, she would giggle. She liked what he was doing. Her fingers dug into his back. She whispered, "More" into his ear. That was so encouraging.

With firm, warm hands, Danny caressed her body tenderly. It was pure ecstasy making love this slow way. It was something they never wanted to lose again. Danny conveyed confidence like a new man as he made love to his wife. She was taken to heights beyond the stars. Now that her love was just as strong, he could take her there always. Afterwards, they cuddled warmly with a light blanket. The moon shone in the window. Tara threw her legs over his, and nestled her backside against his body, so they were tightly intertwined.

"Oh, Danny. I waited for this moment far too long; just to be with you again. I wanted you so badly."

"I know, Tara. I felt the same," Danny kissed her brow. He squeezed her body closer. "Nothing will pull us apart again, darling. We will work together to find our answers, without remorse or anger. We can do this. I know it. This feels too damn good to let it go."

She knew it too. They could mend the hurt. There was no longer talk about divorce. It was a brand new beginning for them. They used the time to sight see around Barcelona and drive up the coastline. They picnicked on the beaches and drank wine watching the sun go down. They went dancing, shopping, and made love at midnight wherever they stayed.

Upon their return at the end of the second week, Sylvia was most happy too see Tara smile. It illuminated her whole face. Even the lieutenant commander beamed with pride while he introduced his wife to everyone outside the building. Even to his friends that stopped by on occasion.

Tara felt on top of the world, except for one minor thing. She noticed that when they spoke about the children, Danny talked mostly about the septuplets. Tara was afraid to mention Tom specifically in the conversation. When he returned to Wiltshire, how would he deal with the child? She had to bring it up somehow.

About two days before Tara's scheduled flight home, the two spent it in bed, cuddled up under the covers. Tara leaned into Danny's body as he sat against the pillows. He attempted to read the local paper with her head upon his chest. His Spanish was so-so, but it was enough to interpret the world news. He turned a page and found an advertisement for a clothing store. All of the infant items were on sale.

"Oooh, I should stop by before I leave," Tara suggested as she saw something in the ad. Danny crinkled the paper in half and a puzzled look came over his face.

"Why on earth for? Don't they have enough?"

Tara pointed at the picture.

"This outfit is cute. That's all."

"It's a size six months. It won't fit the boys or Jamie at all," Danny retorted and went back to his paper. Tara frowned. She sat up quickly. Danny understood that body language. "What? What did I say?"

"I meant it for Tom. You never speak about him." Tara jumped up to go into the other room. There were tears in her eyes. Worse, she was completely naked. Danny scurried to wrap a sheet around her as the curtains were not drawn in the living room. At least, he was in his underwear.

"I'm sorry, darling. You are right. I just overlooked the fact that the outfit could be for him. It was unintentional."

"No, it wasn't. Your attitude speaks volumes," Tara sniffed and then turned around so that they were face to face, "As much as you block it out, the boy exists. When you come home, will you reject him?"

He didn't want to fight, so Danny held her tightly. He kissed her neck. It was definitely time to hash it out. He pulled her back to wipe away her tears.

"You're right. We can't move forward if I remain a coward. This is not about Tom. It's about Ross. I'm unsettled, Tara. Surely, he comes around to see the baby, doesn't he?"

"Yes."

"I can't handle that. Not in my house. Call it my stubborn pride, but we are just getting back on our feet. That one mistake created so much heartache. You may have started it, but you admitted that you were drunk. Still, he damned well finished it. He knew better! We had a friendship too. It's like he spat into my face. Ross can't come within a hundred feet of you again."

Tara couldn't believe her ears. This was about her best friend, but yet, she didn't want to aggravate Danny's feelings further. Still, they had to be fair about things.

She promised to work things out, for good or bad. She had to give up something. So did he.

"Ok, as you wish, but will you stay away from the pub?"

"What?"

"Those women still work there, Danny. Don't tell me that when you come home that you won't have a desire to drop by. You like to drink. You like to hang out with people to socialize. You did it when we met and when there was that crazy celebration after the septuplets were born. Will you stay away for me?"

"It's not the same thing," Danny surmised. He looked at her in the eye, wanting to keep things on a logical perspective, "There are other patrons that go there that I see, like…like Leo. And that celebration was a one time thing. Ok, granted, perhaps I blundered in judgment too, but I walked away from those women."

"And I walked away from Ross," Tara revealed and returned to the bedroom. Danny had followed and she plopped on the bed, "He wanted me to remain in London, but I didn't. I couldn't. I realized a lot then. About you, about me. So I learned what stood important. It was you. I crushed him with cruel words then as I crushed you later. It was stupid! Selfish on my part. Still, when Tom arrived, we made amends. Tom needs his father. You can't deny this as it wouldn't be right. We both grew up with no parents. There is no way I can do this to Ross."

"Well, that may be, but I still draw the line in the sand. I can't trust him, Tara. Not yet."

"So will you stay away from the bar?" Tara asked again, very patiently.

Danny sat down to think it over. She had him over a barrel for sure. Yes, he loved to drink and he loved the chance to mingle with his friends. Now as for the boy, he wasn't sure how he would handle his feelings once he saw Tom, but to be with Tara, he would need to take on this responsibility too. It would be difficult, because he was Ross's boy. Yet once upon a time, they were great friends. Supportive friends. Surely, in time, it would get easier to interact as his father too. As Gloria once declared at the manor, the boy was innocent.

"All right, let's do this. Let's ask Michael or Gloria to help get Tom to Ross in London. Since they travel back and forth, it shouldn't be a major problem. All we have to do is ask for their assistance. As for me, how about if I limit my time at the pub, say to just hanging out for an hour, once a week. Will that be acceptable?"

"All right, fine. I can go along with that," Tara compromised. Her hair was falling over her eyes and her lips were pursed. She looked very sexy and Danny sighed. He was definitely an addict for her love. He would do anything to please her.

"See, as long as we work together, we can compromise. From this day forward, I promise to remain faithful, Tara. This time I really, really do mean it. Those women were nothing compared to you. I swear."

Tara wrapped her arms around the man.

"I believe you, Danny, and I do love you. The words are from my heart this time. I swear it. You will never lose me," She kissed him. They fell into the middle of the bed. She stirred him up again. It was so damn easy to do, but he loved the opportunity to make love. Lately, she made him feel like a man. Her man. He felt on top of the world being with her, in love. That was what was important.

There was no more fear about what to expect upon his return. When Tara boarded the plane for London, she knew that she must discuss things with Ross fully. He would understand and do what was necessary to keep peace. It was what they both wanted for themselves, and for Tom.

Chapter Forty Four

Easing into a civilian world.

A natural progression of events occurred when Danny returned to Wiltshire in late September. First, he arrived two days before Tara's 20th birthday, which fell on a Friday. With a belated late July birthday and the Naval homecoming to go with it, everyone gathered at his parent's house to celebrate. Tara delighted to see the balloons and streamers as they entered inside the living room. The children seemed fascinated by them as they looked up. Helen made a fancy cake while Marta prepared a splendid meal. Michael and Sammy bought too much wine. Everyone pitched in to buy the couple presents for their home and for each other. For all to be together for such a fun occasion seemed overdue.

The whole time, Danny's siblings took notice of how the couple looked upon each other. Tara snuggled close to her husband on the couch, grasping his arm, staring up at Danny's features as if in la-la land. He caressed her face, squeezed her fingers tight. Occasionally, they kissed.

"Well, it's about time," Sammy said by the punch bowl, while observing them lock lips again. His brother didn't agree.

"I suppose," Michael muttered, frowning, forcing tiny wrinkled lines to surface on his forehead. Sammy looked up and stared at Michael in the eyes. His lips thin in a determined grimace.

"It better remain that way. No more interference!" Sammy walked away to stand by the hearth, leaving Michael to feel admonished.

Beside him, Helen beamed at the happy couple. Her heart soared that her one daughter-in-law basked in giddy happiness. In several ways, it seemed reminiscent of the time when she made up with George, after her affair. With strong love and conviction, the couple would see things through from now on.

"It's so good to be home. I missed these little ones!" Danny said as they all conversed after eating too much cake. The icing, sweet and tasty, produced a sugar high for everyone. The children became restless. Vincent fussed over a toy with Jamie. Matt pulled the pillows off the sofa. Tyler tugged on Tara's leg. Edward…well… was just being Edward, temperamental and scowling at Tristan as they sat playing blocks nearby. Eric came to hug on Danny's knee to get his attention too. All of a sudden, tired of redirecting their cooped up energy, he offered Eric something silly to burn off steam.

"How about a pony ride?"

He dropped onto the middle of the spacious floor so Eric could climb on. The boy grabbed hold of his neck and Danny grasped his body too. Then upon his knees, he scooted across the floor, moving his back and shoulders in a ziz-zag fashion, making the boy squeal in delight. Everyone watched for a moment or two.

"Hmmf!" George sputtered and then placed his pipe onto the mantel. He dropped down so Tyler could cling to his back. Everyone opened up their mouths wide. They couldn't believe it!

"Hey, I want in!" Sammy yelped, seeing that his stern father actually smiled. He dropped down to join them. The children clapped with delight to ride their backs. Helen placed a hand over her mouth, trying hard to contain her glee. Grams leaned forward in the chair; eyeglasses perched upon the edge of her nose. She stared down at George, "I'd never imagine he would try!" The old woman laughed. The others helped guide the children on and off safely. At one point, Susan removed Tristan and handed him off to Gloria. Sammy waited for another child and Susan's eyes glowed with an idea.

"Sammy, I want a turn!" she cried out. The younger woman plopped herself on and unmercifully swatted him upon the back side. He stared up in disbelief.

"Don't hit me! Get off, you minx! You're heavy!"

Sammy rose to his knees to throw her off balance. Susan, agile and stubborn, wrestled to stay on. Long legs in blue jeans wrapped around his waist tight. Her arms firmly locked about his head. She refused to be thrown off.

"Ow! I can't see! Stop it, Susan! Stop! We are not kids anymore! For God's sake-Mother, help me!" Sammy complained.

"Oh, my!" Danny gasped, collapsing against the couch. Tears of laughter rolled down his face as he watched the onslaught. He felt so glad to be not the one she picked upon. The children delighted to see their aunt swat Sammy's behind every few moments. The sharp slap held their merry attention. Susan, caught up in the gleeful melee, smiled brightly. A child again, this only brought her joy as she could recall those carefree days of her youth when she and Sammy use to pillow fight or wrestle in the yard. They always had their noses in the corner for getting out of line.

"Now, you're going to get it!" she cried out. Unmercifully, as he collapsed down onto the rug, her fingers ambushed all sides. Sammy's voice rose high in a soprano octave as he gasped for air, "Oh, stop! You win! I give!" She knew the right places. Sammy, now doomed, fell flat upon the rug, his face all red, weakened in snickering anguish.

"Ah, you are such a wimp!" Susan cried out, arms high in the air like a victorious boxer. She was happy to bring down such a strong brother and jumped off his back, looking about the room. All laughed too hard and gasped for air. For once, she delighted in the fact that Tara and Danny brought about this happy occasion. She loved the children being there. It felt like old times, before all her siblings grew up and became wrapped up in their lives.

Tom sat next to Tara on the couch and his cheeks were red from giggling. With dark flashing eyes and a sharp dimple showing, he looked much like his father. Susan could not contain herself and scooped the boy upon her lap as she fell onto the couch. Without a thought, she hugged him tight, such love showering upon him like rain. If only Ross could be there. Susan prayed. How nice if he could gain favoritism again with the family. Somehow, this must happen.

Before Danny left that afternoon, his grandmother cornered him by the punchbowl for a private conversation. She had returned from Cornwall that summer, when Tara was away saving her marriage.

"It makes me happy that you forgave her," She told Danny, "Time is so precious. My brother is not doing so well. He may pass by the end of the year. Of course, at my age, I worry too."

Death was not easy to speak of, but Danny was glad she shared her fears with him. He patted her hand and kissed her brow.

"We love you, Grams. You'll be around longer." he said, but did fear that she would soon succumb to old age. Danny couldn't bare this thought and planned to drop by often just to visit with her alone. He cherished her advice and love.

She looked over at Tara who was busy wiping Matt's hands. He made a beeline for the cake and decided that since it was almost gone, it would be fine to sample the sugary petals made from icing. There was blue and pink icing all over his hands and across his mouth. She smiled to watch them and noticed that Danny had a smile as wide as the sky as he looked at her.

"You seem so happy Danny. Your eyes are glowing,"

"Yes. It is good to be home, Grams. Things are so splendid, that I believe I may burst with glee sometimes. Everything is as it should be."

"It's your lovely wife, isn't it?" she observed. He nodded with heart full of emotion.

"She's totally different, so very attentive and loving. It's hard to decipher how this change came about, but ah, Grams! It's complete magic. We are in another dimension, another world, where I am king. I want to jump out of my skin! I want to shout!"

She placed her hand upon his shoulder.

"Treat her well, Danny, with respect and patience, and that love will only blossom. Treat everyone in your household accordingly. You are a king, at the Briggs House. It's already fully blessed."

During the rest of that weekend, the Cross siblings visited, talked and caught up about everything happening in their adult lives. Sammy shared his usual stories about women and the Navy while Gloria spoke about her photography studio. Gloria bragged about the celebrities she was meeting in certain circles at fashion shows and Michael announced tidbits about the new play he was producing with a co-partner in London. Yet, it seemed inevitable to go about their separate ways that Sunday afternoon. The decorations were put away and the staff busied themselves tidying up the Grand Manor.

Haskell made sure that the servants did a spit spot job. He escorted a servant to the china hutch in the dining area.

"Remove this setting out of the cabinet. It wasn't shined correctly. I'll show you how it's done, so you can redo them," he reprimanded a new servant. She didn't clean the silverware used that weekend to his satisfaction.

"Yes, sir," she said, noting that he didn't sound angry. She went to get it out of the cabinet and turned around to face him again. He wiped his brow and loosened his tie. Then he clutched his heart, "Are you all right Haskell? You look green!" she panicked.

"I don't know," he sputtered and slumped into the nearest chair. His eyes grew wide and then he bowed his head with eyes shut tight.

"Oh, my! I think he's dead! Mr. Cross! Mr. Cross! Come quick!" she called out as she slammed shut the cabinet doors.

The police, summoned right away, deemed that he died of natural causes and so nothing further became warranted from them. Haskell's living sisters in Lincolnshire were notified and the local mortuary service took his body away.

A week went by and the family attended his funeral, which everyone thought the service seemed quite stately for such a noble man. However, by then, the servants in the manor became ruffled. "Who's going to divvy out our assignments?" They asked, "Who gives our orders?" Marta brought this to Danny's attention one day after the service.

"Someone needs to take over, just so no one thinks they can boss another," She said, "I know it will be difficult to do as Haskell was liked by everyone."

"Yes, he was quite a good man and he gave my family long years of distinguished service," Danny remarked, sitting at the table drinking a cup of tea. A smile surfaced on his face and he gazed into Marta's warm eyes, "There were many times Sammy and I played practical jokes on the man while we grew up. Sammy was always inclined to be more mischievous, but I was stupid just to follow along."

Danny leaned on his elbow and Marta joined him at the table to listen. His eyes twinkled to remember everything.

"One time we filled his shoes up with ink. He had black toes for weeks, but he never sold us out to our parents. When we were teenagers, he took us out in the field to learn how to drive a stick shift, and then he let us loose on the road. Sammy almost crashed into a tree because he drove too fast. The whole time, Haskell just held onto his hat and never complained. I will sure miss him, but hope he rests in heaven now. He deserves wings for such patience with us. I learned a lot from that man. I'll run over to speak to father about the matter."

He made the trek to the Grand Manor and found his father in his study, on the phone with some investor in London. When he hung up, Danny brought up the subject of finding a replacement, but George frowned and reached for his pipe. His mind, occupied by incidental meetings in London and the occasional invitations to political and society parties in the county, didn't want to fool with it.

"I can't be bothered with such nonsense right now. Your mother doesn't have time either. She's accepted membership for far too many committees this year. I don't know what she was thinking," He complained to Danny, which made his son sigh. Sammy, still on leave, ambled into the room and perched himself on a chair.

His eyes rolled to hear his father complain. Danny understood. They both knew that their parents were too involved in their social hobnobbing. Danny had time on his hands. Lots of it.

"Ok, fine. Let me see what I can figure out," he told his father. Sammy showed him a plastic bag of sliced apples and nodded his head towards the door.

"Let's take a walk," he offered and so Danny joined him. They headed towards the stable and Sammy sighed, "So, what do you think?"

"It looks like I should just take care of things myself."

"You mean manage your place and theirs?"

"Why not? I have time. Lots of it, so it shouldn't be too difficult. Besides the staff knows me as well as they do father."

"They'll probably complain less," Sammy laughed. The cool air nipped at his ear and his scalp since his blond hair was cut very short, "It's good that you are home full time. You seem relaxed, happier."

"I am happy, more so than I have ever been in my entire life," Danny grinned and offered his brother a pat on the back. There was a spring to his step, in spite of their father's gruff mannerism. Sammy couldn't resist asking a personal question, now that he had an easing opening to discuss it.

"Well I always tell you everything about my escapades and fiascos involving women," he began with a mischievous twinkle to his eye, "I leave nothing hidden about what's said or what we do, so tell me the truth. How are things with Tara? It seemed that you could barely keep your hands off each other at the party."

Yes, now with the tables turned, Danny had something to gloat about, which seemed like a miracle.

"Ahh, it's incredible, really, to have such a tempting, naughty wife! It's like some crazy windfall."

"That's great, but how so?" Sammy encouraged, his curiosity up. He egged his brother on, "Come on and spill the beans. I always tell all the details. Spare me none."

Sammy jabbed at Danny's side, all in brotherly interaction. They grew up so incredibly close and Sammy always had the better outcome with women. Yet, the ones recently were one time flings. There was nothing substantial about the relationships. For once, Danny possessed something very real and strong. Tara looked upon her husband with desire and adoration. Those brown eyes were sexy on one so young. Even for how he admonished Michael to back off, Sammy felt quite envious of their marriage as he watched the couple interact. With all the physical changes she made in the last five months, Tara seemed beautiful and tempting. So what was it like to be with such a hot woman?

"Well, let's just say that she becomes this spirited, willful persona, just as soon as we put the children down to bed," Danny bragged as he followed beside Sammy. His cheeks were visibly red and there was a crazy smile upon his face. Even his voice sounded bewildered, "She comes onto me like clockwork behind closed doors. I don't have to start anything. She takes the lead. What sane man would question that kind of energy? Still, I find myself amazed after all we have endured. If you had told me we'd be this way three months ago, I wouldn't have believed it."

Danny shook his head and leaned upon a rail as they approached a stall. Sammy offered the horse behind it bits of apple that he brought along. There was no one around as the foreman was busy in another pasture. They were free to converse openly. Danny's eyes were beaming.

"With the servants around by day, it's difficult to find a moment alone, but she finagles it. We'd be in the kitchen one minute, and then the next, Tara's grabbed me by both hands to run to the basement. She stands at the door, ensuring that its lock. She has that look in her eye, the one that sends me to the moon. Then she comes running down the steps, throws me against the machine, just to get her way. It's so crazy!"

"Ahh … the quickies!" Sammy said, enlightened with the scenario, "You have turned into teenagers at forbidden play!"

"No, animals actually. Perhaps rabbits!" Danny laughed, "I can't tell you how this blows my mind! So, I want to rearrange the staff's schedule so we can get moments to ourselves more often. It would be embarrassing if one stumbled upon us in a compromising position. Not all the rooms are possessed with locks!"

Sammy never laughed so hard. His brother's wit was getting better. Danny's face turned a deeper shade of red, but he laughed along too. Happy that for once he could boast about his woman and their terrific passion! He did think that the nights were the best times since he came home. As he lay on their bed, staring out the window, holding Tara so tight while she slept, it seemed that the stars finally smiled down upon them. Even the moon bore witness to their love, too. So later, as he returned back to his household, he knew he had to speak to his staff about their new schedule.

Since returning home, Danny respected everyone's place in the scheme of things. The servants in his house were very pleased that he depended on their advice and insight about the children. Especially Marta. The older woman was happy he was home too. She coddled to his every request and cooked tasty meals and baked fresh bread. She knew he loved the scent of it in the house. Danny always wanted a sample as soon as it was pulled from the oven. Even Tara easily allowed decisions to flow without much interruption. Like a commander on a ship, Danny first evaluated how everyone functioned.

All the children slept through the night, even Tom. It didn't seem necessary for twenty four hour help to continue. First, the couple was capable of rising if one child cried out for some reason. Second, this allowed privacy. And Danny wanted that privacy with his wife. When he entered the house, he requested that the servants gather in the kitchen. Caroline and Lila sat at the table and gazed upon him with wide eyes, not knowing what to expect. Marta stood by the stove so she could stir the pot every few minutes. Danny spoke to her first.

"I think its best for you and Lila to continue your role as before, serving meals and keeping up with the house. The children are use to your attention," he said as they stood near him in the kitchen, "You can come around ten and go home at supper. I think we can manage the children's breakfast time. Caroline can come by if needed for a special occasion."

He turned to look at the women at the table and pulled out his wallet to give them a supplemental bonus. The women smiled in delight.

"Caroline, you can return to the manor to your regular duties, now. Over all, you all have done a splendid job while I was away. My great appreciation can never be expressed adequately, but this is a slight reward of our affection. It's just that these changes are inevitable. Tara and I should take over as we are the children's parents. It's only right as they grow that they turn to us more."

"It will be nice to see my family in the evenings," Lila smiled, her green eyes twinkling. She did think it was a good time to make the changes. The children needed a firmer hand to direct their full energy, "Thank you sir. It sounds really good."

Caroline picked up her scarf to place around her brown hair. She walked towards the front door.

"Thanks for understanding about those phone calls," she told Danny before exiting, thinking about the time she was forced to tell him lies, "I didn't have a choice then."

"Yes, I realize now. Tara put you into an awkward position, but it's in the past. I hold no grudges," Danny said and Caroline smiled. She went down the lane to return to the manor.

"It will be a little different, sir," Marta said and went back to her cutting board to sliced up a few lemons for lemonade and tossed them into a pitcher. She added sugar and water, "However, the children need a fulltime father. How happy this makes your wife too. The woman is beaming!"

"She isn't the only one," Danny smiled, with his hands upon his hips, as he looked around the rooms. Marta placed the lemonade pitcher into the refrigerator and took out the ingredients to make fresh bread for their evening supper. She turned on a nearby radio and hummed along with the song. Lila walked about the living room, fluffing up the pillows and placing some of the toys into a nearby playpen. Two loads of laundry lay inside a large basket next to the basement door. There were two loads already downstairs. Lila planned to take care of these next. It seemed like both women would be occupied for a little while.

He could hear Tara's voice drift out from one of the children's room as she read out nursery rhymes. The children were settling down for an afternoon nap. Perhaps they could get one too. The thought seemed tempting. Any chance to lie next to her made his heart beat faster. And so Danny ran upstairs to tell his wife about his sudden idea. For once, he wanted to evoke a reaction. He knew what would happen once they locked the bedroom door.

Chapter Forty Five
A constant father

It was a new role to be a constant father. Danny improvised a lot to get along with the septuplets. They were quite a rambunctious bunch, always quick to get into mischief at eighteen months old, and by this time, were very attached to their mother. They had different temperaments. Sometimes even simple routines could become a battle.

Jamie, Eric and Edward were finicky eaters, taking their time to gobble down what was placed before them at mealtimes. If Edward didn't like something, he simply tossed it over the highchair or flung it towards the wall. For a young tot, a mischievous gleam showed in his eye as he looked upon the mess he did.

"Oh, he's just a modern day artist. He wants to redecorate our kitchen!" Lila teased while cleaning up pasta patiently at lunchtime. Danny didn't like it.

"Let that boy eat sandwiches. He seems to like them," At least it wasn't liquid form and was easy to pick up, but mostly Edward ate it without complaint. This surprised Tara. Such a simple solution to a tyrannical little boy's temperament.

Another thing that bugged Danny was that Tristan easily cried. He was too much in the habit of being picked up to be consoled.

"He must learn to adapt playing alone, Tara," Danny determined. "Otherwise, he'll keep up the bad habit."

She already knew what he thought about this. He had discussed it with Marta. Marta told her. Tara was prepared.

"All right. If you think its best. I'll leave him be," Tara said, depositing two cotton balls into each ear. She grinned at her husband, waved, and then climbed up the stairs to put away towels in the upstairs linen closet.

Tristan stood there. Danny could see what was written all over his face. The tyke couldn't believe it. His mother left him! Eyes blinked, his lips curled, and then he screamed as she disappeared from view. Danny frowned, but handed the boy a toy, patted him on the head, and sat in the recliner to read the paper. He could keep an eye on everyone. The others were playing quietly in the living room. It gave him a terrible headache within ten minutes of it, but soon Tristan tired out. He looked around and stared at Danny a moment or two. Finally, he sat on the floor to play blocks with Erik.

"Thank goodness," Danny sighed, pleased that on this one occasion his idea worked. It took three more times before Tristan realized he didn't gain extra attention by crying anymore. From then on, he stopped. He simply pointed when he wanted something and learned to tag along.

The older boys, Vincent, Tyler, and Matthew were spunky children, ate a lot and liked to get into things. Danny took to playing blocks or building puzzles with them. They especially hated bedtime and would get into a huge tantrum. Whenever Danny picked them up, they sensed they were going to their beds and would cry. To remedy this, he raised them high into the air and then dive them into their cribs, like flying bombers. The toddlers didn't really remember the man, but they thought this game was way too much fun. They begged for more. After a few times, they stopped crying and peered up at him through their cribs, waiting patiently. When he departed the room, they cried out, "Da!"

"What are they saying?" Danny listened closely.

"I think it's da-da, although the "A" sounds like what's in 'daughter.'" Tara explained.

"Hmmm, interesting," Danny said and clicked out the light. They went to sleep.

In Tara's mind, it just seemed to fit. He was "Da" from then on. He headed back down for the next two boys. She watched him whisk both Matt and Edward above his shoulders. They were laughing in delight all the way up the stairs. Edward was tired. He grabbed for his pillow right away. Not Matt.

"My goodness!" Danny bellowed out of breath after the fourth dive bomb. He walked to the door, but the kid screamed bloody murder, "Should we allow Matt to cry like that?"

Surely, the kid could adjust.

"It will be ok," Tara turned off the light and closed the door firmly, "Edward can sleep through anything. Matt will be down in two minutes. Just watch."

And sure enough, Danny could hear the little guy wrestled around his crib. A minute later, he settled down, only crying into his pillow. And then it was quiet. It tugged at his heart. Thank goodness that Eric and Tristan were easy.

Still, there was the matter with his daughter. Jamie. His little princess. Always the last to settle in, the child definitely inherited her mother's expressive eyes. Easily consolable, the child looked for the bottle. From her back, she stared up at him, all eyes intent on his face. Out of all the children, she paid the most attention to what he did. On the pillow, she seemed a quiet little angel. Danny stroked down her curls, hummed a little nursery song. Her eyes grew wide. Again, he could hear a sound escaping her throat. He couldn't get over it. The girl was trying to hum back. Was she musically inclined? At some point, he would have to test her abilities further.

"Go to sleep," he whispered and tucked her in snugly. He turned off the lights. Only a night light remained on the far wall, giving the room a dim glow. Within a minute, the girl was sound asleep, but Danny could not erase from his memory the way she looked. The child was so precious. Forever, he would be deeply devoted.

Tara loved her man. As time moved forward, he was terrific with the children. During their occasional outings, whenever the children got out of line, Danny's voice would sound stern, just to give notice that he meant business. He always bent down to their level to speak, to encourage their best behavior. He was very patient when they were overtired or too rambunctious. His eyes expressed his love and concern.

Tara admired this easy demeanor. She was thankful that the Navy taught him a sense of order. He was the commander of their household. She was a co-navigator. They were all on a terrific voyage together. By mid-November, the children hovered around him quite often, now that he was a permanent fixture to their world. There were lots of times he could be spontaneously silly. They liked that best.

Tom turned six months old that month. His black hair grew fast. Tara didn't want to cut it. He was too cute, a quiet child, that always observed everyone. Tom never minded bath time or being placed in the play pen. Danny eased into the chore of changing diapers and feeding the tyke baby food. It warmed Tara's heart that Danny took to the child, in spite of the fact that Tom wasn't his flesh and blood.

Sometimes, Tara would find Danny in his recliner, reading his paper out loud; a habit he did daily. He held Tom close on his lap, with Eric and Jamie on either side. They were hidden behind the paper, while the other boys played at his feet. They listened to his voice that told world events like he was reading a fairy tale.

"Let's see what our Prime Minister has to say today," he said in big and dramatic sounds while he flipped the pages, "Ms. Thatcher is our new leader, the first woman elected to do so. Things are changing for the better. Do you want to be Prime Minister when you grow up, Jamie? Wouldn't that be spectacular?"

Their eyes grew wide to listen. It made Tara smile. Yes, she loved that man!

After Danny returned home, Michael or Gloria came down to pick up Tom on Friday afternoons. More than often, Susan volunteered, which they all found unusual, but since it eased their busy schedules, it was overlooked. They would drive into the village to meet Ross or sometimes take the boy all the way, depending on what went on. Ross had a car then, so things were easier for him too.

Sometimes it bothered Tara that visitation went this way. There were lots of times she found herself missing her friend, just for conversation. She really thought that Danny preferred never to see that man again. Until one day, he was upstairs packing Tom's diaper bag. She overheard him from their bedroom, speaking to Tom in a playful high voice

"We best put in your favorite stuff bunny. Do you think your daddy has any clue that you like it? Maybe not, but I do. Yes, I do," he said, stopping to pluck his lips onto Tom's belly to do a raspberry. Tom giggled out loud. Danny wrapped him into a warm coat, "Maybe one day, we'll share what we know. Do you think so? You look so cute in this. Your looks come from your mother. Don't tell your daddy. It'll hurt his feelings. He always thinks he's all that. You, my bright young man, have it in spades. Now, we must hurry. Your Aunt Susan is waiting outside."

Danny placed on his lower thick pants, zipped him up, and then swung the diaper bag over his shoulders. He picked up Tom and rushed out the door. Through the window, Tara stared out at Danny. He placed Tom into the car seat. She didn't know what to think, but his words made her feel hopeful. Perhaps in the future, he might get around to talking to Ross again. That was encouraging.

After Susan left, Danny went back into the house. He stopped by the hearth to warm up. Tara was busy that morning, but she did note a strange expression on his face.

"Is something bothering you?" she asked, coaxing him out of a shell.

"Well, it's just that I wish Susan never ditched college to do modeling," Danny sighed, "There's better way to earn a living. She could marry even. Why doesn't she take after Gloria's example? She's a modern woman, but doesn't flaunt her wiles. Not like this."

He showed Tara the hunting magazine that just came out on the stands. Susan gave him a copy to show off. Show off, indeed. There she was, posing on a Riviera Beach with a skimpy string bikini, advertising liquor. He pointed out another where she looked like a hooker out on a hot night in Italy. The makeup was bright. The skimpy clothing showed off everything that Susan had to offer a man. Which was a lot conveyed behind a low plunging neckline.

"I hope you never do this," Danny shook his head. "I mean, Jesus! She is my sister! Just look at her. If you showed off like that, I would be so embarrassed."

"Where would I have the opportunity? I am knee deep in children," Tara took the magazine from his hands. She pulled back the safety gate around the fire and threw the magazine into it, "I am fine just being a wife and a mother."

"Yes, and you look so well for it," Danny agreed, happy that Tara was very modest in her fashion style. It may show off her curves, but never a lot of her breasts. Tara looked best in pastel colors since she possessed a creamy complexion. Her face was flawless with natural makeup or none at all. Now, she would look damn good in a magazine. He felt so blessed to have such a lovely wife.

About once a week, Danny made a trip into the village to swing by the bank or to stop by the grocers. He would only stop at the pub for one drink and then quickly return home to Tara. Rosemary and Eileen knew there was a difference in the man. He was cheerful and smiling all the time. He spoke non-stop about the children. The man was definitely in love, and they were happy for him. Their affair, tucked away in memory, would no longer interfere with the future.

Chapter Forty Six

Tara's Christmas Gift

Christmas time grew near again and for once, it was fun decorating up the house for the occasion. Danny insisted "to do it up right" and went out to the woods to cut down a fine tree. The couple decorated it with plenty of lights, red bows, and bright shiny tinsel. He bought a model train kit to entertain the children. It would be the beginning of a family tradition. The week before the big day, the whole Cross family met up in London to go shopping. They took the children to see a giant tree that was set up near the statue of Lord Nelson in Trafalgar Square. It was brought in from Oslo, Norway.

"It's a thank you gift," Danny explained to Tara. "During World War Two, the King of Norway was exiled in our country when the Germans occupied his country. Later, to express his thanks for his safe harbor, a Norwegian spruce, just like this one, was sent."

"That's remarkable, but it reminds me of New York. We have a large tree set up in Rockefeller Center too," she replied, clutching his arm, and staring at it like a child appreciating the twinkling lights, "This is just as lovely."

"Yes, I remember seeing it when I first went to New York. That seems so long ago, when Harry and I drove up from the Pentagon. We passed the center as we looked for our hotel. Later on that week, we met at that street bar on New Years Eve."

"I wasn't very nice to you then. Will you forgive me?" Tara pouted and blinked her eyes at him intentionally. Danny kissed her lips.

"Of course, darling. You can make it up to me tonight. It'll be good to go out with Harry and Lilly. I know you briefly met Harry, but together with Lilly, they are extraordinary people," He said, his eyes glowing just to see his old friend again. He couldn't wait.

Lila and Marta tagged along on that trip. At the hotel, they watched the children along with Danny's parents in separate rooms. It made things easier than to invade Michael's single flat. It was a great opportunity for Danny to treat Tara out on the town with his friends. They ate at a lavish restaurant and then went out to a ritzy nightclub. They danced the evening away. Tara never enjoyed a time as much as this. She even danced with Harry a time or two. They all had fun but sometime near midnight, Lilly and Harry bid their farewells while Danny and Tara remained. They were younger. They could handle the nightlife better.

"Oh, Danny! You dance so well. You are an expert!" she laughed as they raced off the floor and Danny bowed gallantly. His eyes were as bright as the spinning strobe light above the dance floor.

"The music is great! I love it -all the explosion of sounds, lights, the beat! The stage set up they have here is terrific. I think it's neat that we can jump on one to dance by ourselves. I feel like a rock-and-roll star! Can you imagine being one? What a life!" Danny exclaimed, words tumbling over with his excitement. He reached for his large wine goblet to quench his powerful thirst.

Tara nodded. She, too, felt the rush from the atmosphere. She relished being out with her husband this way. She felt like Cinderella out with prince charming, and her knock out red dress was fantastic. He couldn't keep his eyes, or his hands, off her. It was magical, the ambiance of the club, the people milling about, all the bright lights that sprang from the ceiling, the bar. Just the fact that he was so much fun to be with: a splendid man. What a great way to celebrate Christmas. Yet, the season bore a special meaning for another reason. Tara couldn't wait to share the news.

About two in the morning, they returned to their hotel room. Danny was slightly tipsy, she was not. She knew what she was doing. He sat on the bed to stop spinning for a moment while Tara slinked out of her dress. She stood before him, completely nude, with only high heels, a long gold necklace, and dangling earrings. She let down her curly brown hair and it bounced seductively upon white shoulders. He appreciated that view for a moment and saw a wicked gleam flash in her magnificent eyes. Her hand reached to the wall switch nearby and the lights turned off. A neon sign outside gave off a low glow into their room. Tara dropped upon her knees before him. His eyes went wide in surprise, but he lay back on the bed. With her, everything his wife did was magic. The type of magic he gladly reciprocated. Afterwards, as they nuzzled in the dark, they discussed their adventure that day.

"I had a great time, didn't you, darling?" Danny cuddled closer. Her body was warm, her breasts soft to touch. He sighed, "We should do this more often. We certainly deserve it. I love our children, but sometimes, it's nice having a break, behaving like real grownups."

"I agree."

"Yet, you didn't drink much wine at all. Only a few sips."

"It was fine. I didn't need to drink."

Danny squeezed her body tight.

"Well, if it's the liquor that bothers you, I have certainly cut back a lot in the last three months, by several pints. There's no longer a need to worry. I realize you did once. You had every right to do so." He remarked, glad that he had cut down that demon to size that once wreaked havoc in his actions.

"I wasn't implying anything," Tara giggled, "You do drink less, and I appreciate that. Really, it's ok to drink when we celebrate like tonight."

"But I didn't over do it, and I won't in the future. Still, why didn't you? You love merlot. Did it taste bad?"

"No."

"Then why?"

"Let's say I shouldn't do it."

"Why not?" Danny insisted as his heart pounded. He suddenly realized that Tara was leading up to something specific. He waited for her to drop the other shoe.

"It's not good for the baby."

"What? Which baby?"he cried out. His ears strained to hear what she would say next.

"Ours," Tara declared gleefully and patted away at her slim tummy. She wasn't even showing, but soon would be, and for this, he bolted up. He stared down at her in the dark.

"Great Scott! Are you for real? Are you expecting?"

"Yes. I am," Tara sat up, eager to spill out her secret.

"It was wonderful to have you home again after all that time in the Navy. You opened up our worlds! Your love is so infectious and I truly thought about us. We need to do this now, while the children are still in diapers and playpens. The doctor told me I should wait a year, but I can't. So I threw away those darn pills. I wanted just one more. One more baby. Maybe another girl or a boy. With blue eyes and lots of blond hair - exactly like you."

He never felt so out of whack! This news thrilled him out of his mind! It was like his grandmother said: *Treat her with respect and their love would blossom.* Such pride swelled in his heart now and he burst out loud in delirious laughter. Danny took Tara into his arms. With vigor, he tickled her until she squealed and was out of breath from wrestling with him on the bed. And then he kissed her, again and again. He was so blessed. Apparently, already eight times blessed. What would one more child hurt?

Chapter Forty Seven
Passing of time

Danny waited with great anticipation as 1979 faded away. A new decade beckoned. In the springtime of 1980, so much activity went on in their household and it made it easy for him to mark the time. In February, Tara and Danny celebrated their second anniversary. George and Helen prepared a nice dinner celebration for them. The children were watched in their new playroom by the staff so they could eat in peace. Danny presented Tara with a heart-shaped diamond necklace and matching earrings. She gave him a four-album set of various American artists of the fifties. Danny felt elated. He studied the album cover and tore off the cellophane wrapping. He couldn't wait to blast it through out their house.

"Listen to Elvis, Tara," he said as he played it on his new compact stereo. He sang along to Jail house rock, while he turned up the volume. The children laughed and jumped around him. Every day, he played a different album from the set, over and over again. Tara didn't mind at all. In fact, she fell in love with his voice. He was terrific. Whenever he grabbed her hands to pull her close, so that he could sing "Can't Help Falling in Love", staring deeply into her eyes, she got all goose-pimply. He was so exciting.

"That man sure does love music," Lila remarked as they cleaned out Tara's closet one day. Chubby Checker was singing the Twist. Tara caught herself humming along, shimmying as she tidied up the top shelf. Lila was on the bottom pushing around boxes, snapping her fingers on occasion. It made the work flow smoother. She stumbled over ones with Christmas wrapping and showed them to Tara, "Did you forget these?"

"Yes, Lila I did," Tara said as she plopped onto the floor, sitting Indian style. Lila sat beside her. Tara opened up the first box. A nice pair of leather gloves, from Michael; expensive perfume from Paris, from Sammy, which made Lila's eyebrows rise up, "He likes shopping from catalogues, I'm sure someone helped pick it out, perhaps a lady friend."

This was a good explanation and Lila nodded. There was a nice pair of earrings from Susan. Lila noticed there was another box behind where the presents sat. It was medium size, with plain wrapper. Tara noticed Danny's Falkland address upon it. She tore it open. Inside it was sheet music. They were melodies and lyrics with written instructions on the sides that explained some changes to the music. There was a note from Ross:

Danny! You're a genius, my friend! I beefed up the words. Made a few change-ups- ok, maybe several, but it works! We can argue about them later! Hope you like the majority! We must do this again- Soon! Take care, your friend always, Ross.

"What is it, Mrs. Cross?"

"It's music that Ross and Danny wrote. I bet my husband brought it home last Christmas. He either didn't have a chance to open it up or didn't want to, considering he found out about Ross and I. Haskell scooped up all the presents. He probably didn't realize he brought it here. Perhaps, it's best just to put it up. Danny doesn't speak to Ross anymore, obviously."

"I think that's a good idea," Lila scooted it into the closet, out of sight, "We should never mention it unless they come looking for it."

Tara nodded firmly. A pact made. They continued working.

The septuplets celebrated their 2nd birthday the following month. Since Danny read to them all of the time, they seemed very smart. In just a short time, he taught them valuable independence. They picked up their toys and helped take their plates into the kitchen. They did away with their bottles and pacifiers and drank out of glasses. Danny thought it encouraged their motor skills instead of depending upon sippy cups. In the mornings, the children dressed themselves just enough to where someone could help with the snaps, buttons, or zippers. They loved playing with blocks and puzzles. They repeated nursery rhymes. Often times, they sang along with Danny. It made him smile.

The birthday party was held on a nice sunny day. There were lots of presents and even some of the neighbors came by. "Can I get a picture for the paper?" Mr. Gosney asked, "We can put it into syndication. My office still gets lots of questions about them."

Danny looked over at Tara and she nodded an approval. It seemed inevitable to keep those children out of the limelight.

The septuplets tired out easily after eating cake and playing games all afternoon. They were in bed by seven that evening, going down without a fight. For every passing of an event, Danny grew more impatient for his child to arrive.

In Mid-March, Tom celebrated his first birthday. He celebrated with the family on Friday, even if his birthday fell earlier that week.

"Ross plans to take him to Regent's Park tomorrow afternoon," Susan explained to Tara on the side, "Then we'll share a cake with him. A bit of a quiet celebration."

"We? Will you be there?" Tara looked at her, puzzlement showing in her eyes. Susan's attitude was different lately, as she helped out with Tom. Tara found it unusual that Susan seemed to coddle the boy. The young woman sipped punch and nodded.

"Yes. He asked Gloria, too, but unfortunately, she has another commitment, which is why she's here today. I told him I would help out. I'm Tom's aunt. Why shouldn't I? You don't find anything wrong with that, do you?" Susan asked. There were times she wished she could admit having a relationship with him, but she couldn't, because of Danny and because of Gloria too.

Even if Gloria didn't say things out loud, in her eyes, whenever Ross's name was mentioned, they would glow. Susan never lost sight of this.

Tara paused over Susan's question. The young girl looked sincere, so it didn't raise any other suspicions. Through Susan, Tara always found out the most about her friend. Ross earned his way up to be an account manager, being smart with numbers, investing wisely for clients. Ross was proud that he earned his place in the company on his own.

"No, I don't. I hope it's fun. The weather turned out to be splendid, even if it's still a bit nippy. Just make sure he bundles up Tom well. I don't want him to catch a cold."

"You worry too much. Ross is an excellent father. I'm sure he'll take pictures at the park. I'll bring you some copies."

"Thank you. I'll send you some to give to him too." Tara replied, thinking that this was a thoughtful suggestion.

Later, that month, it was strange placing all the birthday pictures into Tom's baby photo album. She studied Ross's face. He smiled holding his son on the swing set. Their genuine love for Tom could not be shared. It was odd and sad, but there was nothing either could do about it. Tara was sure, that somewhere in Ross's apartment, there was a picture displayed too, of her with Tom.

Helen and Gloria threw a baby shower on Tara's behalf in June at the Briggs House. Most of the guests were old social friends of the family or acquaintances in the area. There were about twenty five ladies in attendance. It was remarkably fun, being the center of attention, playing games. Tara loved the new gifts, all the baby clothes, receiving blankets, toys and little shoes. About mid-way through, Rosemary and Eileen showed up. Lila whispered their arrival into Tara's ear.

"Mrs. Cross, there are two women at the door asking for you. I know them. They are those women from the bar," Lila said as she squeezed a towel tightly. Tara looked up at her, with questions in her eyes. Danny was away with the children at the manor. So why did they come over?

"Excuse me, ladies," Tara walked away from her guests. She didn't know what to think as she opened the front door. This caught her by surprise.

"Hello, Mrs. Cross, I'm Rosemary. This is my friend, Eileen," Rosemary announced. They stood there nervous as she scrutinized them over. The women were in their Sunday best. They looked perfectly normal. Nothing out of the ordinary or trashy. Eileen nudged Rosemary to continue, "Look, we don't mean any disrespect. It's just that we heard about the shower."

"Yes," Tara replied, without giving away any emotion. At that point, Eileen took out a lovely wrapped present from a large bag.

"We brought something for the baby. It'll be exciting when he's born. Danny... err ... Mr. Cross, brags that it might be a boy, because of the way you carry. So, everyone at the pub pitched in to give you something. He's a terrific man. A great friend. Please don't mind."

Eileen showed it to Tara. What else could she do? It was wise to be gracious under the circumstances and let bygones, be bygones. The women appeared so eager to gain her acceptance.

"That's very kind. Please, won't you join us for cake and punch?" Tara offered politely, taking hold of the gift, and opening the door wide. She even smiled. The women gasped, blinking their eyes in relief. They instantly went inside to join the others. Tara introduced them to the guests. Soon, everyone chatted again, as if nothing unusual occurred, but everyone knew what took place. Helen and Grams beamed proudly from where they sat.

When news filtered its way to Danny, it was a big surprise. Even with the time gone by, there was no courage on his part to forgive Ross. On more than one occasion since he came home, his sisters would talk about the man privately. Danny was compelled to listen in by the door. They all sounded quite taken in by the man, for their own various reasons. Somehow, he could relate. They spoke of a person he once knew very well, a gracious, mature young man- an old friend.

"Ross is extremely smart when it comes to making sound investments with my money. He doesn't skim any commissions for himself. He does mine for free. What can be better than that? He's making me bloody rich, rich, rich!" Susan gushed as she deposited a dividend check from the investment firm into her purse. Gloria poured water into a glass. She smiled.

"He is a terrific person. Always so considerate. I got stuck on the metro with a bad flat on rush hour traffic. Michael couldn't come, so I called Ross. I didn't know who else would help me. He came without any hesitation and did it when it began to pour down rain,"

Gloria laughed, "Poor man! He was soaked to the bone. I tried to offer him something- an invitation to dinner, maybe. He just bowed like a gallant man and went on his way. He always asks about the family, especially about Danny, now that he knows he's home."

"They need to get on with life!" Susan snapped, "Danny needs to let go of that bad time. He has his woman, give Ross some forgiveness!"

"What are you two going on about," Tara interrupted from another entrance. She deposited some dishes onto the counter.

"Oh, we were talking about Ross," Susan whispered and pretended to cut her tongue, "I know he's a bad subject to bring up in your home. I hope my brother isn't nearby."

Danny rolled his eyes, but he was safe by the servant's entrance into his kitchen.

"I think he might be upstairs. What about Ross? What did he do," Tara's tone was indifferent. She turned on the water to do dishes by hand. The girls looked at her peculiarly. Tara laughed, "Well, I mean *recently*, ladies. Has he or Michael done something particular? They have turned into quite the dynamic duo, I hear."

"Nothing more than usual. My brother drags him out to the nightclubs, but Ross stays so suave, laid back. It's Michael that uses that handsome man like a glue trap, zoning in on younger girls to come closer to their table. Maybe Michael feels his age now. It's pathetic, really- on Michael's part," Susan revealed. She did hate Michael taking him out.

451

"Well, maybe one day, Ross will meet someone interesting. I guess right now all he wants to do is concentrate on himself and Tom," Gloria said.

The women grew quiet for a moment, all thinking of their own relationships with that man. Just the fact that Tara didn't overdo the conversation made Danny think. She asked questions as a concerned friend would do so, nothing more.

Yet it was too soon to let Ross simply come around again. It would be unbearable if he saw the friends close. What if they slipped up again? Their one mistake still nagged at his pride, even with the intimate time he spent with Tara lately. This alone made him feel protective of his woman. And Ross never even offered an apology like Eileen and Rosemary did. At least not to his face. That was the difference in his book.

Then later that same night, out of the blue, Gloria cornered Danny in Tristan's room. He was getting the boy into his pajamas. Gloria helped Eric. She took this time to admit how smitten she became over Ross.

"I can't help it. He's always there when I need something. Occasionally, he'll drop by the studio. We wind up in these long conversations. He talks about you. He misses your friendship," she revealed, but Danny didn't reply, so Gloria went on further, "He loves his life now, his job. He earns respect the old fashion way. When I see him dressed up, I find him greatly attractive, but he's that way even in blue jeans. I want to push the man into something further. Do you mind?"

Gloria touched his arm then. She searched his eyes for an approval.

"Dearest sister, you are old enough to decide your life. If he has captured your heart, then go for it."

"Really?" Gloria seemed flustered, "Well, it's not like anything will happen. I hint that I'm available. Then he smiles and indicates nothing back. Perhaps he is skittish because of your discord."

"What man can resist you? You are absolutely lovely. You will soon wear him down. I promise, if anything develops, I will be civil," Danny replied. Gloria looked as if she might cry. She hugged him tightly.

"Oh, Danny! Thank you! I love you!" she exclaimed and then she let him loose. Seeing that the boys were in their beds, she smiled and went on downstairs. Danny slumped on the edge of the bed. This was difficult. It was high time that she became infatuated with someone, even with Ross. However, he had a suspicion. The reason that Ross wouldn't date his sister was because of Tara. Perhaps Ross harbored feelings for his wife. No, temptation was best kept far away in London.

Chapter Forty Eight
A Family becomes complete

It was a hot afternoon, late in July, when the baby made his entrance into the world. He came a month early, a few days shy from Danny's birthday. She sat on the porch with a hand fan. The children were on the front lawn, chasing after baby ducks. Danny purchased them around Easter time, along with baby chickens and bunnies, simply for the children's amusement. His plan was to sell them off at a later time. Tara didn't like the idea. "If you sell them, the children will notice they are gone."

"Oh, Tara, the bunnies will reproduce, quickly enough to make them happy again. Besides, I'm raising them for a profit. They must understand about money."

He was out in the yard, sprinkling seed, toasted bread, to attract the ducks to stay, while all of the toddlers chased them unmercifully. Tara laughed at the whole scene.

"Danny! Stop riling up the children! Those poor ducks!"

"They'll be all right!"

He was encouraging Jamie to pick one up, but she wasn't doing it at all. Those little beaks scared her. She ran behind Edward, who took a stance to protect her, like a karate kid. Then he "chop-chop-chop" at the air to scare the duck. By this time, Tara laughed uncontrollably and she denied that contractions were underway again, feeling very strong.

They began the day before and lasted into the night, but were sporadic. It didn't make sense to alarm anyone, or so she thought. Now, they seemed hard and intense. Now she worried, so she stood up, hoping the pressure would go away. Suddenly, it hit in the worst way, just as Michael and Gloria pulled up in the car in the driveway. That's when her water broke.

"Ahhhh!" Tara gasped to feel the warm gush fall down her legs. She looked down then, afraid to move. By the car, everyone stood, making small talk amidst their long hellos. Michael was going on about something, so it took a minute for Danny to look over. He saw the color gone, her face blank. She looked alarmed.

"What's wrong, Tara?" Danny called out then, pausing to see if she would say something. No such luck. He dropped the bread bucket when she bent over suddenly and cried out again: "Ahhhhhh!"

"Oh, my! She's in labor!" Gloria rushed forward to assist too, but they didn't know which way to go, in the house or out to the car. The hospital was too far away for this quick onset. Danny and Michael scrambled to gather the children. They tried not to trip over the baby ducks.

"Lila! Marta! Come quickly!" Danny bellowed towards the house. They showed up at the doorway with puzzled expressions, "Take the children to their rooms. Try not to startle them."

Yet, it was too late. The children looked at their mother quite afraid as she yelled out once more. She reached for the banister to steady herself. She cried out desperately enough to put everyone into a panic.

"Ahhhhhhhhhh! Quick! Quick! The baby is coming out!"

"What?" Gloria and Danny sputtered out loud, while he carried two children up the front steps. Lila ushered them out of the way, towards the stairs. Danny stared into Tara's eyes. He looked at the ground and then at her again, "What do you mean- it's coming out?"

Tara glared at him then. All the forces of the body made her bear down, and it hurt. She *knew*, one way or another, she was about to deliver.

"Just get me inside! Get me somewhere! I'm having this baby now!"

Danny picked her up into his arms. He rushed to place her on the sofa.

"Not here! It will ruin the fabric," She cried out as a huge contraction took over again, "Ahhhhhhh! Danny! I *said* not here!"

Her tone seemed possessed by the devil.

"Well, bloody hell! I don't give a damn! I'll replace it!" Danny put her on it anyway. He looked around. There were two blankets that were on the rocking chair. He placed one underneath her bottom; the other was draped over her legs. She sat halfway up. Her face grimaced, her body shook.

Meanwhile, Michael called the local doctor on the phone. "God, man! Weren't you listening? I said get over here! Now! She's having a baby!" he hollered into the receiver. Then he slammed it down. His face looked very white.

Gloria rushed over with a pair of scissor, a sheet and a towel, and then a pot of warm water that happened to be on the stove to boil potatoes. She positioned herself in front of Tara.

"Ok, Tara. Let's do this. Push!" Gloria instructed. Relieved to be in a safe place, Tara did. She clutched at Danny's hand very tightly. He grimaced too. It hurt! He thought it was like a vice grip. Was his bones breaking? They both cried out simultaneously, "Ahhhhhh!"

Suddenly, a splotch of hair crowned. Danny couldn't help but stare. He seemed pale.

"Great Scott! I can see the head!"

"Don't feint, Danny! You are about to have your son! Right now!" Tara bore down again. She squeezed his hand again. "Ahhhhhhhhhhhh!"

At this point, Michael stood by in case Danny did fall out. He silently prayed that he wouldn't either. It wasn't necessary. Tara pushed with all of her might, and this time, Gloria situated the head, helped ease out the shoulders, and then pulled the child out gently.

Somehow, instinct kicked in. Tara let go of his hand. Danny grabbed the sheet and with the nearby towel, he dipped it in the pan of water, and then wiped the child's face while he hung upside down within Gloria's hands.

She found an old nasal suction bulb used whenever the toddlers suffered bad colds. She used that to suction out fluid from the baby's nostrils. By that time, the child's face turned bloody red. He laid out a wail that could be heard all over the house.

"Oh, Tara! He's here! Our son is here!" Danny cut the cord without any hesitation. He seen it done so many times in movies, he thought he had it right. Then he wrapped the child up within the sheet. Tara collapsed onto the sofa and took a deep breath. Tears came to her eyes as Danny placed the child upon her breast. She looked him over. Everything seemed right. The baby possessed a very nice head of blond hair. Tara cooed at the wriggly, baby boy.

"My! What an all-fire hurry you were to get here!"

"I guess he wanted to chase the baby ducks too!" Danny remarked with a blank expression. Tara looked into his eyes and then they laughed hysterically. Everyone did.

The local doctor rushed over, just in time to take care of the afterbirth. He checked out the boy's weight, measurements and gave him a very good once over. Everything looked great. After that, Tara and the infant were taken upstairs to her bed. The doctor came up too. He filled out the document to take to the county registrar.

"What's his name?"

"Aaron," Tara told him proudly, "Aaron Daniel Cross. After his father."

"Very good. It's a nice proper name. Now, get plenty of rest, Mrs. Cross," The doctor went to the door, "He's a lovely child. Congratulations. I'll come by tomorrow to check on you again."

He went out the door. Tara cuddled Aaron closely. He yawned, resting close to her heart. After a minute, he slept sound. He was a beautiful 16 inch, five pound boy, all very perfect.

"I best get my time in now, little one," she whispered, "I bet after today, your father will keep you all to himself."

After that miraculous day, they both thought the child made their lives very complete. In light that the baby was born at home, she didn't want to go to London just to get her tubes tied in a separate procedure. She had enough with hospitals and all that it entailed. Instead, she thought it best to keep up with her birth control pills. The couple discussed it all, weighing their options.

"If you are worried about another, I suggest you get a vasectomy!" she told Danny one night. He backed away, shaking his head no. He too, made sure she took her pills on schedule. Tara always hated taking medicine, but this one, she didn't ignore. Their lives were too busy. Every morning, as soon as she went down to the kitchen to start coffee, she took her pill.

That time of the month plagued her. It remained, like in her youth, skimpy. She sat down one night and told Danny everything that happened at Hartridge, about Jimmy and the nun, how it seemed mysterious that a halo glowed about her head when she offered the pills. "Don't you think that is weird?"

"It's your imagination, Tara."

"I don't think so." Then she told him about her prayer when he left for the Mediterranean, when she knelt in the snow and looked up to see the light skew into the shape of a cross. She told him about her quarrel with God and her questions.

"I've always been a firm believer in signs, intuitions, and instincts. Haven't you ever experience something cosmic before?"

Her eyes focused keenly upon his. Then, Danny recalled his own conversation with God, too. He was gracious enough to bring Tara back into his life. He had his perfect family.

"I suppose. Maybe we are in the hands of a higher power," He admitted and she was pleased he believed too.

When Aaron was nine months old, he whispered into her ear, "If by chance, another mistake is made, I wouldn't give a damn, Mrs. Cross. Why not leave it in God's hands. Throw away those pills."

Tara stared in disbelief. It would be wonderful to not worry about taking them. They were a pain to keep up. It was crazy too, but she obeyed. For three months, there was no cycle, but she wasn't pregnant. At best, she was lucky to have one maybe two or three times a year. Every time she missed, they held their breaths. Danny was content with their children. Perhaps God, too, thought that nine was enough.

Chapter Forty Nine

Simple Disconnections

Precious time seemed to slip by quickly. Before Danny knew it, summer turned into fall, and then winter, and then came spring again. Another year turned. Their lives were forever wrapped around the children, but he wouldn't have it any other way. He could feel it in his bones that he was meant to be home, to be with Tara too. There love grew strong as the days progressed. He missed the Navy, but he found ways to keep busy in other pursuits.

His father retired from all business matters in London and within their own county. For once, he wanted to take things at leisure, so he gave Danny full reigns of managing the family investments as well. He always hoped that Michael would take over, but his eldest son disappointed him after college. At that point, Michael took off to London to pursue the theater. George didn't see anything practical about that life, but knew that Michael did well in it. At least he could support himself and not fend off the family's money. Now with Danny around, he taught all he could about stock options, dividends, reading the market outcome in the newspaper. George never expected Danny to learn so quickly. His dedication made George feel proud. Their long conversations only made George feel remarkably close to his middle son.

Grams passed away in her sleep one night. One of the maids went to wake her up. She lay in her bed peacefully, with a bible beside her, and the picture of Henry and her in her hands. Aaron was two, Tom three, and the eldest seven were four when this happened. It was a sad occasion for everyone. Danny took it very hard and tried not to weep in front of the children. It was difficult to do.

He dressed in a black suit for the funeral. The children heard him sniffing.

"Da's crying again," Jamie whispered. She urged the others to follow her into the master bedroom. She pushed the door open and scampered upon the bed, careful not to wrinkle her dark maroon dress. Yes, Danny tried to hold his emotions in, as he stood at the long mirror, adjusting a long tie. He couldn't do it. In utter dissatisfaction, he untied it again and sighed.

"Da, come here," Eric said, holding out his arms. Danny looked at the boy. He was pretty bright for a four year old. Tara spent hours one afternoon teaching him to do a tie himself. Danny went over and bended down upon one knee. At that moment, all the children gathered closely to give their Da' an embrace. At that time, Tara returned to the room. She stood at the doorway, tears flowing from her eyes. Danny looked up at her. A surprised look upon his face. Tenderly, he wrapped his arms around them all as best he could.

"Do you feel better now?" Jamie asked after a moment. Her hair was pulled up in a nice ponytail, with long ribbons hanging down. The boys were in dark slacks and long-sleeved blue shirts, looking sharp in their own ties. Jamie's brown eyes focused on his.

"Yes, sweetheart. Much better." He said, grateful that they were old enough to express their sentiments well. He sat upon the bed to gather his wits. It gave an opportunity to discuss how one behaves prudently under difficult circumstances. It was a discussion that would prove timely later in life. The children displayed impeccable composure during the funeral procession. It gave everyone in the surrounding area an opportunity to see the septuplets, to note how the children behaved well. They didn't fidget and didn't talk during the service. It made everyone in the family quite proud.

This same year, in the spring of 1982, Sammy went to war in the Falklands. He was on board the Sheffield when it was struck around 11:00 a.m His letter home, that came about three weeks later, was graphic:

A missile warhead did not explode into us, but the impact and our unused fuel started several uncontrollable fires. We were hit bad and had little power. The frigate "Arrow" came to assist us and "Yarmouth" stood nearby. We fought bravely to save the ship, but we had 20 men dead. Finally the order was given that we must abandon. We had wounded already on board the "Hermes, "Arrow took off most of 260 survivors, which included myself, thank providence. Our Sheffield drifted for four days and Yarmouth finally came about to pull her clear of the TEZ. She finally sank not too far off from where she was hit. We were transported to a tanker, the "British Esk". I'll be so glad when this bloody war is over. I feel so proud of my crew. Danny may have missed this, but it was no bloody picnic.

Danny said a fervent prayer for his brother's safety. Indeed, he was grateful that he was not there. Luckily, Harry and his former crew narrowly missed missile fire during the war. For that, he was delighted and decided not to waste another single day of living. As Grams told him, life was too precious.

Meanwhile, the estate took plenty of work. There were Helen's horses to manage and there were also gardens to seed in the spring, with a bountiful harvest in early summer and then in the fall. Danny bought and cultivated the surrounding fields and then purchased more horses for the stables. Between him and his mother, they made a business breeding out their fine stallions. Danny also purchased three cows and chickens for their new barn. The children delighted in caring and feeding them. They followed their Da' everywhere. He was a huge influence, whether he was aware or not.

About this time, he found his guitar in the basement closet where he had stored it upon his initial return home. He wiped away the dust and cobwebs and poised the dark wood instrument upon his knee. Jamie, Edward and Vincent watched closely as he strummed and adjusted the half-tuned strings.

"What's that, Da?"

"It's my guitar. I half-forgotten it was down here."

"Will you play it?" Edward asked, instantly gathering closer to him. Danny struck up a few bars. He stopped after a minute and sighed loudly. Such a painful reminder of all the times he played with Ross. Jamie tugged on his shirt.

"I want to learn to do that. Will you teach me?" Her big eyes looked at it and then at him in quiet anticipation. Edward nodded too and Danny knew immediately his interest.

"Do you want to play too? If so, I'll have to order small guitars to fit your little arms. If I do this, you must promise to practice often, or you won't get any good at it."

They raised their hands in a salute to seal the deal, except for Vince.

"I'll just watch for awhile," Vincent said. "That's a lot of time to practice."

"Well a good musician honors his craft by being dedicated. When you feel ready to do this, just let me know." Danny instructed Vincent and the young boy nodded. So the next time that Danny went into the village, he ordered special made guitars for them. Eventually, they arrived and happily, Jamie and Edward were eager students. They sometimes went out to the barn to practice with their Da'.

Tara encountered a different situation. Eric wondered into the library to plunk the keys like a bat out of hell. Tara reprimanded him several times not to do it. On the sixth straight day of scolding, she sat down next to him on the piano bench.

"Look, Eric. You can't bang on the keys. You must do them in order, like this," she played the keys of C,

D, E and told him what they were. She continued with G, F, A, B. Then he tried it and hit every note. Pleased, she showed him a different rote. He did that with no problem. With both hands, she played something further, with more notes and two chords. Eric did it without a single error.

"Oh, my! This is interesting," she said. Every chance they could, they practiced. He became better and better. Tara took the contemporary music books from out of the piano bench, the gifts that came from Helen and George. She placed it on the stand, "All right mister. Let's really learn this music, together."

That night, as they went to bed, she told Danny about Eric's hidden talent. She knew about how fast Jamie and Edward were progressing, which Danny viewed as uncanny.

"Jamie is a natural at it, although she still has to toughen up the delicate skin on her fingers. So goes for Edward, as he's not quite as nimble as she. Maybe it's because she possesses longer fingers. Still, I'm going to show them everything I know. Perhaps I can convince Vince to play the base as he is curious. Couldn't hurt, right?"

Tara agreed. She wasn't sure about the other children. At that point, they showed no desire to learn anything. Perhaps it was best. Three avid musicians in the house was quite enough extra noise.

When the eldest seven turned six, they were old enough to attend public schools in the fall. They did exceptionally well and were quite bright. Danny was proud, but the household seemed way to quiet without them around. The next year was just as bad when Tom joined them. Danny spent lots of time with Aaron and when it came time for him to go too, Danny found himself in tears sometimes. Tara understood. She felt the exact same way. Her children were growing up and sometimes this almost seemed difficult, but it was part of life. Lila and Marta stuck around even if they didn't have to do so. It seemed that the parents needed their care and their company.

To ease his mind, Danny began tinkling with music scores on the piano. They were very creative and sometimes uptempo. Carefully, he wrote down his ideas upon sheet music paper. After awhile, the stacks began to pile up. Tara and Marta worked around him as they dusted the books.

"You play very well, Mr. Cross," Marta beamed as she listened to a new score. Tara placed her hands on her hip.

"You always surprise me with hidden talent. When exactly did you learn how to play?"

"Mother forced me to take lessons when I was young. I gave it up when I was around twelve. I always preferred the guitar, but had to learn that on my own." He told her and played the tune on her behalf. She stopped dusting and went to stand by him and watched his fingers move expertly upon the keys. It really was a terrific score, one that Tara hummed as she did the dishes. Since he never wrote out lyrics, she toyed with words in her head to go along with it. It wasn't an easy task and somehow, she envied that Ross liked lyric composition, where he was a natural. . Still, Danny did try to do it himself, but he, too, struggled at it. After several weeks of this, Tara thought she'd go mad listening to the same renditions he dreamed up. If he practiced at night, it disrupted the children from studying or sleeping.

"Danny, why not go to the pub for awhile?" Tara suggested, frustrated that he was stuck again for the third night in a row, "Helbert Finley is turning sixty. I heard Rosemary say to Mr. Merten that they were having a party."

"Are you sure?" Danny couldn't believe that she suggested it. He put the guitar pick down and placed the sheet music on the coffee table, "I could use a lager. These lyrics are giving me fits."

"Yes. Honestly, you are giving me fits! The break may free your mind," Tara picked up his coat. She scooted the man out the door. Yes, it would be very peaceful to get him out of the house for awhile. She had no fear about Rosemary since she married Leo, the barkeep. They were quite fixated on keeping each other in line at the bar. They were making an honest living at it, sprucing the place up to bring about better clientele. A grill was built and the food was better than before. Eileen married too, to a bricklayer and was expecting her first child.

Later, after the children were tucked in bed, Tara sat down to unwind. The sheet music laid everywhere on the table. All those solid compositions. Tara picked up one to study and hummed out the melody. How upbeat and pretty it sounded, but yes, the words needed work! Just then, the telephone rang.

"Hello?" Tara answered quickly so the children would not awaken.

"Tara? Listen, I'm so sorry to call like this, but there wasn't a choice," Ross declared. His deep voice on the line took her totally by surprised. All this time had gone by and they only communicated through the others, "Say, Michael is driving home to pick up Tom for the weekend, so I can't reach him. With regrets, I have to cancel. A business trip came up. In fact, I'm flying out tonight to go with my boss to Brussels."

"Where are you, Ross?" Tara sat up on her knees. She curled up to hear every word, feeing breathless. It was strange how her heart began to beat hard inside her chest. His voice gave her goose bumps.

"I'm at the airport. Look, I don't want to get you in trouble. Should I speak to Danny about this?"

"Trouble? Would you?" Tara retorted. Was Ross truly that brave?

"Is there any other choice?"

"Lucky for you, he's not here. So you are stuck with me."

There was a pause and then it sounded like he sat down. There was a whoosh of his overcoat, a closing of a door, and sounds of moving paper.

"Gosh, these terminals are so messy sometimes. I'm by the gate and they are not boarding yet. I'm in a phone booth. Now, do you suppose that stubborn man would talk to me? That's the real question, my dear. It's been forever."

"No, probably not, but I'm pleased with your attempt. Do you miss us?" Tara truly wanted an answer, but intuitively she knew it.

"Yeah, I really do, and especially you. Gosh, can I really say that out loud? But you know that I like interpreting what is running through that pretty mind. And believe it or not, I miss having a drink with your husband. Several times, I can recall his stories when we were in New York. How is he doing?"

"Danny is fine, but lately, with the children at school, he's bored. It's hard to imagine when there's so much to do around this place. So tonight, I sent him off to the pub. What else to do with a musician who has inept lyrics?"

"Really?" Ross exclaimed loudly, "Is he writing again? I'd love to hear it. There are a few minutes before they line up for boarding. How about it?"

"Ross, I can't play a guitar." Tara reminded him and smiled that he sounded excited about Danny creating songs again.

"You can play a piano. Let me hear it. I'll give a few suggestions."

So, patiently, Tara put the phone down, took the music to the library, closed the doors, and sat down at the upright piano. She picked up the phone receiver in that room and then played softly. She didn't sing the song, but worded it to the beat. They did this for about ten minutes. Ross scribbled on his end. When she was through, she could hear him breathe on the other end. And then he spoke, "Ok, I got it. I think I know what he wants."

Ross suggested a few changes. A word here, change up of notes there. Thank goodness she knew music too. Tara wrote the notes and words in a blank margin so Danny could read them.

"This is terrific Ross. I think you really made a difference. Perhaps the next time he gets stuck, I'll just mail you the melody and then you can send them to me with corrections."

There was an announcement overhead to board the flight.

"That's an idea, but I must board my plane now. I hope Danny finds the new lyrics acceptable. Just explain that they were your ideas in case it miffs him somehow. Perhaps another time, I can call you. If God will allow another opportunity. I miss you Tara. I miss your smile, your laugh. Anyway, that shouldn't be a factor, but it is. Take care and goodnight," Ross sounded rather husky as he hung up.

Tara sniffed for a moment as she laid down the receiver. She walked back into the living room to do the same with the other phone. These simple disconnections were just like them. Each closing the door until some unknown event allowed an opportunity to open up again. She thought about his words. God! She did miss him greatly, but it was not the man's arms or his lips she craved. It was his genuine friendship. It was being a center to his world too. They had shared so much as children. This separation of souls felt so out of place. Tara wiped away her tears. She turned off the lights. She let the sheet music slide onto the table. It was time for bed.

Around midnight, Danny came home. The party was fun. It was good to mingle and drink with old friends again. Everyone was grateful that Tara allowed him to go without any bicker. Danny checked all of the door locks, ensuring that everything was safe, and he went by the coffee table and noted the sheet music with Tara's scribble on the side. For a few minutes, he read it over thoroughly.

"This is so straightforward and perfect," he mused and scratched his head, "No other lyricist can be duplicated like this. This is Ross's doing-but how?"

Danny crept upstairs and found Tara sound asleep with the moonlight shining down upon her. She looked like an angel. The blanket was beside her on the floor as she was restless when he didn't sleep beside her right away. He brought it up to cover her body and saw the exposed satin gown that hugged her developed bosom and curvy hips. Strong desire swept over then and he wanted to wake her up, but reconsidered it. The evening routines usually wore her down where she ensured that the children were fed, picked up their toys and books, and was urged to take their baths in a timely fashion.

He snuggled up to her warm body and thought about what he found downstairs. Did the man happen to stop by? It didn't sound logical since his siblings always picked up Tom. Perhaps he called, but why? Strangely, Danny didn't feel upset or jealous. Ever since Aaron came along, his trust for Tara's devotion developed maturely. She was the best wife that anyone deserved. Instead, as he laid there thinking about it, only curiosity infiltrated his mind. He wondered how Ross would react if he tried speaking to him now. Would he be delighted or insulted that Danny took too long to forgive him? This only made Danny sigh loudly and pull up the blanket to keep the warmth surrounding both himself and his lovely wife.

Chapter Fifty
Let the Music Begin

The next day happened to be Saturday and he knew it would be necessary to ride over to the next village for fencing materials. The leaves were turning colors, the days still warm from bright sunshine. Luckily, the fall was cooperating that year with good weather and not a lot of rain. Danny looked out the window and saw a bright sun hovering over the top of the barn. A car drove by with the windows down, so he knew it to be warm outside.

"What a good day to give the kids a ride on a horse-drawn wagon," he thought and went to gather them up from their sleep.

"If you just have tea and toast this morning, we can be on our way quickly," he suggested as he told them his idea for the excursion. "Be quiet now. Let your mother sleep in for a change."

The children instantly obeyed. Soon they were dressed, chugged down their breakfast, and scampered outside to watch him hitch the horses.

Somehow, Tara woke up, lying on her side, facing a far wall. She reached back for her husband, but noticed that he was already gone. She stretched her arms and legs and let out a huge yawn. Then, she listened for a moment. If he was up, he usually roused up the children too, but she didn't hear a sound. With that many children, there had to be some kind of noise somewhere. So she sat up, slipped on her slippers and robe and ambled out of the bedroom. Going down the hallway, she noticed that Tom sat upon his bed, pouting, "What's wrong Tom? Why do you look so sad?"

"They are going to have fun without me. I wish that I could go," he said as his finger pointed towards the window. Tara rushed to see what he meant just about the moment that Danny placed Aaron squarely into the wagon beside the others.

"Wait here, Tom. Da doesn't know that your dad is not getting you this weekend."

"He's not?"

"No, business came up. I can fix this. Mummy will be right back," She said and rushed to stop Danny before he pulled away.

"Do you have room for one more?" She cried out, wiping sleep from her eyes

"Did you want to go too?" Danny asked and held onto the reins taut. The horses could get jittery sometimes and she had run out of the house too fast.

"Not me! Tom!"

"Isn't he going to London to be with Ross?"

"No, he can't today. I spoke to Ross on the phone last night. He's been called away on a business trip," Tara announced without contemplating the explanation. Her only thoughts were on Tom. Now, what would she do?

Danny put on the brake, jumped down from the wagon, and came up the walkway in a hurry. Tara gasped not knowing what to expect. He doubly surprised her, first with a very calm demeanor, and then by stating: "Oh, really? That's too bad. Let me get Tom ready. I can get him dressed faster than you."

The man ran into the house and within minutes, was back down again, with the young boy drooped across his shoulders like a sack of potatoes. Tom laughed in glee and Danny maneuvered him into a safe place in the wagon. Tara didn't move from her spot the whole time and she kept her hands firm to her mouth. She felt too stunned. Danny climbed up on the buckboard and took hold of the reins again. Watching this, Tara came to her senses again.

"Danny!"she hollered. Danny kept a straight face. The look of surprise in her eyes seemed too cute for him to ignore.

"What, dearest? Is there something else?"

"Well, yes. I was certain that you would want an explanation, about Ross." She cringed. He showed no objection about speaking to Ross. His eyes didn't even blink. For Tara, this was unexpected. The man was way too calm.

"Well, you said the man went on a business trip. These things come up in the finance world. I know. Just go ask my father! If he calls again, just give my kind regards, will ya," Danny declared in a no-nonsense voice and then turned to the children, "Ok, everyone ready? Let's go."

With the crack of the whip overhead, the horses pulled forward and they were on their way. As the wagon descended up the road, Tara swore that there were angels on high shouting, "Halleluiah."

Much later in the afternoon with the supplies tied down, they stopped for a picnic upon a wide sprawling, grassy hill. It was a beautiful spot. The children ate their lunch and then played tag. Danny brought out his guitar to play for six year old Aaron, who listened and watched as his fingers slid on the strings. Interested, the septuplets sat down again, scattered near their Da'.

"Da! Play something for us!" they all requested, "Play one of your songs!"

"All right. As you wish," Danny replied. It was so nice to have a receptive audience as this. The guitar chords riveted sweet music into the air and then he began to sing, a soft passage from the old music he co-wrote back in New York. Yes, the words just flowed along and the chorus was very infectious. *All Ross's words. Damn.* Just then, one by one, the septuplets chimed in and encouraged Tom and Aaron to do the same. As he heard their sweet voices, all in tune, Danny was awestruck. Momentarily, he stopped playing.

"How do you know this?" he asked. "You all sound marvelous."

They looked at each other like they held a big secret. Then they looked at him as his eyes narrowed.

"You play music every night!" Matthew was the first to declare. "And those words are simple to memorize. It's easy! Play more, Da'. I like it very much."

He looked so innocent. Surely, he wasn't pulling his father's leg. Danny wasn't so sure, but the explanation was too logical and he couldn't come up with another theory.

"Yes, I like it too. Do it again." Eric encouraged. They all did, in unison. So Danny struck up the chords again. And the children sang along loud and perfect. No flaws in the words, no flaw in the rhythm, no flaws in pitch. It was a miracle as far as he was concerned. What children ever sounded this good? Suddenly he trembled. Maybe this was a sign. A sign by God. This is what those rambunctious rascals were meant to do. And even if he was their parent, he wasn't biased about this. He really didn't think so. The whole drive home, Danny was fit to be tied. He could not wait to share his plans with Tara.

When Danny came home, he came bursting through the door. All he wanted to do was find his wife and tell her everything that occurred on their ride for supplies. The children were great singing together. This was what they were meant to do. He tried to present his ideas rationally, but by the way that Tara looked at him, he was coming across like a lunatic.

"Tara, I tell you, they were on key. They knew the words. They liked doing it together. We can build on this. I will teach the rest to play, the drums- anything they want," Danny was too excited. Edward and Jamie could play the guitar. Eric liked playing the piano. Now he had to teach the rest, "Once they get good enough, we can show off what they do, maybe put on a little show in the village. It has potential to be sensational!"

Tara was much too busy helping Marta put the picnic items away. Even Lila raised a skeptical brow.

"Oh, Danny. I don't think so," Tara argued, "They are getting adjusted to a new school year. Learning musical instruments could keep them from their homework."

"Please, Tara. Let me try it. It's something they can do together. It will teach them teamwork, how to get along better."

Their Da was so wound up, the children wanted to back him up too.

"Yes, mother! Let us do it! We can do it."

Tara looked at them with a stern face. No sense in encouraging foolish ideas. There Da' was quite capable. Still, Danny persisted. He blinked both eyes, took Tara into his arms, and nibbled her long neck with warm lips, while tilting her body to one side.

"Danny! Stop! You're tickling me!"

"Just say yes!"

"Oh, all right! Do what you will," She said, giving up. He was delighted, but she was eventually right. It was a struggle, juggling school activities, chores, homework and their music lessons. Still, Danny did what he could with their limited time in the evening. They practiced for an hour right in-between supper and getting their baths. From a catalogue, he bought a drum set. When it arrived, he tested all the children to find out who could tap out the best rhythm. The shyest boy, Tristan, wound up with the sticks. From then on, he pounded upon everything in the house.

During those winter months, they held practice sessions in the library, since the piano sat in there. Tyler took to playing it on occasion too. The children, avid learners, surprised Danny with their dedication. Through Gloria's help, she scoured the music stores in London. They found several upbeat children songs written over the years by others, which would fit their vocal range. All of their voices were different, which Danny found odd. While Vince, Tyler, and Matt had deeper resonance, Edward and Tristan were mostly in the middle. Jamie, Eric, Tom and Aaron could reach higher notes. So Danny taught them how to sing in three part harmony. The children seemed content with his song selections. They wanted to make him proud, but there were times they thought the songs were too corny.

With all of the music lessons flooding the air, it was a perfect time to do the laundry in the basement below, just to escape the noise. Sometimes, Tara sang along too. The room, empty and wide, gave her voice a nice echo effect. They couldn't hear her, so she could sing as loud as she wanted. She liked doing it. It was fun.

One night in the late spring, Michael called to speak to Danny.

"Say, brother. I'm having an intimate brotherly/sisterly soirée this coming weekend to celebrate Gloria's success. She deserves some kudos from us. Her business is prosperous, especially with the new facility opening up on the west end. Why not come up to visit? We can have some fun together, like old times. Get out of the country for awhile?"

"Hmm, I suppose I could, for my favorite sister's sake. What time?"

"Come up around 3:00 on Friday. That way, we can do something in the evening together. I'll see you then," Michael said and hung up.

When Danny told Tara, her eyes glowed as she thought about the opportunity that arose. What if by chance Ross stopped by? So, Danny left on Friday around noon. Lila visited a sister in Gloucester while Marta suffered a bad cold. She stayed over at her daughter's house nearby to recuperate and rest. Before departing, the ladies ensured that the fridge was stocked with prepared casseroles and sweet pies. Tara only had to pop them into the oven, carefully noting the cooking times that Lila wrote on an attached index card. For once, Tara looked forward to spending time alone with the children

On that Friday evening, the children heeded their instruction left by their Da' before his departure and took out the instruments to practice. They had something greatly on their minds. Danny arranged a show, the first weekend after school let out, and they needed to be well rehearsed. At first, there was objection by the owner of the pub, which had a ready band stage available, "We can't have kids in here!" the man barked while scrubbing down the bar, "It will chase away business! Besides, we book adult musicians."

Yet, Danny finagled favors with the best of them and decided to put up a deposit, so if the event failed, then the bar would not lose any profit. If it was successful, then Danny would get back his money, along with any extra. The owner agreed with the plan. Everything was set.

Feeling the pressure as the days loomed closer, the children made mistakes while practicing, with missed timing, slow entries into the songs, and singing off key. There were seven songs to get right. They wanted to make Danny proud. If something went awry, they bickered. This weekend was no different. Tara wasn't pleased when she heard their voices escalate as she put away dinner dishes into the kitchen cabinet. She threw her apron upon the table and went into the library to break up their argument.

"All right! All right! Please don't shout at one another!" She declared while stepping in between Edward and Jamie. Their eyes flashed at each other. Edward stood in a defiant stance, but so did her daughter. Tara was amazed that Jamie never backed down from a fight. She always stood up to her brothers. So what if they were boys?

"She's playing the chords all wrong!" Nine year old Edward fussed. "That's not the way that Da' taught us!"

"Well, I like to improvise. I've been practicing more than you and listening to the radio at my friend's house. She likes rock music. It makes a great improvement!" Jamie declared. She stuck a firm nose in the air which made Edward glare.

"Well, you didn't ask Da' if it was all right to change it up. You can't get away with it just because he isn't here!" Edward challenged, his brown eyes squinting as he stared almost nose to nose into her eyes. Jamie drew back her arm, ready to punch, but Tara grabbed her hand before the vicious blow found its mark.

"Now, children! This is not how you should behave! What would your Da's think if you were to fight in front of the whole village?"

"I don't even want to play in front of them!" Tristan cried out, adjusting new wire frame glasses. His vision, for some reason, faltered in the last year and he became near-sighted. The frames were adjusted onto his nose and he pouted, "Can't I please stay home?"

"What will we do without a drummer? We'll stink!" Vincent snapped as his brown bangs fell over his eyes. He hated his bangs and threw the offending locks back on top of his head. Everyone went to bickering again.

"Now, now!" Tara shouted over them, "Please! There's no need to be afraid. The audience will be made up of our neighbors and friends, I'm sure. They will think you are adorable. I bet you can play for them."

The children quieted down to mull this over.

"Will you be there, mum?" Tristan asked with huge, hazel eyes.

"Yes, honey. I will. How can I miss it? You are my talented angels. So now, go back to practicing, and Jamie, stick to how it's written until all your band mates agree on the arrangement. Everyone has to be in sync."

"Band mates?" Jamie declared, rolling these words off her tongue. She liked the sound of it very much and so nodded. Edward seemed content that Jamie would not play in a different tangent. After all, they both played lead and rhythm guitars. They were supposed to be important.

"I don't agree with any of this. The songs stink! Why can't we play something like on the radio that Jamie spoke about?" Matthew blurted out, thinking it was the right moment to bring this up.

"Like what? Do you know a rock song?" Tara wanted to know, surprised by his request.

"No, not exactly."

"Then what do you propose you play?" Tara turned, her jowl twisted and her eyes squinted in his direction. Matt looked at his siblings who shook their heads to keep quiet. Tara was no fool, "Matt. Is there something going on?"

Reluctantly, Matt pulled out crinkled papers from his back pocket and showed it to his mother. She recognized it right away. Danny and Ross's sheet music!

"Matt! When did you dig through that box hidden in my closet?"

"Tyler and I played ball in the hallway, about a month ago. I know we are not supposed to horse around in the house, but Tyler threw it at me. I missed and then it rolled into your closet. We saw the box and were just curious, mum. That's all."

"How could we help it? Mum, we had to see what was inside," Tyler added, running his hands through thick brown hair, "In the barn, on the top loft, we have a hiding place. We took it there to look them over carefully."

"It's great music, mum! We tried it out ourselves. I can play this song by heart," Edward thumped on his guitar. Vince joined in the base. It was great rhythmical effect, "Why can't we play this for the audience, and a few of the other songs, instead of these simple baby ones that Da picked out?"

"Because your Da' expects you to play what he selected. It's designed for children your age level. I'm uncertain if what's expressed here is something you should sing about."

"Mum! We see and hear everything through watching television at our friend's houses," Jamie pointed out, "They watch all the cool movies that you and Da restrict us from at night. We aren't stupid about love and all that kissy, make-up/break-up stuff! Half of my friends all talk about what they see and hear, and there is plenty out there. I hate that we are always so behind the times."

"Yeah!" the boys agreed in unison.

"You can't go against his wishes," Tara mumbled, shocked at the truth. As parents, she agreed with Danny's conservative attitude, to raise their children with a firmer hand and restrict what they watched and who they befriended. Obviously, the times progressed with movies, music and fashion around them. She noted this by reading over the magazines that Gloria or Susan brought over. Models revealed more, movie stars and singers were very high in the limelight, sex was discussed more openly. Scandals with politicians and stars kept a lot of tongues wagging in their community. Sometimes they were not always the best situations or role models, but even Jamie whined about wearing items that were fad, just to keep pace with her girlfriends. So young and impressionable and not fazed by anything, it seemed.

"Can we play them here?" Jamie asked. She looked too hopeful, "Da's not home. It's perfect opportunity.

We just want to do it a few times all together. They are really cool songs! Will that be all right?"

"I suppose. Go ahead," Tara slumped into the couch, weary that they could exasperate her easy at times. Matt suggested a number. The kids poised to play it. Tristan counted the beat. They jumped in, messing up the intro. By the time they sorted out who was doing what, they did it again. The beat seemed infectious. Their rendition bounced off stronger and this time, Tara looked at the sheet music, reading over the words. She sang along some. They sang the bridge and the chorus. They did well and wanted to do the whole thing again.

"We have to get it right!" Matt encouraged. This time, as they played, Tara joined in, standing to sing it out to Tristan who pounded on the drums like a professional. The words and the backbeat turned into a great game between them. Caught up in the momentum of the music, Tara really belted out the words in tune. Why not? They were the only ones at home so she felt no embarrassment. The children stared and allowed her to sing out the melody.

"Wow, mum! You sing out of this world!" Tyler declared when they stopped, "It's even better than Mrs. Gruper, our music teacher, who won all those silly singing awards in college. She brags about it all the time. You're better than she is. Why don't you join us?"

"Yes, mum! Join us! Please! Just do it!" they all piped in unison. She seemed out ranked!

"Only for this weekend, I'm afraid, and as many times as you want. This is quite fun, but you are the products that your Da' wants to introduce to the world. Not me. Besides, once you are up on stage, my job will be to keep all the fans from storming over for your autographs!" Tara teased and they smiled.

What faith! It made the practice really worth while. And they had a blast that night singing with their mother. Her voice: like an angel. With their mother as leader, they sounded very natural. Mathew brought down more samples that he had stored away in his room. They picked out the better numbers to practice. Up until past midnight, no one wanted to go to bed, but their mother insisted. They left the band instruments in the room. As Tara heated up pancakes around noon, they hummed along the songs while they sat at the table. Everyone was hooked. They ad libbed, kidded on what worked, what didn't. Each thought things through and through how to improve the numbers. When they practiced Saturday night, they didn't goof up at all. They were all too serious at this thing called rock-n-roll!

It was very late on Sunday night when Danny returned home. All the children were sound asleep in their rooms. Tara was anxious to know all that happened in London. For once, Danny was talkative, just like Sammy- nonstop!

"On Friday night, we all sat up late and talked until two in the morning. Terrific fun! Sammy missed his calling to be a stand up comedian. He dated a Japanese girl who almost snagged him, but her father! A huge samurai! It scared him to death," Danny laughed, "Anyway, I mentioned about the public performance. Sammy can't make it, but Michael promises to come. Can you believe that? He always fusses he's too busy to get away, but will make an exception for the kids. I found that ironic."

Danny bent down and found a coin lying on the floor. He placed it into a ceramic pig bank on the dresser as he loved collecting them. What luck one could bring if found, he would say. His eyes were all aglow about it and Tara sat down onto the bed to listen further.

"Then on Saturday, we be-bopped around London during the day. At the park, we saw Susan direct a crew for a shoot. She's learning a lot about setting up her own studio, which beats her modeling half-nude all the time. We swung by to see Gloria's new pad. It's quite nice, very convenient to the shopping departments. I met her new beau, Sven, who's also her photographer assistant from Sweden. I think he's too arrogant. He suggested this place up in Soho for dinner and wound up drinking too much wine. He behaved obnoxiously and I think Gloria was quite put out by it, enough to call them off. She just can't seem to meet the right man."

Danny paused momentarily, thinking about his words. Yes, he truly did wish for his favorite sister to wind up with the right man, but since there wasn't anything he could do about it, he sighed.

"Anyway, we did manage to take in a play this afternoon, before my train. Thank God it was a comedy or I fear that I would have fallen asleep."

Danny placed the suitcase into the closet, then plopped down to take off his shirt and slip out of his boots. His shaggy hair went in all directions by the static in the air. It made him look like a youngster.

Tara studied him over. At 33, he still possessed muscular arms and a slim abdomen. He liked to run and would join her for a jog in the early mornings. The fireplace glow now made him look very sexy. With just two night's absence, he was sorely missed, and Tara interrupted the story to push his body onto the bed. Pouncing upon him like a cat, Tara kissed his abdomen, then his chest and found his mouth. She kissed it amorous for several moments. When she let him come up for air, his eyes were wide.

"Wow! I should go away more often!"

Tara disagreed and tossed her long hair over her shoulders defiantly.

"No, you won't, mister! Not ever again! It's difficult to fall asleep. When I do, then I wind up rolling over to seek your body," She explained. Tara stared into his excited eyes and caressed his wild hair, "I find you are not there and then I am wide awake again. I'm a woman gone mad at midnight. It's not fun at all."

Danny laughed at this assessment and rolled her onto her back. With all of their activities with the children, it was easy to push away desire sometimes, for the sake of rest. Yet, it was best not to neglect all of her needs. At least not tonight. She deserved so much for sacrificing so much for their family.

"I understand, darling. I missed you too and wished you could have gone with me to London, but with the help away, it wasn't possible this time. Perhaps this summer, we can go off somewhere, to be all alone for awhile."

"We are alone right now," Tara teased.

"No, no. That's not it. I want to take you somewhere romantic. Just you and me. It's been quite awhile and you certainly deserve to be pampered. Ross said that Paris is really hopping in the summer. You have not been there, so why not go? "

Tara couldn't believe her ears.

"Ross? Did you see him?"

Danny sat up to look away. Tara wasn't sure if she upset him, but when he turned around, there was a mischievous grin on his face.

"No, I didn't see him. It was something he had told Michael. Ross returned to Paris last summer and had a great time. It was a short excursion with someone, but I don't know who went along, but Susan insisted it was a woman. How she knew, I don't know and I don't care. You want us to make up as friends, don't you? Is that why you encouraged this trip to see Michael? Just incase we bumped into each other?"

Tara could not deny this, but she felt two odd sensations, all at once, once he said it. First was the disappointment that they did not make connections, and second, who was the woman that Ross took to Paris? Was he dating someone exclusively? For the first time, Tara wished that her face was not so expressive, because obviously Danny could read every single thought.

"I'm not sure *who* he is seeing. According to Gloria, it must be someone very special, as he never pays her any mind to date her seriously. Now my sister is quite lovely, delicate, and very available, especially after she dumps Sven. After all this time she's chased after him, Ross is a fool for not seeing that. Now, don't worry. Sooner or later, I will bump into Ross. On that occasion, I will talk things out. For you, I will do this."

Tara's head was suddenly spinning. Did she hear the man right? Her greatest wish was that they push their differences aside. At any rate, she no longer felt attracted by Ross, so really there was no longer a need for Danny to worry about them. Her desires remained devoted towards her sweet, sexy husband. What a man! With complete adulation, she tackled Danny down again and smothered his face with sweet, sweet kisses. And this time, she didn't stop until he fell under complete seduction.

Chapter Fifty One
Claim to Fame

Soon, the big night came and Danny was as skittish as a cat. He went around the bar and all the tables, passing out appetizers.

"Please, sit here. How about a drink. It's on me," he said, really wishing to put everyone in an amiable mood. The place had filled up quickly as word of mouth of their performance had spread like wildfire throughout the village.

About thirty minutes late, the children finally came to the pub with their mother. In a single file, they climbed up onto the wooden stage and took their positions, like little toy soldiers in a row. The crowd looked them over closely. The boys wore dark little sequined vests, crisp white shirts, and dark pants and black shoes. Jamie wore a dark sequined skirt with white tights, and possessed matching black shoes and a black bow in her hair. It was something that Helen pulled off in time, as she hardly ever sewed like she did in her younger years. Nine separate outfits was indeed a feat. Still, they were adorable.

Once on stage, Danny looked them all over too, mostly to adjust their standing positions. Matt and Edward seemed quite fidgety as they nudged each other, straightened out their black bow ties and their hair. Vince held the bass guitar stubbed his shoe into the floor and kept coughing. Tristan sat behind the drums and tried to shrink in place, wishing to remain invisible. Staring at the crowds bothered him. He looked over at his mother who by hand gestures reminded him to take off his glasses. Once he did this, he looked down at his drum set and finally smiled. Across the stage, Tom stood with a tambourine and stared about, while Tyler slipped upon the piano bench and tickled the keys. Jamie held onto her guitar, tuned it, and stood close to the microphone, urging young Aaron to do the same. They seemed as confidant as Eric, who played chords upon the Yamaha keyboard that Sammy bought on his birthday that year.

At that point, Eric looked at Da who had gone center of the room to judge them upon the stage. Da's face was taut with anxiety, so Eric gave him a thumb's up sign for encouragement. For the exception of his sister, Eric was excited to try out his new keyboard in front of an audience. It was portable and heavy and sometimes awkward to carry out to the hayloft to practice with Jamie and Edward. If only they could play the rock and roll songs they found in the closet, instead of the kiddie songs that Da had urged them play.

Meanwhile, Tara stood towards the back door, behind a large wooden beam, dressed up in a mini black dress that exposed long, slinky legs. Even with a long, white jacket over this, she felt out place wearing that particular style. Susan had talked her out of wearing her usual matronly, pastel dresses and since there was no time to shop for another in London, Susan lent her this one at the last minute. Nervously, Tara looked around the room and blew out a whistle as she gaped at the people milling about in the room. The family, along with their servants, sat in the middle of the pub. They looked grim and seemed out of place. George puffed at his pipe, much to Helen's dismay who sat next to him. Marta took off her glove and waved it in front of her face to cool off and Lila tugged at her sweater.

As the lights dimmed, Ross finally snuck in the back door with Susan in tow. They kept quiet as Danny stepped up to the stage to make his introduction.

"Hello everyone. I'm so happy to see so many come out. We really appreciate your show of support. The children have been practicing their songs for awhile, but are new to coming on stage like this, so please give them a hand of encouragement as they perform. We hope you will be pleased by their efforts."

The audience clapped appropriately while he took a seat at the front row. He held up his arms, nodded at them, and then began to count off the beat. Edward, Eric and Jamie were the first to play their instruments, but everyone else sounded extremely weak and even Tristan played off tempo. They stopped and tried again. The number began on queue, but their singing efforts this time were barely audible. They looked at each other and then to look about the room, perhaps seeking a way out of the building forever.

"I don't like these songs," Vince complained in a loud whisper to Danny as he stared past him at the snickering audience, "They're too quirky."

The room seemed too dim and he could only make out the folks hidden within thick clouds of cigarette smoke. The beer cans in the trashcan behind the bar didn't smell good either. With such a frightening environment, playing songs he loved would make this performance more bearable. Danny shook his head at him.

"Come on, son. You can do this," Danny encouraged, but at the same time tried to reason out this train of thought. *What other songs did Vince know to play?*

. At this point, Ross approached Tara from behind and whispered into her ear.

"This isn't good, is it? Poor Tom's knees are quivering. I want to yank him off the stage, but I can't."

"No, you can't. It will embarrass them," Tara whispered back, grateful that as a parent, he could relate to how she felt at that moment. It was a surprise that he showed up, but Tara took comfort in his presence and his deep resonating voice.

"Someone needs to do something. This is terribly awkward," Susan whispered loudly, joining them.

"Yes, but what?" Ross whispered back, sounding annoyed at her. Tara felt panic. Her adrenaline had to be pumping because she felt so flushed. Poor little ones! Poor Danny!

He ran up on stage to reposition them, so they could gain confidence from looking at one another. He gave them another short pep talk and then he sat down again, on the edge of his seat. His face revealed his own panic as sweat dotted his forehead and his blue eyes seem wide.

Tara could make out laughter within the audience. There in the middle of the crowd was that awful Mrs. Henry. She was never nice to them whenever they went to her store. She wandered behind the children, scooting them away from breakable items, and rushing them as they made selections in the candy aisle. Tara hated that woman and here she was now, whispering to her friends nearby, giggling uncontrollably, and thoroughly enjoying the humiliation.

Tara looked at her children in a quandary. They stood poised to play, but all of their eyes conveyed their anguish as they now looked at her for guidance. Suddenly, Jamie's guitar reflected the lights from overhead and it gave off a bright glare. It forced Tara to squint and in doing that, she saw a shape take form. It looked like a cross.

"Oh, my!" she gasped as something snapped within. She recalled her argument with God:

"There must be a purpose for the children...I need answers. I need to know your plans. Surely there is one for all this. I promise to stop screwing things up. One day, you'll reveal what you want from me. I'll trust you. I'll do whatever it is..."

Tara's senses boiled over with realization and there was no way to contain it. Those children were terrific and could play their instruments by rote- better than what was heard on the radio. It was that the songs were all wrong for them. Yes, it was high time to prove that they were not the only ones with hidden talent. As any good mother would do, she heeded their cry for help, and seeming to walk in slow-motion, Tara crossed that room, a woman possessed by a higher calling. In a grand upsweeping step, she jumped up onto center stage and grabbed the microphone. She clutched it so tightly that her knuckles turned whiter.

"Sorry, folks! I'm late," she apologized, trying to speak with a purpose. She coughed and then cleared her throat-determined to do her thing. There was no turning back now, "We will do this right."

Danny's jaw dropped in confusion, but he could see that Tara's presence with the children suddenly calmed them down. They looked to her for instruction and were quick to gather near.

"Now lift up your instruments and stand proud. Jamie, we will do things your way – with a little improvisation."

Jamie nodded gladly. Tara nodded her head and looked into Vincent's and Edward's brown eyes.

"Let's do all eight numbers just like we rehearsed Saturday night."

She turned to Tom and Aaron.

"Close your eyes if you have to do so. I want you to sing loud and clear. Imagine that we are at home, in our living room. Believe me children-I'm with you all the way. Let's do: *I'm the only one!* Get it on!"

The children ran back to their positions and look for her lead. So Tara stood, her lips close to the microphone, and she counted the beat out loud: *1-2-3-4!* They closed their eyes and fired up the introduction. By the fourth bar, they were strong. Quite confidant.

When Tara opened up to sing, the entire atmosphere changed. Her voice was powerful, soprano, and gritty on every register. Her vocal range, expansive and on-key, highlighted the voices of the children.

It was a natural accommodation and either way, she came on like a polished singer. All that practice in the basement prepared her for this terrific eye-opening, catch-by-surprise electric night. She trusted her children's words- that she could sing, because every eye in the place was upon her. The song, which started off at a slow pace in the beginning, came across now like a fiery rock song. She loved this song. The children loved playing it this way. It was their arrangement. By then, Tara moved to the rhythm. The children swayed in syncopation. Now, their energy came from their showmanship. It all became magical and spectacular. They backed her up with perfect harmony. Tara had this look in her eye that captured the audience. A look that was beyond comparison. At this point, Michael nudged Gloria on the arm and pointed it out, "See what I mean? That's persona! That's the kind of look that hooks you in!"

Danny stared in disbelief, too! He practically fell out of his chair. Absolutely dumbfounded! This was his wife and children on stage-together-and they were doing their thing like they had done it for years! She looked out of this world! It was a shock that it was his melody they were playing. Where did the words come from? At that point, he looked over his shoulder to check out the room.

Ross stood by the wooden beam. He looked briefly at Danny, but then went right back to stare at the stage.

Those were his lyrics Tara expertly flung out with much bravado, improvising words at whim to give them pizzazz, adjusting her vocal range to give the song life of its own. By this time, the audience clapped along. Tara was great! She was born to do this.

All that constant practice did wonders. Jamie made her fingers fly upon the strings. Edward didn't want to be outdone by his sister. The music jived in tight harmony. They sounded like pros. Tom and little Aaron sang loud enough to be heard over their older brothers. Something was born on that stage and the audience knew it too. Miraculously, at the end, everyone stood up to applaud. Even that nasty Mrs. Henry! The pub owner patted Danny on the back and handed him a beer.

"I thought you said it was just the children tonight. That woman of yours has got one hell of a voice! Why did you keep that a secret?"

"Hell, even I didn't know it!" Danny accepted the beer and drank the whole thing down very quickly.

"Yeah, right! You just wanted to surprise me!" The pub owner laughed, taking a seat beside him. The children bowed professionally. Tara mentioned the second number and they went straight into it. She didn't want to lose the momentum. With each rendition, they grew confidant. They really rocked the house down.

Afterwards, Tara ushered the children off the stage and out a side door. They stood outside with their family, accepting all the kudos and hugs. Danny received lots of congratulations as he pushed his way out. The owner stopped him by the door to give back the deposit, "Bring them back soon. They are good for business."

Out side the building, Ross joined up with everyone. He congratulated Tom and the children. Danny came out then, but rushed towards Tara first. He picked her up high in the air, jumping up and down in delight.

"You were bloody terrific! Why didn't you tell me?"

"I didn't know I could do it!" Tara gasped as Danny held her tight. She was surprised, but happy it turned out fine.

"Where did your courage come from?"

She knew and looked at Danny in the eye.

"There was no bloody way I could let our children be ridiculed, especially by that mob!"

At that point, Ross approached them. He seemed caught up in the moment too. It was a victory. A miracle!

"You saved the show! What an incredible voice! Everyone in there was quite amazed!" Ross held Tom close to his side. Danny placed Tara down and looked at the man. It was the first time that they were face to face. Everyone grew silent. Ross was not sure what to do at this point and Tara waited on pins and needles. Would Danny keep his promise?

"It was bloody amazing! Those songs came out like number one hits! Especially the first number," Danny suddenly declared. Something was greatly on his mind, "It's because you straightened out that first number."

"I did?" Ross reacted, because at that moment, he didn't even recall it. It was the song that Tara sang to him when he waited at the airport.

"Yes! I don't know how, but I don't bloody well care! I know you are responsible. Now, what I want to know is if we can continue. What happened tonight is a damn miracle. The fact that these tykes can get up there to play their hearts out is a sign. It's a sign that Tara can wail out the number too. It all ties together."

"What ties together?" Tara and Ross asked simultaneously. What was he getting at?

"This band! This creation! All of us have a part in it. You and me; with the lyrics and the music. Tara and the children; Hell! By some providence, we have created an outstanding thing. Our music! Not any of that damn nonsense you hear on the BBC radio. This is solid and it can only grow. I always wanted to do this and now's our chance. What do you say?"

Ross and Tara stared at each other momentarily and then they looked at their children, who were delighted to hear their Da' say that they were "*Better than what is on the BBC radio.*" They whispered to each other, nodding their heads up and down, talking excitedly to each other. They looked up with pleading eyes. Ross feigned a cough.

"I don't know," He paused for effect and Danny's eyes grew wide, in disbelief. How could the man not go along? He was a father and Tom was greatly invested in this too. Danny was about to drive it home to convince Ross, but it was not necessary. In the next moment, Ross teased back, "Look, with you, it's always the music. I know what to expect: you'll talk nonstop. We'll go into that pub. You'll describe how I can have it all, but that won't be exactly true. I'll be the one to invest heavily, inherit the grey hair for managing things; while you smile for the cameras, get all the kudos from the press and fans, and get bloody rich once it succeeds. Why do you get to be the one so bloody charming?"

Danny suddenly knew what was implied. It was ironic! Ross could laugh about them. If for nothing else of what was taught to each other in their previous budding friendship, it was to lighten up, take a chance, and enjoy life to the fullest. They naturally complimented and influenced each other.

Yes, this straightforward, mostly no-nonsense fellow who was sorely missed was a long lost brother. Tara was right. It was way overdue to make amends. Danny extended his hand. Ross shook it strongly, much to relief of the family that surrounded them. Susan gasped and threw her hands to her mouth. Michael nodded and hugged Gloria. George and Helen looked into each other's eyes, and then smiled. Tara was elated, but the children demanded to know what transpired.

"Does this mean we are a band?" Edward whined.

"Can we play all of your music? It sounds really cool," Matt piped in. "I want in."

"Yes, you are in," Ross answered sternly, "Now go home and practice. You have to outdo this performance by a milestone next time."

He looked at Tara with a smirk.

"That goes for you too, mummy. There were a couple of notes I discerned were off pitch, although it could have been the mike."

"Critic!" Tara hissed, but she gathered up the children to leave the men alone. They needed their time to mend, to talk out what mistakes were made, their own way. Yet knowing Danny, he would sidestep all that dramatic make-up stuff, just to tell a great story, to someone who would care enough to listen. They went back inside the pub.

After that, it was solid booking every other weekend for a period of almost three months. The kids were pleased to make extra spending money. For every performance, they gained lots of valuable experience. Tara insisted they not perform during the school year. She didn't want the children to suffer in their studies and wanted their lives to be as normal as possible. This was fine with the men, as it gave them time to work on new songs and arrangements.

It was quite ironic how they played things off like nothing ever happened. Tara found it difficult not to do so. She wanted to clear the air. Ross stopped by the house quite often on the weekends. The men talked and worked around everything. Sometimes, Danny would be away and Ross would come over early, and that gave some opportunity for them to be alone to visit.

It was awkward. Sometimes they worried whether Danny would find some fault with their actions. Still, within that opportunity, it was nice to sit in each other's presence, to share a spot of tea, to go over the music and lyrics, or to converse about the family. It was not like anything could happen because they were always surrounded by children. Perhaps this is why Danny didn't speculate anything while he was out for some reason. Ross had worries too, but it was about their future.

"You know, we grew very popular with the village folk this summer. Seems like every weekend, the crowds got bigger. What if we escalate beyond this valley? With the septuplets playing, there is going to be lots of curiosity, as everyone wants to see them," Ross asked one day as she sat cutting out cake recipes for Marta out of a magazine, "Will you worry about the publicity?"

Tara looked at the paper, silently digesting the question, and then she looked at Ross.

"I'm not worried anymore. I'm Tara Cross and these are the Cross children, for the exception of our son. If publicity goes beyond our shores to the states, at this point of our lives, I'm not worried about Jimmy finding out. I don't think he'd have a clue that they were his. He'd probably read the name Cross and skip over anything about it."

She seemed pretty smug and Ross scratched his chin. It made sense, so he didn't think anything more about it either.

Chapter Fifty Two

A band that sticks together

From then on, every summer, the townspeople invited their friends to hear Cross Passage, now the name for their band. The bar became too packed to accommodate everyone as it was standing room only. Since the weather cooperated, Danny moved the performances to a nearby field not far from the Briggs House. It once was a sprawling wheat pasture owned by an agriculture partner who retired, leaving the land unused for two years. Danny purchased it the summer during the year that the septuplets turned eleven.

They bought lumbar to build up a flat stage, along with bleachers. Next, they installed broad lights onto tall poles so they could perform in the evening. Everyone from their own county came out on Saturdays to watch the family perform, along with people from the surrounding areas.

"I never expected such a ruckus," Danny rubbed his scalp, absolutely amazed by this. Several cars pulled into the field across the way from the stage. Several couples with children came; some with older folks too.

"I think they want to see the septuplets, too," Ross said, thinking this must be very true. He was constantly asked about them from people at work, "There wasn't much publicity except for when they were born and on their birthdays. People are just curious, that's all."

"Well, we'll really have to give them their money's worth. I think I may ask my family to help too, if this keeps up. They know how to sing."

This surprised Ross. Even Tara was stunned when she heard about Danny's idea. When Gloria came over to visit, Tara questioned her feelings about it.

"I get nervous going up, except I have fun with the kids. Do you think you can handle it?" Tara asked. Gloria scrunched up her nose.

"Danny talked me into doing something with Michael. We use to sing in choir when we were younger. Michael always liked singing, so it's not difficult for him at all. He's in the theater, after all and they must be multi-talented. As for me, I'll just pretend I'm somewhere else. I note that you are getting much better at performing in front of crowds."

"It's getting easier, especially if I take off my glasses. My eyesight has matched Tristan's, so now I know where he gets it from. We can see close up without them. It keeps him from being gun shy since he can't see the crowds, just his drums," Tara explained, then laughed. She smoothed out the green sequined top she planned to wear for the performance that went well with her black skirt, "I am surprised how we are so popular. I never imagined this at all, but I like showing off Danny and Ross's music. The songs are great. I love singing them."

Mostly the crowds loved Tara's easy going personality. She shined on the stage as she interacted playfully with her talented children and flirted with her husband. When Gloria and Michael finally performed, their tenor and alto voices soared. They sang great together.

George read announcements in a deep serious voice and introduced the music. People paid attention to him. Lila and Marta assisted with refreshments. Helen passed out bulletins and took up donations towards preservation of the wildflowers and wildlife in that area. When Sammy came home on leave, he could not be left out. He joined his brothers to do a few comical songs. The crowds loved them. Sammy scored a few dates, which doubly pleased him.

Finally, someone reviewed them in a popular newspaper to advertise their upcoming 1990 summer show:

"In the last two decades, the US has had their share of family singing groups: The Cowsills, The Partridge Family, the Osmonds, The DeFranco Family, The Jackson Five- so why not one of our own in England? The exception may be in the genuine magic that is displayed in the writing, arranging, producing, and all the creative performances of the variety of songs this entourage takes on stage. Cross Passage are extremely attractive and damn talented:

Danny Cross, guitarist/pianist/composer/singer, is a flamboyant salesman and showman on stage. Half of a successful writing team, (Ross Kelly currently does not perform, but creates their amazing lyrics and most arrangements for the band) Danny soars with a bravado tenor voice, especially in a duet with his beautiful wife, Tara. She can either rock-out a song into orbit around the moon with such a strong, gritty soprano voice or in the next instance transcends dance-pop likeability into a mainstream song. She has unbelievable charisma, with a voice one will not soon forget. A definite star of her own universe, in which we are privy to watch develop. The children have practiced well as you can't even discern any tune off beat or with flat chords. They are a lively bunch to watch interact on stage, even when friends and family join them. They seem to have it all: talent, humor, good looks, and are sure to be a hit with every generation."

"Wow! I like this. That can be our new slogan," Danny said to Ross when he read it to the family, "A Hit With Every Generation! Think that sounds cool?"

"We can put them on the billboards in the village. Perhaps we can create a sign to put on the road to help people find the place."

"Oh, they know how to find us. I don't think we'll ever enjoy privacy again. Ross, you really should join us on stage. At least play the guitar with the boys."

Ross shook his head. At that point, he liked watching what was taking place on stage, but it would not be the first time that Danny requested him to do so. Even the children wanted him to join in sometimes. They respected that Ross could play so well, but even he thought to learn more instruments, and encouraged them to expand their knowledge and to stay competitive.

Together, they practiced learning the saxophone, coronets, and trombones. Even Edward took up the harmonica, banjo, and an electric fiddle. Jamie stuck mostly to her guitar, playing lead, and she was hell bent on playing better than her brothers. Sometimes when Tara tucked her in at night, her fingers moved in her sleep. Being the only girl in such a musically talented family seemed intimidating. She didn't want to be outdone. As a child, she was a tom boy, climbing trees, skinning knees; now she had dreams of becoming more on stage.

. "I want to dress up like a rock-and-roll star, where everyone wants to be like me," she told Danny one day. She turned twelve that year, with long straight hair that went down to her waist. He turned to look at her closely. Much to his dismay, most of her childish pudginess was gone. She was developing curves, wearing a beginner bra, experimenting with soft blush, lip gloss, and chatting with boys about social interactions, instead of discussing rugby. He didn't like it. Where did the time fly too? He couldn't bear to lose his little girl.

Still, in a lot of ways, she remained determined to be true to herself; not so much like an average girl, "This summer, when we have our shows, I want to show off on stage. I want to wear leather boots, a black hat, and a long duster over a sequin shirt, and perhaps wear three earrings on each side with lots of dangling bracelets and beads."

"You can wear the leather and the duster, but you'll be extremely hot in it," Danny told her. He could relate to what she requested, but it wasn't logical, "The lights are bright. You'll feel like an inferno within twenty minutes of playing. As for the earrings and the beads, you'll stick to a few on your neck and one pair of earrings on each side. I won't have you looking weird. You're my daughter."

Jamie pouted momentarily. They were sitting side by side on the couch. She looked into his eyes that reflected he was serious. He also cared.

"All right, Da'. Whatever you say- for now. But when we make it big, playing in front of thousands in air-conditioning, then I'll put on that attire. Ok? In the meantime, you're right. You're smart. I love you," she hugged him tight before leaping over the back of the couch like a slick panther. She ran upstairs before he could scold her, but such was her boyish nature.

On the opposite scale, Erik and Tyler both took up classical music, which Tara taught them. They loved Mozart, Bach, and learned to play violins, the harp, and the flute, which brought a whole new dimension to the songs. They liked to be creative. Whenever Ross came over, the boys would sit with the men to come up with new ideas. It was a team effort and they all loved it.

When the septuplets turned thirteen, all of England couldn't wait to see what venue the band would take next.

"Please Danny, no matter what offer comes in, we must live simply and morally as possible. I don't want to force our children into things that will overwhelm them," Tara requested. For a little while, he heeded her wishes, but it was difficult. He was approached by several outsiders just waiting to market them. There were lots of offers pouring in. Soon they were off to London to visit a producer of a major recording studio.

The first album, a compilation of their outdoor performances, made lots of money, but that particular producer was not happy. At the time, R&B, rap, boy bands, and modern pop rock exploded in the media. The producer insisted that Tara change her style.

"She may be a mother, but she doesn't have to look that way," The man said to Danny one day, "Why doesn't she wear something low-cut to show off those breasts? I can see she has some."

That's all Danny needed to hear before he punched the man onto the floor.

"You're out of line, Fred. No one speaks of my wife in that manner! We don't need your kind of representation. Thank God our contract was project-to-project based. You're fired!" he declared and stormed out of the studio. The band went with another label that helped Danny build on a studio at home so that they could produce their songs under a comfortable atmosphere.

Yet, with popularity, came other problems. In the summer time, too many fans showed up in the village, creating havoc with traffic.

"We've got that field up the road. Why don't we take out a loan to expand that flat stage into an outdoor arena," Danny suggested to Ross, "Do you think we can swing it?"

"Like a mini- amphitheater, with steel seating, precision lighting, and ample parking? I've got money invested, but I wanted to save it for Tom. A loan builds up our credit. I think it's a sound idea."

"Then let's do it," Danny said and so within a year, it was built. .

At the same time, Danny thought about putting Ross onto their second recording effort. He always knew that Ross had a decent voice. It took something more convincing to prove that Ross had star quality. One summer night, quite by accident, Tom convinced his dad to play a duet on guitar. The two had a great time showing off their prowess with the instruments. Then Tom played an old song written back in New York, and Ross knew it very well.

So he sang it to the crowd. It was quite spontaneous; an amazing performance. He had a powerful voice. The ladies in the audience watched him move across the stage, whispering among each other, pointing-almost drooling. Ross was still single. Danny never could get Ross to admit reasons for not dating Gloria exclusively.

"I tell you Danny, he sees someone in London. It's a big secret. He won't even tell me," Susan lied one day, just to get Danny to stop asking questions. He bought it for a little while. Now that Danny was putting on pressure, Susan worried.

"As much as this kills me, take her to dinner once, Ross. It'll make Danny stop butting in. He's driving me crazy." Susan asked one day. She plopped onto the couch and he sat down next to her, taking her hand and patting it gently.

"He's consistent. I'll give him that. Ok, we'll go out just for dinner. You can't orbit the moon about it," He said and she promised. It killed Ross. As he stood in her doorway, his jaw dropped when the door opened up.

"Do I look ok?" she sputtered nervously, but his eyes were eating her up like a wolf. The red dress was fit to form, low cleavage, with spaghetti straps and went well with the black pumps.

"You're a knock out," he proclaimed and she smiled. Like a gentleman, he offered an arm to escort her out to the car, but it took everything in his power to keep his hands to himself the rest of that night. At the restaurant, he fidgeted to contain himself. Her baby blues and striking white features seemed hypnotizing. The usual cool persona he usually possessed had been blasted away by her serene beauty and flirtatious smile.

"You look too ravishing tonight, Gloria. You shouldn't go out with a beast like me. It's too dangerous." Ross admitted, wiping away sweat on his brow. He drank down a glass of water quickly, causing her to laugh.

"Oh, Ross! You are such a kidder, but I like your sense of humor. We always have fun together. It's so easy to get along with you." she conveyed.

"Much too easy," he said and he meant every word of it.

Gloria took another sip of the white wine and stared dreamily into his eyes.

"We should hang out more often," she suggested purposely and touched his hand, "I do realize you don't seem much into commitments, but I'd like us to be close friends. Do you believe that is possible, where we can talk and maybe see a movie once in awhile? My schedule is so crazy, but I'd do anything to be available sometimes."

She batted her eyes and held back a breath, waiting anxiously for his reply. His eyes looked down at the table cloth and she worried about receiving more rejection.

Instead, he leaned back purposely into his chair and gave out a huge smile.

"Someone once told me that relationships are sometimes over rated – that friends last longer. I truly believe this the more time slips away. So yes- let's be the closest of friends," He agreed impulsively and reached over to squeeze her hand, which brought out a smile more radiant than any star in the sky. Being a friend didn't necessarily mean he had to show affection or make love to the woman- although he so desperately wanted to do that. Still, his physical attributes was meant to be shared with Susan; his heart eternally bound to Tara. So what remained could only be something pleasant with Gloria- something grownup and wholesome-and that he could look forward to immensely.

This summation of their friendship was enough fuel to jettison her imagination for quite a long spell. Her determination to reel him in towards commitment just grew stronger and so she always finagled ways to be with him, all quite innocently and much to Susan's dismay.

Even if Ross wanted to be committed openly, it became easy occupying his days away with both women. It was a juggle of time management, but since they all remained very busy with their careers, it seemed to work and every other weekend, he spent it with his son. Things worked out very conveniently this way for about a year, but then Danny finally convinced him to record with the band, Ross didn't realize the major impact this would be on his personal life. Within two months, their new album soared to platinum sales. Ross had a number one hit- then two. In 1992, they put out five singles total that reached the top ten. They were phenomenal and all of the United Kingdom fell hard for the band. And Ross soon became a legend that rock stars only dreamed of becoming.

After the albulm bulleted up the charts, the BBC network wanted the group to do a weekly television show. Jamie and her brothers possessed a lot of youth appeal. The show went into hour long syndication throughout Great Britain, France, Sweden, and other neighboring countries in Europe. Everyone knew their faces, read about their lives, and every girl idolized them. Most fans looked up to their mother. By now, Tara appeared on more fashion covers than Susan. She was drop dead gorgeous in limited makeup. Her style of dress was low-keyed, but very sexy. There was an element of mystery that matched her sultry eyes and natural bubbling smile.

Tara and Danny could not ask for a better lifestyle. The money poured in. Tara went shopping at every opportunity with the children. Danny threw special parties in London often, to hang out with the marketing bigwigs, other celebrated record producers, and recording artists. Harry and Lilly were frequently invited. Danny loved showing off his wife, as she was dazzling in the fashionable glittery gowns.

Tara still kept tight reins on the teenagers, who were now fifteen, fourteen, and thirteen, and for the most part, they were just loveable kids, modest and polite, and sometimes mischievous. However, they had to give up public school, resort to tutoring, in order to keep up with television production scheduling. It was quite an adjustment for all.

In December of 1992, they received a special invitation in the mail.

"We're invited to perform for the Royal Family," Danny announced. His eyes grew wide and everyone gathered around him to listen. "There will be several other artists slated to perform for a children's charity. It will be televised."

"That's so exciting!" Tara said looking over his shoulder to read it too. She gave the children an encouraging smile.

"We have to do three songs," Danny said, sitting down to think it out. He had a few on his mind that they could do exceptionally well. By this time, the band, even if they had youngsters performing, were known for doing a wide range of material, to include songs with adult themes. Tara knew that she would do a ballad and the teens would do something geared for the young people.

"What about the third song?" Tara asked her husband as he studied various sheet music he had filed away. An avid composer with lots of free time to be creative, Danny came out with a lot of ideas, sometimes faster than the band could look over at once. He would write it out on sheet music, mark the date, record the music with an alternate studio band, sing the melody, edit the tracks and then put away one long recording reel into safekeeping. He was the only one who knew where it was stored. In his mind, there was plenty of time for the band to sit down together to go through it. .

"I wrote a new composition for the occasion," Danny declared and showed it to her. She read it over. Puzzled, she looked up curiously.

"Will we do this together? It's a seductive duet."

"I know, but I can't pull off that type of song and come across seriously. I was thinking that you and Ross could do it."

Tara gasped with her eyes wide. She clutched his arm tightly.

"What? This is over the top, Danny. A bit racy in wording. I'm not exactly sure if I'm comfortable singing it. I know you try to keep up with the trends, but…I don't know."

Danny sat into a chair and took her hand. He stared deeply into her eyes.

"I know this, but it's quite catchy. Ross has a seductive voice when he drops to the lower range. He can take to the harmonizing while you stick to the melody. Your different styles blend well."

"I'm afraid that people will get mixed signals in our performance, Danny. There is already a lot of contemplation about Tom in the tabloids. It's no one's business how I ended up with Ross. Yet, the more people know about us, the more gossip is created. Truly, I don't like coming across as gossip for anyone."

"I understand, darling, but we should not hide either. Tom exists. None of us are ashamed. He's a terrific young man, a great son! Yet, there is already a commentator making a big spectacle about why it's hush-hush," Danny revealed. His face was incandescent, "I didn't tell you, but this is what prompted me to write this. He's challenged me personally. I saw it in the paper."

"You're kidding! Oh, the audacity!" Tara cried out. Her face felt warm as she stared into his eyes. He fidgeted in his chair.

"Sure, it makes me steam too, that the man is so arrogant, but he has a reputation of being a bulldog. He won't let this story drop. We should take this opportunity to drive it back into his face, on national television. After all, our friendship and this band endure because we are better people than that mongrel."

"All right, I agree. I'll do it if Ross agrees," she replied and that made Danny content.

Later, the men went out to a local London pub that evening and played a game of snooker. After awhile, Danny pulled out the sheet music and let Ross look it over.

"Your writing is so much better, although it took you years to catch up to me," Ross bragged, but Danny chuckled to ace a ball in the corner pocket. Ross felt puzzled as he read everything thoroughly, "This doesn't need any adjustments. Hmmm, why did you give it to me?"

Ross leaned onto the bar stool next to him. Danny drove another pool ball into the slots. Damn! He was winning!

"I do need you," Danny replied and then reached into his pocket to pull out the newspaper article. After Ross read it, he reacted appalled.

"This guy Blakely is a S.O.B jerk!"

"I agree. So will you do the song?"

"What? Me? With who?"

"Tara. You both can pull this off. She will do it if you agree. We already have discussed this."

Ross blew out a loud whoosh and both his hands smoothed down the back of his thick hair. He suddenly realized what Danny had in mind. It took a lot of guts on his part.

"Are you sure? I mean, this song is really expressive and at the same time, suggestive. It would be an honor to perform it, but you have to bare that in mind. It's a performance –play acting! Can you keep your cool?"

Danny laid the pool stick onto the table and nodded appropriately.

"Sure I can. I will not even be at the auditorium, so you can be comfortable. I'll be across the street at a place similar to this, drinking a tall glass of lager. When all of England gets an earful and an eyeful and the publicity is all in the papers of everything, we'll be the ones that goes to the bank on it. Not that SOB. I have a lot of respect for our friendship. You are like my brother, Ross. You know this. I trust you."

Even if he was declaring this, Ross felt that Danny needed to hear something affirmative. After all, he never came out with a full apology for what happened. He still owed Danny that. Sure, Tara was extremely beautiful these days. A very sexy woman in everyone's eyes, but his deepest respect was for the love she gave their son. She was a wonderful mother, and Danny and Tara made the perfect couple. Danny was his best friend again. Their bond was over the music and the entire family. No one could severe it. Ross would fight over this too.

"Ok, I will do an outstanding performance. I'll have the entire country speculating what took place, but it is our business - no one else's-especially that jerk. I lived for seven years without your friendship Danny. That was way too long. I won't let it happen again," Ross said with a determination that no one could touch, "I never admitted my apology, but I'm doing it now. I did you wrong, my friend. I'm deeply sorry. For you, I will make it right on stage."

Danny was touched and extended out his hand. They shook firmly. Ross lifted up his beer, thinking beyond what would take place.

"Then afterwards, we will return to the Briggs House to eat some of Marta's wonderful pot roast. We will drink wine going over new material for the next recording. Edward and Vincent want to throw in some ideas too. They are growing up, you know, and may give us a running for talent."

And so while the band performed their fiery songs of passion and the human factor, Danny sat across the street at a hotel bar to speak to a well known reporter, to give his own personal interview about the situation, really laying it on thick of what he thought of Mr. Blakely. The next day, the media had a field day. The asinine jerk's bid to make that secret a public shame was slammed dunked by the duo's frank openness on stage. They were all admired for keeping intimate secrets in the closet, where they should stay private; never skirting the issue that it did take place. They did not damage their public reputations to face such rude speculations. The next recordings began before Christmas and finished by mid-February, were solely dedicated to the events in those awkward days. The unique songs that the band created were personal. The fans felt like a part of the family, the band. The entire record topped the charts for months.

Chapter Fifty Three
The premonition of death

Right after Christmas, the band found out they were nominated for several music awards. It was like icing to the cake. Danny was simply overjoyed. Tara felt that way too, but the morning after their fifteenth wedding anniversary, in 1993, she experienced a terrible nightmare about him.

She sat at the bar where they met. He sat alone, all dressed up in a blue suit, one she did not recognize. She walked by; their eyes met. Not once did he reach for her hand. Instead Danny got up and left. Then they were in Spain. Sylvia stood out on the porch. She urged Tara to go after him. Instead of going to his apartment, Danny disappeared up the cobblestone street. If there was no apartment, there would be no reunion! "Danny! Wait! Don't leave me!" Tara raced to stop him. The instant that she caught up and touched his shoulder, they were suddenly at the foot of their stairs at home. Danny looked at her. Did he even recognize her? His eyes seemed glazed over. He gasped, and then slumped to the floor, not breathing.

Tara bolted upright. She wanted to get her bearings. The dream knocked her for a loop! Danny slept deep next to her. They had celebrated that night, then made love. He turned over into his pillow. Tara felt relieved. He was fine. So what was the reason for this horrible dream?

Tara brought the covers over her head. She slid her body as close as possible to his. Her legs glided across his hairy leg. There was no way to go back to sleep after that. So, for two hours, she laid in the dark. The wakeup call at seven seemed like it would never come. They had arrived to London for rehearsals. The upcoming awards show was soon. Finally, the phone rang, loud! Danny answered it and then put the receiver down. He popped open a soda that sat on the table, gulping down aspirin from the bottle he left there. Then he rolled over to touch her body. Peeping with sleepy eyes, he murmured "Good morning, Mrs. Cross. My naughty, naughty baby."

He whispered something else into her ear, something she didn't understand right away, but then he kissed her brow, her nose, and searched for her mouth. He wanted her, but she lay as stiff as a board.

"What's the matter, darling?"

"Nothing. Nothing. Don't stop. I need you," Tara begged and this time slid underneath him. She wanted his love, his fire, his power. She wanted him to force that nightmare out of her mind. To stimulate him further, she kissed him with fiery passion, wrapped her legs tightly around his hips so he really had to work for it, and she moaned at every thrust. He liked it when she moaned. Wild, rowdy sex was unusual for them. Here in the hotel bed, they were free to be as loud as they wanted. The walls were thick and there were no teenagers on the other side who could possibly hear them.

"Oooohhh, I love it when you get stirred up," Danny panted afterwards and caressed her hair, "What on earth provoked you this morning?"

He was always in tune to her emotions. She should have been sighing in ecstasy. He knew she reached it. There were always those little signs one knows well about their spouse, when she dug her nails into his back and pushed her pelvis forward to get the last thrust deeper. Her legs became like vice grips; then slid down his legs, trembling. Still, her eyes were still very wide. She was staring at the ceiling. Her mind was miles away, but her hands caressed his arms like crazy.

"I had a bad dream," Tara rolled into his body so he could hold her tight.

"Yeah? About what, dearest? Are you nervous about all this hub-hub with the show? Everything is going great. Your fitting is today for that fabulous ball gown. I even bought a new suit, just to look great for the press conference today. It's hanging in the closet. I did this while you had your nails done."

"You need a haircut," Tara observed as an afterthought. His hair was always quick to grow out and unfortunately, he liked it long. He didn't have to wear it as short as when he was in the navy. He always liked it when it spiked out. Wasn't that the fashion for some men?

"Ok. I promise to get one later. Was that your bad dream? Did I come out on stage to accept the award with hippy hair?"

"No. it wasn't."

She sounded really afraid, so he took on a serious pose.

"Now, you put me on alert. What was it? Tell me. I'm listening."

"It was horrible. The bottom line is that you never met me in New York, so we never had a reason to be together in Spain. In fact you just walked away from me, each time. You left. You were gone. And then I think you died."

"Good heavens!" Danny sat up quickly, "I'm perfectly all right, my wonderful darling. See, you can touch me in the flesh. And there has never been an occasion in my heart that I didn't need to see you or be with you. We will grow old together and die peacefully in our beds, after we become senile and demented, so it won't hurt as much."

Danny kissed her lips, her cheeks, and squeezed her tight.

"Ah, Tara, I love you! I must chase away those gloomy thoughts. Perhaps what you need is a good breakfast with plenty of hot coffee. You have circles under your eyes. Didn't you sleep well? I thought we had quite the sedative, with all of the Champaign and the terrific sex. After all, I fell straight to sleep. Perhaps that is why you thought I left, or died, since I didn't cuddle up afterwards. I just passed out on my side of the bed, and that always make you mad. You love to be held. You need it desperately for some odd reason. I don't mind it though. I just forgot to last night with the Champaign."

In some ways, this made perfect sense, why she felt so neglected.

"By gosh, that's it!" Tara sat up too and smiled on his behalf, "You know how I crave it. After all, I put up with the bluntness of your physique when we make out. I deserve to be held after all that."

"Aww, that's because you're my girl," He laughed, "I can't help but get overzealous when I'm with you that way. Now, I'll tell you what. Take a hot shower to freshen up. I'll order up room service."

So Tara did as he wished. They ate at leisure, fruit, scones, eggs and bacon. He called Aaron by phone. "Look, son, your mother and I just had a quiet breakfast together. Why don't you and the others check out the buffet downstairs? That way you can eat all the hotcakes you want. Tell them to put it on our tab."

"All right, Da. I'll tell the rest. We'll see you later. Love you."

"Yes, I love you too, but you know that. Have fun," He said and then hung up the phone.

Tara placed on her makeup and jewelry and then he took a shower. Then he dressed in the bathroom. When Danny stepped out for her inspection, she saw him wearing the same blue suit that he wore in her dream. She stared, frightened.

"Don't you like the color of my shirt? I thought gold would stand out. Or is it the tie? Maybe I should switch out the tie," He lamented his choice of it after noticing her look.

"No, no. Don't change it. It's nice. Blue is your color," Tara replied and tried to ignore the nagging premonition in her mind. She then straightened the tie. They went down to the lobby together to check messages at the front desk. He read one out loud to her.

"This is a note from Gloria. She spoke to father this morning. He sounds horrible with that cough. She's concerned. Thinks he's catching pneumonia," Danny squished up the paper to throw in the trash. He had a thought, "Perhaps I should drive home just to ensure he's not getting worse. I don't wish her to worry if it's nothing."

"But Danny, what about the press conference? It's this afternoon," Tara reminded him.

"Let Ross handle it. He's great with the media. Such a suave flirt, but quite dependable. Just follow his lead. You'll know what to say to them," Danny encouraged and then dug into his pocket. He took out an aspirin bottle, "Damn! It's empty."

"Don't tell me. You have another headache?" Tara surmised. The headaches began about a month ago, but just recently were more intense. Danny didn't have a history of them, so it too was worrisome, "Why don't you make an appointment to see a doctor? You are just as bad as your father in ignoring symptoms."

"I'm perfectly fine. My prognosis is that these will disappear, just as soon as we put up our awards on our bookshelves at home. It's just stress, dearest. Nothing more."

"Ok. I'll take your word on it," Tara followed him out to the hotel entrance. The valet brought the car around. Danny embraced his wife tenderly. She looked so pretty in brown. Her hair was long, auburn colored now since she experimented with hair coloring, and the clothing brought out the color of her eyes. She pouted that he was leaving.

"Now, the band must carry on without me. Make sure they keep to the practice schedule. Everyone must be outstanding during the ceremony. It's on live television, you know. Thousands will be watching. I expect complete satisfaction from everyone of your performance. I also want lots of raves in the tabloids, so you must practice to achieve this," Danny insisted. He was a strict task master. One they loved.

"Yes, dear. We will surely knock them off their feet," Tara promised and then kissed him goodbye sensuously and long. He started to turn away, but Tara kissed him again. Danny paused to look at her closely.

"Everything is fine, Tara. I should return tomorrow night, luck be willing, once I figure out what's going on with father. Goodbye, my darling. Remember how much I love you."

He flashed a brilliant smile. Blue eyes were twinkling. He gave a wink just before he slid into the car to drive away, wearing that fabulous dark suit. It was rare thing to be apart, but just this once, Tara thought it would be alright. She looked at her watch. It was 10:00 a.m., Tuesday. She made a mental note to call later that afternoon.

At 3:00 o'clock, the press conference went smoothly. It lasted for an hour. Most of the celebrities slated to perform gave interviews. Cross Passage's pictures were snapped too. Jamie, Edward, and Eric really hammed it up for the cameras. The press was well pleased by this. Afterwards, Ross escorted Tara to the front desk. There were no messages, so Tara borrowed their phone, but to her annoyance, the home phone at the Briggs House just rang and rang. With everyone being away, Marta and Lila were either at the manor or at their own homes.

"I wonder if he's at the manor, too," Tara wondered out loud. Ross smiled, looking over his own messages.

"Danny's probably giving his father a lecture about smoking through his cold symptoms. I'm sure that is why George sounded horrible," Ross elaborated quietly. Tara could just imagine it. George was very stubborn. Even Helen fussed at him more than ever to quit smoking. They were older now, needing more attention. Danny's diligence to his parents was quite touching.

"I'm sure you are right. I'll try again from my room later," Tara suggested and they went to the dining hall to meet the children for an early dinner.

Around nine o'clock, after all had settled in, Tara was alone in her room. Everything was the same as they had left it that morning, except that room service stripped the bed, placed new linen, and made it back up again. It gave her an odd feeling. She remembered every detail from their midnight and morning lovemaking. It made Tara long for her man.

Now, she was very compelled to call. The phone just rang and rang. Tara tried to reason logically why Danny did not call by this time. He was working on new arrangements before the nominations. Perhaps he was busy in the studio and did not hear the phone, or the ringer was off so not to be disturbed. Perhaps he lost track of the time. Just how often did Danny get time alone?

Still, common sense dictated that he would at least call to say goodnight, just to be respectful. So after slipping into a nightgown, she waited impatiently and read a mystery book to unravel her nerves. Sometime before midnight, she finally dozed off. When the phone rang at 6:00 a.m., it put her into a tail spin, but it was only the designated wake up call. It was too early to disturb her in-laws, so Tara showered, dressed and then went to breakfast with the children around 8:00 a.m. They talked excitedly about what they seen and heard around other performers. Tara played along like nothing out of the ordinary was going on. Ross keenly watched her from his end of the table. When they stepped into their own rehearsal room around 10:00, he pulled her aside.

"What's wrong Tara? You seem preoccupied."

"I am, about Danny. He was going to see George, remember? He has not called since and I've tried the house, several times. There is no answer."

"Hmmm, that's not like him," Ross speculated out loud, caught off guard. Danny was crazy in love with Tara. He would never make the woman worry about anything needlessly. He made a suggestion, "Let's encourage the rest to do something on their own, while we investigate what's going on."

So they left instructions and went onto Tara's room so they could make phone calls in private. When Tara reached George, he was surprised.

"Did you say Danny came home yesterday? That's very strange. I have not seen him at all. No one has."

"I'm worried, George. Can you get someone to check the house? I can't get an answer at all."

"Sure. I'll go."

"No, you are sick. Get one of the servants to go in your stead," Tara insisted and George agreed just to get her off the line, but the man was very stubborn. He didn't tell Helen where he was going and went out the door. Usually Danny would encourage him to take these walks, just to get some exercise, but George always balked. This time, it was strangely comforting, as many fears raced through his mind. As he approached the cobblestone drive, George noticed Danny's car in the driveway. Hopefully his son had just pulled in. Perhaps he had detoured to stay at Michael's and did not come straight home. George prayed this was the case.

The front door was unlocked. He pushed the door in, hesitant to walk in to what he might find. No lights were on, except for one in the hall. He adjusted his glasses to focus into the dim lighting. There was something on the bottom step, something in a heap, something blue. It was Danny's body! His eyes were lifeless. George's face went absolutely white. He gasped out loud and backed out of the door in a big hurry. The man clutched his chest. George screamed as a car made its way around the bend. He waved for the driver's attention. The neighbor saw him collapse down to his knees. The car veered into the driveway right behind Danny's car.

"George! George! What's wrong, George," Mr. Franks bellowed as he got out and ran forward to help the old man. Maybe he was having a heart attack, but as he came upon him, this wasn't the case. George was overwrought with grief. Mr. Franks looked around and noticed the door was open, so he went in halfway. In two seconds, he bolted right out again.

"Oh, Jesus! That's Danny! Oh, no! George, I'm calling the police. Let me get you to the car."

Meanwhile, Ross and Tara waited anxiously for news. Finally, after three hours, the telephone rang. Tara nervously answered it, "George?"

"No, Tara, it's me. Mr. Eades," Tara drew a big breath. Mr. Eades was part of the local police force that consisted about five men overall. There wasn't a lot of crime in their village, but the policemen helped the citizens feel safe.

"Yes, Mr. Eades? Is everything all right?"

"Actually, Tara, no," His voice dropped very low. He struggled to get to the point, "George and Helen are too distraught right now, but managed to hand me this number to reach you. I'm sorry, but we found your husband this afternoon."

"Where, Mr. Eades?" Tara wondered if perhaps Danny was in an accident. Perhaps he was just hurt. She could take it if he was just out of it, like in a coma; just as long as he was alive and breathing; but what he said next brought her to her knees.

"Danny was at home. There's no sign of trauma or a break in. Don't know what exactly happened. The body will have to be sent away for an autopsy."

"Body?" Tara slumped towards the floor. The receiver fell beside her. Ross led Tara to sit down beside him. She sobbed, so he picked up the receiver to discover what made Tara cry so. After speaking to

Mr. Eads, Ross held Tara tight. She wept so hard, that she shook. She clung to his shoulders to stare up at him. Her eyes were red, the tears fell like mad, her mouth gaped open like a zombie.

"Tell me this is a nightmare, Ross? Tell me that the vision I had of this happening is a lie! Danny can't be dead! He can't! This is too much! I need him! I want him! Oh, God! *Why*? I can't take it!"

She was in hysterics now. Her body was limp, in a half-feint, zoning out of the real world. It hurt too much to stay in it. He whisked her up to put her onto the bed. Carefully, he wrapped a blanket around her body to keep her from full shock. He picked up the phone to summon the front desk, "Send a doctor quick! Tara Cross has collapsed."

The doctor was there within ten minutes to check Tara over. She woke up, but only went back to full hysterics, so the physician sedated her. He offered Ross something to sleep by too, but he declined.

"No, I have to keep a straight head. This family will fall to pieces," Ross declared, feeling very old. Yes, the horrible chore of informing everyone was on his shoulders. It was now about 4:30 when he descended downstairs to the fancy lobby below. He found the teens hanging out with members of different bands in the large auditorium.

He quietly asked each to go up to their separate rooms. "What's wrong, Ross? You look weird!" Matt asked, but he just pointed to the stairs. They went quickly. They were full of questions, but once he had them together, he shocked them with the news. Jamie cried out. Edward pounded the wall. Little Aaron slumped onto the bed. Tears fell like rain. Vincent held onto him tight. The rest had this wide-eye, glazed look. They were shocked, but comforted each other as best as they could. They worried about their mother. Ross tried to calm them down.

"Look, she's sedated right now. You must be strong, for your Mum, for your family. No one on the outside knows yet. Let's keep this secret as long as possible. I have to get to your aunts and uncles before the media finds out. Once this happens, it will be a circus! Thank God you live out in the country, so it will take awhile for news to spread! Can you remain here on your own? You must keep your wits about you until I return."

"Go, Ross. We'll be strong somehow. Da' would want us to be brave," Tristan whimpered, and the rest vowed their compliance to stick together. They would not tell a single soul what brought them such sorrow. Just until his return. To do it in a short time took a moment of thinking it through, as each Cross sibling was off in different directions in London. Susan was on a modeling shoot at the West end, Michael in a Soho theater with full rehearsals; and Gloria was at an elite magazine studio developing pictures. Ross also had to inform the officials at the awards show, so he did that first.

"This is a difficult thing to say, but I want to inform you that Danny Cross was found dead at home this afternoon."

The officials all wanted to help the band.

"Ross, tell us what you want us to do." Mr. MacAfee replied, waiting for direction. He was head of marketing.

"I need a press release in the morning to convey what I know. The body is being sent for autopsy, so there will be a lot of speculation. Tara doesn't need gossip or malicious rumors floating about, so I want to be upfront with everyone as soon as possible. The family here in London needs to be informed as well. Their teenagers are upstairs, confined to their rooms. They need their privacy to grieve, but while I'm out, they also need security."

"As you wish, sir. It will be done," Mr. MacAfee replied. "Deepest condolences, Ross. I'm quite aware that you and Mr. Cross were extraordinary friends."

"Yes, we were. Thank you," This left a strange taste in Ross's mouth. How does one adjust to state a friend in the past tense? The man was alive just yesterday morning! "Can you do one more favor?"

"Sure. Anything."

"Samuel Cross is Danny's brother. He is in the Royal Navy. I heard he is assigned just off our coastline with his fleet. Commander Sumter is the contact. Here is the number to call. Can you request an emergency trip home tonight? Don't mention what's wrong. Sammy will learn of it soon enough, but I prefer he hears about his brother's death from the family, if at all possible."

The man nodded and went to make the phone call in his office. Ross went out to the main lobby, found a closed phone booth, and made a quick, private call to Susan.

"Hey there! What's up?" She asked upon hearing his voice.

"Susan, we need to talk. Please get Gloria too. You are both needed at Michael's place right away."

"What? We are almost done with the shoot. Can't it wait until later?" Susan scoffed. He knew how important her time was in modeling.

"No, Susan. This is an emergency. I'll meet you there. I'm getting Michael right now," And he hung up the phone before she could argue further. The valet pulled Ross's car around. He drove like mad to the theater. Michael was surprised to see the man walking in, but he recognized the dark scowl and the stern approach.

"What's wrong Ross?" Michael was almost afraid to ask, "You look upset."

"I am upset, Michael. You must come with me," Ross took the clipboard out of Michael's hands. He handed it over to the assistant nearby. She looked up in confusion and even Michael was the same.

"I can't leave. We are in the middle of Act four."

"The curtain has come down Michael. This is urgent! Very urgent!" Ross pulled at Michael to get him moving. This time, he went along. Since Ross was so serious, Michael didn't ask anything further. It was strange that Ross didn't even turn on the radio in the car. The man loved music. They pulled up to a familiar building and parked the car on the street.

"This is my place," Michael declared out loud, "Are you pulling a surprise? It's not even my birthday."

Ross slammed the car door shut, just when Gloria and Susan pulled up too. They parked behind Ross's car.

"What's going on? Why did you summon us?" Gloria quickly ran to keep up. Ross was quickly ascending into the building; going into Michael's flat, as he still had the key. Once they were all inside, Susan reacted.

"I can't believe you pulled me out of the shoot just to come here! What in bloody hell is going on, Ross? You know that I have to work! This contract makes me rich!"

"This is not about the money!" Ross yelled back. He never raised his voice like this lately. He was a happy man, so Susan shut her mouth. It frightened Gloria. She knew something was terribly wrong.

"Ross, what is it. Just tell us," She insisted and touched his arm.

"There's no easy way to say it. Danny went home yesterday to check on your father."

"He did? Well, is this what's it about? Has father turned for the worse? I feared he was getting pneumonia," Gloria was somewhat relieved. My! How dramatic Ross became when delivering news. This was nothing unexpected.

"Father hates doctors," Michael declared and sat down. "I hope Danny made him go to one. He has more influence than the rest of us."

"Ross, this is nothing to get excited over," Susan sat next to her brother. She rolled her eyes. This only made Ross angry.

"Listen to me!" he shouted, "Danny never called. Tara's been frantic to reach him since yesterday, so your father checked the house. Danny was found today. He's dead, I tell you."

Now, he had their full attention.

"Is this a sick joke? My brother is as healthy as a horse!" Susan sputtered and she stood up in his face, but Ross was too upset. He grabbed Susan by the shoulders.

"What the hell must I do to make it sink in, woman? No, this isn't a bloody joke! It's the truth! Tara has been sedated; the kids are bawling their hearts out and are alone at that hotel; the officials have been notified, and right now, the commander on Sammy's ship is sending him home urgently! I've done all that I could. All I had left to do was tell you what happened, but hell! You don't want to believe me!"

Now, the women reacted and wept strongly, so Ross stopped. He was stunned to behave this way, so he escaped to the balcony. Michael couldn't move from his spot, but hot tears fell down his cheeks. He sobbed loudly. His sisters sat down on either side. They wept within his arms for quite awhile. Twenty minutes later, Gloria found strength to call up her parents. The whole grief process began all over again. Gloria needed fresh air after another half hour went by. She went to the balcony door, but didn't go out. She witnessed the man with such steel emotion break down too. She knew he would prefer to be alone.

Chapter Fifty Four
Mourning begins

Two hours later, Sammy arrived to the apartment and they told the whole story again. His eyes grew stern as he looked around at everyone, but he did not immediately react. Perhaps his military training kept him strong. All he had to do was witness what was happening to his family. Michael seemed aged overnight. He looked very haggard. His sisters' eyes were blood shot red. They kept sniffing and weeping consistently. Poor Ross was fidgeting. He was slumped by the balcony door. Something weighed on his mind.

"What troubles you, Ross? What is it?"

"I must get back to the hotel. Tara is sedated. Those kids are alone. They must go home somehow, but I'm uncertain what to expect when we return."

"They need to stay tonight with our parents, so we can all be together. You and I can check out the Brigg's

House in the morning, before we let anyone go back," Sammy suggested and then paused. Certainly everything was in order there. Danny was found slumped near the steps. Still, would the children or Tara even want to go into it? It was still their home. What worry? No wonder Ross was indecisive about what to do. Sammy let out a big sigh and then tapped Michael on the shoulder.

"I know you are upset. Pull yourself together man, to get our sisters home. Go in Gloria's car. Ross will swing me by the theater to pick up your car. This way I can help him drive Aaron, Tom and the rest to the manor. One of us needs to do this!"

Michael nodded slowly as realization sank in. He was the oldest and should be in charge. Somehow he was letting everyone down.

"Yes, I think so." He said and stood up to encourage the ladies out the door. Everything happened in a blur that evening. In two cars, they loaded up nine teenagers with three adults, six equally into each vehicle. Tara was rather dopey. She didn't know what was taking place. Sammy carried her out to the car. They loaded up in the back alley so they wouldn't be spotted. At one point, she caressed his cheek. "Danny, I love you," she said before passing out again. This one thing brought tears to Sammy's eyes. He tried not to show it while he drove home. Still, the teens in that car were very aware of his hurt feelings. They saw tears slip down his face.

Ross stayed on with the family at the manor and slept on the couch. Everyone finally went to bed at three in the morning. Thankfully, Tara rested the entire time in Gloria's room. He woke up at dawn for some reason. He was restless at any rate. Ross picked up a pen and pad. He thought deeply, writing down what he might say at the press conference. He sipped on coffee, scribbled notes upon a pad. He didn't notice when Tara slipped in. She simply sat down beside him. Her eyes were teary. She seemed to hold onto her emotions by a thin thread, so he said nothing, but let her collect her deepest thoughts too. For a long time she studied the fire glowing brightly in the fireplace. Finally, she spoke.

"We barely celebrated our anniversary because of those damn nominations. All this commotion to get to London, to rehearse for a live telecast! He was complaining of not feeling well a few days ago, that he had pressure behind his eyes and some neck pain. He ignored it all once he got that stupid telegram. Now he has died in our home. What I believe is most outrageous is that Danny died alone. How ironic is that: to die in a house full of life and energy? He blew off my premonition that morning. He said that we would grow old and pass on peacefully. I knew he was going to die, but I didn't stop him from making that trip."

"Tara, you don't know for sure if it could have been prevented. Don't torture yourself this way. We must wait to see what the autopsy reveals."

"I know what it will say!" She snapped. She glared at Ross, with a stone, hard expression upon her face. She felt anger, "Something happened inside his head. He was out of aspirin and complained of an oncoming headache right before he left that morning. I suggested that he see a doctor, but he said it was just stress. I knew better. I should have made him go to one, right away. He might be alive now if I had!"

At this, heavy tears fell down her pretty face. Ross took her into his arms and caressed her hair. It was a good cry, not as hysterical as before, and after a few minutes, she calmed down.

"There's so much to do. I don't know where to begin."

"Let me take care of things, Tara. Concentrate on your children," Ross suggested and her eyes grew wide.

"Oh, my God! I'm so terribly, terribly selfish. Aaron! I must comfort our son. I must comfort all of my children. How can I remain knocked out when they need me to be strong," She cried out and immediately went to find them. Ross didn't stop her, as she certainly needed to do this, in her own way. She was their mother. They would turn to her in the hour of their immense grief. They would all cry out their sorrows willingly.

Ross went to London about an hour later. He stood in front of the steps where the awards ceremony would take place. He was dressed in black. His hair flew in the light breeze. He stood tall, proud, in order not to break down. All the reporters crowded around as he delivered the news solemnly. Some even wept openly.

"Will your band back off from the show?" one reporter asked, "There are several nominations pending."

"At this time, everything is in limbo. We have to wait on the autopsy before scheduling the funeral. Then afterwards, depending on the timing of things, we'll make that decision whether to perform. Even if we don't, I will show up to represent the family."

He denied answering any more questions and left the podium. Luckily, the next day, Friday by 1:00 o'clock, the autopsy report was sent expeditiously to the Grand

Manor to reveal that Danny's death was caused by a spontaneous burst type aneurysm. Simultaneously that afternoon, Danny's body was released immediately and shipped to the local mortuary near their village, in Wiltshire.

Mr. Phipps, a respected mortician, took great care to prepare his body. The family had already sent him the military uniform that he wore in his younger days. Danny had always remained in shape, being an avid runner. The dark blue color made him look very distinguished. The family made plans to have a large public ceremony on Saturday.

Hopefully, to do it quickly, would expedite the grieving process for everyone. The ceremony would take place at the amphitheater, instead of having a three day viewing in London at Westminster Cathedral. They opted, too, for a private burial near his home. Tara respected the public's need to say goodbye to the popular showman, but she also didn't want a lot of the pomp and circumstances that usually came with famed celebrities or anyone deemed worthy for state funerals.

Early Saturday morning, Ross drove Tara to the funeral home. She was to view the body for the first time in a private area. The children and family waited outside for their turn. Since she was the spouse, they allowed her to bid farewell first. As she approached the casket, her knees were shaking. Ross could feel it too, so he held on very tightly. Tara drew to the casket. She leaned to look into it. The woman was overcome with the details as she took it all in.

There were already flowers everywhere near the casket, which was dark and made of rich wood. He lay peacefully, dressed impeccably in that supreme uniform that made her fall in love. Danny was clean shaven and his hair was trimmed quite proper. The metals on his uniform were polished brightly, along with the ring on the left hand. The finality of it all was so overwhelming. She collapsed and wept fervently.

"He's gone, Ross! Gone," She stammered with every breath harder to gain, "Oh, God! It's so unbelievable. How I loved him-for everything! For our marriage, for our success, the way he made me realize that each precious moment is so sacred! Life was a grand adventure not to be thrown away. How can our family ever be the same? I need him so much!"

Ross eyes were on the brim of tears, but if he broke down, they may never gain their composure to survive the day.

"Tara, you can get through this. Hold on! Somewhere in heaven, I'm sure he's watching you. You are his light, his angel. Help him move onto the next dimension knowing you are strong because of him."

Tare heeded his words. She regained senses to stand up slowly. Her body posture was straight. She was composed now. She caressed Danny's cold face for several moments and then impulsively leaned in to kiss his mouth one last time. Ross almost lost it when she did this.

"Thank you, my sweet husband," Tara choked back the tears. She nodded her head, "All right. I'm ready. As Danny would say, 'Let's get on with it.'"

Tara managed to handle things that morning. After all the family made their private farewells, a military procession using a gun carriage brought his body to a catafalque at the amphitheater. It was packed full. No one moved or made a sound as the body came in, followed by the family. To the public, Tara was a vision of stoic and regal composure, dressed in black from head to toe. Michael spoke an eloquent eulogy that was brilliantly composed, that spoke about their values and of Danny's devotion to his family. A military band played the "Navy Hymn" on bagpipes. Even Harry, Danny's old commander, came to the podium. He spoke about Danny's outstanding service to his country. The sound of Amazing Grace pierced the air as everyone sang along with the poignant bagpipes.

For the rest of the time, the public were allowed to walk by the casket to pay their last respects. Hundreds upon hundreds of flowers, roses, poems, and letters were dropped nearby. About an hour before sunset, the casket was closed and taken to the private site designated for burial. The Cross family, Ross and Tom, and their faithful servants gathered around to pray with the minister. It was a place at the far end of the garden, that Jamie used as a little girl to grow all of her favorite flowers. The plans would be that once Danny was interred, they would hire a contractor to landscape around it with tall plants, young trees, rose bushes, and cement benches and sculptures, to give it a sense of solitude and privacy. His presence would forever remain in Wiltshire, his home.

Tara and the children were strong throughout everything, but the minute that the casket was lowered into the ground, their emotions got the best of them. Now, they wept openly. The finality of it tore at their hearts. Tara knew that her life would never be the same.

The door was slamming shut. There was no return and no more tomorrows. The fifteen years of their time together now seemed way too short. Danny was gone forever. He would only live on within her dreams and in her heart.

The following week, the award show took place. Everyone was surprised that Ross, Tara and the teenagers showed up after all. They were greeted kindly as they walked inside the grand auditorium to take their seats. When they won the first award, the whole auditorium stood up in standing applause. Tara politely shook hands with those at the podium, took the award, and maintained a dignified pose in front of the cameras.

"I want to thank everyone who has supported us ever since our beginning in Wiltshire and our recent difficult days of my husband's passing. Your letters, telegrams, and flowers meant so much. For you, we will continue on and remain strong. Thank you and God speed!"

She and the band walked off stage to have their pictures taken with the awards. They were poised and brave, and they did this repeatedly because they won four more that night. Ross requested to the officials that the band only perform one number for the show, near the closing, instead of what was rehearsed previously. Out of respect, the officials gave permission.

Tara stood under the bright lights, solemn and proud. The band gave a stirring introduction of what seemed to be a ballad, dedicated to Danny. It lulled the audience along as Tara wept, enunciating the words crisply just to get through it. Then suddenly about midway, there was a dramatic crescendo. Suddenly the song was powerfully upbeat, about how to take on each precious moment with gusto. The music was powerful. Her voice seemed very extraordinary and soared into very high dimensions.

Even if the spotlights were bright, Tara lit up the stage with a magical and fiery performance. At the end, with the dramatic musical climax, there was not a dry eye in the house. There was thunderous applause and again, a huge standing ovation. The band was proud. They could not do this any other way. Their Da' would not accept it if they did not perform with gusto. He would have wanted them to stand tall. They were his lasting tribute. They wanted to make him proud, even in death.

After all the accolades had settled down and the media finally moved on to talk about other news, the family adjusted to a different way of life in Wiltshire. Tara thought it best not to commit the band to any further projects. They all needed time to mourn in their own way. The contractors finished the new landscape in record speed and it was very lovely.

On several occasions, the teens would go out separately to sit on the cement bench to pray. Sometimes they talked out loud, as if Danny could still hear them. Jamie made sure that the area was spit-spot and if she even saw one thing out place, she would straighten it out. The boys managed to get on with their chores around the house without complaining much. Tara thought it was quite strange that they didn't even bicker. Aaron didn't speak much and was so deeply attached to his mother now. Tara couldn't get rid of the boy and nor did she want too, as his presence was quite comforting.

Michael turned over a new play project to a new ambitious partner in order to stay home. The two communicated quite frequently over the phone during this time to discuss business. Michael had to do this. Danny's death took a great toll on his parents. His mother usually stayed secluded in her room. She would look over Danny's old photographs constantly, but this only made her cry. George sat despondent in his chair in the smoking room. He gave up the habit, but it was a familiar room. It gave him comfort. It took a lot of encouragement to convince his mother to go out sometimes and to convince George to go out for a walk.

Michael found ample time to visit Tara and the kids. He helped her go through Danny's possessions and donate his clothing. They boxed up awards and precious memorabilia to place up in the attic. Tara came across an old movie camera and film reels. Danny used it often throughout the years. They sat and watched one of the reels one evening, but it only brought Tara deep remorse. So Michael stored them away too.

Spring turned into late summer and they didn't put on a show that year, but everyone understood. They all waited for an appropriate time to pass for the mourning to end. Miraculously, Tara and Michael renewed a strong friendship. He suddenly found himself in the position to declare true intentions. Tara was always someone desired, yet the arduous responsibility of the children dismayed him. Even worse, they were full blown teenagers, who at times showed conflicting opinions. He was just too old to totally take over. He did love them, but was not one to be a constant father.

One afternoon, the moment of truth arrived. He was anxious and fidgety.

"My new production company is finally taking off. I must return to London on a full time basis now. It is a huge undertaking," Michael mentioned quietly while stirring milk into the tea cup. They were out on the porch, "It will interfere with visits home."

"We'll be fine. Don't worry. Ross has moved up the road into the old vicar's home. Take care of your business. I really should not occupy all of your time," Tara replied and affectionately placed a hand upon his. Normally, he would have delighted that she gave intentions in subtle way, but not today. Michael feigned a cough in order to politely move his away. It was good that Ross left London to live nearby as Tara and the kids needed constant attention. The sun sank low and the wind blew the tall late summer grass in the nearby field. The fence needed tending.

"Since he's back, have Ross look after those boards over there. The boys will fall if they should scamper over it," Michael said and then stared at Tara closely. Over the years, she had blossomed into a mature, outgoing social creature and an accomplished, confidant entertainer who drew fascination everywhere. Her transformation was complete, due to Danny's credit, but Michael didn't feel adequate enough to partake in the final visible product. He stood and placed a prim hat upon his head, "I must leave now."

Startled by this, Tara rose impulsively too. She stared into his blue eyes and his composure broke down. Their bodies were so close. Michael pulled Tara to him tightly. Her ample bosom pressed against his chest and teased his desire. A lovely fragrance graced her body. So much temptation, yet restraint remained the order.

"I can't stay, Tara. Call only if the occasion requires it," Michael felt forced to make the embrace appear merely friendly. Tara knew better

"Michael?" Her voice trembled and now nothing could be denied. How could he just walk away? Looking down and holding onto her this close, the soft delicate features upon her face were beautifully expressive and the ample cleavage was exposed underneath the soft, pastel dress.

"Losing Danny has been difficult for all of us, especially you, Tara. Our deepest emotions are all ablaze. We should not scar this moment with compulsive, selfish desire, at least not on my part. My departed brother deserves that much respect. Tara, my dear, you will always remain the one that I let slip away," Michael said hoarsely.

Tara nodded in understanding. Tears came to the surface. Michael departed with quiet dignity, exchanging a wave as the car disappeared from view. Tara remained on the porch for awhile longer. She thought deeply about their extraordinary friendship that began so long ago. Michael was always on the back burner, somewhere in the corner of her mind. What if by extraordinary coincidence they had met first?

Surely they would have been portrayed in the county as a uniquely happy couple, respecting each others values, sharing many similar interests. Michael was a huge influence in her adult years like Ross was in her youth -always protective and steadfast. Perhaps it was best that he returned to London. He was right that her emotions were ablaze. She missed Danny in that way. Desire was a constant nag as she slept alone every night. What was once a constant thing between husband and wife was now gone. Her loneliness and desires made her ache for a man. What to do now, since Michael was leaving, and Ross was now so visibly close by?

Tara didn't want to repeat an old mistake simply because she felt lust. It was wrong then as it was now. Still, when Ross stopped by for dinner or worked around the place to repair things, she could not help but notice his muscular physique. He tanned well in the summer and whenever he took off his shirt, all she could do was stare. This was all wrong and she decided to work during useless hours, just to occupy her mind on sensible things. She pulled out sheet music, sat at the piano in the studio, and tried to compose songs on her own. Anything to get that man off her mind!

Chapter Fifty Five

A new friend

The next spring, a year after Danny's death, seemed a productive time for Michael. As usual, he snagged customary invitations to either dinner parties or new productions. His popularity was growing. One night, Tara and Ross joined him to watch a historic play by an adventuresome director. Anna Bentley was a tall, blond actress on the stage, that blended well wearing delicate 17th century attire with extended round petticoats. Her voice was crisp and melodious. She was very striking, with angular cheeks and full lips. Sudden interest, like rain falling on a dry desert, forced Michael to grasp the program in the dark. He shuffled it loudly to seek out her name within it. After the final curtain went down, the auditorium burst into thunderous applause.

"I have to go backstage to introduce myself. Perhaps, I can persuade her to work for our production company,"

Michael explained anxiously. He immediately rushed away through the crowded lobby.

"Someone has his attention straight away," Ross remarked as he wrapped a faux fur coat around Tara's shoulders. Ross lingered over this gesture a little longer than he should. Tara tried not to dwell on it. Instead, she kept her focus on the situation with Michael. It left her with mixed feelings.

"That is a good thing, Ross. He deserves someone special in his life."

"Don't we all?" Ross declared softly.

Tara ignored the remark. She worked her way through the crowd and paparazzi that snapped their picture. The morning headlines would list their appearance socially in the commentaries as interesting gossip. By now, all of UK was watching her. She was their new diva, a sensational singing superstar. Who would be the next man in her life? She respectfully waited a full year after the passing of her husband. It was time for her to move on.

Michael didn't run across problems getting backstage as he was frequently requested to give expert opinions about any new production. He found Anna among her peers in the dressing rooms. They were drinking Champaign, eagerly awaiting the reviews.

"Hello. Miss Anna Bentley?" Michael questioned. She nodded, curiously taking the business card offered, "You were fantastic on stage, my dear. I will be honored if we could talk over your future. Perhaps over lunch?"

"Why, thank you, sir," Anna recognized his name. Flattered, she was pleased that such a wonderful producer sought her out personally.

"May I call upon you tomorrow?" Michael asked politely.

"Certainly. I look forward to it," Anna replied. She tried not to sound breathless about it. He was a most handsome man. Someone who made her feel giddy. Michael took her hand and bestowed a kiss.

"So will I," he stated and then departed. Anna was all a quiver about his visit. She felt great expectations. It was more surreal to discover upon their date that Michael displayed more than a casual interest. As they lingered over several alcoholic drinks, he slid closely beside her. He leaned in for a kiss. She could not resist. Those blue eyes stole her heart from the onset.

They took things day by day. Michael fell in love with Anna's subtle humor and kind disposition. She always allowed him to be in control. She was gentle to say if something seemed displeasing. That candor was a very easy pill to swallow. Michael predicted it was a wonderful sign that she shared the same name as his late grandmother. Soon after that, the pair was seen quite often, riding the boat tours down the Thames, spending quiet afternoons at the Botanical Gardens, or dressing up for an enchanting evening.

There was only one hitch to his plans. Anna continued to warn Michael that her stay in London was only temporary. Michael ignored this like one swats away a fly. He wanted to introduce her to the family. Perhaps this would show his keen desire to keep her in England, as something serious did develop. Anna seemed excited when it was revealed that Tara was a fellow American citizen, someone that he shared many confidences.

"The play will be over in a couple of months. At that point, I should seriously contemplate returning home. My father has not faired well lately. Michael thinks I'm simply being overprotective. Still, it is the truth of the matter. If I should leave, I don't know how he will react. Will you help him?" Anna looked into Tara's eyes. The petite woman she observed was breathtaking, but down to earth. Anna liked that about Tara.

"Why of course." Tara agreed. She, too, could not help but admire the tall, Amazon woman before her, who was dressed prim in a pretty black cardigan, black wool pants. Her long bleached-blond hair was worn high and tucked in a coif fashion. Long spiraling curls fell against the nape of her neck allowing a graceful, regal appearance. Tara sensed that Anna possessed Michael's feeling to heart. They were together at the Georgian estate having tea.

"Michael seems so very happy here. He deals efficiently with the theater affiliates. He did mention that he helps out occasionally with business matters for your band."

"Yes, Michael does lend us his sound expertise, especially since my husband has passed," Tara replied, keeping her voice low. Sometimes talking about Danny could bring her to tears. There was much about him she missed, even the sound of his name, "But my band partner, Ross Kelly, is rapidly filling in. Really, it is high time that Michael concentrate completely on your future plans."

"Well, I do wish that Michael truly evaluates our situation, but with his solid reputation in London, how can I ask him to abandon this, just to travel abroad? I would feel foolish if he denied the adventure. I do have some pride. It's a decision that Michael should make. It should matter in his heart," Anna admitted, wringing her hands. Her candor was deeply surprising to Tara and to Gloria, who was sitting on the floor putting together portfolios.

She was in town to meet Anna too. She had sensed through conversation that Michael's intentions were more than with previous relationships. It was difficult to pay attention to the photos scattered around her knees. Anna rose from her seat to look about the wide living room. She studied the family pictures displayed on the walls, those of Michael with his parents and siblings, vacationing at Ventnor on the Isle of Wight or visiting relatives near Eastbourne.

"Such a nice family-that totally supports everyone through every project: the band, the navy, and modeling. It's too bad that Danny is gone. Michael speaks of him often. He says he wished that he could have met me. I guess Michael wanted his approval of our dating."

Gloria bowed her head. Yes, that made perfect sense. They, too, always discussed her love life. Danny was stable and happy then, and for Gloria's romances, he was constantly dismayed that all failed. Even with snagging a date from Ross. Nothing worked out. He wanted her to settle down. Surely there was a man somewhere who would share her adventuresome spirit, to wrestle away the demons that made her find constant imperfection. Danny wanted to beat up everyone that ever broke her heart. Yes, Gloria missed the brother that stood by her so true. Without this kind of support, she felt quite frail and vulnerable.

Anna paused at a faded photo of Danny standing at a pier with a bottle of Champaign. With the other hand, he gave a thumb's up sign towards the camera. He was dressed in a black tuxedo and had a top hat cocked to one side. Tara stood beside him in a white chiffon dress and a flowery net veil. She appeared quite glum.

"Is that your wedding picture?" Anna was completely curious.

"Yes. He sent that to the family to show us off before our arrival."

"Good heavens! If I ever tie the knot, I hope not to look so unhappy. Can you clue me in on your woeful disposition?"

So Tara explained some of the circumstances of their meeting and his proposal.

"I was so uncertain of our future, and it didn't help that he was so strange."

"Danny did everything in his power to convince her to marry him," Gloria added.

"Ahh, it was love at first sight. How romantic!" Anna sighed. Tara scoffed.

"Well, it really wasn't romantic for me, but I did relent to his impulsive proposal. We surprised Ross with our announcement, but he soon went along with our plans."

"Why was it a total surprise?" Anna questioned. "Were they not good friends then?"

"Well, Danny and I saw each other secretly. We didn't want Ross to discover it."

"Why not?"

"Well, the truth is that, even today, very few people know that Ross and I lived together for a short time.

Thank goodness the lease papers were in the owner's name. If discovered differently, it would fuel extreme gossip for the press right now."

"Oh, I see," Anna replied, not knowing how to decipher this information. This was a startling revelation. Tara explained it further.

"We grew up together and I sought him out for a place to stay. I needed time to figure out my future. Ross was very protective, as he remains today. Knowing what Danny had in mind would have ruffled feathers. Once our plans were revealed, everything turned out fine. We all came to England together."

"Well, that is interesting. I am sure the adjustments were difficult to make upon your arrival. I heard something recently. Susan stopped by to have dinner with us in London. In that conversation, she conveyed that early on your marriage there was trouble. She said that your son, Tom, is Ross's son. Michael tried to hush her up, but it was really too late."

Tara frowned, feeling greatly annoyed at Susan. She never once showed an ounce of support. Within her own life, she was terribly self-absorbed.

"Well, Susan is such a sneaky cat. She purrs and moves about as one's friend, but will lash out with sharp claws at some point, revealing a different persona. I'd watch out for her," Tara remarked in a disdainful tone.

"It's true," Gloria agreed, nodding her head. Tara tossed her long curls aside. She took a sip of tea to calm down. Anna took a sip too. Her eyes wide at the disclosures given.

"Well, I will certainly heed your warnings about her. I'm sure you went through difficult times, but somehow got through it."

Tara took the time to explain about her marital discord; the fight about Ross; how Tom came to be. She hated to repeat the history just because Susan brought it all up.

"So that is how it all happened." Anna looked over a picture of Ross, "I met him briefly. He seemed like a decent chap."

Anna turned to Tara and went to sit down beside her.

"Oh, Tara. I certainly appreciate your honesty. Whatever you wish to declare, please have complete confidence in me. I swear never to reveal anything."

This pleased Tara very much. She found Anna quite genuine. No wonder Michael was crazy about her. Later that afternoon, when the couple departed to London again, Gloria and Tara stood on the lawn to wave goodbye. The car disappeared from view around the bend.

"Anna is so kind, sensitive. Do you think that she will leave? I certainly hope not, as I like her a lot," Gloria said.

"Well by what she claims, it is a great possibility. That will be so sad. We must pull together for Michael when that occurs," Tara declared. Yes, for his sake, she had to be strong.

In late March, Anna visited this time at Tara's home. She was given a tour of their studio. Tara explained how Danny excelled in the music business like none other, communicating effortlessly to put deals together;

culminating their sales into the millions. It was easy to recollect every detail.

"Behind that glass partition, Danny would direct our attempts. He possessed a great ear for what was popular, so I would do my best to appease him."

"How did Ross get involved with the band?" Anna looked at an old photograph on the wall, one of the men standing together on stage.

"The boys acquired puberty voices once we reached the greater public spectrum. We didn't have a choice but to keep up with what was popular. Ross participated during our outdoor summer performances. Everyone was fascinated by his talent. Danny realized it was time to get Ross out front and center too," Tara explained.

They looked at the awards and publicity photos on the walls.

"Ross's debut was hotly welcomed. Seems that our versatility sky-rocketed the band into a huge phenomenon. Cross Passage expanded naturally," Tara explained. They headed out of the room. Before she exited, Tara paused to look at a photograph on the wall. It showed Danny with the awards ceremony executives, when they first arrived. It was on the day of their 15th anniversary. The paparazzi snapped his picture outside. Then someone forwarded a copy to Tara after his death. He looked so well that day. So Tara placed it in the studio, where he was always on top of the world.

Tara led Anna to the kitchen so they could eat lunch in a casual environment. Gloria joined them that afternoon. Michael was occupied elsewhere with his father and the kids. They would be out for awhile. So the women were alone. They opened up wine and consumed a lot as they talked. At one point, Anna seemed lost in thought.

"Anna, what is bothering you?" Tara asked, leaning forward to look into her eyes.

"Well you mentioned something in passing today. You said how special it was that Danny accepted all of the children. What did that mean exactly?"

This obviously left Anna quite confused. Gloria and Tara exchanged looks. Should Tara divulge this family secret now?

"Well, you heard correctly. Aaron is our son together. Tom belongs to Ross and my oldest seven have a different father completely, Danny knew that I was expecting when we met."

"He did?" Anna gasped and dropped her fork. This was an amazing admission. "Wow, he was a very special man to accept you in that circumstance. You and your children were so blessed. Living in this area is so lovely. Your home is very nurturing. I can tell in your family pictures that the man made you very happy."

"Yes, completely. After Danny gave up his navy commission, he spent so many carefree days with us. He never favored any child over another. We were a team, a family because of his devotion. Hindsight is everything now," Tara said. Her eyes seemed misty, but she tried to contain them, "It will be very difficult to find another man like him again. I realize I must move on soon. Everyone pushes me to meet their friends, brothers, or acquaintances. I have several single friends that ask me out on a date. I am ready somewhat. There are so many days when I feel so desperate, so alone. I miss having a man around."

Tara suddenly picked up a napkin to dab her eyes. There were so many tender feelings rising to the surface. Anna rose to wrap tight arms around the woman. She understood all of those delicate feelings.

"Everything will turn out fine, Tara. Trust time to heal your wounds. Don't rush things. You are a remarkable woman and strong. If you falter, I promise to support you, even if I am not around physically. We can always talk. You can always call," Anna promised. Tara nodded, struggling to regain composure.

"I'm here for you too, Anna. Thank you," Tara picked up the wine bottle to refill all of their glasses.

"This stuff is really potent." Tara laughed to ease the tension in the room, "Let's drink to our tight friendship." And so the women did.

April arrived with lots of rain. Everyone scurried around with umbrellas, looking for a dry place. Michael stood at the window to watch. He had an appointment at the dentist. Perhaps he should cancel it. He hated driving in that mess. Suddenly, there was a knock on the door. A courier arrived. His partner, Jake, signed for it and then handed it to Michael. He tore it open.

"What does it say?" Jake asked, his face drawn to Michaels reaction. The man seemed shocked, "Is it bad news?"

"Anna's father suffered a stroke. She flew to the states this morning," he explained, feeling deeply bewildered.

"That is terrible news, Michael. Anna was quite amazing. Too bad you lost her," his friend shrugged, thinking that the man would just move on to another conquest. Michael wasn't happy. As soon as he was done with the dentist, he embarked to the manor. Perhaps for the upcoming weekend, he could find more sympathetic company.

"Why hasn't she called?" Michael felt deeply crushed. He lingered over the remains of his dinner as he sat at Tara's house. Ross poured more wine. The teenagers were occupied in their rooms, leaving the grownups alone to talk. Michael felt grateful for the effects of the wine as it loosened up his tongue. How could he hold back his emotions at a time like this? Any objective opinion could sort things out in his head. Tara insisted on clearing away the dishes to leave them a moment alone. Ross studied the man over, who slumped wearily in his chair.

"I'm sure Anna found this easier, Mick. Perhaps she thought it was best, to spare hard feelings in saying goodbye. Plus the news was sudden. I'm sure she had to leave straight away," Ross replied in a gentle tone. He knew exactly how it felt to be dumped.

"Damn. I always blew off Anna's warnings. She gave plenty. I just didn't think her father was so bad off. Balderdash! It serves me right for disregarding such important information. I guess I deserve to lose her."

Michael toyed with a sugar bowl on the table to watch the lid twirl within his fingers. He seemed so sad. Tara stood at the doorway, now totally annoyed at this demeanor.

"Michael, what nonsense and self pity! That woman loves you very much. Ross! Help me here!" Tara demanded. Ross knew that she meant business. As Michael's best friend, it was his duty to find an effective solution.

"You know Michael," Ross paused for effect, "I bet Anna is just too consumed with her father's care to call. She is an only child. We don't know what has happened upon arrival. Perhaps busybody relatives are complicating matters, trying to help. Even with best intentions, sometimes relatives just get in the way."

"It was like that when Danny died too, with so many around," Tara agreed, "I wanted to shelter all of the children, especially Aaron. With all of the commotion at the public viewing, the press got to him. Sometimes, other people manage to interfere."

"I bet that the time difference is an obstacle as well," Ross offered on a whim.

"I suppose you are right," Michael leaned back into the chair, digesting their ideas, "If only Anna asked, I would have flown back with her. I would have followed her anywhere. That woman means the world. She has totally captured my heart. I love her. I want to marry her. She's perfect."

This conviction amazed Tara. Who would ever think the playboy could fall in love? It was time to put the man in motion instead of whining about the circumstances.

"Then Michael, if you feel that strongly, you should do something now," Tara insisted. She sat beside him and stared into his blue eyes, "*"Help her*. Go to her. She does need you. I can feel it."

Her stern words made him react.

"By God, I will! I can't lose her like this! I will track her down in the states. There is much to do before I fly out."

Michael returned the next morning to London, after bidding farewell to his family. His parents were shocked, but pleased with his news. They never thought they would see him become committed either. He sold away his portion of the production company to his partner, Jake, who was equally surprised. Michael tied up all loose ends, even to sublet his ritzy flat to a good friend. After several inquiries were made for Anna's correct address, he reserved a seat on the next flight out. Tara and Ross drove him to the airport. Tara was sad to see him go, but knew it was for the best. A few days later, Tara listened breathlessly on the telephone to Anna's version of their reunion.

"Oh, Tara! What a grand surprise! I had to call to let you know everything. You shared your heart to me in London, this was the least I could do to return the favor."

"Yes, thank you. I do die out of curiosity. It's a weakness of mine, Please go on. What happened?"

"The torrential downpour was horrible. Michael looked like some poor, forlorn, lost puppy ... blond hair all drenched and his brow so furrowed. There wasn't even an umbrella available when he ran up to the door carrying two bags," At this, Anna heaved a sigh of relief.

"Things have been so crazy with the doctors, the tests, and my father's sisters popping in and out. I felt such despair. When he arrived, I needed to *feel* him, to *hold* him again. It was ...completely unladylike! I pulled that man anxiously into the foyer, even with my aunts sitting in the very next room! They were quite shocked as we crashed into the furniture, removing clothing. We made our way upstairs in complete haste. I do recall Michael saying something like, "Excuse us, ladies." Can you imagine our inappropriate behavior? Now that I think about it, it is hilarious."

Anna's happy voice went over the transcontinental phone line, laughing spiritedly.

Tara did feel wonderful for their exciting reunion. She was completely fueled by their urgent physical and emotional fire. Only once did Tara feel this exact same thing, in Spain, when she reunited with Danny. More than ever, she yearned for this fire with someone new. Desperation was taking over. Where would she find such a man?

Chapter Fifty Six
Lies and Secrets

With Michael gone, Tara went about business sparingly. There were several agencies clamoring for her face to sell their products, so Tara did a few commercials. Ross helped set up all the deals. Like Danny, he was very effective. Keeping busy gave her time to evaluate her friendship with Ross. The teenagers were now encouraging their mother to go on with life, too. She was beautiful and lonely. They, too, kept their eyes open for a suitable man.

Jamie hung out with many girlfriends throughout the county. One in particular, Mary Brooks, was someone she admired. They were best friends. Her father was an astute businessman who took many trips to London. One day he invited Jamie and Mary to tag along. They enjoyed lunch in a nice restaurant, center of the busy financial district. Mr. Brooks noticed someone. He waved. A handsome man sat down to converse. As she listened, Jamie felt charmed by his proper mannerisms. Stephan Tessareau was blond, with striking blue eyes. Perhaps this similarity to her Da caused a reaction in Jamie. She and Mary were occupied with their own gibberish, but Jamie listened attentively just the same. Apparently, Mr. Tessareau suffered a disastrous recent relationship.

"Surely, there is an interesting woman somewhere who can capture my attention for more than a week," Stephan complained freely to his friend, "I need to meet someone really outstanding."

"My mother is available," Jamie suddenly blurted out. The man stared at her. The young teen was cute, with her long hair pulled back in a bow. Her hands were manicured, her ears pierced with two earrings on her lobes. Her clothing was neat. He recognized the expensive brand of her watch. She was impeccably neat.

"What?" Stephan asked. He was curious.

"My mom is widowed. Believe me, she is the most fascinating person in the world, a popular entertainer, who does commercials. Everyone loves her. I'm sure you will have fun meeting her," Jamie explained. Stephan looked over at his friend for advice. Mr. Brooks nodded.

"Tara Cross is very well respected in our county. Her husband died over a year ago. She is available."

"Isn't that cute? How often do children want to set up their single parents? Do you suppose she would go out on a blind date?" Mr. Tessareau totally trusted Mr. Brooks assessment of the woman.

"Sure, she would. She's not doing anything in particular this weekend. Why not ask her out on Saturday?" Jamie sputtered, pleased that the man took her up on the offer, "Let me write down our number. You can call her up."

Jamie's knees shook underneath the table. Would her mother just go along? It would take a lot of convincing for sure. Mr. Tessareau promised to call on Thursday. That afternoon, Jamie told Tara what occurred. Shocked, she listened as Jamie went on about the man.

"He's terribly cute. I know you'll have a great time," Jamie insisted. Tara mulled things over. Ross was away on an impromptu vacation with Tom. He would be away for a few weeks. With no man anywhere, Tara felt out of sorts. When Mr. Tessareau called on Thursday evening, Tara accepted to meet him in London

She went inside an exclusive restaurant in Soho. She was nervous, but walked towards the round wooden bar, where they agreed to meet. He said he would wear a white suit, a dark blue shirt with a red carnation on the lapel. She told him that she would wear a simple black dress. Tara could not bring herself to dress up in something bright and alluring. The man must accept her as is or nothing else. He was easy to spot, casually leaning at the bar, sipping a drink on the rocks. He was exactly how Jamie described, tall, blond, and very good looking. Tara heaved a brave sigh. She approached him from behind. She patted him on the shoulder to get his attention.

"Stephan Tessareau? I am Tara Cross."

Stephan turned around. His crisp blue eyes gazed her up and down. It was such a cocky expression on his face. Tara felt qualms.

"Well, now! Your beauty exceeds your daughter's description." the man said. Tara felt her cheeks turn warm. Stephan gulped down his drink to place the empty glass upon the bar. He then offered his arm in order to escort her to a reserved table.

"Shall we?"

The waiter greeted them right away. He handed out menus.

"Sir. Madam. Welcome. Tonight's specialty is the lamb with mint sauce and oven roasted potatoes, along with your choice of steamed vegetables. May I take your choices for your beverages?"

"Allow me," Stephan offered and Tara nodded. He ordered an expensive wine that would go adequately with the special. Without asking, he picked out their entree and vegetables. Tara did not object. She felt impressed by his control of the situation.

"Thank you," she said after the waiter had left.

"No problem at all. It is not often that their specials adequately meet my expectations, but their lamb dishes are exceptional. You will be delighted as it is very pleasing to the palate," he explained. His tone was very snobbish. His blue eyes focused on her finger as Tara still wore her wedding band.

"Your daughter mentioned that you were unattached."

Tara covered her ring. She never felt embarrass to wear it before. Now, she moved her hands underneath the table.

"This ring has been a part of me for over fifteen years. I'm in the habit of wearing it."

"Oh, I see. Well, that is understandable. How nice. Mr. Brooks told me a little about you. There are not many marriages that do so splendidly. My parents have been together for thirty five years. To me, that is a major accomplishment. Everyone seems to get together quickly these days. No wonder why their marriages fail. Still, it's the rage of the jet-set."

Stephan leaned back into his chair. He stared into Tara's eyes, still giving her the once over. She felt goose pimples. Perhaps it was the air-conditioning. There was a high ceiling fan above their head. Stephan seemed to want conversation.

"I don't really hold anything against this fast pace. There are times you can tell a lot about a person on the very first occasion you meet. Unfortunately, there hasn't been any woman who can hold my attention for long, so how will I ever get to marriage? No one has achieved this at all."

"That is too bad." Tara said coyly. She wasn't sure what he was implying. Dating was just a first step. Meeting a man, capturing him, and marrying quickly were far from what she had in mind. Still, there was a nagging thought. Danny fell in love with her the moment he saw her. This man could be doing the same thing. His eyes studied her eyes. He looked over her attire. The dark dress she wore that night concealed much. She wanted to impress him with her mind.

"I don't believe first appearances can be everything. It takes a lot of time to get to know someone, to adjust to a person. Relationships are work. It takes a lot of compromise. I learned that from my husband," Tara admitted. She struggled to keep the conversation going. His cool glances made her feel uneasy, and yet strangely excited. Those blue eyes were striking. His blond hair, long and thick. What would it be like to run her fingers through it?

Stephan seemed intrigued and smug at the same time.

"Why was it necessary to make adjustments? We should not change at all. If a person doesn't accept me like I am now, then what is the point?"

Tara wanted to challenge this reasoning.

"In some ways, I do agree, but I do not proclaim that anyone has to change. It's a give and take situation when you come into a relationship. You can't always be a winner in an argument. Sometimes you have to be the loser."

"I don't like being a loser. I like to win," Stephan leaned forward towards the attractive brunette. He was definitely amused.

"You don't understand my point."

"And that is?"

"If you lose an argument for the sake of making things work, then you are a winner in the end. You wind up with the one you love," Tara hoped that her offbeat rambling made sense. This was a strange conversation to have on a first date.

"Hmmm. Interesting point. So if I allow you to win this argument, then I will wind up with the one I love?"

Tara's eyes blinked quickly. Now she felt really hot. Her thermal temperature jumped by a thousand degrees. How could he possibly love her? He did not even know her. It was a ridiculous notion. *Oh God, déjà vu!* He casually brushed back his blond bangs and smiled provocatively. She panicked.

"Well, my perspective is that when people fall in love, if they compromise, then they both win. Honestly, I was not implying that we… well, heavens! We just met," Tara sputtered. Stephan laughed. The waiter brought over their drinks.

"I was just teasing. You are so nervous, but obviously ready to jump to any challenge. You dive into discussion. I like that. However, in fair warning, I am a man who fights to win, no matter what the situation."

For some reason, she took heed. His eyes were very blue. They pierced at her like a sharp arrow. She felt like she could not look away. He poured their wine. He raised his drink in mid-air.

"Ms. Cross, here is a toast to your spirited opinion!"

Tara slowly sipped her own drink. She felt bedazzled. The waiter returned with their salads. He happened to smile sweetly at Tara, as he recognized her. She smiled back, in spite of herself. Stephan suddenly seemed upset.

"Say, you didn't bring the condiments for the salad. What fool would forget such a thing?" He told the waiter. His words were crisp and rude.

"I'm sorry, sir. I'll be right back," The waiter sputtered and then rushed away. Tara felt embarrassed that she caused this underhanded wrath. *Poor helpless waiter.* It was not his fault.

"I apologize, Stephan. It was not my intent to flirt with him," she explained. Stephan shifted in his seat. His tone was sharp.

"Women who are with me do not find their attention ambling towards other men."

"Well, he was just being polite. There was no reason to bite his head off."

"There is a reason. You are supposed to be my date, my dear, not his. Well, if you are this much imposed, then we can just be done with this nuance. There is always someone ready to take your place in that seat," he remarked briskly. Tara felt humiliated but did not wish for the evening to end this way. She placed her hand over his to calm him.

"No, please. Let's go on. I meant no harm. I would like to get to know you better. Please?" she begged. Why did she ask for another chance when his outburst brought her mixed signals? He looked down at her hand. He stared directly into her eyes. He spoke very monotone and soft.

"All right. Just one more shot, but remember this always, you are with me, not with anyone else. You will bid me all of your attention. All of the time. Is that clear?"

Like a child, she nodded to his command. Why? Any other man she would have left sitting at the table alone. They continued with the dinner. Later, she agreed to see him again.

She saw him a few days later. They met in London again, as she had business there. With a current contract, she was to shoot pictures for an ad at different locations. This required her to go back and forth. Every time she went, they got together. It seemed their conversations were about his wishes, what he saw happening to their relationship. Usually he did things to impress her. If something happened to go wrong, he insinuated that it was all her fault.

It was very frustrating, because somewhere behind that brutality was a man who gave her complete attention. Stephan wanted to be in control of everything. He told her what she should wear, what jewelry to put on, and how she should fix up her hair. For some strange reason, for every small suggestion, Tara listened and obeyed.

When she introduced him to George and Helen, he was suddenly considerate and kind. Stephan invited the teens to a polo match. They sat in the best seats. He bought them dinner. He seemed perfectly comfortable around them, which eased Tara's thoughts. Once, he brought them over to his mansion outside of London. It was a rare invite, as he possessed plenty of expensive artifacts there. He worried whether something might break with boisterous boys around. He showed Jamie everything and told her how grateful he was that she set them up. That was really the last time he did anything involving them.

Tara's business associates were hesitant to accept him. The man seemed too polite. Her hairdresser thought it sounded forced, "He's also very conceited. Why can't you see that? I don't think he's your type at all," she told Tara, while styling her hair. The woman possessed great instincts. They could see through him, but it came too late. Stephan proposed. She accepted. They were married in a private ceremony.

Ross and Tom returned home to find out what
transpired. Naturally, Ross was in complete shock.
Stephan and Tara came home after a three-day
honeymoon in Austria. The family invited them over
for dinner at the Grand manor. It was the opportunity
for Ross to meet this clever businessman who one-two-
three captured Tara's heart. Stephan seemed very self-
absorbed. He spoke too worldly and offbeat. It seemed
suspicious. Ross pulled Tara to the library to speak to
her alone.

"Tara, I don't understand. Why did you get married?
It's so sudden. You did not talk to anyone about this
fool notion at all."

"Ross, it was my decision. Why should I ask for
permission? I am an adult."

"I know, but this impulsiveness seems terribly
childish. How much do you know about him? Even if I
don't, it gets me that he coerced you into marrying so
bloody quickly. What was his hurry? "

Tara felt her temper flare. She reacted defensively.

"Ross! He did not coerce me into anything! We both
wanted this and so we just did it. I should not have to
explain. For heaven's sake! Why don't you like him? He
has everything to make me happy."

"Well, that is one thing for sure, that he does have
money. He won't ask you for a penny. Or at least it's
his family's money and so it will possibly not leave
you penniless. Did you even bother to protect your
assets?"

Tara wanted to slap him. He could really get on her
nerves at times, being so overprotective.

"Yes, Ross. We signed a pre-nuptial agreement that spelled out everything. It was his parent's idea, seeing that I actually appear quite poor in spite of my earnings!"

"No. They did that to protect their son from having financial obligations because of your children. They don't want any one of them getting a piece of the pie if something should happen to you both. "

Tara looked him dead in the eye. Her body was shaking in anger.

"Ross, stop it! Stop it now or risk losing our friendship over this discussion! I will not have you bad mouthing my new husband, his family, or this marriage. What's done is done. There is nothing you can do to change that fact!" Tara warned.

Ross was stunned by her words. He felt mistrust like this before, but it was way back when she met Jimmy at Hartridge, whom she once loved with all of her heart. It was ironic to be put into this same argument again. It was De ja vu. He backed down then, but could he do it again? He was forced to comply. He cared about Tara.

"Tara, I only convey what I feel. It's a gut feeling. Perhaps it is best that the teens settle with you in the summer. It'll give you time to adjust. I cannot pinpoint what exactly is bothersome, yet your friendship is what matters beyond words, so I will keep quiet. Yet, when reality hits bottom, you can always call for help. Don't ever forget that!"

Ross departed the room to leave her standing alone. He was completely right about Stephan. For a long time, she could not pinpoint either what was so frightening about the man. Once moved in, Stephan kept a calm persona around the staff. When they were alone at night, he would change 180 degrees. He was certain to take out frustrations as if she was the most undesirable woman.

"Why can't you get something right, Tara? I thought you were smarter than this," he yelled once, "How can one so beautiful do something incredibly stupid. I deserve better than you."

"I'm sorry, Stephan. I didn't think. I'll make it up to you."

"You can't make it up. It's way too late. You'll just have to suffer consequences," he said, his eyes flashing. She shivered at the implications. He was an actual living Dr. Jekyll and Mr. Hyde. Stephan grabbed her by the arm. He threw her upon the bed only to force his brutality upon her. She wanted him, but not like that.

Tara cried while he whispered sweet nothings into her ear. It was tender, but it was a lie. The moment he slipped inside, the lovemaking would turn into wild abandonment. The man's body bashed into her own so hard that he literally lifted her up out of the bed. It hurt and afterwards, she felt stunned and torn. It was stressful conveying that everything was all right, when underneath the surface, she was falling apart.

"Don't ever tell anyone about us," Stephan threatened as she cried in bed, "If you do, that person will have to contend with me. I don't care who it is."

So Tara remained silent. She masquerade that they were the perfect couple. Everyone believed it. There was no indication not to as they attended all the social functions in London together that summer. His business required him to travel a lot. Tara was forced to go with him. They went everywhere, Paris, Denmark, Rome. By this point, the teens became alarmed. They didn't get to see their mother anymore. Aaron was miserable that she was taken away so often. Even Ross was dazed. How could she abandon them?

Stephan seemed very jealous of the attention she received. He persuaded Tara once too often to cancel out of obligations, usually last minute. He accused her of having affairs behind his back with the photographers. Her husband never really hit her, but threw things at the wall, breaking everything in sight. There were now too many missed commitments. Ross tried to explain away what happened, but just couldn't do it anymore.

"Tara, I just smoothed things over again with the ad agency. This is the tenth time in six weeks. You must finish your obligation to them!"

Ross finally caught up with her at home. He wanted so bad to give her a piece of his mind. He was that angry.

"Yes, you are right, Ross. I am sorry, but it could not be helped," Tara hid behind the towering bush that she pruned in the back garden area. There was a blow up right before Ross's unannounced arrival. Stephan left for a meeting and missed running into Ross by a matter of seconds. Tara kept nerves of steel. She could not let him suspect that there were problems. Her indifference led him to believe other ideas.

"I happen to ask the maid of your whereabouts that morning. She dutifully declared that you two were busy upstairs! This is ridiculous Tara! You do realize that we are under financial contracts with the agency. Every time you don't show up, because there is an animal urge to be with your husband, well ... it costs everyone money! Just get your jollies done at night the same way hundreds of normal couples do!"

How absurd the notion? If only he knew that those jollies were very much like rape sessions.

"Normal, Ross?" Tara was so close to uncontrolled hysteria. It must be contained, but right now, Ross only interpreted that she did not care at all what happened, "Stephan and I are hardly normal."

"Yes!" Ross's anger boiled over, "I can see that quite well now. The next time you screw something-other than that man-then you can fix the problem your damned self!"

She watched him go in a hurried huff. Tara knelt there in the dirt, hidden behind the bush. She broke down. After three months of this, it was a heartbreaking conclusion that she could no longer endure the madness. Yet, she feared that Stephan would keep his threats to bring her loved ones real harm. How best to end it?

About two weeks later, Stephan attended a business meeting in Paris. Tara was with him. This time she didn't even let the family know about these plans. She simply left. Ross blew up over this outright inconsideration. It was high time to have it out. He took a flight to Paris and arrived at the front desk.

"What room is Stephan Tessareau in?" Ross leaned at the counter. His eyes seemed crazed. The man studied the check-in book.

"Room A210. It's on the second floor, but monsieur, the man stepped out. I saw him go. There is this place he keeps talking about, The Luce, a wonderful bar. It's about four miles down this street. Perhaps you can find him there," The desk clerk pointed the way.

"All right. Thank you," Ross was grateful that the man was very informative. It wouldn't hurt to have a few words with Tara's husband, that obnoxious jerk. So Ross found his way to the bar. Stephen was at the back, sitting with some other men. There were stacks of shot glasses and beer bottles all over the table. The man was three sheets to the wind.

"Why, Mr. Kelly, what a surprise. Would you like a shot of vodka?" Stephan looked up with a sneer on his face. The man knew that Ross didn't drink.

"No, thanks. Where is Tara? I must speak to her at once," Ross's tone was sharp and he was greatly annoyed that the man was ripping drunk. Stephan tipped up his drink and laughed.

"There's always some emergency, some pressing urgent business with you. It is interesting that there is always so much to say and it never gets all done in one visit. Now is not a convenient time. Tara is down with a terrible headache. If she couldn't make it out to be with me here, then she can't see you either. In fact, she can't see anyone. She is …er …indisposed."

Ross was disgusted. If Tara was feeling poorly, shouldn't he be upstairs taking care of her comfort? Any decent husband would do so instead of getting plastered with the guys. Ross left right away. His gut sensed that something was wrong. Stephan sounded like he was hiding something.

"That damn drunk! Hey taxi!" Ross whistled as he hailed a cab at the corner. He urged the driver to the hotel quickly, exposing a large currency bill. The cab driver stepped on the gas. They arrived in three minutes.

"Stay here. I'll be back in a few minutes," Ross requested and the driver complied willingly. Ross rushed up to the suite. He banged on the door. He paused to listen, but heard nothing. He jiggled the knob. Luckily, the door wasn't fully shut. This just didn't seem right, so Ross made his way into the living room and then the bedroom, but it was empty too.

"Tara? It's Ross! Honey, where are you?"

His ears listened for any reply. What he got was soft moaning from the bathroom. There on the tile floor, was Tara halfway exposed. Her clothes were in shreds. She laid in a stupor, curled up in a protective fetal position. She was speaking incoherently. Ross was stunned.

"Oh, my God!" Ross picked her up into his arms. Tara was shivering. Quickly, he carried her to the bed, "Oh, baby! It's ok! I'm here. No one can hurt you now!"

Her eyes looked up at him in a daze. Didn't she even recognize him? Ross was angry, but he had to control this feeling to beat someone in half. It hurt to see Tara in this condition.

All he wanted was for her to feel safe and sheltered. Her lips were blue and the skin was torn off where she had bit it so hard. It was bleeding and cracked wide. He tucked the bedspread around her body like a cocoon and it brought her instant warmth. Now her eyes showed recognition.

"We will find the dirty bastard who did this to you!" Ross told her and leaned over to pick up the phone book by the bed. There was a number listed in the reference pages and he dialed it quickly.

"Hello, is this the police! You speak English? Good, I need to report a ......," At that moment, he heard the line disconnect. "Hello! Hello! What the hell?"

Somehow Tara become coherent enough to realize what he was doing. It took all of her strength to reach over and press down the button. Huge tears fell from her face onto his lap. The truth hit him like a shotgun blasting in the night.

"Oh, Tara!" Ross felt bitter anguish. Stephan was the culprit, not some stranger who happened to wonder into the room. This could not be!

"*No!*"

The look on her face told him the hard truth and it was too much. Ross swiftly gathered the woman up into his arms like a baby. He held on tightly. He wanted to shelter her forever from this brutal man. Ross knew what must be done to accomplish this.

"You can not stay with that mad man another minute! I know a safe place," Ross put her down and found clothing to dress her up into. Without another word, Ross carried her down the hallway to the elevator. .

Tara saw the hallway lights above her. The scenery was moving in slow motion. She looked at Ross. His features were so handsome and he was so strong, like Superman. There was love in his heart and she was so grateful for his strength. Once downstairs, the desk clerk saw them come through. He recognized the famous brunette.

"What is it? What's wrong?" the desk clerk demanded. "Do you need an ambulance? Do you need my assistance?"

Ross paid him no mind. He placed Tara into the taxi. He scooted in beside her and barked an address at the driver. They quickly departed. There wasn't much that Tara could recall about that evening, but she remembered Ross's diligent vigil. He took her that night to a house outside of Paris. It belonged to an old business acquaintance. From there Ross called to inform the family of their whereabouts. He begged them not to say a word to Stephan. Ross did not elaborate, but they all trusted him. They hid in that place for almost a month, just long enough for Tara to feel strong again.

She looked at Ross with different eyes now. He was a godsend. There were many thoughts that went through her head during this crisis. She was so lucky that Ross went to Paris to complain. No one really knew what was on Stephan's mind when he attacked her like that. It was sudden and fierce. Tara could not fight him off. She could have pressed charges, but she wanted to bury it all away. She was blessed to have a best friend. She was blessed to have Ross in her life.

Chapter Fifty Seven
Strange Dreams and Intuitions

Tara was so glad, that by some strange miracle, she never conceived Stephan's child. Their ties would be severed. There would never be a reason to see him again. Once they left Paris, Tara filed for divorce. When she walked in at the grand manor, her family was there with very open arms. The teenagers hugged their mother tightly and wept. No explanation was given but they judged Ross' stern face and knew it was pretty bad. Within a few weeks, they all quickly settled into their familiar routines. No one pushed to introduce their mother to any men. They wanted her all to themselves and trusted no one.

Later, Tara heard that Stephan went to Germany after he discovered she had left him. He never called at all, but one business associate bothered to call once, just to say that Stephan agreed to a quick divorce. That early fall morning, Ross went to court with Tara. Stephan showed up too. He didn't look at her once during the proceedings.

The judge read over the assets and in spite of the prenuptial agreement, Stephan gave her a very nice settlement that would last for ten years. Ross thought she deserved ten times more for putting up with that creep. Tara decided to return to her maiden name since ultimately, she was starting all over again. In her view, Danny was gone. She could not bear to return to the respectable Cross surname, now that she felt herself tarnished by Stephan.

When they stepped outside, they noticed him walk up to his limousine by the curb. He took one last look at her. Tara didn't know what to feel. Should it be anger? Pity? For just a moment, she thought he looked very sad. In that same instant, Stephan flashed a very cocky smile before he sat into the limousine. It drove off into the distance. Tara hoped that she would never see the man again.

The disastrous second marriage and that hot summer were now behind them. The only subtle change was that now Tara turned to Ross for everything.

"Ross, the sink is leaking in the kitchen. Can you swing by to fix it?"

"Sure, no problem. I'll run in town for supplies first. I'll be over, say by noon?"

"That's great. I'll see you then, Maybe I'll find something else by then," she told him and he laughed. Yes, she always called for every little thing. If there was wood to be chopped or she needed helped putting in a light bulb, she called. Anything simple and anything just to get the man to the house. It was not as if her sons couldn't do the work themselves.

In fact, they did hang around Ross as much as possible. They naturally chipped in. Living down the road was just too convenient. Ross loved it. In all the years hanging out with Susan in London, it got depressing they never went forward. With fame, things became complicated. When Danny died, he wanted something real in his life. He realized at his passing that time was precious. So was life, love. It should be grabbed with gusto and never be let go. He told Susan what was in his heart.

"Babe, I'm sorry," he said, staring deeply into her blue eyes, "I love you, but I want something more, something you don't want to give. We need to move on."

She studied his face. He was so serious, so handsome. It broke her heart, but she still couldn't marry him. Lately, all she wanted to do was build up her own business. She opened up a modeling agency in London, and soon another would open in Rome. She packed the few belongings she kept at his apartment, a toothbrush, her cosmetics, a few lingerie gowns. There was never a lot because they kept things hidden from Tom.

Susan kissed his lips once more at the door. A sentimental, long kiss. She stroked his chin and then went out of his life with no commotion at all. Through a window, Ross watched her car drive away. He was reminded what she said in Paris, "Marriage is overrated. Friends last longer," In some ways, she did have it right. They would still be friends and he would see her from time to time.

When the Vicar home became available, Ross jumped at the chance to move in right away, seeing that he didn't have a real job anymore. Moving to Wiltshire seemed right. He loved being close to Tara. He loved walking about the countryside. Sometimes in the early morning, when the fog still weighed heavy on the ground, he visited Danny's grave. It was nice sitting there reminiscing about their strong friendship. There were times he couldn't believe his friend was gone. He went there again after he brought Tara home from the courthouse.

"I'm not trying to take over, Danny. I think she needs me. You know I always loved her too. You know I will stand by her, protect her. Allow me a chance to try. She's lonely without you. She doesn't need another mistake. She needs a nice guy like me."

So whenever Tara called, he jumped. It wasn't difficult to do when Tara was so lovely. Sixteen year old Tom was elated that he came over often. It was wonderful seeing his parents interact in the house. They laughed, they talked. Now if only if his mother would kiss his father, things would be so perfect. Christmas time was coming around again. What better time it would make for a wedding?

The septuplets, who were now seventeen, were all in agreement about this too.

"Ross is a perfect match for mom," Edward said as they played a game of Monopoly. He spied his mom showing Ross her car. It was sputtering lately because of the cold. He leaned into the motor.

"He's handsome, in our band, and very dependable," Jamie agreed as she rolled the dice.

"The best thing is that Ross knows us and loves us too. We don't have to pretend to be something else," Matt added. He studied them out the window too, "We have to persuade mom that he's the best choice. Something stops her from going all the way. Maybe we should give them plenty of opportunity to be alone in the house."

"Matt! Watch what you are saying!" Jamie laughed. Tom shook his head.

"Look, nature should take its course. They did it once! I'm here. We are not stupid. We don't need a lecture about the birds and the bees. Let them figure out things their own way. Let's just stay out of sight as much as possible. Agree?"

Everyone nodded. They did have other activities to keep them busy. Public school was out of the picture because of their fame, so they saw tutors. To keep their minds on task, they went to the manor for their studies. Their grandparents didn't take kindly to their mischief making in the house, but whenever they could, they would come up with something.

One day, the tutors left early. There was a large snowstorm expected and it was best to make their way home while it was still daylight. Yet, the teens stuck around. They didn't live too far and figured they could make it home safe if it did snow hard. They knew that trail like the back of their hand. Everyone read their assigned novel as homework. Jamie became quite bored. So did Matthew.

They left the library, went to the kitchen, and rummaged through the refrigerator. They found some left over ham and decided to make a quick sandwich out of it. Then they followed one of the housekeepers around the upper rooms as she busied about dusting. It was just out of curiosity of how she went about her duties and nothing more, but in Helen's room, she went to dusting a bookshelf. One of Danny's trophies hid behind some books and when the maid dusted around the area, it was suddenly revealed to the teenagers.

"Gosh, this is very old, "Matt said as he handled it. The maid went onto the next room and they were alone, "It's a hunting trophy. Isn't that strange? Da' didn't particularly like to shoot, but he didn't mind walking around investigating the woods."

"Yes, that is peculiar. I miss Da'. He told such terrific stories to us," Jamie sighed. She sat on the bed and looked up at the ceiling. Matt sat beside her.

"What are you thinking about? You have a funny look."

"Everything was packed away after Da died. It's up in the attic. I'd love to rummage through it. I would feel so close to him again."

There were tears surfacing to her eyes. Matt couldn't have that.

"Ah, stop that, missy. Don't cry. We've had enough heartache in this family. It's time that we all move forward. Just think, mum is home again and isn't with that horrid man anymore. Ross is this close to being a constant figure under our roof. There's no need to lament, but if it makes you feel better, let's go up and take a peak. I bet we can find other neat things up there."

"Should we?" Jamie speculated, "Grandmother hates us getting into mischief. If we poke around, wouldn't it be considered so?"

"Naw! Let's go," Matt replied and swung his sister up by the arm. They went around the stairwell and behind that, found the entry way to the attic. They pulled down the door and climbed up. By this time, they had been gone awhile from the library and the rest were curious to where they went. Within minutes they found that the attic door was down and climbed up to investigate too. All except Aaron and Tom. They knew better. They went back downstairs to their books.

"What in blazes are you doing?" Vincent boomed. He made the two siblings jump up in fright. They were so terribly absorbed in what they found in an old leather trunk. The tags on it were from New York.

"Blimy! You scared the ghost out of me!" Jamie cried out. She slapped Vincent on the arm as he stepped forward. He laughed. His brown eyes wide. His short hair was highlighted brown and blond. It stuck out in spikes, like a porcupine. He thought it made him look cool.

"I thought you were Grandfather. I could just see him waving at us with that huge pipe of his." Matt agreed. He smoothed back his own brown hair, which was easily tousled.

"He doesn't smoke anymore. He stopped when Da' died," Eric explained and sat down upon a crate. He found a pair of binoculars. He looked around the room with them, "It's so dusty. Lots of cobwebs too. You hate spiders, Jamie. Why are you up here?"

"We were looking for some of Da's old stuff. We found this trunk instead. I think it belonged to Mother."

"Really?" Edward exclaimed. The lean youth grabbed the book out of her hand, "What's this? It looks like a diary."

Jamie grabbed it back and clutched it tightly.

"It's a diary. It's Mother's diary, and reads all about the first time she fell in love."

"Oh, with Da'? It's probably contains all his sea stories too," Tristan declared and adjusted his wire glasses over his fair face. His hair was dark now, not quite black. Even his eyes were a deep muddy brown.

"No, he wasn't the first," Jamie revealed and they stared at her.

"He wasn't? Then who?" Tyler gasped and waited. His muscular arms pulled on a rafter above. He lifted himself up. He loved exercising.

"That's what we were trying to find out when you scared us," Matt said and Jamie flipped through the pages again.

"I was just near the end. Mom and Ross lived at Hartridge- some kind of place for kids with no family. Isn't that sad? Anyway, then one day, this boy turned up. He was the headmaster's nephew and mom wrote about how handsome he seemed. She was describing his features. He liked to play guitar. They read Romeo and Juliet together. Ross was jealous of him. Mom tried to figure out a way to remain friends with both."

"Where's Da in this story? Didn't he go to New York?" Edward retorted. "Yes. That's right. He did say he married her there. So problem solved. Mom and that guy broke up. Da saved her from that dreary place and brought her home."

"No, not exactly," Jamie said as she flipped through the pages quickly. On one particular place she read, "These are her last few thoughts. She was afraid of leaving New York City. She was afraid that she would never return home again. She didn't know anything about her husband or what to expect in England. All she knew was that she was leaving Jimmy far behind and he would never know the truth, and it was breaking her heart."

"Jimmy? Whose is Jimmy? And what truth?" Vincent asked and sat down to listen attentively.

"I don't know. A few pages back, she said something peculiar, that her world was turned upside down. Jimmy was gone. She loved him very much. The headmaster knows everything. He hates her. He is getting rid of her and her sin in the next few days. She must escape to find Ross. She will run away in the middle of the night." Jamie placed the book down on her lap. She stared at her brothers, "Then it skips to being with Ross. She meets our Da. He proposed and she accepted it. They traveled back by ship. So I don't know what truth she implies."

Jamie placed the book back into the box. By that time, Edward poked around another box that contained family files. He pulled out a copy of a form that was filled out by hand. Now, he was confused.

"Say, don't we have our birth certificates at the house in the file cabinet? I swore I saw them," Edward lifted up the form to show them, "Mother filled this form at the hospital."

"What is that?" Jamie sprang to his side quickly to look it over. They all gasped. On the line where the father was named, there was a name written in, but was scratched out with a pen. It was replaced with Daniel Cross. Still, what was originally written came through the thin paper.

"That's mother's handwriting," Tyler said.

"Well, that's Da's writing too. He wrote his name in. I can tell by the way the s's are curved," Matthew declared. They all stared at each other, but Matt was brave enough to ask the obvious question, "Who is James McFadden?"

They were all puzzled. Confused maybe, but based on what the diary said, they all knew.

"We have a different father?" Eric gasped. "What do we do with this information?"

"We keep quiet! That's what!" Edward swiped him on the head. "If mother wanted us to know, she would have told us."

"That's the truth she mentions in her diary. Surely, Da knew she carried us when he took her to England," Jamie cried. She felt stunned.

"Oh, there you go bawling again. Won't you stop?" Matt flung his hat over his knee in despair. He didn't like seeing such a strong sister fall apart like this. Jamie looked up at them and now there was fire in her eyes. What he said made her angry.

"No, I won't stop. Not when I know this secret. How well they all kept it. I cried my heart out when Da' died, and now it says that I'm not even of his own blood? I still feel him in my heart. There isn't a day that I don't think about Da'! No matter what, he's still my father!"

But now... now I want to know my own lineage too. I have a right to know everything. I must ask Mother."

Jamie got up from the floor in a hurry and she was determined to get home right away, but Vincent stopped her before she could climb down.

"No, Jamie. Not yet. We must think smart about this. I understand what you are saying, but it's not fair to Ross to just open up an old can of worms. He loves our mother. I can tell that he's so close to winning her over. They might be married soon."

"She doesn't love him," Jamie sputtered. She stood defiant. She cried, "We can all wish it to come true, but if it was meant to happen, they would have done it by now. I want someone to lean on, in the way that I had Da. If my true father lies across the ocean, then we must find a way there to declare ourselves to him. I want to know all of my history, for bad or for good. I have a gut feeling that mother never forgot him. Maybe that's why she can't marry Ross."

"We all want a man to guide us," Tyler retorted, "I can gather that by our actions. We just have to think smart, like Vincent suggests. In what way can we do this without upsetting her?"

They all paused to think and only Eric came up with the perfect solution.

"We should get back to our music and be done with that television show. It's time to wrap it up. I hear that America is a great place to become an international star. Besides, Uncle Mick is there, and I miss him."

"That's it! Erik! That's perfect!" Vincent shouted. He was terribly excited, "We'll ask to make a trip to the states for our band! We can go over there and scout around for our real father. If we can discover this, then we can discover anything! We are like Christopher Columbus! Let's get on with a new adventure!"

They all cheered, put away the certificate, and went downstairs to plot a way to make their request. At dinner time, they didn't hesitate to make their ideas known. Tara sat there absolutely stunned.

"You want to go to the United States? But why?"

"Mother, it's a great place to make it big! It's a huge market and beside, our band should be known throughout the world. It's the next big step," Vincent explained thoroughly. He looked at Ross quite quizzically. "Don't you think that Da' would push us on? He wanted us to succeed."

"Well, sure he would," Ross thought carefully, but he knew what was on Tara's mind too. An old ghost was coming to mind again. This was not good, but what could he say against this idea? He had to go along with it. "Michael and Anna have purchased a new home. He's proposed to her. Perhaps we can go after the holidays to visit them and at the same time, make a debut. That gives us plenty of time to line up a crew to join us there. We don't want to disrupt anyone's Christmas season."

"Yes, that makes sense," Tara said. She felt nervous. "We should wait until after the holidays. I still have to wrap up my advertising commitments."

Perhaps with time, the teens would change their minds. They were use to traveling close by, in England. They were always near home. Going to the states would mean staying long in order to make it productive.

"Do you think you can say goodbye to your friends and activities for awhile?" she questioned them. "This can't be lucrative unless we stay committed to the area, for at least three or four months."

"Well, I can leave my friends behind for a little while," Jamie replied. "We get bored sometimes doing the same things over again. It will be nice to see someplace new and learn what it's like there. You are both from the states. Don't you miss your own country?"

All the teens looked at Ross and Tara. Ross was the first to reply.

"Our upbringing was limited and confined, so it was not much to miss. There were times that I wished I could travel to different states, like Texas, for example. You hear stories from other people and it's just natural curiosity to want to see it. Like the Grand Canyon or Yosemite geysers, stuff you only read about in geography books. That would be my queue to going back, but like I said, our upbringing was tough. Not pampered like you were brought up."

"Pampered?" Edward sputtered. "I guess we were luckier than most people, but I still earned my keep. I did my chores. Mother claims there are investments in the bank. They are not available to us until we are twenty five, so as far as I'm concerned, I have to work. So what better place to do it than there?"

Matt agreed too.

"That's so very true. Why not start where Uncle Mick lives? In Tranquility City? He said in his letters it's a great place, with clean streets, modern facilities, and friendly people."

"All right, we'll go, but I must call him first. He has to be prepared for when you invade his home," Tara relented and they all cheered.

After they cleaned up, the teenagers departed upstairs to their rooms to leave the adults alone. It was a usual routine lately for some odd reason. Ross didn't quibble. He felt full from a great meal, one that Tara didn't burn. He stretched out his legs, sitting on the couch. He watched the fire burn. Tara turned off the lights so that they sat there in the glow. In some ways it was rather romantic, except that she sat across from him, in a chair all curled up in a blanket. She was staring at him very intently now. That was something new.

"What are you thinking about?" Ross finally asked, only because he was becoming very warm. It wasn't because of the fire. Those expressive eyes were just so beautiful.

"Do you think that leaving is the right thing?"

"It's not like its forever, Tara. It's a trial run, to see how receptive the American audience will be to our music. Sure, we are more contemporary now, as the kids are older and we can do that sort of thing. Still, if we start off in Tranquility and build up slowly, we can stay awhile. And we can come home whenever we want."

"Home," Tara muttered softly as she looked about. "New York was once our home. It was so hard to leave it, but Danny made us come. Now this is home. I have a feeling that when we go, some time will go by before we return. Something will make us stay. I don't think it will be the music. I can't tell. It's all fuzzy. In my head. It's a mystery of sorts."

She was gazing at the fire now. Ross knew what she meant. Tara had this instinct; an intuition which nine times out of ten was right on target. How she did it, he did not know, but he trusted it. Her nose was crinkled up in thought and she looked as if she might cry. He needed to hold her, but how? All he could think of was to pat the side of the fabric next to where he sat. He hoped that she would cross over to join him. And thankfully, she did, bringing over the blanket. She slid in as close to his body as possible. She was definitely afraid, but her gangly legs were straddled all over his.

"Can you tell me more?" he asked and tried not to unravel in the sweet smell of her hair and the fragrance of her body, which was aromatic and sensuous, like her. Desire was spreading through his body like wildfire, but he knew he could not act upon it. *Damn it*, he wanted to so badly. Yet, Tara was clinging to him because he was her best friend, just like when they were kids, and the storms would roll in. She would sneak out of her building and climb into his window, just so he could hold her tight. Those days were so innocent. Now, it only put him on fire. She had too many curves pressing against him.

"Hmmm, I see a strand of diamonds and sapphires and an inscription that has the word unique in it. Then I see a strange charm, also on a necklace, worn by some strange rambling man. I don't like him, but I need him in my life. He's gone away and I must find him."

"Who is it? Do you know him?"

Dare he ask? Ross felt unsettled by what she revealed. Tara's eyes were mysterious.

"No, I don't, but he drives me insane. I think I yelled at him, but at the same time I'm grateful for his presence."

"Sounds like me," Ross teased, but Tara sat up quickly. No, he didn't want this. She had felt so good next to him. But she wanted to make a point.

"No, the man is different from you. Now I know why I'm grateful. He did something to save Jimmy's life. I don't know what happened and I don't know when. You would never save Jimmy even if your life depended on it. You hate him."

"Well, yes, that is true. Still, the man in your vision has a clue to find Jimmy again. Is that what you want?"

Tara stared at him for a long moment. She saw his dark expressive eyes and that familiar concern for her welfare. Ross always thought about her feelings. He cared so very much about this family. She looked at his rumpled shirt. My how quickly she cuddled up to an old friend? But was that why she did it? Suddenly, she was very aware of an electrical feeling floating throughout her body. Desire infiltrated her mind and oooooh, how she liked it.

"Oh, Ross. I don't know anymore. I'm just lost and need a man to show me the way. I want love in my life. There are so many things that Danny gave without question, without hesitation. I never needed to ask. Things were never simple with Jimmy, so I'm not sure whether to do anything; besides his children don't have a clue he exists. What would be the point?"

Tara was flustered and she took the blanket to curl up in it like a cocoon. She stared at him with large, flashing eyes. Her hair was at one side. He suddenly drew very near, seeking something, but what? Ross gathered her up into his arms and kissed her passionately. When he pulled away, her eyes were wide open. Tara gasped, not from what he did, but the way she felt. He stared into her eyes.

"Tara, I would love to be that man. There's never been a moment that I didn't think about you that way. Still, I realize that going back could open up a lot of deep feelings about the past. It's a chapter that was never closed properly. So I will wait for you. If you find that what lies there doesn't satisfy your needs, then you know that I'm close by. Just call out my name. Every desire will be fulfilled. I did it once. You know damn straight that I can do it again."

At this Ross stood up, grabbed his coat, and went home. Tara remained breathless for a very long time. Yes, he could make her sizzle. He always had that capability, but she was right back to square one. It was not love, but extreme lust. Sometimes lust could build to love, if her heart would just allow it. The states beckoned and next month she would seek out a new destiny. The chapter with Danny was closed. Ross could be the next one. Or Jimmy, or that strange man within her dream. Who knew, but she was going to find out very soon.

The End

Printed in the United States
12089LV00003B/2/P